Date Due

Jan 25 '61	Jan 28 '76		
Feb. 61	Jul 12 72		
May 16 '61	Aug 15 79		
Jul 7 '61	Oct 26 79		
Feb 15 '62			
Apr 10 '62			
May 1 '62			
Jun 20 '62			
Jun 25 '62			
Jul 2 '62			
9 00 AM			
Feb 19 "63			
Apr 2 '64			
Nov 5 '66			
Feb 8 '71			
Jul 8 '71			
Jul i 1 '73			
Nov 13 '73			
	PRINTED	IN U. S. A.	

THE QUEEN'S GRACE

Books by Jan Westcott

The Queen's Grace

JAN WESTCOTT

CROWN PUBLISHERS, INC.

NEW YORK, N.Y.

For my family

823.914
W52g

40160
October, 1960

Printed in the United States of America
By American Book-Stratford Press, Inc., N.Y.

BOOK ONE

The castle crowned the hill, its gray stone walls as foursquare and uncompromising as the rugged Westmorland moors and mountains. Beside the river Kent, at its foot, the man on horseback tipped back his head to look up at Kendal Castle.

His eyes searched the walls. They went up to the top of the rounded towers. He sat motionless.

So this was the land, this the castle that had bred her. Helm clouds scudded across the skies, laying a black hand on the hillsides. So this was Kendal, this the border country which accounted for the square shoulders, the small square hands, and the clipped, north-country accent.

"Katryn," he said aloud.

His hands lay slack on the reins. The horse lowered his head to sniff the grass. September's brown had begun to edge it. Slowly he turned the horse's head.

Refuge was near; Burneside was close by. For it is not possible, he thought, for me to enter Kendal's walls—not yet. The past re-captured at Burneside would be pain enough, and the manor house lay near.

He was inexpressibly weary. A weariness of the spirit, he knew, for all that real sleep had been denied him, even when every bone ached with fatigue; and yet, he thought, now when I see the manor house ahead of me, for the first time in two weeks I am conscious of some gladness, some relief. My presence will be a shock. Baron Thomas Seymour, Lord Admiral of England, come riding out of nowhere and out of the past.

And so it was. Dame Mary Bellingham looked incredulous.

"Tom, oh Tom," she whispered. She laid a hand on his arm.

She knows, he thought. I have just come, and yet where before there was bustle and talk and laughter, now all is silent and still, as if my very presence stills voices and laughter has no place on my ears. He said apologetically, "I was overthrown."

Dame Mary bit her lip. Fine lines drew down his mouth. The blue eyes were cloudy. Where had he been for these last two weeks? she wondered.

He answered the unspoken question. "Riding. I came north to Kendal. I tried to find"—he hesitated, hunted for a word—"some surcease. I don't think I've slain the dragon yet. Pray don't weep. You will undo me for sure."

Dame Mary attempted a smile. He said, "That's best."

Her eyes again searched his face. He was freshly shaved.

"I am clean, too," he said wryly, and the blue eyes glinted just a bit. "But I would ask a night's lodging from you, and pen and ink. I must write to my lord duke, my brother. He knows not where I am. Nor when I shall return."

"No food?" asked Dame Mary. A man as big as this should eat.

He patted her shoulder. "Thou'rt kind. Food, of course, later. I've had ale and bread at a tavern."

She heaved a sigh. "Sit you down then, my lord," she said, bethinking herself they were still standing close together in the winter parlor, where a small fire burned on the hearth. Dame Mary glanced about the room. "Daylight is fast fading," she said, "and I shall bring a fresh candle."

He stretched out booted feet toward the fire, leaned his dark head against the wooden back of the one chair. Her footsteps echoed in the passageway. Soon he would have in hand the pen and ink. And what should he say? Words formed in his mind. "My dear brother, I was so overthrown . . ." He closed his eyes. It should take a week to return to London. He reckoned the days. Had it been two whole weeks? The dragon, not slain, turned in his breast. How explain to his brother, Ned, why he had gone forth to live like a hunted animal, to disappear, to sleep in caves on a lonely hillside, to avoid the haunts of men—to suffer thus alone.

The room darkened. Katryn, he thought, this is the same room, the very same room, where first we met.

The shadows stirred. Flame leaped from the logs on the fire. I can almost see her, he thought, in the plain gown of Kendal green,

4

stiff with petticoats, in this same room. Almost could he hear her voice: "But I saw thee first!" she had said. "I saw thee standing by the hearth, just your back and the back of your head, as I came in from the garden."

Nineteen years ago, he thought, nineteen to the very day, mayhap the very hour, nineteen years ago . . .

1

Katryn Parr sat demurely on the bench in the garden at Burneside, her slippers resting on the grass at her feet, peeking out from under the brilliant green skirt. The skirt was girdled in the same green, and a white shawl was over her shoulders, for even though the sun was warm the September day held a chill in its air. Her red curls, caught back under her cap, spilled over her collar. Against her white skin her dark, straight brows were startling. Her eyes were hazel, flecked with gold.

Katryn's white hands lay on her lap, but they were not idle. She was sewing and, as always, she used her sewing to keep her eyes on her needle; then occasionally she would glance up. She did glance up now, across the lawn toward the big manor house, from which there were coming all kinds of sounds and voices, but none of them the one she wanted to hear. She moved restlessly on the bench. Certainly he would come; he had said he could come. Her heart beat fast as she thought of it, and she wet her lips, and lowered her eyes so as to conceal the quick flash of triumph in them.

For this was triumph indeed. A year ago—nay, six months ago—he wouldn't have noticed her at all. Many had been the time he'd passed her by when she came to visit Joan Bellingham, her best friend. It had only been last week that he had said, in a surprised tone, "Why, by the mass, ye've grown up!" And, looking down, his blond head on one side, he suddenly smiled. "Why, Mistress Katryn," he said, and bowed.

She lowered her eyes to let him see the thick, bristly lashes, and she thought, Marry, Hugo is a man; he is twenty. For six months I've been dreaming about him, and now suddenly the knave thinks all he has to do is notice me.

"Marry, sir," she said haughtily, "thou'rt a very dolt not to have discovered it afore. I'm almost sixteen, the same as your sister

Joan." She tossed her head and made a move to pass by him, for they were in a narrow passage between the scullery and the door to the garden.

"Hold on," he said, taking a step back. "I didn't mean to offend thee."

"Pray let me pass, Hugo," she said.

He did so, and she went out into the garden. "May I come, too, mistress?"

She stopped and they faced each other. She regarded him a long moment, raising her eyes to his face to see his sparkling gray eyes, and the good-humored face topped by a thatch of blond curls. "Hugo," she said softly, "I am not a child, and I mislike being treated like one." She ran her red tongue over her lips, for she was a bit nervous about talking with him thus. That's because I've known him so long, when I was so young, she told herself.

Then she saw that he was viewing her with misty tenderness and longing. "I swear I never will again," he said.

"Marry," she said under her breath, and looked quickly at the ground. In silence they walked together to the bench. That had been a week ago, and the seven days had passed in a sort of dreamy delirium.

He is such a gentleman, she told herself a thousand times a day. And he loves me so.

He paid her dizzying compliments, he lifted her onto her horse just as if she were weightless, and yet the touch of his hands lingered on her waist. She thought she could even feel them that night a week ago, in bed with Joan, as she made Joan hush talking so she could dream about Hugo, and repeat in her mind all he had said, and what she had replied. Now, as she waited in the garden, it seemed as though he would never come. "Marry," she said under her breath, and then drew it in sharply, for she could hear new sounds from the manor house—horses and men. She drew a long, satisfied breath. She would take five stitches and then, if she raised her eyes, she would see him coming. So when Hugo did arrive, he stood right over her, and she made an exclamation of surprise.

"I didn't see thee coming, Hugo," she said demurely.

He frowned down at her, squinting his eyes in the sunlight. He didn't answer immediately; he seemed to be hesitating. This was not usual, and his gravity was borne in on her, and she said, "Is aught

7

amiss?" She laid down her sewing, and their eyes met for a long moment.

He said then, "Will you walk with me?" He extended his hand and she rose, laying her sewing down.

Hugo held Katryn's hand tight in his. Suiting her pace to his, she walked fast. Hugo was leading her through the orchards. Presently they would skirt the top of the hill, and she knew he would walk her to the burn. She was vaguely conscious of the odor of horses and leather as the errant wind blew down upon them. It would be fiercer when they reached the top of the hill, for here in the Border counties winter came early, and the thick, tough grass was already turning brown. It was a half after two. Hugo must have been riding hard, she thought tenderly. He was a typical north-countryman, rugged and sturdy; his callused hands were deft on a horse or a sick animal; kind, he was able enough with the long dagger he wore and as his wife she would need feel no fear. She would take her place in the manor house just as John's wife had, even though John was the eldest Bellingham and through the lucky accident of birth would inherit all these acres.

They had come to the top of the hill; on one side stretched the common lands, on the other the Bellinghams' park lands, thick with game, the colors of the trees russet and gold, and the burn sparkling blue. Hugo came to a stop.

"Look," he said, "look. For I shan't see this again for a long, long time!"

Katryn's whole high pile of dreams fell suddenly about her feet, and her eyes were wide and incredulous. Gone were the sparks, gone the long, level calculation only a close observer could catch; gone was everything but hurt and amazement.

"You are going away?" She drew the words out slowly, as though afraid to say them.

But he was not slow in replying. "Aye, I am," he said curtly. " 'Tis my father's wish, and I cannot gainsay him!" He struck his hand in his palm, and turned to face her, taking her hands again in his. "Katryn!" he said desperately. Then, "Come!"

Silently she followed him across to the edge of the burn, where a bit of grass grew, and there they sat. "I'll tell you about it," he began.

She sat dumbly, listening. He was going away into service with

Sir Francis Bryan. It had been suggested by Sir John Seymour, a distant kin of his mother's, whose son Tom was in the same man's service.

"I never heard of any Seymours. They are not of Cumberland or Westmorland," she said definitely.

"They come from Wilts," Hugo said.

She dismissed Wilts. Hugo was going away. Instead of a November wedding—and November was the right month for weddings—she would have to go back to Kendal. Her hands felt cold; next month it might be snowing. She felt cheated and she blinked back a tear. There wouldn't even be the fun of looking forward to her visits with the Bellinghams, now that Hugo would not be home.

"I am a younger son," Hugo said, "and my father thinks I should see the rest of England, even mayhap the rest of the world." He took her hand again in his warm one. "I'll be going to London. Promise me that you will wait for me!"

It was the first real declaration from him. She drew in a long shivering breath, delighted and pleased with herself, but for some reason she did not know, she only said, "Mayhap, Hugo." She withdrew her hand and folded it under her other one, in her lap.

"I know I've no right to ask you to wait," he said. His voice was even, but his eyes betrayed his eagerness. He stumbled a bit. "I love you, Katryn," he told her. "I love you very much. Please promise to wed me!"

She turned her eyes on him. "You love me?" she asked, low, as though trying to judge the truth of his statement.

"I adore you," he said fervently. "You are much too beautiful and lovely for me, I know that well enough! I don't deserve you, Katryn, but I'll do my best to, and I'll make my fortune this winter, and bring you back all of it!" Clumsily he took a ring from his finger and held it out. "Will you accept it, sweetheart?" he asked.

"It is very pretty," she said. She hesitated. The face and figure of her mother floated before her eyes. What would Lady Parr say if she could see her daughter, sitting on the grass with Hugo Bellingham, and contemplating a precontract of marriage? She shoved the thought aside. The ring was heavy gold; she tried it on her finger; it was much too big. She could wear it around her neck on a little chain. She would be betrothed, and have a man in love with her. She looked up at Hugo, and his heart was in his eyes. She tucked the ring inside her bodice, and was unprepared for Hugo's reaction. He seized her hungrily, taking her action for acceptance of his suit; he folded her in his arms, and kissed her cheek, and the tip of her nose, muttering all the time how much he loved her.

"Hugo, Hugo!" She tried to remonstrate. In the back of her mind was the certain knowledge that a precontract could not be broken; that now she was committed, now she had affianced herself, without her mother's knowing aught, and for a moment fear weighed more heavy than excitement or joy or love, and she almost didn't realize she was being kissed on the lips.

"I love you," he said. He hugged her tight.

"Let me go, Hugo," she whispered.

"I wouldn't fright you for the world, Katryn," he said solemnly, and reluctantly released her.

She shivered. The ground was suddenly cold. The sun had gone in. She grasped Hugo's hand and struggled to her feet. It must be late, near suppertime. She caught her shawl close, inadequate as it was.

She glanced up at Hugo. And now of a sudden she wished she were back home at Kendal, safe within its gray encircling ancient walls. She wished she were in the huge hall with the fire blazing; she wished she were not the female she was, but the first-born son her father had wanted. Then she'd have no problems; Kendal would be hers, she its master and its lord. Instead she was a poor, silly wench, with no dowry, not quite sixteen years old, far away from home, and she had done something she shouldn't. She bit her lip.

"We should go back, Hugo," she said, low.

Katryn sat on the edge of the bed in the bedroom she shared with Joan and was thankful that Joan was not here, and that she could be alone for a few minutes. She had excused herself to come up and comb her hair before supper, while Joan helped downstairs and threw glances at the man, Tom Seymour, who had arrived to take Hugo to London. When Katryn came in he had been standing with his back to the room, facing the open fire. She had caught just a glimpse of him, a black-haired stranger, and Joan laughing archly up at him. She hardly cared what Tom Seymour looked like, as she hurried past, clutching her sewing bag, gaining the stairs and the safety of the lonely bedroom upstairs. I must think, she told herself. I must think, and I have a few minutes. She pulled the quilt across her knees and curled up on the bed. The warmth was comforting and she sighed in the pleasure of it, momentarily content. She drew out the ring Hugo had given her, and held it in her palm, so she could close her hand over it quickly should someone come in. She looked at it a long moment, tried to evaluate what she had done, and to arrange her thoughts before she would have to go down and face Hugo and his family.

She found her thoughts drifting to Kendal and to the father she had known so briefly. Her eyes filled with tears and again she wished passionately she were back at Kendal and five years old, and her square, sturdy father were coming in the wide doors, smelling delightfully of strong ale, and leather and horses, and the wide, wide moor-winds themselves. I remember as if it were yesterday, she thought, even to the feel of his rough beard as he kissed me. And the wonderful words of praise he had always had for her. "Aye, she should ha' been a lad, Maud," he would shout in glee. "She should ha' been a boy!" That was the highest accolade Sir Thomas Parr could have bestowed on his daughter. I wish he were here, she thought passionately; he would help me, I would still be his favorite, even though William was born. If father were here now, I'd be finely betrothed—aye, and have mayhap a new length of dress goods for winter, and mayhap even be going to London.

"A lass," she said slowly and aloud to the empty room, "needs a father till she gets a husband." She sighed deeply.

Her father had been dead for ten years. He had died as quickly and with as much gusto as he had lived, ignoring a violent winter cold until it had caught at his lungs. He had hardly been in bed before death claimed him, his stopped breath still redolent of ale and illegal, pale Scots whisky from across the narrow wavering Border. His boots lay at his hand where he had dropped them, his long dagger across the bedside table. Katryn had been five, her sister Anne three, and little Will four. Maud Parr and his family could hardly believe their lord was gone; even when he was laid in the black marble tomb in Kendal church, his wife listened for his booted tread across the great hall, and his daughter Katryn strained her ears for the sound of galloping horse reined to a sudden flaring stop, and the shout of her name in his north-country accents.

It was borne in on his household slowly. Maud Parr sent for a distant kin, a poorer member of her large family, from Norton's Green, where she had grown up sweetly and sanely, she used to say, in comparison to the wilds and moors and lakes of Westmorland. Walter Pickering came, and his wife, Meg, and his daughter, little Meg. Little Meg slept in Katryn's room, as her bed-servant and companion. Meg Senior was the housekeeper, and Walter the bailiff. The garrison slowly disbanded, and Kendal became, not a Border stronghold with its warden commissioned by the King, but a woman's household which was devoted to the raising of its little lord, William Parr. Not that Maud Parr neglected her daughters, but the first care and hope of the Parrs was the son who bore their name. Kendal was his, and he was Kendal. Katryn had been taught that, over the years, and accepted it. She even understood when her mother told her that her own dowry of four hundred pounds—not much, but what her father had left her—even that dowry had gone to secure William's appointed bride, the only heir of the Earl of Essex. This was a brilliant match, and one to which Lady Parr had devoted all her time and efforts and moneys. It was most important to secure William's and Kendal's future; Katryn Parr understood that and credited it as right. That the day would come when he would betray Kendal and his heritage, Katryn suspected, but she did not blame her mother for putting Will first; she understood well the difference in the position of men and women. But she knew that her father would have seen to her, too.

She fetched another deep sigh. In view of her circumstances—and viewed practically they were not happy—she had done very well. A lass could not wait indefinitely for marriage. Hugo was young and well born and honorable. In the excitement of her pursuit of him, she did not doubt that what she felt for him was love. Surely her mother would forgive her; anyway, she did not have to face her yet; she could wait and tell her when she got home; she could wait either hours or days for the right moment.

She got off the bed and looked at herself critically in Joan's polished copper mirror. She refolded the quilt carefully, and went out the bedroom door, closing it softly behind her. Slowly she made her way down the steps, her hand tight on the rail, going quicker to meet whatever the next hours held, going down more surely and confidently now. The door at the bottom was flung open. The two younger Bellingham boys were waiting for her impatiently. They towered on both sides of her. The dogs barked, and the room was full of noise and the smell of wood burning and food cooking.

"You missed me?" she said gaily, looking from one to the other. "Oh, I warrant you're just saying that to turn a poor girl's head." She knew very well that the tall stranger was standing almost in front of her, that the boys had drawn her forward to present him. But she affected not to notice him for a second. So when Hugo said, "Allow me to present our kin, Tom Seymour," she said, "Oh," in pretty confusion, and for the first time turned her golden eyes on him.

The eyes hers met were intensely blue and threw a shaft of mockery enhanced by a smile on a dark face, topped by the black hair she had seen before. Thick and short black hair, as black as the heavy brows above the blue eyes.

She thought swiftly, He doesn't look like Dame Mary's kin. Her eyes widened in real surprise. Openly she studied his face, and then dropped him a swift curtsy and held out her hand.

He took it. His hand was big and warm and very strong, and she jerked her hand away from the encircling fingers hastily. She wondered if she had heard right; perhaps he was someone else. "You're from Wilts?" she asked, raising her eyes past the bulk of shoulder and chest to the dark lean face. "Aren't ye a Scot?"

Hugo shouted with laughter. "Jesu, what a compliment. Usually she's so sweet with words, Tom, 'Aren't ye a Scot?'" he repeated. "Tell him you're sorry, Katryn."

Katryn looked up at Tom Seymour. He was smiling and his eyes held hers and she could think of nothing to say, nothing at all. She heard his voice for the first time. It was low and very amused. The accent was of the South, and she had scarcely ever heard it before; it was soft and slurred.

"My name was originally Saint Mawr," he said. Then he added, "French. Norman." He paused. "So you thought me a Scot reaver, a freebooter, ready to raid on a moonlit night?"

"No," she snapped, and then blushed, for Hugo laughed. Tom Seymour kept his look of amusement, holding it maddeningly on his eyes and mouth; Katryn's eyes darkened and the gold specks swam about. "You're making fun of me," she said.

"Oh, no," he said seriously. "Not at all. You are right. For even though I am kin to Dame Mary—which you find hard to credit—I assure you I have no measure of respectability left, not a shred, and you are quite right." He had hooked his thumbs in his belt and was regarding her lazily from his height. "I might as well be a marauding Scot, come o'er the Border to steal your rings and ravish your honor." He laughed then, bowed, and turned on his heel, going back to the fireplace and engaging Sir John in immediate talk.

She looked about for Hugo, but all she could see of him was his back as he bent over the sideboard with its burden of roast meat. The boys were still at her side, and she paid them no attention, for they were teasing her about Tom Seymour. She glanced over at him, as he leaned against the mantel, one hand resting negligently on the big dagger at his hip, one boot on the fire fender. He was listening to Sir John, and Katryn saw him smile suddenly, his eyes delighted and wicked and amused. She said crisply, "Marry, you're both dolts. What he said about himself was perfect true!"

Katryn usually loved dinner at the Bellinghams'. It was so noisy and yet so cozy, not like the big, drafty hall at Kendal, for Dame Mary had taken over the winter parlor, and a big fire always burned on the hearth near the diners. A trestle table was set up, and the massive sideboard, so near you could almost touch your hand to it, groaned with food. The roasts and stuffed birds made a handsome, succulent display, and the towering silver salts, and the wide-mouthed flagons for ale gleamed as ruddily as the apples piled and polished in a pewter bowl. The fire hissed, John's wife brought the water and towels to Dame Mary, and the meal began.

There was much more variety than there was at Kendal and Katryn usually ate steadily through different kinds of meat and game. Tonight, though, her appetite had deserted her; she picked at her food and listlessly bit into the white bread she loved so much. The men were talking as usual about the King's great matter, and how the realm had no heir, and how his Grace had petitioned the Pope to grant him a divorce.

Katryn was restless. She had heard it so many times before, in the past year. The men always espoused the side of the King, and the women clucked their tongues, and made to say how sad and dreadful it was for his Grace to put aside his loyal and true wedded wife. Tom Seymour had brought up the matter, for he had been in Blackfriars the day the court had ruled on the King's marriage, and he was describing it for Sir John: how the Cardinal's red robes had glittered, but not more than Henry himself, in cloth of gold; and how the Queen had come into this court, and flung herself down before her husband, and cried out about the wickedness of all this talk of her not being a virgin bride! "Who," cried the Queen, "should know better about my virginity than my husband himself?"

"Marry," whispered Joan Bellingham, her eyes round as the saucer of meat Hugo had put down for his dog. "That's right, acourse. His Grace must know true, himself! Whether or not she was virgin!"

Sir John went on to say heavily, with a glance of some reproof at his young daughter, that she had first been wed, after all, to Henry's brother, and no man should marry his brother's widow. No good would come of it for it was forbidden by the Scriptures, in Leviticus. Sir John named the chapter and verse, and bit into a strip of leg of mutton and chewed hard, the juice running down his chin.

His wife took up the argument. "But she was not true his wife, John! She was never his true wedded wife!"

"Nonsense," Sir John said boldly. "They were put to bed together and they were both sixteen."

Joan blushed. Katryn was thinking she should blush, too. Tom Seymour looked across the table at her, and, annoyed, she stared back at him, her eyes narrowed. Let him think what he pleases, she thought defiantly. I have other matters to worry over than Queen Katharine; she is old, over forty. Besides, Katryn privately thought the Queen was making a big fuss over nothing. The King had offered her the honorable title of Princess Dowager, putting her back to the position she had had as Arthur's widow. Why didn't the silly woman accept it, and let the King wed again?

Joan said, "Katryn was told by a fortuneteller that she would be queen, and that her hands were ordained for scepters."

Tom Seymour smiled, and Katryn felt her cheeks growing hot. "Did she believe it, Joan?" he asked.

"Aye," said Joan, "and she wouldn't do her needlework, saying why should she bother, with hands ordained for scepters?"

Now Katryn did blush. Tom Seymour leaned across the table to speak to her, his big hands idly holding his dagger. "If you list to your dreams," he said, "you'd best not stay here in Westmorland."

She raised her eyes; they looked straight at each other across the polished board. On her lap her hands were clenched tight over her handkerchief. In her hazel eyes the gold flecks swam and glittered for a moment; and seeing her eyes, and what was in them, so plain, his mouth curved down at the corners deprecatingly.

"I have no wish to be a king," he said. "Why does a woman wish to be queen?"

Her thick lashes dropped. " 'Twas just a jest, and many years ago —aye, I believe at least three."

"Nonetheless," he said, "I shall expect to see thee someday in London."

"You'll not," she told him, and for some reason her voice was low and furious. "You'll not!"

She shot Hugo a glance, and he smiled at her reassuringly, almost as though he had squeezed her hand. I'm contracted to him, and I shall wait for him forever. And I shall love living here. She looked around the table again, at all the familiar faces; Hugo adored her, the two boys were half in love with her; Joan was her best friend.

She could feel Hugo's ring lying in the hollow of her breasts, a lovely secret to hold and cherish, and even though they couldn't be wed this November as she had planned, mayhap they could be wed the following spring. 'Twould not be long.

The evening had a dreamlike quality; she found herself trying to push aside the mist of her own thoughts. There was no chance to see Hugo alone. She tried by long, pregnant glances to tell him she wanted to speak with him, that there was something of vast importance they should discuss. But he just smiled at her absently. His mind was obviously on the talk that swirled across and about the table, cleared now of food and cloth, and with the dice rolling and clattering across its shiny surface. There was the clink of coins, and the noises of the flagons being raised to bearded lips and lowered gently, thoughtfully, as the hand paused mid-air to watch the roll of the wayward die. Dame Mary sat close by the fire, with Joan and Katryn on either side. She seems content, Katryn thought. She wondered if Lady Parr would be so content to see Will leaving Kendal in the morning.

At nine Dame Mary laid aside her sewing. She rose, and the two girls rose, too. Sir John looked across at his womenfolk; he shoved back his stool.

"Time for all to be abed," he said in his gruff voice.

Dame Mary smiled at his usual peremptory tones, softening them for their guest. "Sir John probably thinks you and Hugo have a long ride ahead of you tomorrow."

Tom Seymour was on his feet in a moment. "Aye, and he's quite right," he said easily.

The good-nights were said. Katryn tried to hold Hugo's eyes with her own. A delicate frown crossed her brow. She was almost at the door, and no one was watching her. The rest were all in a group, a circle. She went over to the fireplace, laid down her sewing bag, and returned to the door, just as Joan reached it. The two girls made their way upstairs together, with John's wife and Dame Mary following close behind. The parlor door closed, and the low murmur of talk within it receded from her ears.

Underneath her red curls her brain was busy. It would be dangerous, and downright shocking conduct, to descend the stairs in her dressing gown, unless of course she had all her petticoats under it. She removed her dress carefully and laid it away. "I'm so sleepy," she said, and yawned.

"So am I," said Joan.

Katryn sighed in relief. "You wash first."

Joan was in bed in minutes. Katryn took up the candle from the bedside and set it down on the stand by the bowl of water. She washed slowly and quietly; when she finished she blew out the candle. Moving softly in her slippered feet, she made her way to the door; she opened it gently; it made no sound. In a moment she was alone in the dim hall. Carefully, gingerly she started down the steps.

Under the door of the winter parlor she could see faint light. Yet there was no sound from within. Surely Hugo waited for her there. Cautiously she took hold of the latch, lifting it swiftly; in another second she was inside, with the door shut noiselessly behind her.

The room was lighted only by firelight. It danced on the whitewashed walls, flickering ruddily. In front of the fire was Sir John's chair, drawn up close, and in the chair was a shadowy figure, turning now, and Katryn saw with dismay that it was not Hugo. In the unbroken silence Tom Seymour was rising and turning to face her.

"Oh," she whispered. She came forward, to him, toward the fire. Her bag lay on the floor, to the side of the chair. Her eyes fastened on it, as her excuse for being here. She gathered her robe close; then she was alongside him. The fire blazed suddenly, an extra flame licking hungrily at the side of a charred log. She said, "I forgot my sewing bag."

She watched him bend to retrieve it; he had followed her eyes. He held it out wordlessly; his eyes, studying her, narrowed a bit because of the uncertain light; he held out the sewing bag and she reached for it, and their fingers touched.

Katryn Parr drew in her breath; his fingers were warm. She took the bag and, puzzled, she eyed him narrowly too. This was such a strange encounter, here in the dim, firelit room; silent as the grave, it was. His face was in shadow. But the angle toward the light showed the powerful jaw. The blue eyes were darkened now, regarding her from under heavy brows; the mouth in repose was wide and strong. He was taller than Hugo; her heelless slippers accentuated his height compared to hers. She stepped back to see him in better proportion. He had the narrow waist and flat stomach of the jouster and swordsman. His physical prowess had elevated him to the position he held now, as the first of Sir Francis Bryan's gentlemen. Sir Francis was called by the King the Vicar of Hell. One-eyed, he saw more than most men, and there was no deviltry that he could not get into, or any that he could not be rescued from by Tom Seymour, who bore his colors victoriously into games, contests and tournaments besides. Tom Seymour wore Sir Francis' badge on his left arm, stitched on the soft chamois. Hugo would wear it, too.

"I left my bag," she repeated, her hands clasped over it. She took a backward step.

"You expected Hugo," he said. "I guessed there was something between you. But Dame Mary wished him; he's with her, in her chambers." His voice was low and matter-of-fact. "She wished to bid him Godspeed, her second son, for all that he's older than I was when I set forth. But I mind me my mother talked to me, that night afore I left home, for at least an hour. You will have a long wait."

The unreality that had plagued her all evening persisted. She forgot the rest of the manor house, sleeping, dark, with maybe just a candle burning in the room where Dame Mary talked with her son. She forgot that she shouldn't be here, talking to a man almost strange to her. Her breath came lightly; the fire threw out a shower of sparks. Tom Seymour brushed at her robe hastily and she watched him, her own hands clasped over her bag. She said, "What did your mother say to you when you left?"

18

He glanced at her quizzically. He seemed about to brush the question aside. Then he frowned a little, dark brows drawn, as though he were trying to remember the right answer to her question. While he hesitated, she asked, "How old were you when you left home?"

"Sixteen," he said, "lacking a few months."

"The age I am now," she put in.

He nodded, as if he had known. "That was four years ago, and I am trying to recall the answer to your question. For surely you must guess what mothers say to their sons, about honor, and family responsibility, and the name one's father has made at court, and not to disgrace it by wild talk and action."

She sighed. Then she frowned. Didn't they mention about women? she wondered. Wouldn't Dame Mary tell Hugo to keep away from tarts and be true to his love, which Dame Mary didn't know he had?

Tom Seymour's eyes lighted a bit. "That, too," he said.

"How did you . . . ?" she began.

"I guessed, lass," he said. "Shall I tell Hugo you said to be true to you, as you will be true?"

There was an expression on his face she couldn't read. She bit her lip. What did he imply? He looked unbelieving and there was a glint of mockery in his eyes. Or didn't she read aright? His glance swept her, openly now.

He said, "You have no dowry?" It was a question.

She stared at him in shocked surprise. Then she rallied her forces. Her mother could always promise a little, say a hundred pounds, paid in five years. "I have a dowry," she said passionately.

His narrowed eyes were intent on her face. "Hugo said you did not; I asked him outright."

Amazed, she could say nothing. A thousand thoughts rushed through her brain. Ordinary men didn't go about asking about a maid's dowry; could it possibly mean he was interested in her himself? She shot him a glance under her lashes. "Why?"

"I was curious." He rubbed his hand over his jaw, thoughtfully. Then he said, "Lass, you're very young, you know. And the world is a big, big place. Westmorland is a very small part of it."

The fire flared and he turned aside to pick up the heavy poker. She watched his hands, capable, and brown; she watched the ease of the stance, as he bent to lift one of the heavy logs; she saw the badge on his arm. It swam before her eyes. She could vision it on the London streets, streets she had never seen; she could vision it blazoned on a suit of shining armor, as the horns blew and the gates opened and the armored steeds came thundering onto the tournament field; she could hear in her mind's eyes the music of the King's court and see the colors of the ladies' gowns. She fastened her eyes on that badge. Four years he had worn it, he said. He must be a younger son, too.

"Have you a brother?" she asked.

"Aye," he said, straightening, and laying down the poker. "A brother Ned, some years older."

"Does he look like you?"

Tom Seymour nodded. "Ned is very dark, like me, but his eyes are brown, and he wears a little beard, but you would know we were kin. And I have an older sister, a sister Jane, who is as fair as thee; fairer, for her hair is gold and her eyes blue."

Fairer than thee, he had said. She raised her eyes to him, and he smiled slightly. "She is serene, her beauty is. Your beauty is arresting, disturbing; there are depths in your eyes, and warm fire in your hair. And I think . . ." She knew he was going to say that she should go up to bed. After all, he was four years older, and seemed to her to possess a wealth of knowledge and experience; to her his body and mind seemed to move together with ease, with assurance, without fear. Her mind raced. She had had no counsel from men, ever, save Walter Pickering, whom even her mother discounted, and the boys she met, and then Hugo. Yet she harbored a belief, inherited from the memories and shades of her father, from long generations of teaching, and her woman's mind, that there were many things that only men knew the answer to, and it would be well to discover what it was they did know. And surely it would do William good to do as this man had done. Suppose this man were Will; she'd have no fears about Kendal.

She said, breaking into his sentence, "What do you do for Sir Francis Bryan? What do you do in London?"

"By God's most precious soul, lass," he said in a commonplace tone, and she had rarely heard an oath used so casually. She glanced at him, surprised by his language.

He made her a little bow, and gave her a rueful smile. "I learn, lass," he said. "I try to learn to be the gentleman I was born." He surveyed her. "I didn't look like one to you, did I?"

"No," she said gravely.

"Well," he said abruptly, "one must learn to fit oneself to a world with which one is sometimes, ofttimes, at odds. And it is too easy to be at odds with oneself. What do you want from life, for instance?" He bent his gaze on her. He said then, "You see, I was going to send you to bed. You shouldn't be here—not that I mean harm to you. But then I have not much use for caution, and neither, I warrant, do you. But you see, to pursue one's own way—there's a penalty for 't. Are you prepared to pay it?"

"Aye," she said directly. She pulled over a leather-topped stool and sat down. "You take the chair," she said.

He threw her a glance of amusement, and met her open gaze.

"Are ye wed?" she asked.

"Nay, for God's sake," he expostulated. He stretched out his legs, and the heel of his boots rested in the ashes on the hearth. Once again it was brought upon her almost by physical force, the insolent, lazy strength of his big body, and of his mind, and of his quick, sure tongue. He was an enigma to her, a maze in which she'd get lost surely; 'twould be a foolish woman who'd lose her head over this man, she was sure. He spelled danger, for of a certainty he would take and not give, conquer and be unconquered. A gentleman? Nay, not the kind she knew.

"What do you want from life?" she asked softly.

He raised his thick brows and said, "A great deal. Now you answer my question. What do *you* want? This?" He flung out his hand, to indicate the room, the very nature of it, with its trestle table and its single chair, its white walls and its rush-strewn floor. His wave of hand included the manor, the stretching fields, the little village, and hidden lakes, and Hugo.

"I don't know," she said.

Once again she heard his voice at dinner describing the scene at Blackfriars. But it was not just the thought of London, and the King and court. Often she had heard her mother talk about her days in London, of the pageants at court, of the panoply of royalty and royal living, of urban living, of politics, of war, of streets with shops, of everything she didn't know. It was something deeper, something evoked by the restless spirit opposite her now—something new, something vital, a stirring, an ambition, a clearing away of the veil of uncertainty. She leaned forward.

"If I were in London now," she said, "what then?"

Tom Seymour frowned at her. In his mind's eye he could hear his master's low whistle of approval if he should lay his one wicked, all-seeing eye on Katryn Parr. His description would be apt and earthy; his tactics immediate and easily prescribed. But if Tom Seymour guessed aright, 'twould be to no avail, for along with all the notions this wench harbored, she'd make no mean opponent in the battle of love. He grinned; he leaned over and patted her knee.

"Stay away from London," he said.

She drew a deep breath. "I was going to ask you to take me." Excitement raced in her; she could be frank and direct and honest with him. He would understand. He would know she couldn't just spend the rest of her life at Kendal, or just sit by supinely while youth ran out. All the restless stirrings she had felt, she thought now she knew what they were. Why not ask Tom Seymour for help? Why not?

His blue eyes studied her. There was surprise on his face, and some concern, and some laughter. Lounging there, in his chair, his eyes glittered as they regarded her. "No, I won't, Mistress Katryn." His voice was gibing and low. She would have interrupted, but he shook his head and held up his hand. "Be quiet a moment and listen. You can get a lot from men, Katryn, but not that way. Jesu, you've a look in your eyes like a usurer. Use your woman's wiles, whatever they are. You should know that better than I. Take you to London! Thou're a mad wench, madder than I even, and that's saying a good deal. Look you, Mistress Katryn, you've a natural-born way with men."

Her eyes swam with the deep golden specks. "But you are different," she said. "I thought you would understand."

He scowled at her. "I'm not flattered," he said. "You want something from me. Well, you can't have it, and there's an end to it. I take you nowhere."

Anger sharply swirled Katryn's blood, doubling her heartbeat. She balled her fist tightly on her knee. She had asked him, straightforwardly, to do her a favor; he had insulted her and refused. He leaned back in his chair, his face inscrutable, and Katryn sat back on her stool.

"I am a fool," she said icily. "I read you wrong." Aye, indeed she had, she told herself. I read him as the gay adventurer, with whom I could bargain. It was her woman's estate that hampered her, of course. And yet she had thought it would make no difference to him, and that he would understand.

"Never try to use a man—with his knowledge, at least," he said evenly. "You stay here, then, live here and raise a big family. Stay away from the follies and foibles of the rest of us. I'm not so sure that I shouldn't do the same. I'm not so sure, if you were going to inherit the Kendal I heard about, I shouldn't marry you now. There is part of me hankers for this kind of life; I'd be a good Border warden, never doubt it." He grinned at her. "Aye, there's much appeals to me here, and yet I'll forgo it. What's amiss, lass? You said you liked my directness; aye, you used it on me." His glance was mocking, and she could feel the anger.

She said, "And what makes you think I'd wed with a knave like you?"

"You should be complimented. You're the only woman I ever considered marrying, even though I didn't consider it long."

She said coldly, drawing herself up, "You're much too late. I am already contracted." She rose and held her head high. How had she ever got mixed up with this man? "I can't think why I even talked with you," she said, eying him. "I must have been mad! In any event, sir, you misread me complete. I wanted you to help both Hugo and me."

"I see," he said. "Well now, mayhap I did. I had the notion Hugo and I were to stand by you, in London, till you found a more munificent benefactor than either the penniless Hugo or me." Lazily he drew from his belt a leather pouch. He shook it at her, the jingle mocking her. "Those are base coins," he said. "Not gold. And Hugo wouldn't be able to summon that much."

She said in a strangled voice, "How dare you? You, you knave!"

Tom Seymour said, "Mistress Katryn, if I've done you an injustice, I apologize. You see I am none so good with women." He looked at her long. He saw her standing there, her robe clutched close; he saw the perfect oval face, the skin white, and the deeply fringed long eyes, swimming in gold. "I'm rough-spoken ofttimes," he said, "and yet a doubt keeps persisting, for which I apologize again."

She said, "Apologies are unwelcome, sir; any further speech with you is unwelcome." She picked up her bag; he stood, quickly, to face her.

"Good night," she said haughtily.

He smiled at her, a quick flashing smile. "I suspect a kindred villainy, Katryn," he said, and bowed gracefully. "I know a precontract of marriage is a solemn thing. Yet, for the life of me, I'll be surprised if you respect it."

"Oh!" she exclaimed.

"Oh," he mocked. "Good night, sweet wench, and may thy dreams be of thy Hugo." He said this to her back, as she marched toward the door.

It was an hour and a half before sleep claimed Katryn. All the retorts that would have vanquished him came readily now to mind. Oh, the villainy of the knave! To suggest she'd sell her charms! How could he? She clutched the pillow tight in her hands and squeezed it hard. She had just meant to stay in London with Hugo and Tom Seymour till mayhap she could get a position at court. After all, her uncle was in London; she could have appealed to him. She would not think of being a light woman! She would marry, of course. What else? Then she remembered again she could marry no one but Hugo; she had promised.

She wet her lips. Joan lay insensible at her side, almost snoring; she had no troubles. Anyway, she could not think now, for that man kept mixing himself up in her mind with her other problems. It was impractical not to sleep. Obediently she closed her eyes, pushed her arm up under the pillow, and thus she fell asleep.

Kendal Castle crouched gray and solid on the hill outside the town, the Kent River encircling its foot, the hills of Westmorland stretching out to the seas beyond. It had been built in the eleventh century by the Norman Ivy de Tallebois. Its masters had guarded this side of the English border for centuries, and the castle had spread its protective winding walls for refuge.

In one of the tower rooms, before a fire, Maud Parr wrote slowly, often resting her hand on her brow. Occasionally she glanced toward the door, but nothing could be heard through the thick stone walls of this small cabinet.

She was excessively thin. There was little left of beauty in her face; it shone now in her children. The inner serenity that had always been hers now spoke only through her clear hazel eyes; her fair hair was gray, almost hidden under her coif, and her lips were pale and narrow. There were times when Maud Parr had found the burden of widowhood and three growing children almost insupportable; each time she regathered her forces to cope with what must be done, she thought she emerged weaker.

She laid down her pen. No matter how much she totted the figures, something was wrong. There was not the sum she thought there should be, and she wondered how her ambition had driven her to expect more. Worse than that, a letter lay on her table, a letter which completely dashed her hopes for Katryn.

The letter was from old Lord Dacre, lord and lieutenant of the Border, and bearer of a fine, ancient name. For three years, unbeknownst to Katryn, Lady Parr and Lord Dacre had been corresponding and settling the terms of a hoped-for marriage between Katryn and Lord Dacre's grandson. Now it had come to naught. For Maud did not have enough gold to pay for Katryn's finding and board—nay, nor a dowry proper in Lord Dacre's eyes.

She sighed deeply. Her husband had left each of his girls—Anne had been only three years old when he died—a dowry of four hundred pounds. Now it was gone, spent because Maud Parr had a son, William. Through her industry and foresight, she had affianced him to the only child of the Earl of Essex, and it had cost her much, in sleepless nights and in hard, cold money. For a moment the thought of a convent for Katryn ran across her mind; then she dismissed it: Anne was thirteen, and sweet and yielding; Katryn—well, even her mother would have to admit she was not suited for convent life.

She picked up her pen. At court she had a brother-in-law, William, for whom young Will was named. She would write to him; mayhap he could help. In Lincoln she had a cousin in the fourth degree, who had two unwed sons. North-country people had a strong sense of family; Lord Borough would help, she was sure. Aye, when he received her letter, with the pink sealing-wax rose of Kendal stamped on it, he would immediately come to her aid.

Lady Parr took up paper and pen again. She wrote carefully and steadily. She sanded her letter, rolling it up; then tipped the rest of the sand back into the silver bowl. Then she gathered up her woven shawl, and made her way down the outside staircase, across the court and through the postern gate. She was going to church.

Kendal church was cupped in the brow of the descending hills. Its doors stood open to the warm air; inside it was empty. In the south choir there was a black marble tomb, bearing the name, the effigy, and arms of Maud Parr's husband. Had it been ten years? It was difficult for her to know how much she missed her sturdy, four-square husband; the sharp edge of grief and loss had been so dulled that it was almost impossible to grasp once more the clear, forceful image of Thomas Parr. All she felt now was a sense of injustice, as though she had lost something but didn't remember quite its shape and meaning. She laid her hand on the black marble, and she was brought sharply to the present—for how thin her hand was and how raised the blue veins.

She walked up to the nave of the church, and knelt. She prayed briefly for Katryn, and for herself—for the Lord to help her in her travails.

Outside, the sun was dying; the wind was sharp and swift. The helm, they called it, in the northern counties, coming in the winter like a gale off the tops of the mountains.

Lady Parr started up the grassy path; thick, tough grass it was, tough as the sheep and people it bred, this land, these fells and moors, these steep valleys and craggy hills, these sheltered, deep-wooded lakes. Across the top of the hills, the low-lying black clouds parted suddenly, and the sun made a path through, and the hillside turned green. The sheep grazed, she could see the figures of two shepherds, and the castle bell began to toll. It would soon be dark. "The priest will be late for complin," Lady Parr thought. He was inexpressibly independent and would probably smile if she reproved him.

Down the path toward her hurried Meg Pickering, her steward's wife. She flapped like a rooster, her cloak blowing. Lady Parr smiled to see her.

Meg came to a flurried halt, for her legs were going too fast to stop at once, and the wind was blowing her along.

"Ye remind me o' Katryn," Meg said. "When ye smile like that, just like the girl that you was so many, many years ago."

"Meg, what a stupid thing to say." Maud Parr went more slowly. "God gave you good intentions, but he certainly should ha' left off your tongue."

At the castle gates Meg remembered what message she brought. "Mistress Katryn's home, my lady."

Katryn was waiting in her mother's cabinet. When Lady Parr entered, Katryn rose hastily and gave her mother first a curtsy, then a kiss on her white cheek. Then Maud Parr held her daughter off and looked at her critically, as she always did.

"Thou art pale," Maud Parr said.

"Aye, m'lady," Katryn said. She did not dare contradict. She had arrived home about an hour ago and she had unpacked her things, as she had been taught, and laid all away, carefully. She had changed her shoes, and brushed her hair, and washed. And at the last minute she had taken off Hugo's ring from around her neck, and put it away in her small jewel case, with her silver chain and her gold brooch and her little pearl cross. Then she had locked the case and come to her mother's room.

Now with the ring locked away, she did not feel quite so guilty, nor quite so transparent. If she had been wearing the ring about her neck, she would feel quite sure her mother could perceive it, right through her clothes. She bit her lip and wondered if she would ever dare wear it, here at Kendal; Anne might see it and tell. That thought made a frown across her brow. Lady Parr was sitting down on the bench before the fire. Katryn took a stool and sat, too.

"First tell me the news," Lady Parr commanded.

Katryn told about Hugo's being sent into service and about Betty's expecting. She had messages from Dame Mary about the death of her aunt. The poor thing had caught a terrible cold and pain in her stomach and expired in two days.

Maud Parr said, "I thought you were going to bring Joan back with you."

Katryn's eyes widened. "Marry, I forgot," she blurted, and then was silent, for the reason she had forgotten she could hardly tell. When she thought of kissing Hugo, instead of saying to him, primly, he would have to speak with her mother, her face went even whiter.

"What ails thee, child?" Maud Parr asked sharply.

"Naught, madam," Katryn mumbled. Tentatively she eyed her mother, essaying a smile. Inwardly she prayed the Lord to forgive her for lying to her mother, for it was a terrible sin to lie to one's mother; and, certes, she didn't really deserve a mother like hers. She said, biting at her lip, "I wish I could be like thee!"

Maud Parr said crisply, "You shall be, one day."

Katryn swallowed. Mayhap she would be. There was time, and

she would try. "I try to remember all you teach me, madam," she said. If she could only remember!

"You should certes know all my dictums," Maud Parr said. "I've said them oft enough, to you and Anne. 'Be always kind and polite to other women, setting them first, and be circumspect and always a lady with men and boys.' "

"Aye, m'lady," Katryn said.

Maud Parr studied her older daughter. "You are near sixteen," she said, "and I think to get you wed soon. I have writ a letter and you may as well know it. To a Lord Borough, our kin. You have met him. He has an eldest son."

Katryn's eyes grew wide with horror. Her mother said, "Sometimes you amaze me, Katryn. I thought you'd be pleased. And the eldest son will inherit, for Lord Borough is a baron."

Katryn said, "But . . ."

Lady Parr cut her short. " 'Tis no need to talk more now, for it may come to naught. Indeed it may. You may go now, and get your needlework, and you and Anne may attend me in the parlor."

2

The name had originally been de Burgh. But now, after more than four hundred years, it had been Anglicized, and the big, burly man riding ahead of the small group of horsemen spelled it Borough.

Lord Borough was fifty-five years of age. His mane of thick hair was dark gray, his eyes brown. In the saddle he sat like a man half his years. His shoulders were powerful and so were the hands that held the reins. He was hawk-nosed as one of his falcons, and his mien was lordly. The Norman blood ran proudly in his veins, and his possessions were many and rich. He had come from his principal dwelling place, his great manor house of Gainsborough, which lay seventeen miles from Lincoln.

Lord Borough rode ahead of his two sons, Henry and Thomas. Behind them came eight serving men, all well armed, for this was wild country. There were no roads in Westmorland, nothing but tracks across the wild moors, down the steep valleys. They were riding hard, because they wished to reach Kendal before nightfall.

The wind was strong. Lord Borough had ridden this way but once before, a long time ago. He had responded to Maud Parr's summons quickly. Although he was related to Maud only in the fourth degree, she had few male relatives to turn to except for him; accustomed to authority, he was ready to wield it far away from home.

They topped a rise in the hill. He raised a gauntleted hand from the reins. "Ahead lies Kendal," he shouted.

Behind him Henry called back, "Thank the Lord."

Lord Borough made a grimace that twisted down his big mouth and heavy jaw. He had enjoyed this ride; Henry was too soft. Lord Borough spurred his horse to a gallop and motioned the men to follow.

The castle gates stood open, for it lacked an hour to sunset. Borough remembered it—its great circular tower, the oldest part of the structure. All was enclosed within gray stone; stretching off to the right of the court were the stables, the brewery, the guest stables, the chicken houses, and pigpens at the very end. On the other side lay the kitchens and storehouses. Doves sat cooing on the roof of the dovecot, and far in the distance, through the clear, winy air, the pipe of the shepherds could be heard.

Lord Borough stamped into Kendal as though it were his. His sons followed in his wake; the serving men had already led off the horses. Maud Parr came forward to greet them.

She kissed Lord Borough. He patted her shoulders clumsily; his eyes were kind as he thought swiftly how much she had changed. He would not have known her, he swore to himself. He stepped aside and presented his two sons.

Maud bestowed a kiss on each young man, who were twenty-nine and twenty-seven. As she had told herself all last week since she had known of their coming, even if nothing came of this visit it was good to have three big men stamping into the house.

She was a bit flurried by them, too. She took Anne by the hand and presented her to her cousins.

Lord Borough put his big hand on Anne's shoulders, and asked her how old she was.

"Thirteen, my lord," she said.

He laughed. "And how fair a lass she is, Maud."

"And my son, William," said Lady Parr proudly.

So this is the heir of Kendal, Borough thought. Dark, with a frailty of feature and face. He will grow tall, but will he grow strong enough?

William had taken Lord Borough's hand in his slender one. He raised one black eyebrow. "And I am almost fifteen, sir." His black eyes sparkled, and Lord Borough smiled.

"A fresh young one you are, my lad," he said genially, and swung around to survey the hall at his leisure.

His two sons had already divested themselves of their boots, and their servants were bearing the stained footgear away. Anne was standing alongside her mother; she had a sweet demureness that men would relish, Borough thought. He approved of her, and he gave her another quick friendly smile. William was watching him out of alert eyes. Borough let his eyes go over the ancient hall, with its raised dais and huge open fire pit. A great table stretched along one side, and the balcony off which other rooms opened was supported by carved wood pillars a foot thick, blackened by smoke.

Lord Borough thought of the great Norman who had built it. What days those had been! Now—his jaw jutted out. He was deep in the past, and he absently took a tankard of ale that a servant was bearing and drank it off.

"What an inheritance thou hast here, Maud," he said. He brought out a fine linen handkerchief and wiped his mouth.

"Thank you, my lord," Maud said. "But you have still your boots! Won't you let . . ."

He cut her short. "I seldom wear other. My boys will bear me out." He indicated them with a wave of his hand.

"Supper will be soon; you must be hungry," Maud said. "Should you like to see your quarters, my lord? And your servants . . ."

"Thomas," Lord Borough said, "get thee out to the stables and see the accommodations. Especially for my own steed, Maud." He felt he should explain. "He's a great unruly beast. My pride and joy. I thought," he continued, "you had another daughter." He looked around as if to make her appear.

Lady Parr said nervously, "Katryn is—well, to be truthful, I don't know quite where she is."

Lord Borough remembered that Maud Parr had been a widow for ten years. "You probably have spoiled her, Maud," he announced, "and not used the rod enough."

"I'll send for her," Maud said hastily.

"I shall find her myself," he announced.

The walks of the first court were circular. Lord Borough went through an arch and emerged into the garden. Flowers grew along the paths, and neatly fenced in was the herb garden. It was free of weeds, he noted approvingly. He went through the gate to the big court with the stables to another, larger garden, rather haphazard but pretty, with fruit trees. The doves cooed. There was a small wooden building with its door open right in front of him. He peered in.

A young girl sat on the dirt floor, peeling rushes. Over her stood another, wrapped in a green cape, its hood back. "Nay," she was saying. "Look thee, wench." And she took the rush from the sitting girl's hand and neatly divested it of its outer shell.

Suddenly she turned, aware of another presence. "Oh!" she gasped.

Lord Borough was bent down to peer in the low door. He reached out a hand and drew her into the fading sunlight. He looked down at her from his height.

"I remember thee," he said, "from five years gone now. Do you remember me?"

"Acourse, my lord." She smiled and gave him her lips to kiss and he bent down and touched her mouth with his. Then he drew back and looked at her closely.

She said, "Oh, an that you should see me like this!" She flung out her hands to indicate her disarray, and pushed back a loose curl. "Indeed, I apologize; the time fled—I am . . ." She stopped short.

"Uncommonly fair," Lord Borough put in. "Thou hast grown up."

For a second her eyes showed gold. Why, she thought, he said the same as Hugo. And he looks at me like Hugo. She shot him another glance. Mayhap men are all like no matter what their age, she thought rapidly. Lord Borough was speaking.

"That green suits thee," he said flatly, nodding his head, "with thy red hair."

She said demurely, "'Tis Kendal cloth, my lord. We are most proud of it here."

Lord Borough's dark eyes were narrow and sharp. "With thy red hair," he repeated, "and thy white skin, and thy remarkable eyes."

Katryn drew in her breath. She looked straight at him. His face was tanned and creased, his eyes sharp as a hawk's, his bearing lordly. And he was paying her extravagant compliments. Frantically she hunted for the right words to say. I should say something a wee bit reproving and a wee bit pert, she thought desperately. Is this how men in London act? Or in the South? She remembered the brief warmth of his lips. She tried to remember how old he was or whether he was widowed. She had heard of married men making advances to maids. She saw him smile, a wintry smile.

"You must answer when you're spoke to," he said.

She cast down her eyes. A ready answer came this time. "I'm but a country lass, my lord," she said. "And I lack the city manners." She thought this time she could look at him from under her lashes, as she did with the Bellinghams' boys, to show she was jesting, just a little.

Lord Borough smiled. Then he sighed, a little, satisfied sigh. "Come along," he said, "your mother will be afretting herself. I' fact, she is already."

Katryn gathered her cloak close, for the wind was blowing sharp now. Lord Borough reached out and took her ungloved hand. The leather of his gauntlet felt smooth and warm from his fingers. She felt him squeeze her fingers under his, and she made a motion to draw her hand away, for she was startled.

"Nay, nay," he said patiently. His hawk eyes were on her. "You like this country, do you?"

"Aye," she answered. "Much, my lord," she added. She would not apologize for Kendal!

"You've a proud heritage, do you know that? Your grandmother was the granddaughter of John of Gaunt."

"Aye," said Katryn Parr proudly.

"And your great-grandfather . . ." He hesitated.

"My great-grandfather," said Katryn, "was the Earl of Westmorland."

Lord Borough chuckled. "So you know it, and are proud of it. You should be. Have you always lived here?"

Why is he asking me all this? she wondered? Still, a wench should be flattered by so many questions. "I was born here, my lord."

Borough remembered that well enough. "Aye, ye certes were, lass. You were born when the signal fires of the Border were blazing high. When you were born, I was riding north with Surrey to Flodden, and I saw your father there, with his moss troopers dressed in that same Kendal green. Yea, Mistress Katryn, whilst the King was playing at war in France, we of the northern counties truly fought a battle! And brought Scotland to her knees. For a time, anyway," he added and threw her a smile.

They were entering the hall. All the young men rose, and Henry and Thomas Borough stared, smiled, and came forward quickly. Maud Parr, too, hastened forward.

"Katryn, you must change your dress," she said. "But first I shall present Henry and Thomas, your cousins."

Katryn curtsied. To each of them she gave her lips, and a small smile. "Welcome to Kendal," she said.

Lady Parr said from behind her, "Now you must change, Katryn."

Lord Borough held up his hand. "No," he said. "She looks well. Let her be." Maud Parr looked amazed. Borough said, "I wish her to remain, Maud."

Katryn looked up at him. He removed her cloak, lifting it from her shoulders. As though he already has spoke for me, she thought swiftly. Jesu, but 'twas for one of his sons he came! Her eyes met his in a long look; she felt her stomach turn over. But I am betrothed to Hugo, she thought desperately, and I cannot marry anyone else! But I cannot think now what to do. I'll have to wait. Till later.

"Anne," she said, "pray tell Jack to fetch some towels, and some warm water, for all of us."

The dinner was wonderful. Katryn thought, I've been looking forward to it all day, smelling the roasting fowl, and the thin slices of veal warmed in wine, and now I cannot eat any of it, not even the wild-bramble jelly. This is the same thing that happened to me the other day at Bellinghams'. I am a silly wench with a silly stomach, by the Mass.

Fortunately there was no need for her to talk. Lady Parr and Lord Borough were reminiscing, and the two younger Boroughs and William were busy eating; even Anne, who had a small, dainty appetite, and was always twitting Katryn about hers, was eating. The stewards and Meg Pickering and her two daughters, and some of the other servants, ate farther down the table. Just the same, every once in a while Lord Borough would look over at her, a long, long look. She could feel deep down inside her that she knew exactly what he meant.

She was so excited her hands shook. If he speaks for me, she kept thinking, what shall I say? Oh, Mother of God, what shall I say?

And how can he know, so soon? He knows my family, of course, and he has been two years widowed—he had said so bluntly just before supper. He wants a wife mayhap; a young one, so he can have more children. She knew all men, especially those with titles, wanted children—sons mostly, strong, sturdy boys. From king to baron, they wanted sons. And that means . . . Her mind whirled.

But I am already affianced, in the eyes of the Lord, for Hugo and I pledged ourselves in a precontract. It nullified any other marriage; it surely did.

Lord Borough was saying, "I have rebuilt Gainsborough and I would wish you to see it, Maud, with its many windows, and great fireplaces, and most of the rooms paneled, and carved so cleverly. This," he said, flinging out his hand, "is like living a hundred years ago."

Katryn raised her head. "I love Kendal!"

Borough smiled. "Aye, and so you should, my dear."

"We cannot have windows because the walls are too thick," Katryn said.

"But what do you do here in the winter?" Thomas Borough asked.

"Why," said Katryn, "the castle is the center of life hereabouts. We throw the hall open for all festivities, saints' days, Christmas. There are troops of entertainers and troubadours."

"And you like it?" Thomas asked her brother.

Will Parr hesitated. He grinned. "I catch cold," he said. "I'd prefer London."

Kathryn said, "Will!" She shook her head; she could not understand her brother. Kendal would be his someday. "I love it," she repeated. "If all are finished, we can roast nuts, as we do on a winter's eve."

The table was pushed back, and the servants took the food. Benches and stools were pulled close to the enormous hearth. Katryn sat on a low stool, and Lord Borough found his place beside her instantly. He poured her more hot wine, and she could hear Jock strumming on his lute in the background, while two of the menservants sang songs of the Border. Rush lights—for Maud Parr could not afford candles—burned in thick cups on the stone mantel, and cast an eerie light. The smell of roasting nuts and wood smoke escaped into the room.

"This is what winter is like at Kendal," Katryn whispered, for Lord Borough was listening to the music of the ballads.

"They're singing about Flodden," he whispered back.

"Aye, I told them to; I thought you'd enjoy it."

She felt curiously as though she had made her decision, during dinner. Once she felt his hand on her hair, and she tipped her head to look up at him. A lazy look, she thought, as if I were asking, do you want me? If you do, speak out. I cannot wait for Hugo, she thought suddenly. I cannot wait, and I will do penance, every night. For just a second it crossed her mind that she would never have courage enough to confess to her mother what she had done. But she pushed that away. Acourse I would, she said to herself; but it might be three years afore Hugo returns, and I'll be old. What is the use of telling my mother? She would never forgive me, and Hugo might not come back, contract or no. Lord Borough's description of his manor house and spreading acres lingered in her mind. The heavy gold chain he wore glittered like the money he must have in his money boxes. He was a baron. His hand reached out and caught hers. "It is time for you to retire, my dear," he said. "I wish to speak with your mother."

A kind of sanity returned to her. Once more the enormity of the sin she might commit unnerved her. I should say "No!" she thought desperately. She gave her mother an imploring look. She saw her mother's sweet, calm face, thin and white, and the beautiful hazel eyes, so like to her own. How those eyes would look if I said I was contracted! I cannot, she thought miserably. I'm a poor coward. I'll go straightway to bed and pray for my soul. If I can get out of this room without showing my distress, I'll thank the Virgin.

She wore a little cross of pearls. She clutched it tight in her hand. "Good night, my lord," she said. Her knees felt weak. She kissed her mother good night; she knelt for a moment, and felt her mother's hand on her head.

"The Lord bless you, my child," her mother said as always.

Katryn struggled to her feet. Her eyelids were cast down. I'm a wicked woman, she thought; I've committed a mortal sin. I'd best get right to bed and pray hard.

Katryn Parr was married to Lord Borough in Kendal church, at eleven of the clock in the morning, the second of November. The day was cold. The helm clouds wreathed the mountaintops; the sun sent shafts of gold into the valleys. Winter had come to Westmorland.

Three days later, at noon, she mounted the new mare Lord Borough had brought her; she rode away from the gray castle, through the village where men and women and children came out of the small houses to wave and cry out their good wishes. She brushed away the tears with her gloved hand. She turned about to watch the rumbling cart coming behind with her possessions. It had all happened so quickly; the whole month had passed in a welter of terrifying changes. She was leaving Kendal. In a short three weeks she had left her home and become a woman, a wife. She glanced over at her husband, taking her eyes off the rutted track for a moment. She should not show tears, she thought; she should smile. She remembered well her mother's words: "A wife is happy only if she loves her husband."

It had been three weeks ago to the very day that her mother had called her in, early in the morning, and told her of what had transpired between her and Lord Borough the night before. Maud Parr was amazed that her daughter herself was unsurprised, as amazed as she had been when Lord Borough had said, "Your Katryn is not for my sons. They are milksops. She is too much woman. She ought to bear children, Maud, not wed wi' one. Don't you know what I'm saying, Maud? Your Katryn does. I want her for myself." Maud Parr looked sharp at her daughter. Then she amended her suspicions, for although Katryn seemed unsurprised, she had gone white, and pressed her hand to her breast in Maud Parr's own gesture, which she often used when she was distraught. It made Maud smile.

"Are you undone, child?" she asked. "'Tis a great honor, and Lord Borough a fine, good man."

Seeing Katryn's distress, she went on, saying how fine a family he had and what an old name, of great honor, and that she was proud that such a man as Lord Borough had spoken for Katryn. It showed that she was a good girl, and properly brought up, or else Lord Borough would not be so willing to take her as he had—without a dowry. It showed that Katryn herself was a big dowry, and her mother was glad to see that she reflected how well she had been raised.

Under this overt praise Katryn's face lost its pallor. She basked in the glow, for ofttimes during her sixteen years she had been severely reproved. "Sometimes," Maud Parr said, "I thought you'd never learn."

Maud studied her face a moment; true, it was an arresting face—and her eyes! Maud Parr wondered briefly if she had ever looked like that, but certes she had not; part of Katryn's spirit had come from her Borderer father, the master of Kendal. Maud thought how quickly her problems had been solved, for Lord Borough had said he would lend her a hundred pounds. She and William and Anne could reside in Greenwich this winter; and perhaps she would prosper more, in health and mind, if the long winter in the North were avoided for one year. It would be good for Anne, too, for she was thirteen and needed a glimpse at a gentler life, a more social one. The North was naught but sheep and mountains, and icy lakes glistening in the frosty air. Yet it had produced this daughter of hers.

She said, "We should go down on our knees and thank the Lord for his blessings this day."

She was surprised at the alacrity with which Katryn knelt and cried, "Bless me, madam!"

Maud Parr was touched. She looked down at the curly red head and the glimpse of white cheek. "Why, my child, thou hast always my blessings!" She laid her hand on Katryn's head. She thought, she is grown now, to a woman's estate. Soon she will know what that is; now she wonders what lies ahead. I could tell her—and I shall try during the next weeks—what it means to be a woman and thus to hold men dear, from one's father, to one's lusty sons, to the husband she should most like comfort in the sickness afore death. All this I have done, Maud Parr thought, and ofttimes it is cruelly hard. "Katryn," she said, "I bless thee forever from my heart and, no matter what haps, I shall always love thee." Then she added, "Prithee do not weep. There is too much to do. We must sort out of the chests the cloth and furs that can be recut for thee. I may have to send thee to thy husband without a dowry, but God forbid you go unclothed."

Katryn wiped her eyes. "Furs?" she asked.

"Aye," said Maud. "That court robe of your grandmother's that lay away for so many years. We could line a cloak of Kendal cloth with the white fur; 'twould be magnificent."

Katryn sat back on her heels. "Aye, it would truly," she said.

The whole castle was busy. Lord Borough left the next day, for he had much to do, he said, afore he was wed; and, he told Katryn, he was impatient for her. "I am too old to wait more than two weeks," he said. "I shall return the first of November to claim thee. I shall bring you jewels," he added. "If I must send to London I shall bring you topazes to match those eyes, to lie against thy white throat."

"Thank you, my lord," she whispered. "But you need not bring me aught." She bit her lip; she knew what she should say. "Except thyself," she added.

He put his hand in her red-gold hair. "I love thee, Katryn."

He said it just the way Hugo had, she thought. She set her mouth stubbornly. She certes owed it to Lord Borough never to dwell on Hugo again; she must banish him from her thoughts, and she would.

She kissed Lord Borough on the lips and bade him Godspeed. She stood on the battlements and waved good-by with her shawl. When she could see only a dot in the distance, she still leaned on the stone parapet, deep in thought, and smiled happily to herself.

During the next two weeks Maud Parr regretted having acceded to Lord Borough's demands to be wed in so short a time. After a week of intense activity, great weariness seemed to claim her, so that even after she got into bed at night, her limbs ached, her head ached, her chest pained her, and she coughed. Each morning she struggled once more to cope with the enormous task of readying the castle for a wedding, and wedding guests. From nearby Sizergh would come the Stricklands—kin, of course. From farther away would come the distant Parrs, and Greens. The Bellinghams, they must come. Joan arrived three days before the wedding, bringing gifts and food and a fresh-killed buck, plus many messages from Dame Mary, who would follow her daughter in twenty-four hours.

Joan thought both Lady Parr and Katryn white and exhausted. She wondered why Katryn seemed so changed and didn't seem to sleep. She attributed this to excitement. "After all, a lass only weds once," Joan said, laughing. "It is very exciting, Katryn," she whispered, when they were in bed.

Joan didn't know she herself was a kind of badge of Katryn's guilt. "Please stop talking," Katryn cried. Surprised, Joan was silent, and soon she slept.

On Katryn's wedding day it snowed a little. Great white flakes drifted down on the gay wedding party as they streamed down the hill to the church. After the ceremony the warmed brideale was drunk and the loving cup passed around, right below the altar. The banquet was a tribute to Maud Parr and the generosity of her kin and neighbors. After the banquet, when darkness fell, Katryn was taken upstairs. A huge old chamber had been cleaned and aired, and the straw mattresses shaken, and the new down mattress laid carefully on top. Katryn was put between the linen sheets. Two candles burned. The door closed on her mother and Joan and Cat Strickland, her cousin. Cat was twenty-seven and a widow; Katryn, lying there waiting for her husband, could hear her giggling in the hallway. She put her hands over her ears, rolled over and felt herself sink deep into the feather bed. It was comfortingly warm. She waited.

The next day she was very annoyed with herself for her continual blushes. Even Meg, her youthful companion and now her personal maidservant, received a hot blush when she asked in a whisper how m'lady liked marriage.

By afternoon Lord Borough took charge. "We're going riding," he said, and he took her out.

They rode to Lake Windermere. It was cold and blowy. When they stood on the trail beside the lake, looking across it at its encircling hills, Lord Borough seized her and held her tight. "This is you," he said. "This wild, wild land. And I love thee. Tomorrow I am going to take you home."

"It is best," she conceded. She was through with Kendal now.

"Come, m'lady," he said, holding out his hand.

She smiled at her new title.

That night she talked again, for the last time, with her mother. Maud Parr reminded her of the great household she would soon have under her command. She reminded her again of Borough's daughter, Lucy. "She is older than you by some seven or eight years. I'm afraid difficulty lies ahead for you."

Katryn said, "I shall deal with her."

Maud admonished her. "But softly, Katryn. One can understand how jealous she will be, and the fact that she did not come to your wedding . . ."

The two women nodded together. The sickness Lucy Borough had announced as an excuse not to come to Kendal to see her father wed might have fooled her father, but not his new wife or her mother. Katryn briefly wondered how easily Lucy Borough did fool her father. If he credited every word she said, Katryn's task would be doubly hard. Katryn know instinctively that by not coming to her wedding Lucy had flung down the gauntlet and cried for war. She shall have it, Katryn swore silently. I'll take no nonsense from any wench that's reached the age of twenty-four or so and isn't wed. She's probably ugly as a horse, and wait till she sees me. She tossed her head and smiled. "I'll settle that wench," she said. "There'll not be two mistresses in my house!"

Maud Parr said, "Be kind, Katryn. As I have taught you to be with Anne."

Katryn looked down at her shoes and felt guilty. "Aye, my lady," she said.

"You are leaving your father's house, your ancestral dwelling. Pray take with thee all the good things you have learned, all I have taught you. Remember me, my daughter; remember me, in thy dreams and thy prayers and thy everyday living. It shall be a long time afore we meet again."

Katryn cried, "Oh, why? Why so long? Cannot you come and visit and stay with us?"

Maud Parr said, "Thou art still such a child. Acourse I shall come. When you have your first child I shall come." She smiled and she added, "Say good night now, daughter."

Katryn knelt. Her mother blessed her. Still kneeling, Katryn clasped her hands. "Try very much every day," Lady Parr said, "to deserve the Lord's blessing. Since you shall no longer have mine."

"No longer have yours?" Katryn whispered, her eyes wide and suddenly fearful.

"I mean," Lady Parr said, putting her hand to her breast, "that I shall not be able to lay my hand on thy head every night, as I have done since you were a wee bairn."

She bit her lip. Her mind searched the past, the days that were gone. When Katryn was a wee bairn, Maud had had her husband by her. "How happy I was," she said. "I pray God you shall be as happy." For just a moment it occurred to her that her husband had been young and full of gusto; there was no doubt, Maud Parr thought, that Katryn would have a different sort of marriage. But it was a good one, and the child seemed satisfied and happy. "Godspeed, my daughter," she said, and she said it once more, the next day at dawn; then Katryn rode off from Kendal.

Lord Borough had sent a horseman ahead to warn the Fountains Abbey of their approach, and when Katryn saw it, just at dusk, with the bells of the tall tower ringing out for complin, she gasped in delight. The evening was still. Over the symmetry of square stone abbey, leafless trees stood gaunt and tall, and a few leaves rustled along its walks and cloisters. Firelight glowed ruddily through the small-paned windows, and the chapel windows gleamed like jewels, hand-cut. Torches flared at the gates, and smoke curled from its fat chimneys. Katryn heard the sound of singing in the chapel; the monks' voices were full and reverent, the Latin sonorous in itself. "This is a famous abbey," Lord Borough said. "And you shall be comfortable after such a long ride."

She looked into the courtyard eagerly. It seemed full of men and horses, part of whom were their own escort. Lord Borough noted her glance.

"There will be other travelers, my dear," he said. "There always are, here; 'tis a famous stopping place. But you shall have the finest room for guests, the room over the gatehouse, for I've seen to 't. Tonight you and Meg will sleep well there. I shall probably have to share a room."

He is looking at me expectantly, she thought. "I shall miss thee, my lord," she said obediently, and was pleased to see by his smile that she had said the right thing. 'Tis not so difficult, she thought, to get along with men, long as you sweet them a bit. He patted her hand, and they rode into the courtyard. She reined to a stop. Lord Borough dismounted and came toward her to help her himself. At that moment, fifteen feet away, through the gathering dusk, she saw a long, lean face topped by a rakish hat, and from under that hat a one-eyed man had fixed upon her like a beacon. But it was not until she saw Hugo himself that she realized what dreadful coincidence had occurred. She and Hugo were met again, unexpectedly and with horrifying suddenness. She gasped. A thousand terrible possibilities rushed through her head. What if Hugo spoke out? She clung to the pommel with both hands, and Lord Borough's voice brought her to her senses.

"What's amiss?" he asked, his voice sharp.

She steadied her voice and dropped the reins. "Naught," she lied. "I'm of a sudden weary, I warrant, my lord." She kept on talking, forcing herself not to look to see if Hugo had seen her. "It came of a sudden, as I said, my lord; I fell all undone."

She looked very white and stricken. Lord Borough made an exclamation of concern. Mayhap she would faint. To his right was a tall, black-haired man with Sir Francis Bryan's badge. "Here, sirrah," he said peremptorily. "My wife, Lady Borough."

Tom Seymour turned on his heel, in response to the appeal for aid. He noted Lord Borough's gray hair. Katryn had bent over in the saddle, so Hugo would not see her. Tom Seymour tossed the reins of his own horse to his servant, and without a word lifted Katryn out of the saddle, scooping her neatly into his arms. She turned her head into his shoulder, but not before he had time to see whom he held.

"By God's most precious soul," he muttered, very low. The oath reached her ears, muffled as they were in her hood. She even heard the hint of laughter in his voice: a see-what-did-I-tell-you voice, now you have gone and done it and got yourself into a barrel of trouble what with your husband and your previous contracted!

Aloud he said, "Lord Borough, may I assist you and her ladyship further?" Katryn, suspended in those heavy arms, wanted to squirm free and ask to be set down, and could not. Helpless, she felt him squeeze her, just as though he were mocking her plight. Yet his voice was respectful as he spoke with Lord Borough. "Aught I can do, my lord, I'll be most glad."

Why does he just stand here, holding me? she raged inwardly. He squeezed her again and said, "Let me carry her ladyship to her room, my lord. I fear she has fainted dead away."

Oh, the liar, the knave, she thought. He knows perfectly well I've not fainted! She almost spoke; then she lay limp again. Mayhap he is right, she thought; he might be trying to help. He knows perfectly well what's undone me. And what if Hugo should cry out at the sight of me. She could just hear his voice, excitedly crying, "Katryn! Katryn!"

She felt Tom Seymour move now, with Lord Borough leading the way. Oh, I pray I get past Hugo, she thought. She kept her head turned into Tom Seymour's shoulder; under her cheek she could feel the steady beat of his heart. She kept her eyes tight closed. A door banged behind them; now narrow steps must be ascended. Tom Seymour gathered her close, to keep her away from the walls. She had got safely past Hugo, and he had done it for her. She felt vaguely grateful. He bore her with such ease, too. Clasped so close in his embrace, she sighed a little with some unbidden pleasure. He was so very strong. All manner of thoughts raced through her mind—Hugo, and how Tom Seymour had pre-

dicted all this, and how he had said, "I suspect a kindred villainy."
She heard Meg's excited tones. Meg bustled past Tom Seymour and
his burden, and was in the room when Lord Borough and Tom
entered it.

"Lay her ladyship on the bed, if ye please, sir," she said.

Tom Seymour laid her down gently, lifting back her hood. Meg
pushed past him clucking. "I'll do it, sir," she said. "Poor, poor
lass. The trip was too much, I warrant."

Katryn opened her eyes. The first thing she saw was a pair of
blue eyes regarding her, mockery glittering in their depths. From
under straight, level black brows his eyes looked into hers for a brief
instant, though his face was as dark and lean and impassive as it
should be. There was even concern in his voice, as he inquired
gently, "Art feeling better, my lady?"

Lord Borough was holding her hand. She looked up into his
troubled face. "All's well," she said shakily. Lord Borough removed
his pouch and handed Tom Seymour a gold piece.

"Thank you, my lord," Tom said. " 'Tis too much for so small
a service, and one which I gladly performed. But I thank you and
her ladyship, and mayhap 'twill bring me luck at the dice table
tonight."

Lord Borough frowned. "Here?" he asked gruffly.

"Sir Francis will not forego his gaming pleasures, my lord," Tom
Seymour said; there was laughter again in his voice. "And I do
confess I concur with Sir Francis."

Lord Borough frowned deeper. Katryn thought, Now why did
he say that? He didn't need to. She opened her eyes wide and tried
to give him a reproving stare. Instead he grinned at her, bowed
deeply. "I hope you feel better, my lady," he said politely. Then he
was gone.

"What a knave he is," she said aloud.

"Aye," Lord Borough agreed. "He is one of the new breed.
Daring all, almost godless, disrespectful, and unmoral. We've been
breeding them, aye, and they cluster about the King. You mark
my words, Katryn, he and his master are here to inspect this
monastery and go over its books. We've fallen on evil days and are
left to the mercy of rogues." He walked over to the window. Since
the room was above the gatehouse, he could look down into the
court.

"Aye," he continued. "There must be twenty of them down there, and this one the leader, save for his Sir Francis. And only God knows what dark deeds they've all done at one time or other. List to that one here openly boast and confess his villainies. He's proud of them, and I wouldn't put it past him to steal from the priests."

Katryn's eyes widened; she was thinking of Hugo. "I think they'd not steal," she said, sitting up. "I don't think they're all rogues."

"You're young, too," he said heavily. "You're young."

This was an indictment she could scarcely deny. For a second she was tempted to argue hotly that he had wanted her young; that she couldn't help her youth, and aye didn't want to help it, for she was proud of it. With some difficulty she restrained the very essence of youth, its arrogant delight at its own years, and the wonderful, timeless years that stretched ahead. Years and years and years, and all of them certain to be just like now. Instead Katryn Parr closed her eyes, masking her face, leaving it in sweet repose, guileless. "I think I'd best retire, my lord," she said wanly.

Lord Borough said, "Acourse, and forgive me."

The faintest smile touched her mouth. This was ridiculously easy. Her woman's mind noted that and at the same time her young stomach stirred rebelliously. "I think a little food," she said, casting quickly about for something suitable for both a fainting woman and a starving one. "Some buttered eggs." Oh, the thought was delicious. "And some white bread." Surely a monastery as rich as this would have big loaves of bread, mayhap crusty from the ovens. "And pray don't forget, my lord, that Meg will be very hungry. Indeed," Katryn added urgently, opening her eyes, "she's probably weak with hunger, and she eats hearty, that wench. Aye, just cast your eyes on her, and ye'll see."

Lord Borough nodded, as Katryn leaned back and closed her eyes again. He bent down and kissed her cheek. "Good night, my sweet wife."

"Good my lord, the saints bless you," Katryn murmured.

Lord Borough closed the door. Katryn sat straight up. "Lock it, Meg," she said, and hopped off the bed. She went over to the window and looked out. Down in the courtyard there were still some figures: men and grooms and their horses. There was a great deal of laughter and she leaned her elbows on the sill and watched until the bells rang forth calling all to the chapel.

Katryn wiped the last bit of butter and egg off her plate with the crust of a fresh-baked loaf. The fire burned merrily in the whitewashed rounded fireplace. The room was cozy and warm; the wind rattled the tiny diamond-shaped panes and was a delicious reminder that while outside the raw wind blew cold and bone-chilling, within was warmth and safety and a full stomach. She sighed, wiped her mouth, drank the last of the ale in her cup, and rested her feet on the hot bricks laid near the fireplace, which Meg would wrap shortly and put between the white linen sheets.

The bed had a feather bed upon it. Inviting as it looked, Katryn found herself full of excitement, wondering what the next day would bring, when Lord Borough would show her the new domain, her new-found woman's world. Her eyes sparkled. What lovely dis-coveries would lie ahead! Imagine having the keys to a large manor house; imagine being its mistress, complete. What might its rooms not hold? What treasurers were in its chests, its old jewel cases, its wine cellars? And it was so near Lincoln. Imagine the luxury of being near a town as great as Lincoln. The mind was beggared for words.

She had discarded her fear that Lord Borough would meet and talk with Hugo. Such a contingency was remote, and knave that Tom Seymour was, he would not give her away, she was sure. She was safe and, with luck, she would never meet Hugo tomorrow. Even if she did, it was cold enough so that she could cover her face with her furred hood. Indeed, there was little or no danger; and it was well, too, for Lord Borough might conceivably reject her, his religious tenets were so strong. He'd not be the man to keep a wife who had contracted herself to another, for how could children be born to such a marriage, he would think. Of course he didn't know how she prayed every night, and did penance. Surely in time the Lord would smile once again on her; she thought truly He al-ready had forgiven her, for certes she had been showered with good things, and a good husband, even if he were much older than she.

"You should get to bed, madam," Meg said.

Katryn smiled. She could not accustom herself to Meg calling her madam. After all, Meg was four years older than she. But this new mark of respect, a fresh reminder of her new and important estate, made her eyes shine and her mouth turn upward in a dazzling smile. "I should, Meg," she agreed, and in the silent room, just on the heels of her words, came a new sound, a tapping, insistent.

Katryn whirled. Meg looked frightened; her eyes searched the room. It was Katryn who went to the window, loosed the latch, and swung the casement inward. A booted leg swung over the sill, then another. Tom Seymour swung by his hands for a moment, and then slid into the room. Meg gave a cry of dismay. Then, seeing her mistress had actually admitted this man, she clapped her hands to her mouth, and her round black eyes were wide. Her mistress and Tom Seymour had words, low and furious on Katryn's part.

"You villain," she whispered, but her voice shook. "How dare you? And whence came you? You'll be my undoing, by the Mass! I cannot credit it, that you truly dare! And why? Tell me, why! I never gave you a moment's notion you could come here, like this, full of stealth—"

Tom Seymour was closing and latching the window. Finally he turned and said, "Oh, for God's sake, hush, hush, hush!" He advanced toward Katryn, raising his fist in mock gesture. His blue eyes went toward the door, seeing it securely bolted. He loosened his jacket, easing it back off powerful shoulders; his rakish cap sat on the back of his head, and a jeweled dagger gleamed at his belt. He had removed his spurs, so his booted feet made no sound. He sat down, at his ease by the fire. Katryn stood glaring at him, hands on her hips. He turned his head slightly, to glance at her. "If you'll cease your clacking tongue for a moment, Mistress Katryn," he said lazily, "I'll tell you why I came."

Something important it was then. Of course he had not come to try to make love to her. She almost blushed.

He noted it; he said wickedly, "Did you truly think that I was nigh mad for a kiss from you? Or that I couldn't stay away from your bedchamber?"

"Acourse not," she cried indignantly.

"Something in your manner must have suggested it to my mind," he said. "But no matter." He turned to Meg. "Climb up on the bed, girl, and put the pillow about your ears."

Meg's spine grew stiff, and her beady black eyes snapped. Tom

47

Seymour grinned. "I do believe," he said conversationally, "that she'd listen in any case." This thought amused him and he laughed, stretching out his legs toward the fire. "My dear Katryn," he said without preamble, "Hugo saw you and is aware you have got yourself wed."

There was silence in the room. Katryn's heart plummeted. She clasped her hands to her breast hopelessly. "Oh, marry," she breathed. "Oh, by all the saints! What in God's name am I to do?" She stopped then, for she saw that Tom Seymour was not finished.

"Your husband would boggle at a precontract, would he not?"

"Aye," she whispered and nodded her head, coming closer to him. "Aye, he would, certes, sir!"

Tom Seymour scowled and rubbed his hand over his chin. "Hugo is trying to make up his mind whether to speak with Lord Borough in the morn." He said this as if he thought Hugo an arrant fool and as though she should know how silly she had been. "How little able you are to read yourself, my lady. One should know what one values, what one wants."

She said passionately, "I know what I want now!" Her face was set and white, and her eyes gleamed, narrowed and calculating. She breathed hard. Here she was on the very threshold of stepping into Gainsborough Hall as its lady. She had already paid the price for it: wedding a man almost four times her age. Her eyes narrowed as she stood by the fireplace, looking into the flames.

"I'll not kill him for you," Tom Seymour said.

"Jesu," she said. "I think not of bloodshed!"

"You look it. And you look just as guilty as Father Joseph down below when he wins at dice."

"Father Joseph?" she asked. Then she said, "I wasn't thinking of bloodshed, truly! But you could put something in Hugo's ale so he would sleep tomorrow morn!"

Tom Seymour shook his head. "I carry no drugs with me, my lady. Odd but true."

"I don't dare see him myself," she said hopelessly. "I don't dare go creeping through this house." Her eyes grew full of horror. "I'd faint or die if someone saw me!" She swallowed. "I must think."

"Sit down," said Tom Seymour, pushing forward a stool. He glanced over at Meg, who was staring at the two of them with amazement and disbelief, not comprehending how her mistress could have got herself into such a godless situation. Tom Seymour gave her a brief, pitying look. He said to Katryn, "I can do naught with Hugo; he just listens to me and says naught, but he might listen to a priest."

He watched her out of the corners of his eyes. He watched while she digested what he said, while she added and calculated and figured out what she must do. He almost smiled; she was so intent she did not notice.

"Remember," he said softly, "you once loved Hugo. So you said."

Virtue spread across Katryn's face. " 'Tis my duty to my husband not to think on Hugo."

"How convenient," he murmured.

She gave him a reproachful look. "I don't expect you to understand duty," she said. Then she pushed that thought aside, gazing at him speculatively. She rose, keeping her eyes on the back of his head, and retrieved her small purse. When she returned to his side, she held out to him all her worldly wealth: three gold pieces, a small pearl cross, and Hugo's ring. "Will you help me?" she asked, very low. She began to be afraid their voices could be heard, and to realize the danger in Tom Seymour's presence here. What if someone should try to enter?

He looked up at her, frowning a bit. "I'll be out the window in a few seconds, mistress. What else do you want me to do?"

"I want you to see this Father Joseph you spoke of, the one who dices," she said. Offer him these to tell Hugo 'tis God's will I'm wed."

Tom Seymour raised one black eyebrow. He studied her a moment. "No," he said flatly.

Her face fell. "Why not?" she whispered angrily.

"Because I have a peculiar conscience, which I shan't trouble to explain to you. I subvert no priests, nor bribe a man of God, no matter whether he is bribable. I don't know exactly why, Mistress Katryn, but it sticks in my throat." He got to his feet, and she saw he was on the point of leaving her. She paid no attention to the expression on his face, one of distaste both for himself and for her; he was fastening his jacket.

She cried, because there was not much time, "Take a note to Father Joseph for me then!"

He shook his head. He said, almost bored, "Poor Hugo. He never stood a chance with you and me as his rascally opponents, did he? Now, Mistress Katryn, I'll give you a word of warning. Never, never commit to paper what you wouldst not have known to any." For a long minute he looked down at her. Then he said gruffly, conceding some aid, "I shall tell Father Joseph you will be waiting to see him before Mass tomorrow morn. I shall tell him you wish to see him alone, in the chapel. There's no harm in that; there must be much you have to confess, after all. And I hope this is all worth it."

Before she could say good-by, he had opened the window. She saw his hands reach out for an unseen cornice, and then he was gone.

She made Meg hush. She sat down before the fire. The way ahead was clear, then. She would see Father Joseph early tomorrow in the chapel. She would ask him to see Hugo; she would give him all the money and the few jewels she had. That was the best she could do. If Father Joseph failed, she still had a card up her voluminous sleeve. She would have to convince Lord Borough that Hugo was lying, that she had rejected him. This thought was comforting. All would be well and tomorrow she would see Gainsborough Hall. Tom Seymour's last sentence lingered in her ears. Of course it was worth it.

It was almost dark and it was very cold, a deep biting cold borne on a shrill, wet wind. For several hours Lord Borough had spoken of stopping, and of continuing their travel in the morn, but they had pushed on, regardless of weather or aching muscles and bones, weary of the saddle.

Katryn was conscious not so much of weariness as of discomfort. For a while during the morning, she had been buoyed up by her successful speech with Father Joseph. She was able to bask in remembering a task done, and an unpleasant consequence averted. But before long, the sun hid itself behind sweeping clouds, as though to tell the visitor to Lincolnshire that here was a land nearby sea and peat marsh and great rivers. These streams flowed as though their banks would not contain the water—as indeed many times they did not, but spilled across the land with all the fierce suddenness of flood. Aye, it was different from Kendal, much different, low-lying and so damply cold. But soon they should see the welcoming lights of Gainsborough Hall.

" 'Tis on a slight eminence, nigh the river," Lord Borough shouted across the wind, his voice coming less strong than usual, for weariness assailed him. He glanced at his bride. Her face looked cold, but her eyes sparkled and her youth sustained her, he thought enviously.

He peered ahead into the growing dark. Gainsborough Hall should be within sight, but there were no lights ahead, and he made an exclamation of anger. Katryn turned to look at him. "There are no lights," he shouted, waving his riding crop.

She peered ahead, too. For some reason dismay struck her. They rode on, the pace increased. Beads of rain clung to her clothes and her face. The wind sighed mournfully; then out of the darkness gleamed a single flickering light, far up, as though in a tower. She craned her neck to see; a ghostly glimmering came from the top of a tall pile of house, now there, now gone. She shivered in the saddle; tight were the reins in her wet gloved hands. Impatiently, fearfully, she tried to see ahead, for indeed this was Gainsborough.

The curving drive went up toward the house, the whispering sibilance of the river following them. Katryn tried to see. There was a great oblong ahead of her. Brick it was—this must be the new part—with tall windows, from which light should be shining and was not. The great new doorway, flanked by two sets of windows twenty feet high and almost twenty feet wide—there were no torches in the polished niches beside the doors. Yet indeed there was a light, and not a ghost light, high in the house; Lord Borough saw it too, and even in the dark she could see the anger cross his face. He leaped from the saddle, and was at the doors, hammering on them with his whip. Speechless, afraid, and filled with foreboding, Katryn sat quietly on her horse, looking at the silent black house. Finally one of the grooms was at her side. She dismounted and came slowly to stand by her husband in front of the closed doors of Gainsborough Hall. Then, without sound, they began to open inward, creaking a bit. Lord Borough nearly stepped in first. Then he remembered Katryn. He took her arm. She glanced at him; she was icy cold; her knees trembled. Unreasoning fear took her, and she shrank back. Lord Borough was impatient, grasping her arm.

"Come, come!" he said peremptorily. " 'Tis just that mad Lucy, forgetting! Soon there will be light and warmth. Come, come!"

She obeyed, coming forward in his wake. She gasped then, for what she saw gave meaning to his words. Fearfully Katryn fastened her eyes on the single figure in black that stood before them, holding her candle high, shielding it with her hand from the drafts of the open doors. That candle played across a long, narrow face, like Lord Borough's, atop a long, lank frame, slightly bent; and the face possessed a pair of eyes startling in their black intensity. The mouth was moving; the eyes had gone past Lord Borough and were fastened on Katryn. "Welcome to Gainsborough," the moving mouth said. The eyes stared at her, almost unseeing. At this minute the candle flame sputtered and died, and Katryn uttered a loud cry of terror.

She would have turned and run if Lord Borough had not seized her arm and pulled her close to him. Behind her she could hear two of the serving men, and Lord Borough raising his voice in a loud shout. "Light," he shouted. "To me, Gib!" Gib was his personal body servant, and Katryn heard Gib's feet running across the hallway. It was a huge hallway. She had never seen anything like its immensity. Even in the light of one candle it had stretched ominous and black all about. A door crashed, and from the very back came a man with a torch—from the warmth and fires of the kitchens, Katryn thought, where surely all would be normal. Lord Borough squeezed her waist. "Don't fret, sweetheart," he said, in a more normal tone. " 'Tis all explained. Lucy forgot we were coming. She is saving; she didn't light the torches or candles."

The man with the torch was close now. In its light Katryn could see the stairway rising, a heavily carved stairway with painted scutcheons on it. And now she could see the glitter of paint on the paneling, gold and blue. She took a deep breath. Lighted, the hall would be beautiful.

"You see, my sweet," Lord Borough said, squeezing her again and proud now, as her eyes roved over the immense hall. At the top of the stairs appeared more light. An older woman stood up there, with a branched candelabrum which she set down on a great sideboard.

"There's a gallery there," Katryn said excitedly. Galleries were wonderfully new, with long windows and a place for all one's guests to sit in cushioned window seats or stroll along its length to chat and parade their new gowns. Ahead of her loomed an open door. Within was oak paneling, and Lord Borough was propelling her toward it.

"We'll go into the winter parlor," he said. " 'Tis a warm room, and we can sup there."

For a moment she demurred; she would have preferred to go right to her chamber and change her wet clothes; she thought with longing of her warm robe of white Kendal cloth, cunningly woven.

Then Lord Borough said, "Nay, I know what you think. But I wish to have Mistress Dawson properly arrange thy chamber, so that there are no more bad surprises." He said it jokingly and glanced at her, but she saw not his glance. Instead she saw the eyes of Lucy Borough, deep-set and satisfied.

Katryn narrowed her own eyes. She said sweetly, "Marry, we'll economize no more on light and candles, dear daughter." I'll see to that, she vowed silently. Then she swept ahead of Lucy into the parlor, showing her neatly who had precedence.

But when Lucy came into the small cabinet, lighted now and with a fire blazing, she said, low to her father. "I had the fires laid against your coming, my lord."

Katryn took the time to look at her closely. She saw the great ruby cross on a pearl necklace Lucy wore. How utterly and completely beautiful it was, the enormous rubies winking in the firelight. And when Lucy curtsied to her father upon her words, and then kissed him, Katryn saw gold-lace petticoats. She had naught so fine, she thought. Gold lace on one's ordinary petticoat! Or had the girl truly expected them? Why would one wear gold lace when guests were not coming?

Lord Borough was saying, "You did wrong, Lucy. And how oft must I command you not to revisit the dead past? How oft must I forbid you the room?" He bent his stern eyes on her, and yet his face softened. The two were remarkably alike: the father's face creased and tan; his daughter's drawn and brooding. Lord Borough patted Lucy's shoulder. His voice was kinder, as to an errant child who has been punished. "One cannot regain the past, no more than one can stay the future." He sighed heavily. "You retire now, Lucy. You need sleep."

"Aye, my lord," Lucy said. Then she turned her black gaze on Katryn. She stood uncompromising, silent.

Angry, annoyed, and her feelings hurt, Katryn stared back. Mean horsy wench, she thought. Who does she think she is, flaunting gold lace? Much good it may do her, with those long shanks. Marry, what feet she has, too; I've never seen such an ungainly creature. And she must be twenty-five, at least. Marry, thought Katryn contemptuously, she might as well be dead.

Katryn threw back her cloak. Her own dress was plain gray woolen, for riding, but it fitted neat and tight across high young breasts, and it was caught up at the side for fullness. Her little boots were dainty, and the silver spurs her father had given her jingled merrily, as though to say, Look at me, Look at me, as she walked across the room toward the fire. At the fireplace, alongside Lord Borough, she took her place. My rightful place, she thought. From that vantage point she surveyed Lucy, and the silence in the small room deepened.

Then Lord Borough said heavily, insistent, "Kneel for your lady mother's blessing, Lucy."

Lucy, in her black gown, stood as thin and stiff as the black poker that rested alongside the fireplace. She gave her father a look of mute appeal, but it availed her not. Dropping her eyes, she knelt as she'd been bidden. For a moment Katryn was shocked. There was no need for this; she was too young to expect a daughter's homage from Lucy. She bit her lip. Pity stirred in her; she laid her hand on Lucy's head, shrinking a bit at touching her. She said, low, "The Lord bless you and keep you this night. Sleep well."

Lucy struggled to her feet. Katryn felt sorry for her. Keeping her eyes averted, Lucy slipped out of the room like a wraith. Katryn spoke impulsively, low, so the departing Lucy wouldn't hear: "Why does she wear black, my lord?"

Lord Borough's mouth drew down at the corners. He decided on the truth. "She mourns her mother," he said.

Katryn felt a kind of cold horror come over her. She said slowly, "But it's been two years!"

Lord Borough nodded. Then he said, "As God's my witness, Katryn, if you could help her, I'd be in thy debt forevermore! If you could help her—" He broke off and flung out his hands. "But no one can, I fear. I have tried. Her brothers have tried. She has a big dowry, and she'll not wed; indeed, I can scarcely insist, her state being what it is. I shall explain it to you later, but not now, not now." He shook his head, as if to rid her of the notion he would talk further, and also as if to shake himself free from a constant, nagging worry.

He looked to the doorway, and Katryn saw that Thomas and Henry were there. Lord Borough pointed his finger at them. "Just say good night," he ordered. "Then leave us."

There was a moment's silence. Thomas essayed a weak smile, which did not quite come off; Henry succeeded better. He grinned and gave Katryn a glance, as if to say that was the way his father was and what could one do about it. He said, "We welcome thee, our little mother." He bowed and blew her a kiss. "In the morn we hope to show you Gainsborough."

"Good night, my lady," Thomas said stiffly. His eyes were on her for a second, devouring, and then he, too, bowed and they were both gone.

Katryn, standing yet by the fire, felt a chill go over her. Lord Borough smiled his creased smile.

He said, "You find me peremptory? Strict? You will see I must be. But you, my little one, I adore." He took her hand and held it gently. "Fear not, my sweet. We will go upstairs to thy chamber now. I have had it redecorated for thee with new paneling and hangings. I pray you like them. The fireplace has been refaced. The feather bed is new from Lincoln, the sheets newly weaved and the quilts new-fashioned. There is a broidered chair, and I shall try to be a good husband! I swear I shall! And perhaps, with thy warmth and youth and love, you can bring order to this house. Come now."

He took her arm. Outside in the great hallway lights burned on the brave blue and gold. The Gainsborough crest blazed over the entrance and its heraldic devices adorned the great stairway. At a low landing the steps branched both ways; truly elegant, Katryn thought. As she mounted them, the lighted gallery swam opulently before her eyes. Step by step she went up to the very top. At the end of the gracious gallery was an open door. A woman stood in the doorway, and as Katryn came nearer she curtsied. "Welcome, my lady," she said. "Welcome."

3

The little desk was covered in pink velvet. The quills were plumed and pink. The inkwell was silver and the sander gilt. Katryn dipped the pen and began to write.

My dearest mother:

The messenger who will bring this should reach you afore Christmas, so this carries our best wishes and our heartiest greetings. He will also bring the New Year's gifts for all of you, but pray do not open them before New Year's Day! I have worked hard to get them ready, too, for it seems like the days have flown past with so much to do! I never realized before how much you did. I shall try now to tell you all that has happed betwixt our leave-taking and my coming here.

The hall is beautiful, but I shall not describe it much, for you heard what my lord said of it, and it is all true. I have a waiting woman, Mistress Dawson, who is fat and kind, and Meg does extremely well. I am so glad she is here with me. So you see I am well took care of. I have three gentlewomen, too. Two are sisters, kin of the Cobhams, for Alice Cobham was my lord's first wife. The other is from a nearby manor and will stay here with me. Her name is Maud Bishop, and she is a likely lass. They are all very respectful, and ofttimes I have to smile. Imagine me! At first I could not give them orders, but now it comes easy. At present they are chattering loud, so I cannot think, and you would be surprised to hear me say, quite like you, "Hush, hush your clacketings! Ply thy needles," or else, "Maud, pick up thy lute and play for us." I know you would smile, and, my dear mother, I wish you could come and be with us, for truly sometimes I need you very much.

But I do very well in all manner of endeavors. For instance, you should have seen the state of the manor here. All the chests needed repacking and airing and fresh herbs. The stillroom looked as though it had never been cleaned, and its vessels were encrusted with dirt. I had two men set to scrubbing them with sand. The wine cellars were dirty, filthy. From buttery to pantry to kitchen itself, all was miserable, and I cannot think it took only two years to get all in such case; one would have deemed years of neglect had preceded the housekeeping. So you see I am not near done yet. And such waste! Lucy would not have the candles lighted oft, but the ends were all thrown away, or else the servants took them; and great huge slices would be cut off the end of each loaf of bread because Lucy thought crusts produced ill humors. So I summoned all the servants, even the dressers and warders, and I told them all was clean as a pin at Kendal and it shall be just as clean here. All the keys were handed over to me, and every morn and every eve I make my rounds of inspection. My lord is very pleased, also, with the suppers and dinners I contrive, but I must tell you true, there is no wild fowl in all England like we have here. Partridge you think is tasty, and so do I, but you should taste our smaller birds—I've learned their names—like dotterel, puits, godwits. With a wine sauce, or just roasted, they are truly the most delectable I've ever put in my mouth, so tender.

Acourse the housekeeper, Mistress Bell, and Lucy don't approve of what I do, but I have tried to be nice with them, albeit firm. I have tried hard with Lucy, even though she is so distressing. For instance, I sent to Lincoln for two new lengths of goods to make new gowns for her, for she was still wearing black! I told her she must put her black things away. Instead I found her secreting them in her chest in her bedroom. I had to order her to remove them. But she is tractable, even though she is so odd. For when I said to her, "Why, folks will think you're daft," she gave me the most violent look. That was the day I found out the mystery. I shouldn't write you about it, if it still troubled me so. For this house was very queer. When I got the set of keys, I found all the locks right enough save one. And one day in the topmost story, I found the door for that; I was looking for a storeroom. When I went in, I was nigh mad with fright, for what should it be but the small chamber that had held my lord's wife for the last two years of her life. She must have been utterly mad! There was a bed in it, with gyves and you could see where she'd gnawed at them. It was horrifying, and there was a *prie-dieu*, and I think that's where Lucy was the first night we came, up there praying. So I locked the door, and the key is on my chain so Lucy cannot go in. But she is most strange. For instance, she worships her father; and I think the reason she wanted to wear black was for penance, for her brothers have told me she always fought with her mother and they never understood why she mourned her so at death. So I said to her, "We'll lock the room, and we'll never go there again." She cried at me, "How can I do that?" And I said, "Well, I can; I can lock things out, and if I can, you can."

And I said, "Don't think of it further, it's done and past. Even if you didn't treat your lady mother right, she'll forgive you where she is now, in heaven." That made her feel better, I think. Still, I can never tell what she truly thinks, for she looks not at me but at anything else in the room, then she flashes sudden a black gaze on me, or the keys at my belt. So I tell her, no matter what, she may not have the keys; it cannot be good for her, surely, to go up there. I should think it would lead one to certain madness.

Katryn laid down her pen for a moment. She reread the words she had written and a little shiver ran up her spine. Then she looked over to her gentlewomen, grouped about the fire, sitting on their stools, their billowy gay skirts resting sedately on the floor, their young voices hushed but excited, their hands and tongues busy. The room was pretty and just as it should be; if there was a locked room upstairs where a madwoman had agonized out her days, one should banish all thought of it. She picked up her pen again.

Lord Borough's two sons are very kind to me. Henry is gay and sweet with words, and always busy; he is outdoors even in the most inclement weather, and he likes much to play at cards, which he is teaching me. Thomas, my lord's eldest son, is quiet and reserved, but very steady, quite grave, much the opposite of Henry. He manages a lot of my lord's work, and is in reality the manor's bailiff, doing much the same as Walter, what with his long accounts, and his riding out every day to supervise and oversee what is being done and what is needed, in the manner of houses, and repairs, et cetera. One can always depend on him. I know it seems odd they've neither wed, but I sometimes get the notion that their father wishes to keep them about him, although they could bring their wives here.

She laid down her pen again. She looked over the last paragraph. My handwriting is neat and clear, she thought, and I wonder if some of my disquiet is clear, too, for I do not want it to be. She felt a bit hampered by pen and ink. Unaccustomed to using it, she found correspondence laborious work, and yet she owed it to her mother; a dutiful daughter must write all the news, especially so momentous news as this, her daughter's house and the new relations and her lord. Her mother would say she was growing up. And her poor mother, left alone with that silly Anne and Will, who was never much help at anything, probably missed her much. Katryn let out a long sigh. A bit of ink clung to the end of the pen and she wiped it carefully so as not to spoil her velvet desk, before she began again.

The hall looks beautiful decorated for Christmas. Henry and all of us gathered pine branches to festoon the stairways and walls, and long ropes of ivy for twining about. We are going to have a huge Yule log; 'tis already cut, and I swear 'twill have to be dragged in. And we shall have singing, and mulled wines and ale, and a boar's head, proper roasted.

She frowned. Was there much more to tell? Should she say she was disappointed about the odds and ends of jewelry in the case that Lord Borough had handed over to her? That it had just a few chains, not too heavy, and that Lucy had already taken all the best pieces and always wore the great ruby cross? Every time Katryn saw that cross swinging over Lucy's flat bosom, she wanted to seize it. No indeed, she could not confess such a thing to her mother! I wonder why, Katryn thought fretfully, I have to entertain such wicked thoughts so constantly? I'll try to forget I want that cross; mayhap my lord will give me a new piece for New Year's.

She looked down at the long letter she had writ. The mood of satisfaction which had been hers when she had begun it had now vanished. She felt baffled and annoyed. That Lucy, she made every day unpleasant! Looking at me from her sly, mean, black eyes as though she hated me! She probably does, too. Jesu, I would like to slap her face sometimes, and someday I will! You cannot hurt her with words; she turns sullen, and mutters under her breath. She is as mad as a dotterel; it wasn't fair to ask normal happy people to live in the same house with her. Katryn picked up her pen and wrote furiously, ink flying and words spattering across the white paper.

Ofttimes Lucy annoys and angers me so I don't know what to say, nay, nor how to control my anger. Yet I know, my dear mother, that she is my lord's only daughter, and I know how he must feel about her, even though she's so queer and distrustful. Ofttimes I don't know what to do!

She felt a trifle better; looking down at her scribbled words, she felt some measure of relief; it was good to be able to confess this much. She wet her lips; mayhap she should go to the priest, and speak with him about Lucy. Her eyes brightened, and she decided to end her letter.

Pray send news back, and pray do not pay my messenger, for I've recompensed him enough. I have not said much about my lord, but I can tell you he is happy and well, and so am I, your loving daughter. With my greatest respects, your loving and obedient daughter,

KATRYN, LADY BOROUGH, K.P.

She sanded the letter, and shook off the shiny grains into the gilt sander. For a moment she wondered why she had affixed her maiden initials to the letter; mayhap, she thought, it is because I am so proud of my heritage, my people, and Kendal itself. She drew a long breath, now she was indeed satisfied with herself. It was a fine signature, and the *Lady Borough* looked nice. This is the first time I have writ it, she thought; aye, and for a wench just sixteen, I have done very well, very well indeed, and I'm not going to let Lucy spoil it.

Her eyes narrowed a bit. Were this two centuries back, and she the lady of Kendal with a lord of the Border for husband, she'd have disposed of Lucy, right enough. In some ways the old-fashioned days were best, truly. Now the very air was charged with change; Lord Borough complained daily they were entering on godless days, with soft-headed ideas of every man being able to seek his god by himself and not through candles lit on an altar, and the Bible being read by all manner of men. Oh, well, she thought, I have too much to do to fret about this and that which makes no matter to us; what haps in London is no concern of ours, even though men like Tom Seymour say it is.

She folded her letter, and dropped on it the hot wax. Her seal was an old one, the roses of Kendal, and she resolved suddenly to use it always. I could have it regilded, she thought; the next time I go to Lincoln, joyous thought, I shall have it done. Oh, I must make a list of all my errands in Lincoln. She rose and said to her women, " I go to the chapel to pray, and I shall include all of thee in my prayers, so mind you be good whilst I'm gone and keep busy. When I return, we shall practice some carols."

They all rose, and curtsied, and said, "Aye, my lady." On the heels of such sweet homage, Katryn swept out of her rooms and down the long gallery, her keys swinging at her belt, like the chatelaine she had suddenly become.

The chapel was small, but artfully worked in dark wood, with an arch above the altar and a stained glass window through which the winter sun was transformed from paleness to glowing ruby and gold. Father Blake, Lord Borough's chaplain, knelt on the first step on a red cushion; when he heard Katryn enter, he rose rather laboriously, his bony knees protesting.

He looked at his mistress as she came toward him. As the light from the window fell on her face, he acknowledged the arresting quality of her eyes, the level dark brows. She moved proudly. Nearer now; her hood fell back, and she made no movement to replace it. She can be selfish and godless, he thought.

He said, "Cover thy head, daughter. Hast thou forgot thou art in the Lord's presence?"

The great eyes gave him a long level look. Then with one white hand she rearranged her hood. She stood before him; he got the swift impression of pride and impenitence. "Judge not, that ye be not judged," he spoke aloud.

Katryn jumped. She gazed at him with some respect. Was he reading her mind about Lucy? "I have come to confess."

He nodded, knowingly, and with compassion. "We shall seek the booth."

"No," she said. "No, father. I want to speak with thee not as a confessor, but as a friend."

Father Blake's face set in sadness. As a friend, he thought ruefully. How can a priest practice his profession in such a world as this? When the old forms were being called to account, held askance? I should insist, he thought. But he said, "What is it you wished to speak about, my lady?"

"About Lucy, father, and about how I can exorcise the devil in me that hates her so."

Father Blake waved his hand. "We should seek the booth."

"Why?" asked Katryn, impatient. "When you know me and I know you? Why must I be prisoned in that booth?"

Ah, the arrogance of gentility and youth! "My daughter," he said "thou hast much to learn of humility."

"I am repentant," she said. "Else why should I come?"

"Why, indeed?" he asked, himself and her.

"Tell me," she said, "about Lucy, father. It's been your privilege to know her, as a child, as a young woman. Tell me what you know that I may be some measure of help to her, and thus to myself."

He was silent a moment. Then he said, with more acuteness than Katryn gave him credit for, "She is not mad. If that's what you're thinking, 'tis not true. She is the victim of wicked and evil emotions, and if she could spew them up, she would be saved." He crossed himself, and bent his head; he was praying for Lucy, Katryn knew. Politely, she bent her head too, and told the Lord she would be glad if He would help Lucy. Father Blake said aloud then, "She is jealous, she envies thee. Her mother was a strange woman, and she and Lucy were never close; it seemed difficult for Lady Borough to love Lucy. In turn she worshiped her father. She should have been wed long ago," he said sadly, shaking his head at the unwisdom of the world, and his own helplessness against it. "I urged it, but no heed was paid to my words, for Lady Borough said Lucy was unfit for marriage."

His tired eyes searched Katryn's face. He put a hand on her shoulder. "Kneel with me, my daughter," he said, "and pray for forgiveness, for thyself and for Lucy, and I want you to forgive Lucy and her envy of you. When you are done, you should feel free of thy burdens."

There was silence in the small chapel as they knelt and bent heads. Finally Father Blake rose, and Katryn did too. She murmured a word of thanks and squeezed his hand. "And thou art sure, then, that she's not mad?"

"Not she, she is not the one," he said, thinking not on his words, nor what they implied. He turned from her, back to the devotions that she had interrupted.

Katryn hesitated, and then, head bent, made her way from the chapel through an old doorway into the oldest part of the hall. She came to a flight of narrow steps and her eyes went part way up. There, at the very top, was the locked room. She swallowed. Lady Borough must have been quite, quite mad to have had to be cuffed to her bed by hands and feet. Mayhap she had tried to do away with herself, or harm another. "Jesu," Katryn whispered under her breath.

She gave the stairs another surreptitious glance. Her feet felt like lead, and she tried to walk past, but her hand was clinging to the old post at the bottom. The words of Father Blake echoed in her ears, "No, she is not the one." If Lucy were not, who was, then? Were they living with a madman they didn't know? For surely it couldn't be Henry, or did his gay good humor in the face of his father's dictums conceal a cunning, unrealized depth? And surely it could not be the serious Thomas!

"I must go on," she told herself. She gathered up her skirts. Then she stood paralyzed with fear. Someone was coming down the steps; someone with a heavy tread was coming nearer and nearer.

She knew she should run, but fear and curiosity held her motionless. She waited, hardly breathing, her hands icy and her heart pounding, till at last she saw who it was.

"Thomas," she said. "Thomas!" She stared at him, and backed away.

His eyes, like Lucy's, were black and he gazed at her blankly for a second. Then he said, "What do you here, Katryn?"

His voice was even and normal. He looked as composed as always. If he even got a glimpse of what she were thinking, he'd think her mad, and quite rightly too. She gave a shaky laugh.

"You startled me," she said. "I was coming from Father Blake."

"Oh," he said. "Well, do not stand here; you'll catch cold."

This evidence of his concern was heartening, and just like Thomas. They walked together down a passageway and into the great dining hall. There they parted. She was halfway up the great stairway to her chambers when she remembered she hadn't asked Thomas what he had been doing there himself.

4

Katryn was removing the Christmas decorations. Holly and ivy and great pine branches lay piled on the floor. All the gifts had been given, and Katryn was still busy exclaiming over the petticoats and partlets, the caps and coifs. The new table-covers were already in use, and two little silk screens were standing in front of the hearth in the winter parlor. Katryn had a new gold chain with a gold pomander, and four new pairs of gloves, one from Spain. She had a new gold damask underskirt, from Lucy, and she had even been able to give Lucy a kiss in thanks.

Katryn's mother had sent gifts for New Year's; her sister Anne had sent six linen and lace handkerchiefs, and her mother a purse for her girdle with three gold nobles. The familiar face of her mother's messenger had made Katryn homesick. They had taken him in and fed him, and listened to the news from Greenwich, where her mother and Anne and Will were staying.

The King had quarrelled again with the Queen, the messenger reported. It had been Henry's habit to dine or sup occasionally with Queen Katharine and her twelve-year-old daughter, Mary; mayhap, as her enemies said, to escape Anne Boleyn's sharp tongue. Now his Queen was sharp-tongued also. Henry found not his usual ease when he lounged in her apartments watching her sew; she argued too. "I dare say," Katharine once said, so loud she was heard in the anteroom, "that for every learned doctor you find who declares our marriage invalid, I could find a thousand, if you'd dare to give me leave!"

Henry shouted, "By God, I'll declare the Pope a heretic, and marry whom I please!"

Katharine snorted. "Take our case to Rome!"

Henry stamped toward the door. At it, he turned solidly. "Get thee to Richmond!"

Katharine had picked up her discarded sewing. She flashed him a look which was not lost on Henry, who had been married to her eighteen years. He backed down. "At least, keep to your own apartments!"

Katryn was listening breathless. "Then what happed?"

"Then there was a banquet, and Nan Boleyn's father was made Earl of Wiltshire and Ormonde, and Nan the Lady Anne Rochford, and she sat at the Queen's place, above the Duchesses of Suffolk and Norfolk, with a smile on her face like a cat. And then at Christmas, did not Henry reverse himself, and bring Queen Katharine out into the halls at his side. Marry, m'lady, 'twas a rare thing to be at Greenwich this Christmas."

Katryn had misliked to see her mother's messenger go. She had had another letter from her cousin Catherine Strickland. Cat was widowed; she was twenty-eight and had a son, and she lived near Kendal, in great Sizergh Castle. She wrote that it had snowed heavily all during December: "from the great windows of Deincourt tower you could see nothing but snow; we even had difficulty cutting the Yule logs, but at last it was done."

Katryn was reading the letter to her husband. "If this Cat is a widow, why don't you ask her to come visit us?" Borough asked.

"I wanted to, my lord," Katryn said joyfully. "She sounds lonely at Sizergh, all alone with her son. And she is so very fair." She was thinking to wed Cat to Henry Borough. "May I write her back, with her own messenger?"

"Certainly," Borough said. He was afraid she was lonely, too. He was away much.

"I'm sorry I must leave you so oft," he said.

She said seriously, "I warrant most wives who see more of their husbands aren't as proud of them as I am of you."

Katryn was making silk covers with tassels for the stools in the solar. "My sweet wife," Borough said. "I shall be gone two weeks."

As the King's warden of Pontefract Castle, it was his duty to see to its armaments, tally them, and check over its muster and rolls for the Crown. "When I come back," he said, "we shall go to Tansfield. The manor is part of your jointure, and I wish you to see it."

Lord Borough rose and went to the fire, and stirred it. "Wilt ha' wine?" he asked.

Katryn said that she would not relish it. Borough swung around; she looked pale, and she had been eating little. "You need fresh air and sunshine," he said. "Promise me you'll ride out tomorrow; you could go part way with me."

The morning was frosty and clear. If Lord Borough had not been riding away for two weeks, it would have been a memorable ride, for the January sun had outdone itself, and its shafts fell warm on brow and cheek.

After the riders had covered about seven miles, Lord Borough called a halt, and leaned over from his high saddle to kiss his wife's gloved hand and to whisper a word of farewell. Then with a flourish of caps they were gone down the rutted road, leaving Lucy and Katryn alone. Katryn said nothing, and wheeled her horse. Lucy trotted along at her side, saying nothing either, looking dark-faced and stormy. The grooms had galloped on ahead and Katryn called to them, but they did not hear. She waved her whip.

Lucy said, "I told them to ride ahead!"

Katryn checked her horse with her knees. "Why?"

"I wished to have a word with you."

Lucy said nothing further, and Katryn, determined not to show curiosity, concentrated on her animal.

Lucy finally spoke. "You dismissed Wat, the cook's helper that I depended on, who was so deft with the medicine making and herbs!"

Katryn retorted, "Marry, he was about the kitchens half naked, dressed in a lewd fashion and unfit to be wi' the maids!"

Lucy said coldly, "What have you done with him?"

"I should ha' had him soundly beat," Katryn said. "I sent him to take care of the pigs, where he belongs."

"Oh," Lucy said with some relief. "Look you, m'lady, I meant what I said about his talents. If I—if I find fit attire for him I should wish to have him in the kitchen, for which he's been well taught. She paused. "Wat is most odd, I grant, but I have taken an interest in him since he was young. When he was young, he spoke hardly at all, and now no one can understand him save me."

Katryn said, "He's a dreadful creature, mistress. I cannot conceive—" She shot Lucy an appraising glance. "If I consent, he must scrub himself, and have the barber cut his matted hair."

"Pray try to be merciful." Lucy clenched her hands on the reins.

Katryn said sharply, "How dare you speak thus!" She spurred her horse, and as she did she felt a rush of blood to her head and she swayed in the saddle. She caught hold of the pommel. Lucy leaned over, staring at her. Katryn murmured, "I feel faint." She tried a deep breath, and her head cleared a little. She met Lucy's eyes; they were dark and full of venom, as though searching for weakness. Lucy bent over like a falcon ready to strike, and she seized Katryn's bridle.

Katryn struck at her hand viciously with her whip. She was breathing fast in sudden inexplicable terror. The grooms were nowhere in sight. She raised the riding whip again. Lucy backed away, and Katryn spurred her horse and galloped ahead.

She was panting. She could hear the hoofbeats of Lucy's big horse coming behind. She rounded a curve in the dirt road, and saw the grooms. She gave a long high shout. "Halloa, halloa there!"

"Merciful God," she muttered to herself, for one of them heard her. She saw them wheel their horses at the same moment that Lucy galloped up alongside her. Waves of dizziness went over Katryn. For fear of falling she slowed her horse to a walk, and Lucy did the same. Katryn could hardly speak. "Thou'rt mad," she whispered, her huge golden eyes fixed on Lucy's face.

Lucy sat stiff and frozen. "Nay, thou art," she muttered, holding her arm; the first signs of blood were beginning to show on her sleeve. "You struck me."

"Aye, and I'll do it more, if you come near me," Katryn said. The grooms had arrived. Weakly she surrendered her reins to the head groom. "I am faint," she said low. "Pray lead my horse."

Katryn was well enough at supper time to dine in the hall. She sat straight on her cushion on the bench next to her husband's empty chair, her back to the fire. Henry served; he was kind and jolly. But halfway through the meal, she began to have pain and nausea again.

Lucy said, "I warned you about these crusts. They make unhealthy humours."

"There's nought wrong wi' crusts," Katryn said. "It's an old wives tale, and wastes too much bread." She felt the nausea rising. "I'll leave you," she murmured.

She stood unsteadily. Thomas was very concerned. His dark eyes shone with fear and apprehension. He came toward her slowly, his eyes fixed on her like a magnet. He put his hands on her waist, to steady her.

She swayed, and her eyes met his. Under his gaze she felt odd, almost as if hypnotized.

"Loose my waist, Thomas," she whispered.

His eyes seemed unblinking. He gathered her up in his arms; she tried to free herself, but it was no use. He carried her all the way to her bed.

The next morning she felt better. Meg was poking up the fire and Mother Dawson was brushing her hair, when Lucy knocked on the door. She brought breakfast for Katryn, and it was carried by Wat. Lucy had indeed dressed him fitly, and had even snipped off his long greasy locks. Lucy said, "Oh, my lady, I hope you feel better this morn! And I have brought food." She kept right on talking, as though she were afraid Katryn wouldn't let her finish. "There is warmed wine, and a fresh egg cooked in butter, and little planchets of white bread with the crusts neatly cut off. And in a hot pewter dish, and sizzling slices of pork. I wanted to show you how well Wat cooks, and how this is but one of his talents, my lady."

"Thank you but get him hence," Katryn said fretfully. She realized that Meg and Mother Dawson were looking at her strangely but she didn't care.

"He's but a poor speechless thing, my lady," Lucy said, but Wat had gone. Katryn saw that Lucy wore a bandage of linen on her arm. She gave a curtsy and withdrew slowly. Katryn watched her go, thinking she should stop her and thank her, but no words came.

Mother Dawson said, "Mistress Lucy says you struck her by mistake."

"I did it apurpose," Katryn said. "She was about to push me from my horse!" She bit her lip and sipped the wine; it tasted good.

Mother Dawson said mildly, "Mayhap you think too ill of her, my lady. I knew her when she was but a babe."

"I wish you'd strangled her in her cradle," Katryn said.

"Nay, nay, thou'rt not thyself," Mother Dawson said, worriedly.

Meg said brightly, "Master Thomas gave the candlemaker a rain of blows this morn—for speaking ill words and saying you sent him to the stocks. I was right in the court drawing water I was, when he done it."

Katryn felt a stab of pain. "I'm going to be sick," she cried.

Mother Dawson ran to the bed and looked at her mistress. "She has fainted," she cried to Meg. "Fetch some water. I'll bathe her head. Quick, Meg—Lord help us, she's all undone and the master not here. If aught haps to her whilst he's gone, he'll beat us all!"

White and worn, Katryn stayed in bed all day. In the afternoon a messenger arrived bringing a letter from Cat Strickland. She was coming. If that were not enough, in two days Katryn felt better, and in a week her sole reminder of her former trouble was a little dizziness.

That week, at the end of it, Cat came. Katryn was never so glad to see the boxes piled in the hall, the shouts of men outside, and the bustle that meant arriving guests. She flew down the great stairway, and Cat took her in her arms.

Cat was twelve years older, but she had lived near, and they had known each other since they were little children. She brought Westmorland right into Gainsborough Hall.

Katryn wiped her eyes. She held Cat off and looked at her. "Thou'rt just the same," she breathed thankfully. "Just as pert and pretty as ever!"

Cat bridled and tossed her head, and said archly, so Henry could hear, "You are a flatterer, my lady."

Katryn giggled. Henry looked at her with surprise and relief. It was the first time he had heard Katryn laugh for some time; now that she did, he realized how long it had been. The faintest shadow crossed Henry's face as he made his way up the stairway behind the two women, listening with but half his mind to the questions that flew back and forth between them. He noted Cat's neat ankle ascending the stairs ahead of him as absently as he began to realize that she was a widow, with a seven-year-old son, and that she was the mistress of the Sizergh Castle. But when he laid down Cat's little box, which he had carried up for her, he took Cat's hand and kissed it.

"I'm glad you came," he said directly.

They were standing alone, near the door.

"Thank you, Master Henry," Cat said, demurely. Her round face was full of good humor and her eyes were merry. Her bosom was full, her hips generous, her cheeks dimpled. She said then, her eyes sparkling, "I'm glad I came, too!"

It was wonderful, Katryn thought, how quick she had regained her spirits from the very minute Cat had set foot in Gainsborough Hall. She showed Cat all her new domain, all her treasures. She even managed to present Lucy with some degree of unconcern, as one would present any one woman to another.

They had supper all together in the great hall. There was much laughter and songs and lots of wine and beer. Henry was careful to give Cat fine succulent choices of fowl and meat; Lucy sat up straight, throwing both women glances and tentative smiles. But Cat was tired after her journey, and covered her mouth politely when she could no longer restrain a yawn. She and Katryn were going to share a bed, and so Katryn suggested they seek it afore she fell asleep at table. Henry lingered over his good-night, and Cat was still smiling after he left the room.

"Your brains are busy with plans," Katryn accused her.

Cat shook her head, dissembling quickly. "Nay, how could you think thus?" she reprimanded. "Even if you do, don't say it, or Henry might smell me out." She gave Katryn a merry look.

"I'll not say a word," she promised; naught scared a man so. But she added seriously, "I shall truly hope, though."

"What nonsense!" said Cat airily. She sat down on the stool before the fire and thoughtfully gazed at Katryn, who was struggling to unfasten her gown.

"Henry said you had not been so gay in some time. What's been amiss?" As the words were spoke, Katryn pulled off her gown. She looked across at Cat, hesitating.

"I've not felt well," she said slowly. "And Lucy upsets me."

"Aye, I can see that," Cat said. "She is strange, but I think you can help her. I mind she is probably jealous, but she is rather pitiful, and sometimes one thinks she wants to please and be one of you."

Katryn said, low, "Do you think she would try to harm me? Sometimes"—she bit her lip—"sometimes I fear for myself, at her hands." She gazed at Cat. "I truly do. I've been so ill, so weak and faint and nauseated, I am a little afeared . . ." Her voice trailed off. She looked at Cat and was conscious of her pretty room and the fire burning bright; probably Cat thought her mad.

But there was a smile of understanding on Cat's face. She rose, patted Katryn's bare shoulder. "Why, Katryn Parr," she said, slowly, shaking her head in disbelief, "Why, Katryn, how could you not see what's the matter?" She giggled a little. "Look at thyself," she commanded. "And how long since your last flux? Why, you're blossoming out and getting rounder, and you're going to have a baby!"

Katryn stared at her.

"Aye," said Cat. "I can see your blossoming out, and you said your sickness has passed!"

Katryn put her hands to her breast. "Marry, I never once—" She shook her head from side to side.

Cat said, "If I were thee, I'd go to chapel tomorrow. When does Lord Borough return?"

"In two or three days," Katryn said. "Pray thee, Cat, say naught to anyone! About me and the babe!" She felt the cold on her bare arms, and slipped on her warm night robe, holding her hands out to the blaze, waiting for Meg to come with the warm water for her to wash. She gathered her robe close about her. "I must not catch cold," she thought, gravely. "I must be very careful." It seemed quite incredible: she, Katryn Parr, was going to have a baby.

5

The day dawned blustery and with a smell of spring in the wind. Katryn wakened early to hear the sigh of the wind; she stirred deliciously, for in the winter there was no greater luxury than to lie snug and warm in bed.

She wakened Lord Borough. He smiled at her sleepily, and asked in a foggy voice what she did astir so early.

Katryn laughed. "I'm so very hungry," she confessed. "You know what I crave? I can just see and smell them. Woodcocks. Stuffed, with gravy. I could eat six of them. I wonder why it is I crave woodcocks?"

Lord Borough, thoroughly awake now, laughed aloud. "You shall ha' them, sweetheart." He drew back the bed curtains. Gray light seeped into the room. "The sun's hardly up, wench," he said, "and you're dreaming of food. That must be a big knave you carry." He leaned over and patted her stomach, chuckled, and, regarding her fondly, got out of bed. She heard him open the chest where he had laid his hunting jackets.

"Put your shirt and hose on afore you hunt that jacket," Katryn called.

"I'm not cold," he said. He disappeared into his closet, and Katryn could hear him splashing water. After a while he returned, fully dressed. "Are you going to stay there in bed whilst I go hunting?" he asked. "Or are you going to breakfast with me?"

"Acourse I'm going to breakfast with you," she answered.

He told her he'd go summon Henry and Thomas. And Katryn, yawning deeply, rose and dressed.

An hour later, the hunting party galloped off. Katryn went back to the solar and sewed, for the whole household was employed in outfitting the expected babe. But when the sun was well up, she put on her cloak and went outside to the inner garden. The garden was well sheltered behind stone walls. A few fruit trees grew there, and there were two stone benches. Katryn sat down on one of them and gratefully felt the sun on her face. A few crocuses showed their golden heads at her feet.

But the day that had begun well proceeded badly. Katryn had brought out her sewing, but when she saw a big black cat sitting on her basket, she gave a cry of alarm. Cat Strickland came rushing out and shooed the cat away. Both women sat on the bench, a bit shaken.

" 'Tis a bad omen," Katryn said.

Cat tried to be cheerful. But she felt moody and depressed. She was afraid that Henry was not interested in marriage, and had been thinking deeply on whether or not to enlist Katryn's aid. She could not come to a decision. "I should soon take my leave," she said low, and felt at any moment she would burst into tears, which was most unlike her.

The March sun went in. Great black clouds whisked across the skies. "Oh, list the wind," Cat murmured. It moaned about the sheltered garden, blowing fiercely across the grass and the stone benches. "We'd best go in," she said. Katryn gathered up her sewing in her basket, and stood up. Just then a crack of thunder rolled. Katryn hurried toward the gate; she gave a last look at the lowering sky. "I hope m'lord soon comes home," she cried.

The long hours passed. After dinner Katryn went down to the cosiness of the paneled winter parlor. A bright fire was burning there. She sat in the window seat, with cushions behind her back to protect her from drafts, and kept listening for the sights or sounds that would herald the return of the hunting party.

"I wish by the Virgin I'd never dreamt o' woodcocks," she said to Cat. "I swear I couldn't stuff one down my throat now."

The gentlewoman named Maud came over and solicitously slid a footstool under Katryn's feet. Katryn thanked her, and reflected how sweet and pleasant a wench was Maud, and how she had a hundred pounds for her dowry. She should soon be wed; there was a family near with three young sons and ample place in their household for such a good lass as Maud. If her husband ever came home she would speak to him and get him to offer the girl, and the wedding could be a spring one.

"Maud, I want to get thee wed afore the summer."

Maud smiled, and Katryn told her not to drop a stitch thinking about a May wedding. Cat went on to say what a lovely month was May, to think on the sunshine and the fresh smell of the earth and the flowers. And all the time Katryn was listening for distant sounds.

The door opened. Lucy said, without preamble or shutting the door, "Where i' the name of God can they be?"

Katryn felt a wave of distaste for her. "Marry, you stupid girl, shut the door," she commanded. Lucy closed the door with a bang, Katryn said more calmly, "I know not where m'lord is, and I am distraught, Lucy, so hold your tongue and sit quiet."

Lucy obeyed. She was using a small loom, making an intricately patterned bright carpet; the other women were sewing on the babe's wardrobe. Lucy clattered the shuttle back and forth in the silent room. Katryn started to say she wished Lucy would sew and be more quiet; then she checked herself, for Lucy misliked sewing, and that made Katryn remember her own words to her mother. "Why should I worry wi' sewing when these hands are ordained to wield sceptres?" Life is strange, Katryn thought suddenly. I would not have been surprised to be a queen, but I am very surprised to be sitting here, a woman with child, running a household and waiting to hear my husband's voice echoing in the courtyard.

"What truly haps to a knave or wench is more surprising than his youthful dreams," she said aloud. "And more exciting."

"D'ye think thus?" Cat asked.

"Do you not?" Katryn returned, surprised. Then she smiled. "Alas, cousin, you have no imagination; but never you care, for there's many would say you're best off that way. Now there's no true reason why I should be jumpy as a witch on a broomstick, save my mind's awhirl with dread and—" She broke off and jumped to her feet. Lucy flew out the door, once more leaving it standing wide.

Cat started for the door to listen, for something was amiss. There'd been no shouts nor horns, yet Cat could hear Henry's tread. She left the room, and she saw Henry; he was white-faced, and he was saying something to Lucy. Cat's eyes flew back to Katryn, who was coming slowly down the small hall that separated this side of the manor house from the great hall. She reached the end of it, and she could see Henry. Lucy turned.

74

"It's my father," she said clearly, her voice coming steady and even. "He was thrown from his horse. He's in the abbey of the Franciscan friars down the river. He is dead." She raised her finger, and pointed to Katryn. "You killed him." She turned and made her way up the great stairway to her chamber.

In disbelief and horror Cat watched her ascend the stairs, her skirts swinging from side to side. Then she turned to Katryn and put her arms around her, and she and Henry took Katryn back to the cushioned seat in the room she had left a few moments before, where the fire still burned unheedingly bright and welcoming.

Katryn was dressed completely in black. Her veil covered her hair and her white face, and a pall black as sable streamed from her shoulders to the tips of her velvet slippers.

The great house was full of family and friends, who had come to mourn and lay Lord Borough to rest under the floor of the great cathedral at Lincoln.

All the women in the household wore mourning, and would wear it for six months to come. Servants came and went on hushed feet; the whole great house was still and silent; only outside in the courtyards did the hounds still bay, the doves flutter in the dovecote, and the chickens cackle. Even Lord Borough's horse mourned for him, in fits of wild neighing and stamping in his stall.

"Oh, list that horse," Katryn would cry, and Henry would dash out and try to calm him, and take him out for a wild gallop.

They had fetched the body of her husband from the friary on a horse litter, and Katryn had helped to bathe and dress him, and lay him in the chapel. She had prayed there, kneeling at the side of his bier, and each time her lips stopped moving the remembrances of him would be sharp agonizing thrusts. Henry would come and find her there, and lead her away.

"He suffered not," Henry said over and over.

"Aye, ye told me."

" 'Tis God's will."

"Is 't?" She flashed him a glance.

"Ye pay no heed to Lucy, mind, or I'll beat ye both," Henry said.

"If I hadn't wished for woodcocks," she cried out helplessly.

"Nay, nay, wench; 'twas the child you carry made ye wish, and that's the Lord's will too. My father lived the life he wished to live, and he died the way he wished to die, Katryn, galloping o'er the countryside, on a wild, wind-ablowing afternoon."

But she could neither believe it, nor accept it. Unprepared, she struggled as though each day were a nightmare from which she should surely awaken, but did not. For each day brought anew the slowly mounting horror that the child she carried would be forever fatherless.

She ate almost nothing. Her huge eyes burned fierce and full of desperate frustration. "If only I'd been there," she would cry. "If only I had not sent him forth."

"What could you ha' done?" Thomas would cry back.

"I would ha' saved him! I would ha' seen the rock on which his horse stumbled! I would ha' done something!"

"It is almost supper," Cat put in, coming to stand by Katryn, who cried then, "I cannot eat! Not a morsel! I'd just as soon die!"

"Nonsense!" Cat then said coldly, "I ha' lost my husband, too. And I acted not this way!"

Katryn whirled on her, fury in her eyes. "I shall act as I please!" Katryn shouted. "D'ye dare challenge my right? I am the widow!" Suddenly overwhelmed, she sank down onto the floor in a billowing heap of lace and black gown and bright head. Her shoulders shook.

Thomas leapt forward and leaned over her, putting his arms around her. She felt his hands on her and at his touch she recoiled sharply in terror.

"Let me be!" she shrieked. She sat back on her heels, putting her hands out to ward him off. "Let me be! Let me be!"

When Cat returned from supper, Katryn was asleep in bed; there were three other women in the room, and Mistress Dawson, and a distraught Meg. They made way for Cat with respect, for she was kin. Cat sat by the bed, silently. The little clock ticked. Katryn, she thought, I knew thee as a child, and child thou still art, only with a woman's body and a wayward wilful mind, wanting much, desiring greatly, lusting much. What will hap to thee, who in acting badly have all this attendance and attention? What is there about thee that keeps all these women hovering. A sense of drama? Do you do the things they wish they could? Or dared? I should not dare. I should swallow my grief, as I did, as Lucy has. If Lucy comes here tonight, she will look upon you with hatred. She will think, and rightly, why should this woman get all the attention when I mourn too, and just as much, for I have lost my father, dearer to me than life itself.

What will hap to thee, Katryn, in the years to come? I who sit here am widowed too, none the less bereft because six years have passed. But I know well what I want: one man, named Henry, who will help me bring up my son, and look after me and Sizergh, and come to love it. I am a simple soul. What do you want? Do you know? Cat looked long at Katryn's face. She is like the sleeping princess, she thought. Who will wake her with a kiss? Will she ever awaken?

The long night passed, and the long gray dawn heralded the day on which Lord Borough was to be interred in the great tomb below the cathedral floor in Lincoln. For the burial of the dead, all was in readiness, the bearers, the mourners, the guests, the stricken family, the choristers whose voices would implore the Lord's mercy, the gaping hole in the vaulted tomb. For the living, there was sustenance. Huge platters of fowl and meat, a capon sewed ingeniously to a suckling pig, great mountains of white bread, and cheeses, and yellow butter. An even greater fire roared on the hearth, and the hall was full of trestle tables and benches.

It was a dark day, and torches flared in their sconces on the walls. At the head table, tall candelabra shed light.

Katryn had been composed throughout, but Cat and Henry watched her narrowly. She ate surrounded by her gentlewomen; Lucy sat apart, with streaming eyes. Neither of them took food, but drank wine. Cat thought the meal would never end, for they were feeding the priests and heralds and choristers; even the torchbearers would get food and dole. But finally it was over, and the food cleared away to be distributed to the poor of the countryside who had thronged to the manor.

Thomas motioned to Cat. "Take Katryn to the solar," he whispered.

There were few men and women remaining in the hall. Katryn made her way through them slowly, saying good-by. At the foot of the great stairway, she gathered up her skirts in her hand and started slowly to ascend. Cat came right behind.

They paused on a double landing halfway up the stairway. Below stood Henry, with Thomas too now, and three men dressed for riding. They raised their crops in salute, and Katryn waved back. Then once more, she slowly began to ascend the turn. She reached the top.

From below, Henry saw Cat hurry ahead of her, and he saw Lucy slip out of the shadows. He saw Lucy's black-robed tall figure come closer to Katryn; had she been waiting there? There was an ominousness about those two women. Where was Cat? He couldn't see her. Then he saw Katryn clumsily take the last step up, and heard Lucy say: "You killed my father!"

Just then Cat reappeared to see why Katryn was not following her; she too saw the two black-robed figures. She seemed to hesitate, and then Lucy whispered something Henry could not hear and Katryn laughed, mockingly.

Wildly Lucy advanced on Katryn; Cat flew forward as Katryn flung up her arms to protect herself. Henry gave a leap, pushing aside the men in his way.

He heard Cat scream at Lucy. He saw Katryn try to regain her balance; at the top of the steps the two black-robed figures swayed.

He was too late. Only Katryn's thin high cry of real anguish pierced the huge hall as she began to fall, down, down the great curving stairway. By the time Henry reached the landing she lay, a little heap of black clothes, at his feet.

The wind had died. The candles burned steadily, and by a trick of light the vapor from the torches in the stairwell threw a shiny pool on the landing as though the blood spilled that night yet lay ominous and uncleaned.

Thomas paced back and forth. The house was almost still now. Death had struck twice here. It had already claimed his father and the unborn infant; for the woman who lay unconscious in a chamber near by, Thomas could but pray. A maidservant slipped past him, carrying a covered bucket. " 'Tis Katryn's blood, soaked in linen," he thought, clenching his hands; for the anger he had originally fought to control was settling. It was cold rage now, and he could wait to fulfill it.

A door opened and closed and Mistress Dawson's white-capped, white-aproned figure came rustling toward him. Her gray eyes were sad. She looked up at his face worriedly, as though she were sore afraid the night's violence had not yet ended. It was quite plain to Mother Dawson that this boy she had known so long had gone clean mad with love and anxiety over his father's widow, and God knew naught but harm and evil could come of it. Her hands sought for her beads. "I go to fetch the priest." Thomas resumed his steady pacing.

Presently Mistress Dawson returned, the priest in her wake, his head bent, hands tucked in his sleeves, his plain silver cross swinging. He told Thomas he would speak with him as soon as he had seen Katryn.

Thomas remembered he was now Lord Borough. "I shall come too," he said, and dismissed the priest's protests with a lifted hand, like his father. "I shall stand within the door."

The bed curtains were pulled back. Meg had sprayed rosewater in the room, and thrown sweet herbs on the fire. The linen was fresh and clean, but there was an odor to the room which no perfume could dispel, the odor of vomiting and blood, of pain, of sickness, of death. Thomas brought himself to look at Katryn's face.

Her eyes were closed. There was a thick bandage around her head, hiding the lovely white temples where the red curls usually clung. There was blood on the bandage, and under both eyes were heavy bruised smudges of deep blue. He cried out like an agonized animal; he covered his face with his hands. Mistress Dawson plucked at his sleeve.

"I told you not to come in, my lord," she whispered. "She is mortally sick. Go thee to the chapel and pray."

Katryn felt the pain in terrible waves. Great noises surged in her head; then great black clouds would come nearer—heavy, so heavy, they would crush her, and she would open her lips to scream for mercy.

She did not hear the priest. She did not hear any voices. She did not think of dying; she thought of nothing, and knew nothing but pain.

So the night passed, and the next morning and the next day. On the following morning another need thrust itself on her—thirst. Someone must be there, for she felt cool water on her lips; this was pleasure. Her eyes opened, and closed again. The black clouds were pressing closer. "Oh, God, please!" she cried. Her hands raised a bit and fell back on the counterpane helplessly.

Had two days passed, Thomas thought? He stood by Katryn's bed, looking at the bruised face. But her breathing was quiet and even. She had swallowed water and, an hour ago, a clear broth. But I cannot be swayed, Thomas thought.

It was almost suppertime. Henry was waiting for him in the hall. Henry told him Cat could not join them, she was asleep; Henry would have one of the women take her up some food later. Cat had labored without stint of self or love or pity.

The meal finished, Thomas took his leave to go into his closet where he kept his accounts, and Henry went back into the dresser, and picked out some choice morsels of cold meat, and some cheese. These he put on a pewter tray, along with a flagon of ale and made his way upstairs to the small room where Cat lay asleep. He knocked gently on the door. It was a sleepy Cat who opened the door. Henry set down the tray. He put his arms around her and squeezed her tight.

Surprised, Cat tipped her head back to see his face. Henry looked at her, soft and warm, and sleepy. "I adore you, Cat," he said, and grinned at her.

Her face changed, sobered, delighted. She wet her lips. "I adore you, too, Henry," she whispered.

"Will you marry me?" Henry asked.

She nodded, her face solemn and smiling at the same time; not trusting her voice, she nodded again, and two big tears stood in her eyes. She blinked them away. The miracle of love had happened to her; surely it was no time to cry. She raised her lips to Henry for their first kiss.

At ten the manor house was quiet. Thomas picked up the candle by which he'd been working, tucked his riding whip under his arm, and made his way toward the unused staircase. There was no sound from above.

Step by deliberate step he went up to the locked room, unlocked it, and then went in, setting down the candle. In its light he saw Lucy on her knees. "Thou art full of evil spirits, and it is my duty to exorcise them." He tried to be calm, but as he stood over her his voice thickened. In the unsteady light of the one candle, her eyes were huge and full of fear.

But he was not ready yet. "Take off your shoes," he said, quite calm now. "When you leave this house you go on naked feet, to exact penance." When her slippers and her hose lay in a little pile, he kicked them aside with sudden violence and raised the whip.

He struck her across the side of the arm. Lucy gave one short cry of pain, but after that she was almost silent. Finally Thomas gave her a last blow across the buttocks, then leaned down and pulled her to a sitting position, by her long hair. He twisted it about his hand, and pulled her after him down the stairway, and flung her outside the chapel door, which he then locked and bolted. There was no need to bar it, Thomas knew. Lucy would never come back to Gainsborough Hall.

Katryn opened her eyes, and closed them again quickly, lowering the purpled lids against the stabbing pain of the light. Safe again in darkness, she experimented, turning her head slightly, gingerly lifting one hand to feel at her temple. It was padded thick with bandages. She brushed her face with her fingers; I am not disfigured, she thought; I will have no terrible scar running across my cheek. She moved the toes of her left foot, rotating her ankle. Her leg was stiff and aching, but she could move it. She tried the right foot; the ankle protested, sending a tremor of pain. She lay still and opened her eyes again; before she closed them she saw a shape.

"Close the curtains," she said low.

Meg gave a cry of joy. She came to stand over her mistress, clasping her hands this way and that, sending up thanks to the Lord, the Virgin, and all the saints.

"Close the curtains!" Katryn repeated fretfully.

Katryn heard the pull of the rings on the bedside curtains. One closed, then another. She opened her eyes.

"Ah," she said. Nay, that is enough. What good is it to pull all of them, for then I cannot see aught. By God's most precious soul," she ended. She had heard the oath from Tom Seymour's lips. What had recalled it? "I feel quite strange," she said aloud.

Meg said, "Oh, thank the Lord to hear you speak, madam!"

Katryn frowned. She did not bother to answer Meg; it was too much effort. She felt so weak, her body was like a piece of crumpled paper; her mind kept dwelling on the oddest scraps, like that oath she had just used, for instance. How strong his arms had been, what a knave he was, teasing her in front of her husband. Her husband . . .

Memory reached into her now, swift and shattering, destroying the half world. Her husband was dead. He was buried. And the night of the funeral, Lucy had pushed her down the stairway. Terror and grief were for an instant one with her. To dispel that reliving of terror at the start of her fall, she opened her eyes wide; she breathed swiftly, trying to raise herself from the pillow regardless of pain, regardless of the searing throb of her head and the misery of the muscles of her back and shoulders.

She said, struggling with her body and her fears, "I lost my child!"

Meg leaned down, a big bundle of black. Was she crying? "Aye, my lady. Aye, bless thee, my lady."

Katryn repeated, "I lost my child."

She saw Meg clearer now. Meg had taken her hand. "You shall be blessed with more childer," she said.

"Nay, nay," said Katryn. How could that be? She was a widow. When she could arise from her bed, she would dress in black. Aye, for a long year or more. Meg's face swam dizzily before her. She felt Meg put an arm around her, and let herself sink back onto the pillow. She had lost her husband and her child. Her eyes filled with tears; soundlessly, they slipped down her cheeks. Meg laid something on her forehead, where there was no bandage and wiped at Katryn's cheeks. She whispered, and Meg leaned down close to hear.

"Why didn't I die?" Katryn was saying. "Why didn't I die, too?"

Cat held Katryn's hand as, still crying noiselessly, she lay white-faced against her pillows with the tears rolling down her cheeks. And Cat was impelled to say, "Take heart, Katryn! Courage, my little one!"

Katryn didn't answer. Her breath felt hot to Cat, and her forehead was beaded with sweat. She was only half conscious, Cat saw; her dreams would come back, and she would soon mutter and her bruised body would turn and toss.

Cat was in despair. If only Henry would return! Although his love for her, and hers for him, was a miracle that lighted her days and nights, the tragedies and mounting horror of life at Gainsborough was taking its heavy toll. Henry had tried to spare her much. When Thomas had told him what he had done to Lucy, the shock to Henry had been shattering; for Henry was a man who lived by the code that human beings should love one another, especially brother and sister. He had said only, "I am going to find Lucy."

Henry wouldn't bring Lucy back to Gainsborough. But he could see her safely to another manor house with relatives, or a nunnery, where she could recover. He set forth immediately, only telling Cat briefly what had happed.

A spatter of rain beat at the windows. Cat looked across to the streaming panes. Pity for Lucy, out in this storm and barefoot, vied within her for concern for Henry. Although it would soon be April, no hint of spring seemed in the air; the wind was bitter cold and whistled mournfully.

Cat squeezed Katryn's hand again. "Courage," she whispered, as much to herself as Katryn.

Katryn felt the clasp of her fingers. She heard the word *courage*. She knew Cat had spoken it. She pushed it aside. She could feel the tears filling her eyes. She didn't want Cat. She wanted to go home.

She dreamed of Kendal. It was spring, the month of May, and the sun shone and the sky was a clean sweep of blue. She was lying on her back in the grass; there were wild flowers in her hands, and her mother said, "Oh, Katryn, how many times have I told you not to lie on the ground!" She fell asleep.

She slept all afternoon. About four, Cat fed her some broth, and after it, she slept soundly. Cat waited by the window.

The wind and rain were not abated and darkness was coming, but Henry had not yet returned. Cat drank a little wine, and tried to sew. At half after five, Henry rode back to Gainsborough Hall. He had not found Lucy.

The next day he rode out again, and the next day and the next. On the morning of the fifth day, the tension had heightened for Cat till it was almost unbearable. She ran down the big stairway to say good-by to Henry; almost desperately, he took her in his arms, to say good-by. Thomas saw them as he came out into the gallery.

Thomas came slowly down the stairs, and they waited for him, hand in hand. His face was unnaturally pale and his eyes burned. He never removed his eyes from either of them as he came slowly towards them.

"You have disgraced our house," he said. "And I must ask you both to leave!"

Katryn had had some porridge, and was propped up in bed, still white, still sore. Her clean white bandage looked like a coif about her red head, and her eyes were only partly smudged now with blue shadows.

"You look better this morn," Cat said trying to be cheerful.

"Aye," she said listlessly.

How to begin, Henry wondered. And although this might come as shock and surprise to Katryn, he knew it had not to him; for it now seemed perfectly reasonable to suppose that since Thomas had got rid of Lucy he had wanted to get rid of Henry too. Thomas, who had waited so long to hold the reins, now wanted them fiercely.

"Katryn," Henry said without preamble, for pleasantries did not seem to break through Katryn's lassitude, "Cat and I are leaving Gainsborough today, and we shall be wed at Sizergh as soon as possible."

Katryn stared at him. She struggled up to a sitting position. "You are leaving?" she said incredulously.

"Are you not glad we are going to be wed?" Henry asked gently.

"Acourse, acourse," she said. "But—" She frowned at him, seeing his kind, calm brown eyes; he was waiting patiently, she knew. "You have all my best wishes and my love," she said. She bit her lip and caught at Henry's hand. "Why cannot you be wed here?" she whispered. Involuntarily she gave a glance at the door.

"You have guessed it, Katryn. Thomas wishes us gone." He hesitated. "You will be perfectly safe here, with your women. And I want to explain about my father's will. Of course Thomas inherits, as the eldest. You have your manor of Tansfield, and the right to live here at Gainsborough forever, as long as you please, and Thomas is beholden to take care of you. The bequests my father made toward your child are of course nullified." Her grip on his hand tightened. "Katryn," he cried. "We shall come back soon!"

She said softly, "If you don't, I shan't be able to endure it."

"You can come to Sizergh. As soon as you're well enough to travel, I shall come and fetch you. But this is your home."

"My home?" she whispered. She looked around the room; she drew a long shuddering breath. "Aye, Henry."

Cat leaned down and kissed her cheek. "Good-by, Katryn," she said, "and God bless you."

"God bless you both," she whispered back. Cat gave a last glance at Katryn's face; she looked haunted and miserable. Poor child, she thought. But this will pass; she is young, and will recover quick.

The door closed, and Katryn sank back on the pillows. Dimly she listened to the last bang of the big doors, the sounds of horses in the court, and the last shouts of farewell. She heard all those sounds, and then there was another sound she did not expect. The great gates clanged shut. She frowned, wonderingly. It must be a mistake, she thought. Someone has shut the big gates to Gainsborough Hall.

Two days passed. Then Maud Bishop met Thomas on the stairway and was taken of a sudden by an unreasoning terror. "There's something strange and queer about him—his lordship," she whispered to Mistress Dawson.

"Nay, nay," said Mistress Dawson. " 'Tis just there's been so much sadness here."

"I feel it in my bones, and I want to go home," Maud said.

Mistress Dawson could not dissuade her. Maud packed her two boxes and tremblingly sought out Thomas. He almost dispelled her disquiet; he was as stolid as ever.

"Of course, Mistress Maud," he said. "You live not far. I'll send you home."

Was he glad to see her go? she wondered. Tearfully she bade Katryn good-by.

"When I am better," Katryn said, "you can return, and I'll find a good husband for thee, as I promised." That promise seemed to have been made so very long ago, she thought. How happy she had been!

The next day the house seemed unnaturally silent. Katryn said, fretfully, "I miss Maud." She looked to Mistress Dawson, as though she should make Maud appear. Katryn turned restlessly in the big bed. Outside the sun shone fitfully, and Katryn asked suddenly,

"What day is it?"

"April the first, my lady." Mistress Dawson said this with some pride, as if she was sure anyone would be glad to know 'twas April, and she was making her ladyship a gift of it. She smiled, fondly, and patted Katryn's hand. "April first," she repeated.

There was a knock on the door and then Thomas came in. Katryn looked over at him, a bit surprised, for he had not waited to be admitted. She passed a white hand over her forehead, for her head plagued her still.

"Good morrow, my lord," she said.

He came close, to stand by her bed, and he took her hand. His hand felt clammy, and she was conscious of a flicker of dread and dismay. He said nothing, after a greeting word, but stood looking down at her in such a manner that she felt the first shock of fear.

I cannot bear him, she thought wildly. She blurted, "Pray leave me!" There was no movement on his part, and she glanced up at his face. His gaze was intense and devouring. She gasped, "My head! It's bursting!"

She fell back on her pillows as though in a faint, and kept her eyes tight closed. Only after she heard Thomas leave did she open them. "What's wrong with him, Mistress Dawson?" she asked, direct and almost frantic. "What's wrong? Tell me, or I'll have you soundly beat!"

Mistress Dawson, her lips quivering, came closer to her mistress. After a long pregnant silence, she cried, "As God's my witness, madam, I don't quite know!"

Then the truth was too awful to be said. Meg made a little whimper, sat down on the stool, and began to say her beads. Katryn and Mistress Dawson fixed their gaze on each other, in a sort of dawning horror.

Finally Katryn whispered, "Ha' ye seen the way he looks at me, or is it one of my imaginings?"

Mistress Dawson looked helplessly at her.

"Answer me!" Katryn screamed.

"Madam, madam," sobbed Mistress Dawson, "I've known him since a babe. How can it be true, and you his father's lawful wife?"

Katryn gave her a look of revulsion. 'Twas a mortal sin for him to covet her, 'twas rank evil and bloody sin. "He's horrible," she breathed, "horrible. If he touches me, I'll die, I'll die, I'll die." She turned over and buried her head in the pillow.

For a long time she lay thus. Then she roused herself. Her voice was even. "I'm not sure but that he isn't mad," she said. "Lock the door, and bring me pen and ink. I shall write to my mother, an innocent letter but one that will bring her here. He cannot refuse to send a letter to my mother, telling her I've been ill. Surely he cannot refuse!"

Thomas did not refuse. After supper that night, he took the letter from Katryn and went to his closet. He didn't bother to read the painstakingly composed correspondence. He sat for some time, staring at the white paper and the waxy pink seal. Then with a slight grimace, he tore it carefully into small pieces and put it on the fire.

6

In the palace garden at Greenwich, the King's wench, Nan Boleyn, was dressed in gay scarlet this morning, with red petticoats and red hose. She sat on a bench whilst the King played at bowls, and it was a noisy gay throng that gamboled by the river bank.

Sir William Parr, the King's lord chamberlain, hurrying up the path toward the knot of men who stood watching the bowling, bowed briefly to Nan Boleyn and hastened on. She and her ladies watched his stiff square figure stumping along mid the crushed-stone flower beds that were so new and popular.

"His mind is as uncompromising as his figure," Nan murmured, her black eyes snapping. She fondled the gold pomander at her belt thoughtfully. But the King was laughing, and there seemed to be no cares under the April sun.

Sir William came to an abrupt halt before John Dudley. He eyed him a moment. Dudley's father had gone to the block; the heavy taxes he imposed had bled the county families—among them the Kendal holdings of Sir William's own brother Thomas Parr. The elder Dudley had been an unwelcome holdover from the reign of Henry VII, and young Henry had dispatched him quickly, an execution which had won him much popularity with the English people. But this young Dudley—there was a force about him, too. Like father, like son. He will come to the same bloody end, Sir William Parr thought, but whilst his head is still on his shoulders, I can beg him a favor. "Good morrow," he said, and bowed.

Dudley's voice was unctuous as he presented the three young men who attended him. Sir William evaluated them swiftly and fixed on one, a towering, lithe young blade with a dark face. Sir William said, " 'Twas you I saw at the joust yestermorn!"

He was momentarily diverted from his mission, as his mind went back to the drama on the tournament field yesterday, when this man's great black charger had balked and thrown him. Sir William could still envision him sprawled on the grass while his mounted opponent wheeled his steed to make an end to the duel. There was was a concerted gasp from the gallery, as the figure on the grass doubled up and away from oncoming man and horse, and with one gloved hand seized the reins of his own horse standing nearby, gaining the saddle in a swift bound, stirrups flying. Sir William was close enough to see the powerful neck and haunch muscles of the black horse as it reared, to see the hard gloved hands twist the reins tight and back, and to see the blood spurt from the black flanks as the spurs dug in and the horse wheeled just in time to meet his opponent's charge. All the gallery had let out a hoarse cheer. Sir William, his broken tooth showing in a wide smile, looked up at Tom Seymour. "You acquitted yoursel' nobly, my lad," he said heartily.

"Thank you, Sir William," Tom Seymour said.

"Aye," said Sir William, "and I know thy father well." He nodded his head and pursed his lips, and Tom Seymour knew he had been given the stamp of approval.

"If there is aught I could do to accommodate you, Sir William, I'd be glad."

"Indeed, sir," put in Dudley, bowing.

Sir William turned to Dudley, "I've a favor, sir. My sister—my brother's widow, poor soul—lies very ill in Greenwich, and has had no word from her daughter in Lincolnshire for two months gone, now. His Grace, the King, told me last eve that you ha' business in Scotland. I would deem it a great boon for you to carry letters for me, and bring news."

Dudley bowed again; he would be delighted to do any favor at all for Sir William. "Attend Sir William, Tom," he said, "and fetch from him the letters and instructions."

Sir William gave his thanks. Dudley said as he stumped off, "He's like to a bear, sturdy, and his virtue's as unassailable as the Queen's."

Sir William heard none of that, for he was well up the path and was thinking of the young man who strode at his side, and the man he served. "To do a master's bidding, lad," he said gruffly, "a man must well respect him."

Tom Seymour gave him a slow speculative smile. Sir William

89

grunted and said no more until he laid the letters in Seymour's hands. "Do you take these yourself?"

"Aye, sir."

"See that you complete your commission," Sir William commanded.

Tom Seymour's blue eyes were grave. "I shall, sir."

Sir William gave a sigh of relief. He thought the task was in the right hands.

Tom Seymour left Rising Castle before daybreak, and by the time the skies were red and gold and violet with the sunrise he was at the edge of the causeway across the Wash. Straight out, where fishing craft were already leaning and dipping in the wind, the sea glittered a dusty blue and then caught the colors of the sun. The air smelled like salt and sand, and he reined his horse for a moment to drink it all in. Then he gave the signal to ride on, and the small troop of men began to cross the Wash.

By midday they had sighted the Lincoln heights, and they had dinner at the Golden Arrow. He ate quickly and then brought a tankard of ale and sat outside on a bench under a huge chestnut tree, stretching out his booted legs and listening to the men talk. He told them what was happening in London.

"Nay, the Cardinal's got no hold on the King's ear," he said. One of the rustics said ribaldly that Nan Boleyn had hold of Henry in another place. Tom Seymour laughed.

"You think 'twill pass—this passion, this madness of his Grace?" one of the older men asked, soberly.

He shrugged his wide shoulders. "God knows, man," he said, standing up.

They wanted him to stay. "I cannot, my hearties. I've business in Gainsborough." He tossed the tankard to one of the boys, mounted and flung down some coins. Then he was off down the narrow cobbled streets, past the great cathedral, and thence to the river road.

At three he had reached Texford, and the ground was rising a bit; his eyes searched the countryside for he had not been this way before. The woods and brush and bracken betokened its fame as a hunting land. A flock of wild duck circled up. He shouted to his body servant and pointed with his whip.

To his left stretched hills that looked as though they had been patted out of clay by a child's hands and then painted rich green. Sheep dotted the sides of the fat round hills. They reached Gainsborough at four o'clock.

He looked ahead at the great house rising in the distance from the thick walls of the outer court. Its mullioned windows reflected the afternoon sun. With quickening curiosity he rode forward, pushing aside the vague feeling that something was wrong as he remembered Sir William's last words, noted the lack of bustle and the general air of unkemptness that clung all about. When he reached the gates, he saw they were shut tight, although it lacked at least two hours till sunset.

Tom Seymour reined up sharply. There was an unnatural silence about the whole demesne. He raised his voice, to shatter the quiet. "Halloa, there! Halloa!"

His voiced echoed in the silence. There was no immediate answer. Then he saw an elderly man come out of the gatehouse and look through the barred gates. His voice was surly.

"What want ye here?"

"I've business here. Open me those gates!"

The old man squinted up at horse and rider. "What business, my master? Tell it me, and I'll go see."

Tom Seymour made up his mind quickly. "I' the King's name, ye'll open me those gates, or by God, ye'll suffer for it!"

"In the King's name?" The old man peered through the gates, across the heavy chain.

Tom Seymour knew him for a country dolt, so he said, almost patiently, for he wanted those gates open, "D'ye not see the green and white of Tudor livery, my man? Now open me the gates." He fished in his pocket and held up a coin.

The old man unhooked the chain; he drew back the first bar, lifted the second one and then the third. Slowly the gates swung inward, and Tom Seymour pressed forward, motioning his men to follow him. Once inside, he reined up. He tossed the coin to the old man. "Leave them open, for me," he commanded, "for my business is not long, and I'll soon be on my way again."

The old man said doubtfully, "Aye." But Tom Seymour did not trust him. He waved a man to his side. "Stay here, and see my order's obeyed," he said. Wheeling rapidly, he clattered across the court and into the inner court, and thus before the big doors of the hall itself. He flung himself off his horse and ran up the two wide steps, lifted the heavy knocker and banged it sharply—back and forth, back and forth.

Within the house the clang of the knocker, which had not been heard for long weeks, sounded and resounded, echoing through the dusty halls, into the kitchens, even up to the top room where Thomas knelt at the *prie-dieu*. He rose and dusted off his knees, thinking idly to himself that the whole house was dirty. He went on down the stairway, wondering who had been let in. His staff had orders. If anyone knocked they were to come into the hall and help him, for it might be Henry, or even Lucy. As Thomas came down the last steps, he saw with satisfaction that twenty of his menservants were already within the hall. He went over and opened the doors. And Thomas' first thought was one of relief.

He saw Tom Seymour, with two men at his side and another seven ahorse in the court. A pitiful force, one with which he was amply equipped to deal. He bowed.

"Pray enter," he said. He opened the door just wide enough to admit the three men; then he closed it sharply.

Out of the corner of his eye, Tom Seymour saw two knaves sidle past him and take up a stand next the door. He frowned deeply as he faced his host. This was not the Lord Borough he had seen. He said, sharply, "Who are you, sir?"

"I am Lord Borough," Thomas said. "My father is dead."

Tom Seymour glanced about, seeing the knot of men grouped under the shadows of the stairwell. How had Lord Borough died? By violence? And where was the little wench with the red hair?

Thomas' voice broke the silence. "Howbeit, I would wish you to surrender your weapons, master. I know you not, and you and these knaves are armed." He waved his hand to indicate the full protection of his own men, their swords ready to their hands. "Surrender your weapons, and then you can tell me whyfore you are here."

Tom Seymour smiled and said easily, "Why, certes, m' lord." He drew his sword, proffering it to Borough hilt first. His men, their eyes darting to their master and thence to the ring of men who had moved closer, hesitated, but he gave them a nod, paused to see they did as bidden, and swung back to Borough.

"Now," he said, " I forgot to introduce myself. I am Thomas Seymour, my lord, here on a mission from Sir William Parr to deliver letters into the hands of Lady Borough. "Lord Borough," he asked curtly, "where is the Lady Borough?"

"Upstairs in her chambers, sir, confined there by illness."

"Illness?" asked Tom Seymour, taking a step forward, keeping his eyes on Borough. "What kind of illness?"

"That is none of your concern," Thomas said, distantly, as if from a great eminence. "Each day she betters a trifle. She is beginning to walk some. Although now she is confined to bed."

Tom Seymour quickly weighed two plans. Should he retreat and enter this place by stealth after nightfall? Should he insist on seeing Katryn now?

He would try the latter. "May I deliver my letters to Lady Borough, then, my lord?" he asked. "I have a long way farther to ride, and the day's going fast."

Borough hesitated, yet his suspicions were not allayed. "No," he said, "you cannot see Lady Borough. I shall take the letters." He held out his hand, and, to gain time, Tom Seymour nodded. He started to unfasten his jacket. At this moment Katryn appeared at the top of the steps.

She was trembling with excitement. She had heard the hammering on the doors, and the sound of horses in the court. Ever since writing her mother she had been prepared to leave—her slippers to hand underneath her pillow, her cloak and shawl under the quilts. Not only that; she had had Mistress Dawson stitch into her sturdiest petticoat her jewels and finest gold chains. In the time that Tom Seymour had been speaking with Borough, she had donned this special petticoat, grasped up her reticule, her gloves. Now she stood at the top of the stairway with a trembling Meg at her side. When Katryn made sure the voice she had heard was coming from the lips of the man she thought, her whole body was seized with excitement and joy. It was some kind of miracle!

"Oh, God be thanked," she cried out, her voice echoing down the stairwell. "God be thanked, it is thee!" And even though the sight of those stairs unnerved her, reminding her of her horrifying fall, she started down them fast, with one hand on the balustrade, one hand outstretched to the man who had come to rescue her. She called out joyously, "Oh, Master Tom!"

She had reached the last step before Borough fully digested her words and her appearance. She had tricked him; she knew this man! Borough stepped between Seymour and Katryn; he pointed to Tom Seymour.

"Seize him!" he cried. With intense satisfaction, his eyes gleaming with hatred, he watched two of his men lay hold of Tom Seymour, hooking their arms through his and holding him thus, stiff, shoulders back. When he was fully satisfied that Tom Seymour was truly helpless, Borough swung about to Katryn. He advanced on her slowly. "You tricked me," he snarled.

She looked as though she were about to faint. Then words spilled out, desperate words. "You can't keep Meg and me here any longer! Unhand Master Tom, and leave us go!"

Borough smiled. She looked at Tom Seymour, and the two big men on each side of him. Katryn's heart sank.

Then Tom Seymour's voice cut into her sudden despair: "My lord," he said, easily, "Lady Borough is right. You cannot keep me here. Have you not noted that these knaves of mine are the King's men? Do you realize that I am on the King's business, traveling north to Scotland? Under my coat I have royal dispatches, and if I do not return to the royal castle at Rising, the garrison will set forth to look for me here, for they knew my destination. But I am willing to bargain. If your men will leave go my arms, I shall give Lady Borough the letters, and we shall go."

"No," sobbed Katryn. "No!"

Tom Seymour said, "I cannot prevail against such superior force, my lady. I have no means. Be quiet now, and let my lord and me talk."

"No!" cried Katryn despairingly.

"Aye," growled Borough. "Get the letters then, and ye can begone!"

Tom Seymour said, "Loose my hands, masters, whilst I procure them."

The hard hands loose their hold, and Tom Seymour made a motion of easing his shoulders, flexing his arms. His hands went to his inside breast pocket and he withdrew a thick white packet, which Borough could plainly see was an ordinary letter. Tom Seymour held it forth, but when Borough reached for it his hand was seized in a grip of iron, so cruel that he cried out in pain. Tom

94

Seymour had swung him about, his arm doubled uselessly behind him, and the letter fell to the floor. Borough felt another arm pass about his body across his shoulder and under his neck, and he let forth a howl of pain.

Tom Seymour said grimly, "If any man comes near me, I break your master's back; not his arm, lads, his back! Now stay your distance, whilst I give the orders!"

For a moment there was no sound in the hall. Katryn stared at Tom Seymour's face; the blue eyes glittering as they swept the men, the dark face set; there was no mask of good humor now. He said in the silence, "It would pleasure me to exact a heavy toll from you, my lord, for I mislike you much. Softly—softly, now, or I shall show you what I could hold in store for you. Now, lass, come and stand aside of me, and my lord's men will give you my sword and dagger. They will also return their weapons to my men."

Woodenly Katryn obeyed. She heard Tom Seymour's voice again.

"Have ye retrieved your arms, lads?"

"Aye, sir." They had come forward, and were standing on each side of him. Katryn faced him, his own sword in her hand, the light playing down the length of bared steel.

"Then back up and open me those doors," Tom Seymour said. "Lass, you and Meg go first."

Katryn faltered past him; the late sun fell into the hall as the doors opened. She breathed the fresh afternoon air; she went down the steps and turned. The two men came right behind her, and then Tom Seymour, backing out, carrying his hostage like a clay figure.

"Mount," he called. He took no chances now.

"We are mounted, sir," one of his men called.

"Now," Tom Seymour said. "All of you within the hall, back to the stairway and under it. Quick!"

They obeyed him. Seymour stood motionless for a moment. Then Katryn heard Thomas Borough's agonized gasp as his prisoned arm was twisted and the bone snapped. She saw Borough crumple and Tom Seymour fling him down on the steps of Gainsborough Hall, in an unconscious heap. Then she felt herself lifted by those same arms, and set in the saddle.

"Put your arms around me, and hang on," he commanded.

Dimly Katryn did so. The big horse wheeled, and was urged to a canter, even within the court. She saw the gates open; she saw them fly past. She shut her eyes, and leaned against his back, her face turned sideways. She hung on tight, as the graveled drive ended, and the rutted road to Lincoln began.

Katryn had never stayed at an inn before. She sat on the edge of the bed watching a boy light the fire and listened to the sounds from the busy yard.

Outside darkness had fallen. It had pursued them into Lincoln; they had raced with the night to obtain shelter. Halfway to Lincoln, Tom Seymour stopped long enough to tie her skirts around his waist in a big knot; with Katryn thus hitched to him, the pounding ride was resumed with never a word spoken, so that all she could remember was the jolting of the big saddle, and the protest of her muscles and bones. She remembered how she had hung on, desperately as though life itself depended on it, and how cold her legs had got, dangling there. She remembered the feel of his jacket against her cheek, the hard chest around which her arms clung. This was indeed a man, and their physical proximity made a oneness that struck her deep.

In the inn yard, he untied her and swept her out of the saddle into his arms. Cradled in them, her head tipped back against his shoulder, she was but half conscious of the sounds of men and horses in the inn yard. She was fully conscious of herself and the man who held her like a piece of booty that already belonged to him, as though she had not the power to say him nay. The savage strength he had demonstrated in Gainsborough Hall before her very eyes was like a prelude to the act of possession. Unsmiling, he regarded her; his arms tightened. She sucked in her breath. How very easy it would be to be swept into an unpremeditated act of passion and love. How very easy it must have been for him to conquer the other women who must have preceded her. Swift scorn for those nameless others filled her, plus scorn at herself. At the same moment she heard his voice.

"Open me that door, lad," he said, his tone peremptory, curt.

He plans to carry me right into that inn, she thought. She found her voice; it was clear and even, to her own surprise. "You may put me down, sir," she said. "I am well able to walk."

He stopped in his stride. For a wild moment she wondered whether he would obey. Then she felt his arms relax, and he set her on her feet, keeping one big hand under her elbow. She swayed a bit; and he steadied her.

"Thank you," she said.

But he blocked her path. Looking down, there was a glimmer of unwilling admiration in his eyes. "Will ye sup wi' me?" he asked, with a hint of a smile.

She clasped her hands tight. "I could not do that, sir; 'tis hardly proper." She reminded herself she was Lady Borough, and he wore a badge on his sleeve. She looked levelly back at him.

"Hardly proper?" he asked, his voice a little mocking. "Why, 'tis done every day in London. 'Tis most fashionable, in fact."

She gave him a brief angry glance. He is telling me I know naught of the fashionable world. She said haughtily, "Howbeit, I think not tonight, sir. You would find me a poor companion, at best. Also, I am unfamiliar with inns. If you could procure a room for myself and Meg—" Of a sudden she remembered Meg. "Where is that wench?"

"Right here, my lady," Meg cried, stumbling forward to open the inn door.

Katryn stepped inside and went up the narrow stairs. The room at the top seemed clean, at least, small though it was. Having surveyed it swiftly, she turned to Tom Seymour.

"Could you have some food sent to us?"

He nodded.

She drew a deep breath. "May I thank you for all you have done?" she said.

"You may, madam. However, there are a few matters I wish to speak with you about. I will come later, after you've washed and supped." He gave her a little bow, a very correct one, then turned on his heel. She closed the door and sank down on the bed. "I must think," she said to Meg. "I must think."

Even though she had ridden far and it was the first real exercise she had had in weeks, she was not hungry. She forced herself to eat a piece of bread, and washed it down with ale. She knew she must get to Greenwich to her mother. Her mother . . . Maud Parr's sweet face floated comfortingly in the distance; the vision made tears rise to Katryn's eyes. Oh, what joy to feel her mother's arms around her, to know she was home again! She blinked back the tears. Tom Seymour would take her to London, and she would be safe. But she must have money. She stood up and wriggled out of her petticoat.

"Undo some of the jewels," she commanded Meg. "The gold chain —'twill be easy to sell."

She sat down again on the bench at the foot of the bed. He would come soon; she must try to strike a nice note between gratitude and hauteur. I shall not be one of those silly women who lose their heart to him, she vowed. Absently she took the chain from Meg, and listened for his step, the knock on the door.

He came soon. She waved Meg to the door, and saw the curtsy Meg gave him. She rose, the gold chain dangled from her fingers.

His glance went briefly about the room and returned to her. They looked at each other, in the manner of two duelists, measuring.

"Pray sit," Katryn said in the silence, pointing to the bench.

He said conversationally, "Ye look none the worse for your ride, save you're a mite white. Ye must ha' tricked the Lord Borough neatly."

"I was forced to," she said. She gathered up her skirts in one hand and sat down on the stool. Tom Seymour took the bench and stretched out his booted legs. Now it begins, Katryn thought, and I shall tread carefully. She heard Meg's skirts rustle as she sat on the edge of the bed, unseen; the fire hissed. Katryn heaved a sigh which could be plainly heard.

"I cannot quite credit it—that I am truly here, and safe." She threw him a small smile. "I would hope you deem me properly grateful, sir. For indeed, it may well be I owe you my very life and sanity!"

Tom Seymour said diffidently, "I don't deserve such an accolade."

"Lord Borough was quite mad, sir," said Katryn, warming to her theme. "Indeed, completely mad! And obsessed with the"—She hesitated, searching for the right words—"the idea of keeping me there and looking after me. And I his father's widow!" She clenched her hands. "Still," she said, "when I think on how you left him, lying there—" She made a grimace.

"Now do spare me your show of pity. At any rate, I broke his arm and pulled that shoulder out of joint not for the pleasure of hurting, but to keep him from following us." He got to his feet and faced her, his back to the fire, uncompromising, looking at her narrowly.

There is something in his eyes, she thought, when he looks thus at me. I am not going to succumb to it! I'm going to forget the daring quick rescue, the wild ride. She dropped her heavy lashes; over her head his voice came.

"The marauding Scot," he said.

She raised her eyes then. He was reminding her of the first time they had met. He had that same taunting look, only this time more devilish, she thought angrily. She composed her mouth. He is like to a Border brigand. And he wears a badge. She looked at it, and saw suddenly that it was the infamous ragged bear and staff. Her eyes grew wide in astonishment. "You serve a new master," she breathed. "And of all wicked men, Dudley!"

He grinned. "What sharp eyes you have, kitten. Aye, and shall I be as infamous as the badge I wear? Now?" He took a step toward her, and since the space betwixt them was very small, he towered over her so close she had to lean back to avoid touching him.

Katryn started to speak. He was teasing her. "I don't apprehend you," she said, and tried to divert him. "Pray give me the news of Hugo."

"Are you looking for a man so quick and you still wearing your black?" he asked wickedly. "I hesitate to acquaint you with this fact, but London did not suit Hugo, except he got himself wed. Then he went back to Westmorland. He is very happy, and his bride is all pink and white, and sweet. He has forgotten you completely. I'm sure you will be glad to hear it, for I know you would not want to cause Hugo pain."

"Shut your mouth!" said Katryn.

He laughed. "So this is the thanks I get."

"I've already thanked you," she mumbled. Why did she even talk to this knave? He makes me say all manner of things I never should! Again she set her mouth. "So you are not with Sir Francis then?" she said.

"Nay."

Why had he chosen Dudley, of all people? She forgot her anger. "You know," she said, "I cannot but remember how my father hated that name, and how the elder Dudley made us suffer, how bitterly he was hated. Take care he does not bring you grief!"

"A man brings grief to himself," he said. "But however infamous you deem Dudley and his name, he is a fine sailor, and when I finish this mission, I go to sea. On the flagship *Grace de Dieu*. Lord Dudley commands her."

His blue eyes danced, and she thought, Why, he truly means it.

"I shall make a good sailor, lass," he said. "And we are going to have the finest navy in the world. The King—" He was about to tell her of all the new ships, of the docks abuilding, of Henry's rampant interest. Instead he said, "Henry has a love for ships. And so do I. And now the hour grows late and I came to tell you I have procured horses for you and your woman." He sat down on the bench once again.

"Thank you," said Katryn stiffly. She should have been the one to say the hour grew late. Annoyed with herself, she said, "I have little money." She held up the chain. "Will this recompense you?"

The chain swung between them. Tom Seymour made a reluctant motion, as if to wave it away. Katryn was touched. Surely he had little money—unless, of course, he'd had luck in gambling, in which she knew he indulged.

He asked, "How much money have you?"

"I have three rose nobles, ten shillings, eight pence. Meg had ten crowns," she added.

"Save the chain, then," he said. "Ye have more than enough."

"But you—"

"—have paid for your lodging, and hired the nags. But I still have enough left." He frowned slightly, trying to remember how much he did have left. Stretching out as far as he could on the bench, he leaned back against the bed and yawned; he had been up at dawn and was sleepy. "I'm soon for bed," he said, and then his eyes opened wider and he gave her an impudent smile; his eyes glinted merrily.

Katryn said, "By the mass, you're a knave, sir." She looked at his almost recumbent figure, sprawling with a certain animal grace even in his awkward position, his head back against the bed, dark as sin against the white cotton cover. He had closed his eyes; in repose his face, even with the roughening growth of a day's beard, looked young as his twenty-one years. He seemed less formidable, and she was conscious of a certain tenderness. Was he asleep? Of course he shouldn't sleep in the presence of a lady, but he lived by no rules. She envied him a bit. How lovely to break rules! I'd never have the courage, she thought. But at least he had offered to help her, like a gentleman. He'd not taken her money. Mayhap she had judged him too harshly. She would feel no fear either, with him as her protecter on the long journey south to London. It seemed unbelievably far. How fortunate she was to have him at her side. She leaned forward to see if he were truly asleep, and Tom Seymour opened his eyes. He rose to a sitting position and rested his elbows on his knees. Lazily he reached out a brown hand and captured hers.

"I must say good night," he said.

Her hand lay within his. He turned it over, inspecting the smooth white skin, the carefully cut and polished nails. Gently he raised it to his lips and kissed the palm. They were quite close; she felt a desire to touch the dark head so near. Then she stiffened as she felt his lips on her wrist, where the pulse beat was quickening like a signal beat. To break this spell which seemed to envelop her, she said, "Master Tom." She pulled her hand from his and set it in her lap. "I'm glad you are going to take me to London and very grateful." She gazed into the fire, and when his answer came she did not dare look at him, for she could not believe what she heard.

He said, incredibly, "But I am not taking you to London."

Had she heard aright? He was going to leave her here! Miles from London, alone. Ahead of her stretched unknown roads, sometimes impassable from spring rains. Ahead of her stretched long hours on horseback, with fields and forests full of all manner of ruffians. She would be killed! In real terror, she turned her huge golden eyes on him. "You cannot leave me here!"

He had risen to his feet. "I cannot take you, mistress," he said, and there was a note of finality to his voice; it was flat and there was no appeal.

Hatred and fear stood her on her feet. "You villain!" she sobbed. Her thoughts swirled around crazily. He was leaving her! And a moment ago she had actually felt tenderness! A moment ago he had dared to make love to her! A rush of anger such as she had never felt before suffused her; she sprang at him, hand clenched.

"I hate you! I hate you!" With both fists she was pounding at him, trying to reach his face. If he spoke she heard him not; all she knew was that he was trying to seize her; kicking and struggling, she beat back at him, a wriggling mass of arms and legs, and contorted face. Tears of anger streamed down her cheeks as Tom Seymour finally caught both her wrists in one hand. While she struggled wildly, he passed another arm around her body, lifting her off her feet. She tried to kick at him, but gradually he increased his hold on her till the arm about her waist was crushing. Collapse came then; she could hardly

101

breathe. Her head dropped to his shoulder, and she shook with sobs.

"Sweetheart, stop, stop, for God's sake," he was muttering. "You'll have the whole inn here!"

"I hope I do!" she cried, with all the breath left in her body. If she could do nothing else held this way, she could scream. She opened her mouth to do that, but swift as a cat, he took one step to the bed and laid her down on it, pushing her face into the mattress. He stood over her holding her thus while she writhed and twisted. Tom Seymour lifted one big hand and hit her hard across the buttocks, once and then again. Then he pulled her around to a sitting position.

"You be quiet or you'll have more of that!"

Abruptly she closed her mouth. She bit her lip and started to cry again; he had hurt her. Huge tears rolled down her face. "You beast," she stuttered.

His hands still held her, hard.

"Listen to me." He looked from Katryn, and his eyes found Meg, who stood frozen in one corner, her hands clasped, her eyes fearful and wide at this quarrel between her betters. Abruptly he began again. "You listen too, woman. Tomorrow you will make an early start. I've hired two knaves to go with you and your woman. You will stop each night at a wayside convent or nunnery; do not stop at inns." Katryn was looking at him through tearful eyes. "D'ye hear me? No inns!"

Her mouth puckered. "Aye, I hear you."

He smiled grimly. "You know, the next man you strike may not be as gentle as I."

"I wouldn't strike another man," she said brokenly. "It's you I hate and despise!"

His hands left her shoulders, now that he was satisfied that she was quiet. She looked helpless, like a tearful child.

Katryn caught back another sob. He looked so tall and strong. "Why can't you take us?" she whispered. "Why are you leaving us?"

His jaw hardened. "Because I have a duty to start north immediately, to Scotland, where I deliver letters."

"Letters," she said, contemptuously. "If you were a true gentleman, and a lord, you would not have to carry letters!"

He stiffened. "That was an unfair thrust," he said, "and I mislike treachery in swordplay!"

"Aye, and you dared to make love to me! And then would leave me!" Perched on the bed, her legs tucked under her, her face defiant, she waited for his answer. His level gaze swept her.

"Love?" he asked. "There was no talk of love."

She shot him a glance from under her lashes.

She set her teeth and was about to say more when Meg came round the side of the bed, holding up her apron as though she would fling it over Katryn's head to stop her.

Tom Seymour was at the door. "Good night," he said, politely.

Katryn raised her head. "Good night," she said as evenly as he. Then she couldn't stop the next words: "Get out!"

Tom Seymour gave a shout of laughter. He looked helplessly at Meg, and then, flinging out his hands as if to say, what could one do with her mistress, he shut the door. Katryn hopped off the bed and ran over to the door, intending to open it and hurl an insult at his departing back. Instead she shot the bolt with the violence she would have used on him if she could. She leaned back against the door, breathing hard.

"Prithee let me undress you, madam," Meg cried. "We have a long journey tomorrow!"

"Journey?" asked Katryn. Memory returned. Her eyes grew wide. "Oh, by the mass!" she said. "Oh, by the mass!" she whispered. Now she began to cry again, while Meg drew off her hose and slippers. Here she was, abandoned at an awful little inn, and not only that, he had insulted her and laughed at her.

"How can he be so cruel?" she sobbed.

Absently she stood up for Meg to unhook her, and when her dress had been drawn off, and her other petticoat, she felt gingerly at her backside and raised her chemise. "Look," she said tearfully. On her round white buttock was the imprint of Tom Seymour's hand; black and blue it was turning, and Meg averted her eyes hastily.

"Pray come to bed, madam," she implored.

"I'll not sleep a wink," she said. She crawled into the bed, and pulled up the quilt. A long sigh rent her. "Oh, the villain," she muttered. "Leaving me here! But we'll get to London somehow, Meg! That hellish knave notwithstanding, we'll get to London!" Oh, to see her mother! "Oh, my lady," she whispered aloud, "my lady mother. Soon I shall be with thee. I wish thou were here to bless me!" She stifled a cross between a sigh and a yawn. I should pray, she thought, but that means I should get out of bed and kneel, and I am too sleepy. "Bless me, mother," she said, into her pillow.

London lay one hundred thirty-five miles to the south, almost a week's journey for Katryn and Meg and the two knaves Tom Seymour had hired. Katryn did not see him the next morning, for he had departed before sunrise, leaving behind a scrawled message that said simply, "Godspeed, my lady." She crumpled it furiously, threw it on the floor, and stepped on it. Making mock o' me," she muttered.

Nonetheless, it was her anger with Tom Seymour and that message that did much to give her courage that day and the following ones. Each jolt of the saddle was like the blow of his hand on her sore backside, and the recurring memory of all he had said and done so filled her mind that she hardly noted the long lonely road, and the poor place they stopped to have bread and cheese at noon. Anger was her companion all that first day, and fear did not make itself known till just before dusk, when out of the gloom a nunnery came into view. Its welcoming lights meant harbor and safety; and yet once within its walls she realized that the next day they must not wait so long, but stop long before nightfall to make sure of having safe lodging.

As the road led further to the south, more travelers appeared and she learned much. By the third day, she was able to enjoy the fresh spring air; the sound of horses in the distance meant greetings to her instead of trepidation. She learned to enjoy the sights and sounds of new towns, and new faces; she talked merrily and easily at table every night, surrounded by all kinds of different people, from the nuns or monks themselves to the travelers stopping just as she was. She heard bits of gossip long denied her concerning king and court; on the fifth night she went to bed full of wine and high spirits. How exciting life could be! And all the time she was drawing nearer to her mother.

The morning of the fifth day, the nuns crowded about to bid her good-by and Godspeed. Their friendly faces smiled up at her as she sat in the saddle; the sun shone; how marvellous it was just to be alive in this world! Around a bend in the road a London gallant galloped by, accompanied by six men. He stopped his horse beside hers for a moment.

"By God, madam," he said gaily, "I wish I could turn about, and ride with thee!"

Then he was gone, with a wave of gloved hand. She smiled as she said to Meg, "How impudent! And I in black!"

Her dress was getting worn and rumpled. Every night she carefully sponged and pressed it. The badge of her widowhood. Even as she wore it, it was sometimes hard for her to remember all indeed that had happened, and sometimes she felt it so far in the past—her husband, her lost child, and even the horror of being shut in her rooms with Thomas' step hovering outside in the hallway. Had it all been really true? She was Katryn Parr again; soon she would be home. And yet, when she thought of her estate, from her worn gloves to the only chemise she owned, now on her back, she felt a twinge of disquiet. Who would wed with a poor widow? Certes not a young man of estate. Her quick wit knew that her face and figure were her fortune; outside of the manor in Tansfield that Lord Borough had left her, she had naught to her name. The sunlight shone on her red curls. "Tomorrow," she said, "we'll be home!"

She rose the next morning before dawn and dressed with trembling fingers. Even Meg was excited, and as the road bore southward and the sun climbed the heavens, Katryn became conscious of tightness in her stomach. She became conscious of weariness, too, for the journey had been long and hard.

At noon she was beginning to droop in the saddle, and they stopped for refreshment. The bread and strong ale lay heavy on her stomach. Her hands and face were dirty, but she didn't wash. She was ahorse again, and although fatigue and excitement and journey's end were one with her, she felt assured and hardened and even brave. Ungiven to introspection, she was even aware that the Katryn Parr who rode toward Greenwich now was vastly different from the one she had left behind in Gainsborough. My mother will be proud of me, she thought—except that truly she should have washed, for her mother might say immediately, "Katryn! Your face is filthy! And you a lady!"

At two they crossed the river, busy with traffic. Twice Katryn had to ask her way. Her ears rang with unaccustomed sounds; the bustle of London reached here. Through the new budded trees rose the towers of the royal castle at Greenwich; from its gilded pole flew the royal flag, splashing color against the pale April skies. It had been eleven years since Katryn had seen her mother's house at Greenwich; nothing was familiar. Asking their way, they pressed on, past the castle, down the river road, in the direction of London. Her eyes darted this way and that.

"There it is," she cried suddenly. She would approach from the back, for the house faced the river, its gardens sloping down to the silvery banks. It was very pretty, and it made her proud, for she had not remembered. 'Twas a fine residence. A whole rich life here, near London, blazed before her; then she flung off her horse, and to the postern gate, set in a brick wall. She was through the small garden enclosed within, and through the side door into the house itself, calling out, "Mother, mother! It's I, Katryn, come home!"

Her voice echoed through the house. Her flying feet carried her forward, toward the center hallway, "Mother," she cried again, savoring the joy she knew Maud Parr would feel to hear her first-born daughter's voice after so long a time. She whirled at the sound of sudden footsteps.

"Anne!" she shrieked. She had never thought to be so glad to see Anne. She seized her sister, hugging her tight, laughing. "Anne! Anne!" she cried. "I'm home! I'm home!" Anne was crying. Was it with joy? It must be, for Anne grasped for her again. And there were more persons about, too, an aproned wench and two serving men, come on hasty feet. She paid no attention.

She squeezed Anne again. "Silly goose, you! Don't cry, you'll set me abawling!" She held her off and looked at Anne's tear-stained face. "Where's your smile?" she asked. "Where's that pretty smile? Have ye not a one for your sister you've not seen for six months or more?" Suddenly she stopped talking and stared at her sister. Anne's face was white. Katryn looked at her again. Anne was wearing black! She and Anne were dressed alike! Why? She couldn't believe her first dreadful thought. It couldn't be true! But what had been in the letter that she had left lying on the floor at Gainsborough Hall? She felt herself stiffen all over. Even her lips were stiff. She grasped Anne's arm.

"My mother!" she whispered. "Is it my mother?"

Anne didn't answer. Her eyes grew huge; she looked as though she were going to faint. Katryn almost shoved her into Meg's arm, for there were heavier footsteps coming down the stairway. She whirled toward them. "Will!" she screamed, her voice echoing out through the silent hall. She paused, then spaced each word. "Will! Where is my mother?"

Will had stopped just above her, one hand on the stairrail. His voice came then, deeper than she remembered.

"Our mother is dead, Katryn," he said. "She died two days ago."

I was too late. The words repeated themselves, awake, asleep, adreaming. I was too late, too late. Never again will I feel her hand on my head, never again will I know the comfort of her arms, her smile, her soft voice. I am alone, alone in this vast world, alone without husband or father or mother. What will I do? Where shall I seek safety? Here, in my old, little-remembered child's room? Here, where the candle at my bed is shaped as it was when I was a child, like a brass doll? "Oh, God," she said aloud. She knelt on the bare floor and began to pray. "Please help me," she begged, "please help me."

She had seen her mother in death, and now she tried to wipe the memory of that cold face from her mind. Will and Anne had tried to tell her how her mother had gradually wasted away, but she had cried out to them to stop, she couldn't bear it. "Later," she said, "later, not now. Leave me, leave me alone." At her door she had turned to look at both of them. They were younger than she, Will by a year, Anne by two years. She felt the inevitability of what was going to be thrust upon her; she was all they had, she forced herself to think. Standing there at the door of her old room, "Is our uncle at court?" she asked, wearily.

Will nodded.

"Send him my respects, and ask him to wait on me on the morrow." It was growing dark. "I shall attend to all in the morning. Go to bed, and try to sleep. I must try, for other I shall not be able for the next day—nay, nor its duties." She turned from them, then paused again. "God bless you both," she said. "It is well I came. You can depend on me." Then she shut the door.

Outside the moon shone; it cast a shaft of palest light across the wooden floor and onto Katryn's head as she knelt by the rumpled bed. "Please help me," she repeated. At dawn the singing of the birds wakened her. April was being almost wantonly kind and warm— like a mockery, Katryn thought, to my heart, my heart which aches so I can almost feel the pain in my body.

Later she did not know exactly how the days had passed. First Sir William had come, early. Wifeless and childless, he was gruff but steady as a rock, and she took a good measure of comfort from him. It was he who had made the funeral arrangements; Maud Parr would be laid to rest in Blackfriars, as she had requested. "In my letter, I told you your mother was gravely ill," Sir William said. They were in the garden and the soft April sun was warm. "I told you that I had asked the King to send his own physician, which his Grace, from the goodness of his heart, did. But there was naught to be done, my dear. I called a lawyer for your mother and she made her will, but her affairs are in bad case, and it may well be a full year afore they're straightened out, or the will proved. I tell you this plain," he ended heavily.

After a while he left her, leaving also three of his men servants to help ready the house for the funeral. Katryn worked hard that day, instructing Anne and Will, too, for there was the whole house to be made ready; for our mother, Katryn thought proudly, was much loved, and there will be many mourners.

Just before the funeral, she almost collapsed. She remembered how little time had passed since she had done this for her husband, and a fit of crazy laughter shook her and she trembled all over. Then the strange fit passed, and she could feel the frenzy drain from her limbs.

"I warrant I can manage," she said to Meg. "It won't hap again, and I shan't cry."

She didn't cry. Not until her mother's body was interred beneath the stones at Blackfriars did the tears spring into her eyes. She drew her black shawl across her face and put her arm around Anne, who sat shaking at her side. That night she took Anne into her bed, and they slept together.

That week passed, the first week in May, with many callers. Exhaustion claimed Katryn; she slept long, and even late, wakening but to another day of sweet May weather and bitter grief and sorrow. "But you are young," Sir William said, "and time will heal your wounds. How old art thou?"

"Sixteen and a half, my lord," she said. "And I feel forty."

He chuckled. "Even at forty," he said, "one has a future. You must ponder yours." He took her white hand. "In two days, I shall come and have dinner with you, and we can talk. Sleep, eat, and sit outside here and get thy strength."

She watched him stump away. "Thank God we have him," she said to Anne, who sat on a cushion at her feet, "for we have no one— nay, nor nothing else." She said the words aloud, and even as she said them, she knew they were false. Her heart leaped. Into her mind came a sudden vision, clear and sharp and so real it shone right before her eyes. "Jesu!" she cried. "I almost forgot. We ha' Kendal!"

She explained her decision to go back to Kendal to Sir William two days later. While she watched Anne and Will at dinner to make sure their manners were exemplary, their voices low and well modulated, and full of enough respect for their uncle, she waited to speak. But first, as proper, Sir William told his own decisions.

"I shall take Will with me to court," he said, "till his marriage one year hence." In a year Will would be seventeen, and of suitable age.

Katryn thanked him. She asked him then if he would speak with his Grace, the King, on Anne's appointment to be a maid-in-waiting. Katryn said that through one of the ladies who had come to call she had heard Queen Katharine had been permitted to reorganize her court in April, and therefore 'twas just the right moment for Anne to put forth her request.

"Quite so," said Sir William approvingly. "She must not be permitted to join Nan Boleyn's ladies." Sir William leaned over and patted Anne's hand. "For though she would like it much—they have masques, and go about London dining with gentlemen in public places, and one can hear their barges coming back up the river late at night, full of laughter and songs—yet Anne would be overcumbered by them, unfit, and no one knows which way the night crow will fly." He meant Nan Boleyn herself, for no one knew when Henry would of a sudden tire of the chase and be done with the black-eyed Nan. After all, Henry still had a wife, a queen, and it was best that Anne join the Queen's court. "You will go to mass five times a day, and do your needlework," Sir William said, his eyes twinkling.

Anne made a little face at him. "Aye, sir," she said.

Then Sir William turned his eyes on Katryn. "And what of you, my dear?"

"I have let this house, sir. The moneys can be paid out to Anne and Will for their expenses. And I shall go back to Kendal!"

Sir William was silent. He frowned slightly. He reminded himself that someone of the family should look after Kendal; it was a vast estate, with its villages, its towns, its moors and hills. Nevertheless the responsibility was that of his nephew, his namesake. Sir William glanced at Will, who was eating steadily, not pricking up his ears at all at the mention of his ancestral dwelling. Charming is Will, he thought, with wit and kindness, but a jelly of a man. Maybe he could help the boy; although maybe he didn't need help but could slide through life on his charm. Sir William looked again at Katryn. Even with her manor at Tansfield left her by Lord Borough, she was too poor to apply for the post of lady-in-waiting, and widowed—

He took a bite of bread and chewed reflectively. "Take care you're not retreating to Kendal to lick your wounds, my dear."

She flashed him a look of complete bewilderment; she hadn't understood at all. He said then, "You have a talent for living. Any talent is both a burden and a joy; one pays high for 't."

She tried to be polite. "Aye, sir," she said. "But someone has to look after Kendal, till Will does!"

Three days later Sir William sent for his nephew. The leave-taking was not tearful; Will seemed pleased, and eager. Two more days passed, while Katryn frantically remade her mother's clothes for herself and Anne. Then the message came that Sir William would escort Anne to Queen Katharine's court at ten of the clock the following morning.

Late that night Katryn wrote a long letter to be delivered to Anne on the morrow, a long farewell letter full of instructions she had forgotten to give her sister. Katryn wrote of always being industrious and willing, and of keeping up with her lute and virginals, or memorizing quickly the new songs the Queen might like, of never fidgeting at mass, of never gossiping.

> Thou wilt have no privacy [she wrote], so strive to like and love all those about thee, seeking what is best in them, and blinding thy eyes to their faults; for what shall it profit thee to list them and brood over wrongs or insults?
>
> Be circumspect with all men about thee; never meet any alone or at night; and I warn thee, stay well away from Master Thomas Seymour and his friends. A wench has naught so precious as her virtue; she must bring it to her husband.
>
> And thus good night, dear sister. Prithee take heed of all I writ, and keep the letter by thee, and learn to live well with others.

The hour was four of the clock in the morning. The air was warm and dewy; the birds had not yet arisen. But the front doors of the house stood open, with Katryn in their center and Meg to one side, holding high a hastily lit candle. On the top step knelt Lucy Borough.

"I have found thee," she had cried, and fallen on her knees.

Katryn pushed back her tumbled hair, and tried to realize that this was truly Lucy who knelt before her. She looked further and beheld the huddled form of Wat. Lucy was praying, and then suddenly she lifted her head and began to speak.

"We pilgrimaged barefoot to the shrine of Our Lady of Walsingham. Only there could my immortal soul be saved. I entered the shrine, and went on my knees to the altar, and Our Lady spoke to me. It was like a shaft of light—though indeed there was little light, and only the mute glowing of colors, of jewels. Candles burned."

Katryn saw Wat shift in the shadows beyond the doors. Lucy continued. "Our Lady spoke, and I heard as though she had spoke aloud. My madness was gone; and though I was not cleansed of my sin, I saw in what manner I should atone for it. Then we set forth, Wat and I, to find thee, my lady, and make restitution." She held out the great glittering cross of rubies on the long pearl chain.

"Jesu!" whispered Katryn, shrinking back. It flashed through her mind that both of them, Lucy and she, had managed to slip jewelry out of the house at Gainsborough. Pity for Lucy and sudden remembrance of the past stirred her.

"Lucy! Oh my poor, poor Lucy!" she said. "I want not thy mother's cross!"

"You must take it and wear it always!" Lucy said. "And it will protect you, and hold its blessings on you. And I shall do the same, my lady." She glanced down at the pearl chain. "I do not offer this as a jewel. Nay, when I began to lay it on the altar, I knew 'twas a false offering, for it belonged to you. I was jealous, and to erase my jealousy, you must have it and wear it, so I may see it on you and be reminded of my wickedness. I shall see it daily, whilst I aid thee and am at thy side, for this is what I've sworn to do."

"Sworn?" whispered Katryn. A thing sworn could not be undone.

"Aye, I devote my waking and sleeping hours to thee." Lucy stood up, and beckoned to Wat, who slipped forward and babbled a greeting. "And as Wat is my servant, so is he thine. Forever."

"But I do not need thee, Lucy," Katryn began.

Lucy said, "Nay, mayhap not, but we need thee! To redeem our sins."

Katryn flung out both hands almost in supplication, and looking for words, found none. Lucy placed the ruby cross in her hand; Katryn felt its weight. Lucy cried, "It has lain on my body, and comes to thee warm from my breasts, and rich with repentance. May God will that someday you will forgive me."

Katryn blinked back her tears. She said low, "I don't deserve it, Lucy."

"Oh, my lady," Lucy whispered. "Pray accept us."

"I shall," Katryn said. There was no choice; the memory of Lord Borough was sharp. This was his legacy to her, and one which she had earned through her own follies, her mistakes, her vanity. Instead of a child of her own, she would take his child, Lucy, who knelt at her feet. "Rise up, Lucy," she said.

Lucy struggled to her feet. Suddenly Katryn was aware of her physical appearance. "Oh, by the mass!" she cried. "Ye cannot come into the house like that! You are crawling with lice, I warrant!" She pointed to the path. "Ye'll have to enter by the kitchens."

In the kitchen, Lucy undressed and cast her chemise onto the fire. Katryn threw a shawl about her. "When you ha' washed, and made thyself clean, we shall find clothes for thee. This morning we start north for Kendal."

"Aye, my lady," said Lucy, a bright smile on her face.

Katryn left her to Meg. Upstairs she laid the ruby cross on the mantelpiece. She glanced at her tumbled bed. It was too late to woo sleep again. She threw off her robe, and stood shivering and naked in the cool room. "By God's most precious soul!" she muttered. "How do all these things hap to me?"

7

The great residence of the Earls of Essex was dubbed New Hall, and when Katryn first glimpsed it she was conscious only of wonder. It was enormous, and so were its spreading acres and parklands. How pleased her mother would have been, she thought, to see Will wed the heiress of these vast estates and grand titles.

It was very hot. The July afternoon sun burned down, and dust flew from the horses' hoofs. She would look a sorry sight before she arrived there.

She had been so proud of herself this morning, as she stood dressed in green Kendal cloth with great roses embroidered on it by Lucy, and the morning sun bright on her red curls. Lucy had stood off and admired her. "Oh, you're an entrancing sight!" she had exclaimed. But now as she led her small entourage of Lucy, Meg, and four men servants nearer the magnificent dwelling of the Earl of Essex and reminded herself of all the personages who would cram its walls, she began to doubt she would make the impression Lucy had thought; she felt as insignificant as her Border-bred animal, also trapped in Kendal green.

At least she had left off mourning clothes; she had been able to pack them away in the late spring, soon after she had received the long letter from Anne, telling her the news.

The King has left his wife [Anne had writ, baldly]. On the first of June, I and the other ladies were working with wool for tapestry, and the Queen was using white wool; she had it round her neck. The hour was nine in the evening, when of a sudden we heard a commotion in the hall, and all of us were fearful, for we did never know what was being planned against the Queen. All of us cried out, save the Queen, who took another stitch and bade me inquire who was without. I obeyed, though I was full of fear, for only God knows what deviltries the Boleyn party will brew.

In the hall was a deputation of noblemen, and two dukes, one of them Suffolk, the King's good friend. We all stood about the Queen's chair and heard them speak, as she bade them do before us; for she said she had no secrets, as they did.

Then Nan Boleyn's father, the Earl of Wiltshire, began to speak of a wife's duty to her husband and prince, and that an absence of duty could be construed as treason. The Queen did not falter at that terrible word, as I did; on my soul, I trembled all over, for we all think what might they not do to her, our queen? And the Queen said, "I shall always serve and obey my husband, but as to the spiritual realm, it pleases neither me nor God that I should consent to a nullification of my marriage."

Then Suffolk said, "Madam, the King considers you his brother's wife, and he considers the Pope has no power to transcend the word of God, as it is writ in the Bible. What o' the King's conscience?" he asked, and that is what all that party asks, for they say his Grace is deep troubled, and feels God has cursed the marriage.

But the Queen does not list to that. She said, "The Pope is the true Vicar of God, and he alone has the power to judge, not kings."

Suffolk said, "Madam, you take a hard course, and one which indeed comes close to disservice to your King."

The Queen did not answer this, but bid them good night.

We slept almost not at all, that night, what with whispering and talking. I have in my room Jane, and Kate Willoughby, who is in love with Suffolk.

Jane who? Katryn wondered, raising her eyes from the letter a moment. And why did she put that in about Kate Willoughby being in love? Is she trying to say she too is hankering after a man, when I have already betrothed her? She says naught about her betrothal! Katryn read on.

But a month passed, with no further word to us. Then one morning at dawn, we were awakened by the horns of a hunting party. I got up and looked out the window, and there was Nan Boleyn, dressed in green, with a new hunting cap on her head, riding off with his Grace, and the yard was full of baggage carts! We knew they were off and away, and so it happed. We were told the next hour that the Queen was to leave Windsor and not return, but to go to Moor Park and await the King's pleasure.

We helped the Queen pack her few belongings, for she was not allowed to take even the worn hangings, nor her bedstead, nor the carpets and furniture. It was a meager train that set forth, with just her physician, her confessor, and a handful of personal servants. It made our hearts ache, for she was so stoic and brave, and kissed us all good-by. We all sobbed and she told us to be brave. But she will never return; we are all sure of it, and we hope and pray every night they will not send her to prison. She is not in good health, either, poor Queen. And so now, we are still at Windsor, awaiting the King's return, and we are told we must join Nan Boleyn's ladies when the court returns. How we shall ever serve her, I do not know; but Sir William says I owe allegiance first to his Grace, and that we do it for him, for he truly thinks his marriage was cursed and that he has sinned in living with his brother's wife. It is very hard to know, indeed, and I feel sorry for both of them, for they are unhappy, I think.

But I shall see thee at Will's wedding, next month. Until then, my dearest sister, I remain your loving and obedient sister,

ANNE P.

Katryn had laid down the letter in amazement. Why, she said not a word about her betrothal, nor about the dowry—and so much too, three hundred pounds!—I've gone without to save. Katryn couldn't believe it! How could she forget to mention it? Or didn't she realize how I had to scrape for that money? Anne was still young, but fifteen and a half, and yet—Sir William, who had helped arrange the match with Sir Robert Trywhit, had written that Anne's betrothed was a fine man, widowed, who would make a good husband. Katryn had planned to settle it when she saw Anne; they could be wed at Kendal, in November, a fine month for weddings.

Now, riding nearer the great looming dwelling, she thought of Will, too. How pleased he would be when she told him all that had been accomplished at Kendal this past year—how much cloth had been woven, how the last of their mother's debts had been paid. Twelve new fields had been enclosed for new flocks, and through her efforts and patronage, the monastery at Kendal, where much weaving was done, had doubled its brotherhood. Much, much had been done, and she glowed with pride when she thought on it.

Through the thickly leaved groves of trees, she saw the castle plain now. I warrant there must be four hundred rooms, she thought. By the mass, how ever will I even find Anne and Will? Her spirits drooped. A troop of gaily caparisoned horsemen trotted by, paying her no attention. All about now, on the lawns, were little gay tents where the county gentry had gathered to see the wedding and its festivities. The King himself will be here, she thought, as she spurred her weary animal forward through the great gates and into the outer courts of New Hall.

The court was full to overflowing. Men and horses, servants and baggage, dogs, women, little boys dressed in bright livery. Everyone is shouting, Katryn thought, completely bewildered. She sat on her horse, looking about. Her own servants dismounted, and one came over to aid her down from the saddle. Afoot, she tried vainly to see a familiar face. Lucy and Meg came alongside of her, and cast her appealing looks as to what they should do next.

Katryn said to her groom, "Find the stables, and then pray return and help us with our baggage."

"Aye, my lady," he said, touching his cap. At Katryn's side stood Wat; he smiled up at her. "I shall find a proper place for you, Wat," she said. He hardly reached her shoulder. Still, she was proud of him, for he was quite distinctive, almost like a toy man, and devoted as a puppy. Two liveried servants were at the great outer doors. "Come," she said, gathering up her skirt in one hand, and holding her red head high. She marched ahead to the doors. "The Lady Borough," she said clearly, and passed into the dimness of New Hall.

This hallway too was crowded. Men and women stood about, waiting for their boxes, or such. She glanced about, wishing desperately to lay eyes on Anne or Will. Instead she found herself looking straight at a tall man, slender, with hair almost the color of gold. His eyes were gray, and rested on her a moment; then, incredibly, he was coming toward her, a welcoming smile on his face. He stooped a little from his slender height. He bowed in front of her, and said in a voice cultured and soft, "I heard you speak your name. I am Lord Latimer, my dear. We are kin, and I have been waiting for you.

Sir William writ me, and he, unfortunately, is unable to attend the wedding. Shall you mind if I look after you?"

"Oh, how kind!" she exclaimed. Oh, what a real gentleman, she though dizzily. So tall and fair, and grave and smiling, all at the same time. "Are we kin?" she asked, looking up at him.

"I should have told you my family name, Neville. Your grandmother was my cousin. We are related in the fourth degree, and the sight of you makes me very proud of it." He took the hand she held out, and kissed it, in a most polished and courtly manner. "Will you present me?" he asked then, inclining his head toward Lucy as though to remind her.

She blushed. What a dolt he must think me, she thought. She found her tongue, and presented Lucy. Her voice was very low, and she cast about for something further to say, but she was conscious of her dirty face. She blurted, "This is so kind of you, my lord. Could you help me find my sister Anne? In this vast place, I know not where even to begin to look! And we are weary, and wanting water for washing." His manners are truly elegant, she thought, and here I stand talking about washing. At least I didn't say I needed to sit on a jakes, which I do. She caught her lip with her teeth, and looked up at him again, a golden gleam in her eyes. "Will you help me find my sister Anne, my lord?" she repeated, meltingly.

"Of course," he said. He raised his hand, and beckoned to a servant. With nice authority he established the fact that Anne was indeed here, and where she was. He placed Katryn's hand on his arm, and they started off together with Lucy and Meg coming just behind.

As they went along, Katryn said, "I should never have been able to find my way, least of all Anne, without you, my lord. Oh, I cannot thank you enough!"

"I'm glad to help," he said.

But he looked pleased at her words, and it was reassuring. For I've almost forgot what men are like, she told herself. She asked, "You are familiar with New Hall, my lord?"

"Aye, I've stayed here," he said, offhandedly.

He must be important then, and used to wealth. She admired his coat and its cut, but she thought she should not say so, yet. When he took her hand, his own was so gentle, and slender and so well cared for. She noted it as she took her farewell of him, and she noted the big diamond on his finger, cleverly set in heavy gold, as became a man's ring. She started to say she hoped she would have the pleasure of seeing him again, then stopped. No, that wouldn't do; he must ask her that. She waited, letting him hold her hand.

"I shall see you at supper. I hope so."

"Of course, my lord," she said, and her smile flashed out, radiant. He had said it! "But I may be a poor companion, for I'm so very hungry!" She gave him another dazzling smile. "Good-by till then." Then, head high, she opened the door and flew into Anne's arms.

But were Anne's arms as tight and welcoming as she had expected? Freeing herself from her sister's embrace, and paying no mind to the other women in the room, Katryn held Anne off. "But you look so fair," she exclaimed. "You grow more lovely!" She smiled, "Mother would be so proud of you!"

Anne's face softened; she sighed and their eyes held. Then she said, "I *am* glad to see thee, Katryn!"

"Weddings are so exciting!" another voice said, and Katryn turned to see the speaker. She must be Kate Willoughby, she thought, for she is half Spanish, and she looks it with her tawny hair and great black eyes and her sinuous grace. But why had she said that, and why is that look passing between her and Anne? Katryn drew Lucy forward, and presented her—she had been right, it was Kate Willoughby—and then Anne said, gesturing to a tall girl who stood by the window, a pale serene girl, with palest hair and deep blue eyes, "And this is Jane."

Jane? Katryn wondered again. The tall girl smiled at her. "My name is Seymour," she said. She was unhooking her dress, and she stepped out of it. The figure revealed by her chemise was full and voluptuous. Seymour!

"I know your brother, I think, Mistress Jane," she said.

"My brother Ned?"

"Nay," said Katryn, watching her.

Jane said warmly, "My brother Tom?" She smiled. "I adore him," she said. "Would you mind handing me my silver brush, Kate? You have it, to your hand there." She sat down on the edge of the bed and began to brush her golden hair. She had to get her travel-stained clothes off, too. She felt Lucy's fingers at her cloak, and since the others were doing so, she let Lucy undress her while Meg unpacked.

119

The room was so crowded they could scarcely move. Open boxes spilled out their pretty contents: lacy chemises, vivid robes, little feathered slippers and mules, gleaming satin dresses. On the only table stood bottles of perfume and open jewel boxes and a dainty pile of combs that Kate Willoughby was using expertly to pile up her hair. Katryn felt a little left out. They must be very close, the three of them. They all seemed to be wearing each other's clothes, borrowing each other's jewels and hose and anything else that came to mind. And they talked constantly.

"The black gown is cut very, very low, and it looks beautiful," Anne was saying. "And she says she will prove his Grace wrong, for he thinks he mislikes black."

Kate said, "And do kings like to be proved wrong?"

"Who is 'she'?" Katryn asked, fascinated.

Jane Seymour said matter-of-factly, "Nan, the goggle-eyed whore. And don't use all the water, Kate."

"No," said Katryn, "for God's sake, don't!"

Kate threw her a merry glance, an accepting one. "I shan't," she said, throwing perfume around with abandon.

Katryn was washing, and as she brought the edge of her towel from her face, she saw all three pairs of eyes were watching her. She affected not to notice. Then, a bit puzzled, she threw down the towel.

"Anne," she said, "you didn't write about your betrothal."

Anne's eyes got huge. "N-no," she stammered.

"Why not?" asked Katryn reasonably.

Anne sighed deeply. "I know Sir Robert, and I don't like him for a husband," she brought out finally. "I—"

Looking about at the three of them, Katryn said sharply, "And is 't the new fashion to pick and choose? Do you all think you can pick your husbands?"

Kate put another pin in her hair. "Aye," she said. Her eyes challenged Katryn, and then flew to Anne's face as if to give her encouragement.

Katryn turned to Jane. "You think thus, too, mistress?"

Jane said sweetly, "Aye, my lady."

"Anne," Katryn said, "I've paid your dowry, and—"

Anne said, "We cannot talk here! Later, mayhap. Please, Katryn."

Katryn, unwilling to give up the battle, hesitated, when from below came the sound of bells being rung lustily.

"Supper," cried Anne with great relief. "Supper!"

It took ten more frantic minutes, of powdering and fastening garters before they sallied forth—as though to battle, Katryn thought —eyes flashing, jewels gleaming, throwing out clouds of perfume. She felt a brief envy; they were so carefree and gay and pretty. They had not the slightest notion what it meant to be married; they had no troubles, no one to look after. That made Katryn remember Lucy. "You look lovely, Lucy," she whispered, as they went down the hallway. She had spent hours on Lucy's dress, cut from a robe of her mother's. She was conscious, too, of her own dress. It was white satin, creamy with age.

But Katryn still didn't know how well she looked, with the great ruby cross catching the colors of the red embroidery, and the aged satin against her skin and hair, until she saw the look in Lord Latimer's eyes as he came forward to greet her.

Then she saw Will. "Will!" she cried. They kissed. "How much you have grown," Katryn said, holding his hand and looking up at his face. He was a good five inches taller, and grown broader, too. He looked so handsome and fit. Sir William had certes done well for him. Smiling Will presented his bride.

Bess was slim and dark and possessed of an elfin beauty. Her smile was quick, and she had an odd quality of imploring one's acceptance which Katryn thought strange for a great heiress, yet perhaps it was just an engagingness. She was vivacious.

"To think I'll be wed tomorrow," Bess cried, "and you shall be my dear sister! I've never had a sister!"

"You've never had a husband, either," Will said, with a merry look in his eye.

Lord Latimer and Katryn laughed. "Thou'rt just the same, Will," Katryn said.

They sat together near the very head of the table, as befitted the bride and groom, and his kin. Only after they had started to eat from the great platters of food the servants brought, did Katryn realize that Anne had eschewed their company and was with the maids-in-waiting, farther down the table.

Katryn herself was near the King and Nan Boleyn. She was indeed garbed in black, an evening gown of black satin, cut well away from her throat and shoulders, and through the overgown of net her white skin glistened. Katryn could not hear the King's conversation. But once she saw Nan lean close to him and whisper something, whereupon Henry laid his hand on her throat. There was a savageness in the gesture that was as though the King desired both to caress and destroy. Nan laughed, and laid her white hand against his. Slowly Henry released her.

"Marry!" Katryn said under her breath, meeting Lord Latimer's eyes. Lord Latimer raised his handkerchief to his lips, as if to wipe away the picture he had seen. Lord Latimer then asked Lucy, who sat on his other side, how she liked living in the North. Katryn didn't hear her reply. In the big doorway, she saw two men, alike and unlike, cutting a swath as though they bore themselves clothed in shining armor. Katryn had never seen Ned Seymour; she had never seen Tom Seymour dressed in aught but leather. Now in sober black, with white shirt, a swinging black cloak lined in red, the glitter of jewels in the dagger at side, with his brother dressed in dull red, he moved into the great room. Katryn could hear Jane's high voice, as she called, "Tom! Ned!"

Lord Latimer raised his head. He too looked across the room, as did everyone else who heard Jane. "The Seymours," he said. "They manage to look different from every other man in the room." He bent his gaze on Katryn. "Do you know them?" he inquired.

She did not answer for a moment. The question had fallen on other ears than hers, and she knew it. Across the narrow trestle table was the gaunt face of William de la Pole, member of an ancient family and boasting the blood of the Plantagenets. Next him was one of the Courtenay women, kin. It had not escaped Katryn's notice that she sat amongst the oldest and greatest of the old families; she knew they formed a group hostile to Nan Boleyn. The party that supported Nan did so for a variety of reasons—some of them a belief in the New Learning, the weening away of England from Rome and the Pope (there were even those persons who leaned toward Luther, although they didn't say so aloud). Against them—aye, and even against the upstart Henry Tudor—stood in an almost solid block these oldest names. And no wonder Henry distrusted them so, for what was more threatening to a monarch than someone else who claimed royal blood, and that blood older than his? What Yorkists were left were here, about Katryn. She was impressed. They were true ladies and gentlemen, just like her mother, serene, reserved, restrained, lofty.

A sigh escaped Katryn. Did she know the Seymours? Katryn thought with horror of the scene between Tom Seymour and herself. What would Lord Latimer think if he knew that her hip had borne the marks of Tom Seymour's hand? And what would he think if she told him of that scene of violence in Gainsborough Hall? Such raw adventures belonged to the past of a tavern wench; no decent girl got herself fought over by men, men who used their hands. Lord Latimer would not realize that she had never encouraged Thomas Borough save by civil talk. Lord Latimer would be distressed; he would be repelled. I mustn't even say a hello to Tom Seymour, she thought rapidly; I must hardly acknowledge him, and God knows I never wanted to see him again, anyway. Yet her eyes continued to stray over to him where he stood talking. Aloud she said, to Lord Latimer and the Countess of Courtenay, across the table,

"I know Thomas Seymour but slightly, and Sir Edward I know not at all."

"Sir Edward," said the Countess, "is an iconoclast!"

By the mass! Katryn thought, whatever is that? What shall I say? "I didn't know that, my lady," she whispered in tones of horror.

The Countess nodded and leaned forward. "Frightful, is it not, that we have such amongst us? And more frightful when one realizes that his mother is the granddaughter of the Duke of Clarence."

Now Katryn did truly look surprised. Her eyes went over to Thomas Seymour with some respect. "He is direct descended?" she asked.

"Aye, my dear," said the Countess. "And young Master Tom looks like a Plantagenet; he has that strong face and jaw. Edward's lineaments are not so marked and male."

Katryn thought, Well I could tell you a few things about him that would turn your hair. He's a knave, disrespectful and hateful.

"I've a soft spot for Master Tom," the Countess was saying, with a smile.

"You have?" asked Katryn in amazement. "I cannot endure him," she said, haughtily. Blood of the Plantagenets indeed! she thought angrily; no wonder he had laughed when she had accused him of not being a gentleman! A flush stained her cheeks and she took a big swallow of wine. Lord Latimer was regarding her with some surprise. I shouldn't ha' been so vehement, she thought; he'll think it strange.

She smiled at Lord Latimer, "It is just that his manner is so bold and ungentlemanly, my lord," she said. Her eyes told Lord Latimer she considered *him* a true gentleman. "We are so glad you are here, Lucy and I. We should feel lost without you!" A dazzling smile accompanied these words.

"You are so young," Lord Latimer said. He said it almost plaintively. Does he mean I'm too young for him? she wondered, now thinking only of the man beside her. She studied his face for a clue to his age. He looked so distinguished, and yet he must be over forty. She leaned slightly toward him so he could catch a whiff of perfume.

"I'm not so young, my lord," she said. "I am almost nineteen." She would be in three months, so it was not a lie.

"Nineteen," he said, and sighed. "A wonderful age, my dear, and one to be proud of." His smile was fond, she thought, but so removed, as though he viewed her from a great eminence. He has such aplomb and restraint—I wonder if I could ever break that down. I wish I could; I am half in love with him already. She gave him a melting look. He turned away from her, almost quickly, to speak to William de la Pole across the table, asking some inconsequential question. Katryn was taken aback. I don't understand him, at all; if he likes me, why doesn't he respond? Mayhap he is shy; maybe the very fact that he turned away from me means he was affected, because I almost told him plain that I was old enough for him. I'll wait, and sometime tomorrow I'll let him know again that I like him. Now I'll be reserved too, a real lady for the rest of the evening. I'll just lean a little close to him once in a while when we dance.

The trestle tables were cleared away, and food and wine were placed on the great sideboards along the wall. In the great rooms opening off the hall, gaming tables were set up, and the dice rolled and the cards slapped, and light glittered on the piled gold coins. The doors stood open onto the gardens; a few torches were set out there illuminating the green paths.

Katryn danced with Lord Latimer. She danced with Will. She thought the music wonderful; when Lord Latimer said it was a bit loud she look surprised, and he smiled at her—fondly, she thought with a catch in her throat. He looked straight at her. "Would you care to walk in the garden?"

Her heart leaped. "Aye, my lord," she said primly. "I think the fresh air would be most salubrious."

He chuckled at the choice of word. They had left the hall and its music behind and walked slowly along the path. "There is the maze," he said, pointing.

"Oh, let's try it."

He put her hand on his arm. "And what if we get lost?"

She didn't answer that. "I wish there were a moon," she said, wistfully. Then he could see her face better.

"Then we would not get lost." He squeezed her hand. "Now we have a chance."

Why he's making an advance! she thought. But I shan't answer that, because of all things I don't want to scare him off. So she said, "I know we are kin, but I don't know you very well, my lord."

He drew her into the first path of the maze. "Why, I'm old enough to be your father," he said gruffly.

Katryn stopped walking. She looked up at him in the darkness. "Mayhap," she said steadily, "but you are not my father."

He was silent and then he said, "True, and I'm glad. Are you?"

She hesitated. "I don't know."

In the darkness Katryn's eyes gleamed gold. I'm in love, she thought dizzily, and I think he's in love too.

They walked for half an hour; they did not get lost. Katryn had an inner knowledge that Lord Latimer never got lost. He was deliberate and always in command, of himself and events. He told her his principal dwelling place was in Yorkshire. Snape Hall, he called it. He described it briefly, especially the bookroom, his favorite, and how its shelves were cleverly encased in glass panes; she could almost see it, and the carpet on the table with its silver writing implements. He told her of his London town house on the Charterhouse, and of his two children—for Lord Latimer was a widower. Two and four they were, a girl named Margaret and a boy named John, named for his direct ancestor the Duke of Warwick, who had been dubbed Neville the Kingmaker. When they reentered the hall, she looked at him proudly. He was so distinguished!

I'm in some kind of spell, she thought. I don't think I had best even talk with him more this night; it will be better if I retire. She said aloud, "It is eleven, my lord. I have so enjoyed myself, but would you excuse me now? I—we—have had a long journey."

He looked pleased. "I mislike staying up late myself, preferring to rise early and enjoy the day. I am glad you do, too."

He bowed. As he made his way from her, she spied Lucy across the room. Gathering up her skirts to avoid the whirling dancers, she started across the floor. At the door Lord Latimer waved to her, and she waved back. She sighed deeply; I'm so happy, she thought. Her shining eyes rested on Tom Seymour, standing almost in front of her. She came to an abrupt stop.

"Good evening," he said. "And where have you been?"

"I was in the garden," she said absently.

"Ah," he said. "I suspected as much. And with what luckless knave?"

She said haughtily, "I think that choice of word is not very happy!"

He grinned. "But true. Will you dance?"

She looked up at him. His blue eyes were merry, and she almost smiled; her foot tapped to the beat. Why do I want to dance? she wondered. "I think not," she said, forgetting to add her thank-you.

He looked a trifle taken aback. Perhaps she should make some explanation, some amends for her refusal. "I am most weary, sir," she said, essaying a small smile.

Tom Seymour said, "That's the weakest smile I ever saw. What's the matter with you? Could it be," he wondered, "that you are setting snares for the gentle Lord Latimer, and do not want to jeopardize your standing with him by being seen with me?"

She was not going to answer him, but another thought slipped into her mind just then. "Pray tell me, Master Tom, what is an iconoclast?" She hesitated over the syllables, frowning slightly.

He said, surprised, "An iconoclast? But I am not—" he too frowned, gazing at her with narrow eyes. "Was that epithet applied to my brother, Ned?"

I'm not going to answer that either, she thought defiantly, but Tom Seymour just nodded.

"I thought so," he said. "Well, an iconoclast is a destroyer of images, one who disbelieves in images, in church, for instance, and thus an advocate of the New Learning, though perhaps stronger in his leanings than others hereabouts. Does that answer your question?"

"Aye."

"Well, say thank you, then," he prodded. "How was your trip to London, by the way? Did you tramp on heads and hearts all the way down?"

Katryn was truly speechless as she remembered. "You villain! You left me in Lincoln!"

"You're none the worse for it," he said casually, sipping his wine.

"I hope you choke on that!" she whispered, furiously. "Good night!"

Her skirts swished as she went away from him. She gathered up Lucy and they started up the stairs together. Lucy was talking about the evening and how lovely Will's bride looked, and Katryn was paying no attention to her until Lucy suddenly said something that brought her up short. She turned on Lucy, incredulously.

"Lord Latimer told you about his children?" she repeated.

"Aye," said Lucy.

Katryn had seen that expression of misty tenderness on Lucy before. But always it had been Katryn who caused it. She felt a twinge of jealousy, tempered by dismay. Then Lord Latimer's conversation had run about the same with both of them. "When did he tell you that?" Katryn asked.

"When we danced," Lucy said.

Katryn looked at the girl's face. Then she dismissed her fears. Lord Latimer could not possibly be interested in Lucy! She yawned. Bed, even a pallet on the floor of the overcrowded room, would feel good. Lucy would hang up her dress, and attend to everything.

The little room was empty of all its occupants. "Unhook me, Lucy," she said.

The wedding ceremony early the next morning was as moving as always to Katryn. Through her head went visions of her saying those words to Lord Latimer, and at his side she cast glances at his face, which remained averted from hers. He is so restrained this morning, as though I were a child, she thought petulantly.

Will's bride looked radiant, her dark beauty against her white dress; against the profusion of white satin and lace, her hair flowed over her shoulders. The day was warm, and the sun brilliant. Not a cloud in the whole sky, everyone said. Not a single cloud! Katryn's eyes were bright; there was so much laughter on the way down to the church. "Weddings are such wonderful fun," she said, happily. Oh, this was different from Kendal. Every gay gown seemed to proclaim, Isn't life a heady drink!

Lord Latimer said, "Marriage is a solemn sacrament, though, my dear. I think its solemnity gets lost in weddings such as this."

"I think so too," Lucy said, and Katryn flashed her a stormy glance. What was she trying to do, sweeting my lord Latimer?

In the church, Katryn bent her head with all the rest while the priest prayed; certes if Lord Latimer looked at her, he would see how prayerful and sweetly composed was her face. I'll think on my mother, she vowed. I'll ask the Lord to bless this marriage, as she would have. "Bless Will and Bess," she murmured, over her clasped gloved hands. She wondered whether to add a prayer for herself, but decided the Lord might think her selfish, and she had better not ask for aught.

Then the organ pealed forth, and Will and Bess rose and so did all the guests. It was time to celebrate.

All day long the feasting and dancing and games went on. Music poured through the halls, through the gardens. There were entertainments, and morris dances, and matches and contests of skill. Everyone wagered on their outcome, and crowded about and drank more wines, and spirits. "It is almost like a huge county fair," Katryn exclaimed excitedly. She had never laughed so much. Almost convulsed by the fools, she sat on the ground and held her sides. "I'm truly weak," she cried. Even Lucy's eyes sparkled. "Oh," said Katryn, "think on the moneys this must ha' cost, too! How wonderful to ha' so much money!" Her eyes shone. To spend thousands of pounds on entertainment! "Even I won two gold pieces."

At supper she again ate ravenously and quickly, for she and Kate Willoughby and Anne were to help the bride get ready for bed.

Katryn was still bubbling from the events of the day. When the time came, she and Kate seized Bess's hands and ran, stumbling over their gowns. Pursued by a goodly number of young men, they fled the hall and raced up the wide stairway. Shouts from below and giggles from Bess and Kate rang in Katryn's ears. When they finally gained the sanctuary of Bess's big rooms, redecorated for the occasion, they leaned weakly against the door, helpless with laughter.

"I've never laughed so much," Katryn said. "Never!" So many men had paid attention to her. The whole long day swam before her eyes. She had danced innumerable times; she had even danced with Tom Seymour, whirling around in his arms. It was he who had lent her money to wager with, she had won, too!

"Put your money on the fellow in the red hose," he had said. During the match, she forgot herself and leaped to her feet and called out encouragement to the wrestler of her choice.

"Kill him!" shouted Katryn, shaking her fist.

Tom Seymour pulled her down beside him. "What if Lord Latimer should see you?"

"I had forgot," she blurted, looking about. But she didn't see him anywhere. She gave Tom Seymour a merry dimpled smile. "I truly didn't mean kill him."

He chuckled heartily. "I know that," he said, pulling at one of her curls which had come loose.

Then she forgot everything again in the excitement of the match. After it was over, she said ruefully, "How you laughed at me!"

Her words brought a big smile to his face. There is something odd betwixt us, she thought rapidly. Mayhap it's as he says; anyway, I can be myself with him; somehow he understands me. She shot a glance at him. "But you wouldn't ever breathe a word to anyone about Thomas Borough, would you?" she asked. "Especially to my lord Latimer?"

"No," he said shortly.

Was he angry, she wondered? Lord Latimer had come up then. How elegantly handsome he is, she thought. For the first time, truly, I am in love.

"The whole day was wonderful," she said now, turning to see Kate and Bess and Anne, and Jane Seymour, and some other girls Katryn didn't know. Bess's personal servants were in the room, too, two older women. While Katryn and Anne undressed her, they put away the bridal clothes, and readied and tidied the room. But when Kate drew the gown off Bess, she stumbled and almost fell. Katryn caught her and steered her to the bed. Over Bess's head her eyes met Kate's. Bess closed her eyes and leaned back.

Kate whispered, "She's had too much wine. Aye, as we all have," she added, rubbing her head. She lifted Bess's feet up onto the bed— it reached all the way to the ceiling and its curtains were gold damask, looped up and hanging down against the wall with a wealth of material—and started to take off her slippers and hose. Then Bess's eyes opened and she sat up, blinking at them. With horror Katryn saw huge tears pour down her face; her whole body shook, and she cried on, soundlessly, even while Kate went on efficiently undressing her. Bess stood up and slipped off her chemise. Katryn was a bit shocked, for Bess made no attempt to cover herself with the shawl at the bedside. She stood there stark naked and cried, then she flung herself face downward on the beautiful bed.

"I've seen her do this afore," Kate whispered. "She often cries when she's had too much wine."

"Marry!" whispered Katryn, wondering helplessly what they were going to do with her. Her women stood against the wall, wringing their hands. Katryn suddenly said, "Where's Anne?" She looked about the huge room; certes Anne had come in with them. Now she was nowhere to be seen.

"Never mind about Anne," Kate said. "Get some cool water."

"Fetch us cool water, and a cloth," Katryn repeated to the serving-women.

Kate said then, "And bring me a basin." She was leaning over Bess, shaking her. "Bess! Bess!" she said, commandingly. "You'll have to retch that up! Now sit up!" She dragged Bess over to the side of the bed. "You have a husband coming in here, immediate!"

Bess still cried, but she obeyed. She's done this afore Katryn thought, mayhap many times. The serving-women were about her now, and Katryn backed away so as not to stain her gown. Kate had backed away too, now. "She always cries and feels sorry for herself."

Katryn watched as Bess's women sponged off her face, and Bess rinsed out her mouth with water. Kate went over and got the perfume, which she sprinkled lavishly in every direction. Then she carried it to the bed and began to apply it to Bess and even the edge of the pillows. Bess lay on her stomach and sobbed.

"I love him so much," she cried. The rest of her words were lost.

Katryn's eyes grew horrified. She stared at the naked figure on the bed, the import of the words unmistakable. Katryn said incredulously, "She's been seduced!" In God's name, what kind of a woman had Will married? Katryn felt the sly eyes of all the women present upon her; she felt as naked as Bess, naked with the shame Bess had put upon her and Will—poor poor Will, coming as a young bridegroom to this woman! How the ladies would talk!

"And to think you bear our name and will be mistress of Kendal!" The words were wrung from her. Eyes wide, her hand pressed to her breast, she came closer to the figure on the bed; the women made way for her, silently withdrawing from her path. She said furiously, "Aye, listen! Listen well! All of you!"

A tense silence fell. Bess struggled to a sitting position. She looked like a sulky child, her lips curled, her face contorted with sudden hate.

"Mistress of Kendal!" she screamed. "And what is that? The same poor puling mess your brother will be after Tom Seymour!" She sat back on her bare haunches, her hair falling over her face, but not concealing the cunning gleam in her eyes. She started to laugh; abruptly she stopped and cowered back, looking vainly for protection which was not there, for Katryn was advancing on her, hands outstretched.

Fury had seized Katryn. The name echoed in her ears. This woman had lain in his arms and had his kisses. Katryn Parr seized Bess by the hair.

"Shut your wicked mouth!" Katryn cried. She yanked her head in jerks as she talked. "You miserable, whining, drunken whore! If you betray my name, I'll kill you! You try! You're never to go near him again! Never!" She still had Bess's hair in her hand. Although her whole body was shaking with anger, she knew if she struck Bess the marks would show, and Will would see them.

She released the tangled hair and she dropped her hand, letting it fall to her side. The room swam. I must escape this place, she thought. I must not be here when Will comes; I couldn't bear it.

Only when she was out in the hall did she realize Lucy was beside her. She stumbled along to her own room, with Lucy following, silent and horrified. The little room was empty. Katryn sat down on a narrow bed and put her head in her hands. What a dreadful scene! And on a wedding night! Her heart ached. Poor, poor Will! And this was the match her mother had labored so long to bring about. What bitter fruit it had borne, and she felt with certainty it would bear worse than this. She raised her head. Her eyes were dry. She said miserably, "I screamed like a fishwife. But what else could I ha' done?"

"My lady," Lucy said, taking her hand.

"Thou'rt a comfort to me, Lucy," Katryn whispered, holding her hand tight. "A true comfort."

"Oh, my lady," Lucy said, almost in a moan. "I shall not be this night. No indeed I shall not!"

Katryn frowned, puzzled. What could she mean? Poor Lucy, so inept with speech. "Lucy," she said kindly, "you are always a comfort, and there is naught you could do or say to undo your kindnesses."

"Aye, but there is," said Lucy, desperately. "For what I have to tell you will truly undo you, madam!" She went right on. "I have to tell you Anne has disappeared, run away with a man named Will Herbert!"

For a moment Katryn did not take in her words. Then she gasped. "Run away?" she whispered. Surely it were not possible! But Lucy was nodding her head.

"Oh, God," thought Katryn. It cannot be! Double disgrace falling thus upon me and our house! What had she done to deserve this? She almost staggered to her feet; she had to stop Anne, to find her, to find her quick before the world and her betrothed knew her for the light wench she had become. What they said of Nan Boleyn's court must be true, then; they were all wicked and drunken and unprincipled, and somehow they had caught Anne in their toils and taken her away from her loving sister. "Oh, God," she said, moving toward the door. "I'll have to find her, and you, Lord, will have to help me!"

Where would Anne have gone? As she started down the stairway, blasts of music and laughter poured upward, almost engulfing her, almost physically shaking her very bones. There they were, all those people laughing and making merry, while for her, her whole world had collapsed. She couldn't seek out Lord Latimer, for he must not know the events of this night—no, surely not, never. So, halfway down, she stood and looked carefully at those below her, her eyes searching frantically for the one man whose name came to mind—odious name, but the only one who could help. Faces and masses of color made a huge blot of the whole room. But right below her was a familiar face; he was turning away from her. Desperately she called, "Sir Edward!"

Ned Seymour turned. Down the steps toward him came Will Parr's sister. He stopped and bowed; he didn't know her name. Thus for the first time they met, and Katryn said, "Sir Edward, pray find your brother for me! And send him here to me!"

Ned Seymour raised one eyebrow in a manner similar to Tom's. "Certes. I shall tell him a lady in distress. But I do not know the lady's name."

"Lady Borough," Katryn whispered, her voice shaking. "Tell him I shall wait here!" He bowed. "Hurry," she commanded, and Ned Seymour obediently hastened his step.

Katryn saw him coming, making his way through the crowd, managing to look purposeful and unruffled at the same time. Some of his aplomb reached her; by the time he stood in front of her, she had walked a few feet toward him. She felt his hand under her arm, and all the words that Bess had said came flooding back. She felt herself tremble as she looked at him, and she thought passionately, Till he tells me what he knows about Anne and this Will Herbert, I must conceal from him everything I know about him and Bess!

"What's amiss?" he asked calmly.

"I—" she began, "I can't find Anne!"

"Ah," he said only. Then, "Come. Will Herbert is one of my finest friends."

"I might ha' guessed," she cried unsteadily. "But where? And Anne, she's gone! You must help me find her!" She had stopped and was facing him, but he shook his head at her warningly.

"We cannot talk here," he said, and steered her toward the nearest door to the gardens.

"But Anne—" she began. "And if he's your friend it's part your fault!"

"There is a long way to walk, Katryn," he said, "and people are looking. Smile. It will be quiet in the garden."

Katryn cried, "But she's but sixteen! And to run—"

"Smile!" said Tom Seymour. "And remember you were the same age when you became involved with Hugo. Here is the garden."

Katryn stepped down onto the path. What an unkind thing to say! she thought. Here she was, alone and unprotected in this vast world, and one would think he would be gentleman enough to be kind. Her toe caught in her gown, and she stumbled; she caught tight at his hand. If I've torn this gown I shall surely cry, for 'tis my only one. "My gown," she whispered, and held up the edge of it. It was torn, a bit.

His voice was sharp. "Are you worried more about this dress than Anne?" he asked. "Come along, we'll try the maze."

Katryn bit her lip. She trotted along at his side obediently, but her eyes, sharp as an eagle's during the daylight, failed her during the hours of darkness. "I'm as blind as a bat at night," she mumbled. He didn't answer. She trod carefully. She could see the outlines of the tall hedge about them. She blurted, "And last night I was so happy here!"

There was a moment's silence, then he said, "With that parfit gentil knight, the Lord Latimer?"

"Don't dare mock at him," she cried.

"I am not mocking at the Lord Latimer," he said. "He is a fine gentleman, much too old for you, my dear—much too old. Why do you always want what you shouldn't have, Katryn?" He looked down at her. Her mouth was open, her eyes bright even in the darkness. Tom Seymour grinned. "Are you stuttering with rage? May I ask why you didn't ask him for help tonight?"

"I wish I could have!" she cried. "Instead I had to turn to you! You—" She broke off. The despoiler of my brother's wife, she was about to hurl at him.

She had stopped in time. But she dropped his hand. I'd just as soon fall and break my leg, she thought fiercely, as hang onto the hands that have made love to Bess. "I had to ask you," she burst out, trying to keep her mind on what was happening to Anne. A hummock of ground almost tripped her; she felt his hand under her arm again. She stopped to face him. "Pray don't touch me," she said.

"We have gone far enough. You said you— Oh, tell me what you know about Anne afore I—" She flung out her hands.

Tom Seymour hesitated a moment, his eyes studying her in the darkness. Then he said curtly, "Anne is perfectly safe. True, she has run away, but by this time she is honorably wed. Will's father was born of a true love match." A kind of smile touched his face, and he added harshly, "Something you know nothing of. And if I were you, I should not fret over Anne. Anne may be the Countess of Pembroke; for her husband is the only male heir, whether or not his father was legitimate. Anne may outrank you shortly, and I warrant be much happier, rank or money or no. Anne is gold; you, my lady, are half dross." He took her by the elbows. "What did you mean, 'Pray do not touch me?' By God—" He broke off, anger roughening his voice.

"I meant exactly what I said!" she cried, her voice shaking. She was trying to take in all he had said: Anne was safe; her husband might inherit; this was better than she could ever have hoped for, and no disgrace would fall upon her, either. She was conscious of nothing but relief. "Thank God," she said devoutly, and clutched at her great ruby cross.

"Are you thanking God for yourself or for Anne?" he asked. "Or are you thanking all the stars that your name won't be tarnished in the light of Lord Latimer's noble ideals? Were you afraid you'd lose your chance with him? Was that it? I cannot believe you were worried so about your sister! You are far too selfish for that, Katryn, far too selfish and too wilful. You should be more careful, too, when you address your God, and make sure you know what you're thinking; for He does, and someday the thunder and lightning may strike!" In the darkness his eyes glittered, and she was afraid. Perhaps he was right! She put her hand to her bare throat.

The only excuse she could make to the Lord came to her lips. "But I love Lord Latimer," she said. She loved him and certes she was thankful about Anne! Anne had a good husband, and probably a wealthy one—she hadn't known about his being the only male heir. How lucky Anne was! Suddenly the disparity between her sister and herself filled her eyes with tears; her shoulders shook, the lump in her throat got huge, and she tried to swallow. I'm not going to let him see me cry, she thought stubbornly, but the events of the night were so heavy on her she didn't know how she could bear it. For another thought had just occurred to her, and with shattering suddenness she knew it was true. She might never live at Kendal again, not any more—surely not with Bess. In a short twenty-four hours she had lost what she had labored for during the past years. She might not be sure of loving any man, but she knew she loved Kendal. Now that Will was married, and going there in a short week, she would have to leave. All the woes of the evening piled high. "Oh," she said, but anger stiffened her voice and stopped her tears. "Oh, I wish to God I'd been born a man!" Her hands flung out in passionate longing for something she could never have.

He took the outstretched hands in his and said gently, "What an impassioned childish protest, sweetheart. You are so very young. And how your mind hops about, like a rabbit! A true female mind you have, Katryn, and it bewilders me entirely."

She shook her head to deny the words. But she said nothing, for suddenly the whole garden seemed to stand on end. I'm going to faint, she thought and grasped at his coat.

"The wine is catching you up," she heard him say, as if from afar. He was holding her now; she braced her knees against his legs, her eyes half closed; the darkness swam about.

"Open your eyes and fix them on me," he said.

She tried to obey. She tipped back her head, and looked up at him. This was better, with her eyes open; she smiled weakly. "I feel dizzy," she whispered.

"It'll pass," he said. "Breathe deep, and keep your eyes open." After a minute he asked, "Better?"

She nodded, and laid her head back against his arm. She blinked her eyes rapidly.

"Can you listen to me?" he asked. "You red-headed wench, Katryn, I love you."

He isn't serious, acourse, she thought, for he has that smile on his face which I never understand.

"And," he went on, "I covet that spirit of gallantry I perceive in you."

"Gallantry?" she asked, thinking that was an odd word to apply to a woman.

"You know so little of yourself you don't know what I mean," he said. "Did you work so hard this past year, and all for nothing?"

"Aye," she mumbled. I have nothing in the world but my manor of Tansfield. And I am even too weary, she thought, to tell him it is part his fault, too. "I am so weary."

"Good God!" Tom Seymour said. "I tell you I love you and you tell me you are tired. Listen, Katryn, I go away tomorrow, early. I have my own command. I have been given five smallish ships with which to sweep the narrow seas of pirates."

He was holding her close. The buckle of his belt pressed into her stomach, his legs were warm and strong against hers; her limbs seemed to feel heavy and weightless at the same time. It was very dark; the hot summer night folded her as tight as his arms. He began to kiss her.

What is happening to me? she thought. I can feel his kisses even in my stomach. I must be drunk, she thought dimly. She knew that her arms were around him and her palms pressing against the muscles of his back; she could feel them, heavy, powerful. His mouth was on hers again.

"I am going away tomorrow, Katryn," he whispered.

I am being seduced, she thought wildly. I am just like Bess—half drunk, I am—and he is kissing my breast right through my gown. Words she should say, and images of Bess in these same arms, rushed through her brain. "Oh!" she cried. She raised her hand and struck at the side of his face, pulling away from him with all her strength. "Oh, you false seducer," she sobbed. "To think that you would—and that I—" She felt him free her, and she stood by herself, her knees trembling. "You false seducer!"

"What a silly epithet, Katryn," he said, his voice cold. His face was unreadable in the darkness; she saw just the outline of it, unsmiling, the eyes studying her as they always did.

"I know about you and Bess," she gasped. "I know what you did to her so don't you ever touch me, or come near me again! And you needn't bother to deny it! I warrant you'd try, to act like a gentleman!"

"I ought to act just like a man," he said, "and lay you flat on the ground and undo your dress." His voice was a bit weary and a bit mocking, as though at himself.

"How can you?" she cried. "How dare you!"

"It's either that," he said, "or leave you to the mercy of your own vagaries during the time I'm away. However, my dear, I doubt that

Lord Latimer will marry you, and he is far too honorable to be seduced, as you put it."

"Don't you even dare mention Lord Latimer's name to me! You aren't fit to black his boots!" Suddenly she wanted to rail and scream and spit at him; she clenched her hands, and her face grew red. He stood in front of her, as big and hateful as ever.

"When I come back, wench," he was saying, in his slow voice, "I shall as soon cuckold Lord Latimer as any other man. I mean it. And don't count on your precious Latimer, for I think he's going to marry Lucy. He is quite right, too, for she would be perfect for him. You go to your manor in Tansfield, and wait for me."

"Never, never, never!" she cried. "And leave me! Leave me!"

"Turn right twice, Katryn," he said. "Good night." He gave her a little bow and turned his back.

He's gone, she thought dully. When she could see the outlines of his broad back and shoulders no longer, she sank down onto the grass, uncaring about her dress. She put her head in her hands, and tears squeezed out between her thick lashes. He had said Lord Latimer wanted to marry Lucy! What if it were true! He was so often right, damn his eyes. Wait for him, he had said. How dare he! Before he comes back I'll marry the King! I wish I could. I'd make him kneel to me. Her eyes snapped, and her brain whirled. I'd have him thrown into prison, I would! In the Tower!

She struggled to her feet. She wiped her eyes, and shook out her gown. Turn right twice, he had said. She started to walk purposefully down the grassy walk between the hedges, toward the sound of laughter and music and voices.

8

Katryn had never seen her manor at Tansfield; all she knew of it was its location, in Yorkshire, with the river Ure winding through its acres, near Jervaulx Abbey and Norton Conyers, only fifteen miles from Richmond. So she had sent Lucy and Wat and two kitchen servants ahead, and early on a warm August morning, with rain beating down, she made to leave Kendal once more. Will I ever return? she wondered. And yet I cannot stay longer, for Will and Bess are coming; I cannot bear to see Bess as mistress of Kendal.

Her eyes took in the small cavalcade of belongings which they would need to keep all their bodies and souls together. There were three fine looms, the best, and three carders. There were four sturdy carts filled with sheep; they baaed mournfully, and bits of grass still stuck in their mouths, as they peered down from the wooden carts. But that's the only way I know to prosper, she thought—wool. The carts went slowly past her. Household items came next: feather beds, and quilts and wools in boxes; silver plate, salts, and all manner of kitchen utensils—for suppose Tansfield didn't have enough? Where was money to buy? When the last cart finally rumbled past, she nodded her head with satisfaction. I have forgot naught, she thought; we can live. Even Mistress Nell and her daughter Goodie rode on the second cart. Mistress Nell was the Kendal midwife and Katryn's nurse. "I couldn't bear to be parted from you," Katryn had said.

"Nay, nor I you, my lady," Mistress Nell said. "And I'll bring Goodie." Goodie was thirteen, the child of Mistress Nell's middle age. "Ugly as a cock's wattles, she is," her mother said cheerfully. "Aye, whether she marries or not, at least she'll know what a wedding bed brings, won't you, Goodie?"

Katryn had difficulty keeping her face straight. She waved them on. I'm the rear guard of this army, she thought; but although she was outside the walls, still she didn't mount. She turned for a last long look at the castle that had bred her. But surely I can never forget, she thought. They shall not grow dim, either, my memories. In the gray sky the castle melted into the heavens itself, looking ghostly. She leaned down and picked up a tuft of thick grass; wet earth clung to it, and she crumpled it tight in her bare hand, feeling its texture, its warmth; the grass cut her palm and a bit of blood oozed out. She loked down at her hand, and opened her fingers and let the grass fall to the ground. Then she mounted and rode away from Kendal.

Tansfield seemed small to her. It was built in the old manner—almost a square—around a court. Its walls were weathered timber and old brick; ivy clung to its chimneys and the garden walls. As she stood in the garden, at the foot of the narrow outside stairway that led up to her room, some impulse seized her, and she leaned down and took up a handful of rich brown loam. It crumpled finely in her fingers, as good earth should. This now is mine, she thought.

Later, propped up in her own bed with the curtains already hung, her own table in view with its tiny mirror and her silver brushes and her silver candlesticks on the mantel and her pink satin quilt over her knees, she felt that she was home. She looked across at her bailiff, who sat, cap in hand, on the bench, looking extremely uncomfortable.

"The two fields that slope down to the river we shall enclose as quick as possible," she was saying. "For the sheep."

He twisted his cap. His lady went ahead so fast. He said, "They aren't about to like it, though; that's good farming land. And there's a wee forest with game in there."

"There are sheep now penned in the courtyard," Katryn said crisply. "And whether they like it or no, 'tis my land, Master John."

"'Tis good farm land, my lady, and they get part of the crops."

"They can help with the sheep and wool, and they will get paid, in money."

"Aye, my lady," he said, standing up. "I'll bid you good night, then."

"And tell all my tenants that I shall inspect tomorrow, and see that all is well kept and well mended and clean, including their children."

He was at the door. "Their childer?" he asked, amazed.

"Aye, their childer," said Katryn. "Good night."

Lucy closed the door after him. Meg was employed in making up her trundle bed in a corner of the room under the eaves.

Katryn waved her hand to include all her new possession. "I am going to buy more land. Someday you shall see my fences running for miles and miles!" Her voice stopped. She did not usually confide her plans; if she were going to do something, why bruit it about? The world would know soon enough. And she had other plans, which hadn't been confided. Certainly a woman would be a fool to tell anyone at all about the man she had set her heart on. Still, she thought, there's many a slip 'twixt the cup and the lip, specially when there's a man involved. If he didn't succumb to her, she would have Tansfield to fall back on.

"Did we pass the Lord Latimer's demesne on the way down the Swale Valley, Lucy?" she asked idly.

Lucy flushed slightly. "No, madam," she said. She threw Katryn a covert look; even weary as her mistress was, with her hair loose against the pillow and her huge eyes shadowed with fatigue, what man could resist her, Lucy thought fearfully. "Lord Latimer lives three miles down the river road, madam, in a manor he calls Snape Hall. I've not seen it, madam."

Katryn nodded. Then a thought occurred to her. "But you've seen him?" she asked, an edge in her voice.

"Aye, my lady," Lucy said low. "He called. And he brought his little boy. Oh, madam, you should see him! Fair as his father, and strong and sturdy, and with great gray eyes that laugh! He's such a beautiful lovely little boy! Six years old soon he'll be. There is a wee girl three, and I cannot wait to see her! I told my lord, pray bring her."

Katryn said sharply, "How clever of you, Lucy!" Lucy flushed deeply, and Katryn heaved a long sigh. "I meant only," she lied quickly, for Lucy must not think she was jealous—there must be no semblance of fighting over Lord Latimer—"that it was clever of you to be so friendly, for without near neighbor and kin, and with a household of women mostly, we may have to ask Lord Latimer for advice and aid in the manner of things we know naught of, like taxes, and such, and tenants' rights."

"Acourse, madam," Lucy mumbled. "I will get out my needlework. It's still packed away."

"There is much mending to be done, Lucy," Katryn said. "Then after that you can start to practice your needlework again."

"I just thought," Lucy blurted, "that if my lord calls tomorrow, 'twould be nicer for him to see me doing needlework than my mending."

"My lord is not extravagant, but sensible. He will think it good of thee to mend," Katryn said. "And think you he will come tomorrow?"

"Aye," said Lucy. "He promised us four pheasants, already trussed, madam, for your homecoming to Yorkshire."

Tomorrow would be a big day. She must look fresh. "If you'll bring me a cup of wine, I'll sleep, now." She was accustomed to a cup of wine before she went to sleep; it was a small luxury, and she enjoyed sipping the wine, leaning back against the pillows, thinking of the day and what it had brought, and thinking on the morrow and all that might happen. She took the silver cup; it had been her mother's. "Good night, Lucy," she said. "God bless thee, and sleep thou well."

The baaing of the penned sheep beneath her windows and the raucous crowing of the big rooster she had brought from Kendal wakened her early the next morning. For a second she savored the feel of the cool linen sheets and the softness of the feather bed in which her body was cradled. She rolled over and stretched; she sniffed the air and opened her eyes. Palest young sun gilded the tiny window, and she sat straight up in bed. "Oh, wonder of wonders," she cried. " 'Tis going to be a beautiful day!" She hopped out of bed and ran to the window.

Below her the sheep milled, some of the black-faced ones making a dot of color in their grayness. Over the ivy-laden walls morning mist lay gentle against the green meadows, and the silvery river wandered in the distance between its tree-lined banks. The rooster crowed, and from the small village a mile away there came an answer, sounding faint through the morning air. She pushed the window open wide, much to Meg's consternation.

"Oh, madam," she cried, "and you almost bare!"

Katryn paid no attention. Only three miles away the Lord Latimer would be awakening, too, to this fresh lovely August morning. She turned from the window. "I love August," she exclaimed. "And I think I'm going to love Yorkshire!" And if he were coming, there was much to do, for he should see how accomplished she was at housewifely endeavors, how pretty would be the dining hall when she finished with it this morning. "Meg," she said, her mind racing ahead, "go you right down and gather flowers, afore those damned sheep trample them all! For the Lord Latimer may dine with us, this eve!"

By three o'clock the outside of the manor had an entirely different look. The ivy had been cut back from the windows, and every one of them sparkled clean in the westering sun. The brick walks had been swept, and the big oaken door rubbed with wax. Within the house, Katryn surveyed the dining hall, and it was then that Lord Latimer rode up.

Katryn didn't hear him come. She saw him first as he entered the dining hall. Its windows stood open, and the air was fresh from the sweet herbs scattered among the pine branches in the empty fireplace. Its brick floors were scrubbed, the fireplace hood gleamed brassily. Katryn had found two big brass bowls; now they were full of flowers, their color gleaming bright against the polished oak of table and sideboard. The sun slanted into the windows, touching her hair; she turned to greet him, making him a little curtsy, then holding up her face for a kiss from a kinsman, as a lady should. He kissed the edge of her cheek, and held her hand.

"The whole house looks different," he said, "inside and out."

"Thank you, my lord," she said. "And you come bearing gifts! Are they not beautiful birds? And you must stay and share them with us."

Lucy had come into the room. He looked from one to the other. "I am glad you are here," he said, a warm smile on his face and in his gray eyes.

While the birds turned for an hour on the spit under Wat's carefull supervision, Lucy and Katryn and Lord Latimer sat in the garden and had a cup of cool ale. Mistress Nell gathered lettuce for a salad, and Goodie scrubbed the trenchers till they shone. Meg clucked and fussed till she found a cloth white enough.

At dinner Lord Latimer insisted Katryn take the big carved chair. He sat on a stool, with Lucy betwixt them. During the meal Katryn herself kept Lord Latimer's wineglass full, leaning toward him solicitously. After she had gone out into the front court and bid him good-by, she leaned against the door, feeling almost dizzy. He rode so well! Her eyes misted and grew tender. So much in love am I. So much in love!

The days passed, a month passed; he came almost every day. Once he gave a big dinner and invited all the gentry round, including some of Katryn's distant kin whom she'd never met. How kind they all were! Old Lord Darcy, seventy-eight if he was a day, and big bulky Rafe Bulmer, with his pretty gay wife who chattered incessantly of London and clothes. And Stephen Hamerton—he was distant kin, and knew Cat Strickland; one of his girls was already betrothed to Cat's son Walter.

Katryn learned the county families were as close here as they were in Westmorland. But she had so much to do there was not time for gay living. "Later, in the winter, I shall go about more," she told Lord Latimer. They were walking down by the fence to the river. "See how much has already been fenced," she said proudly.

He nodded, thoughtfully. "Sheep are increasingly profitable."

Lord Latimer had immense tracts of ground. Snape Hall was huge, bigger than Gainsborough, and it boasted not only what seemed to Katryn miles of farm lands but three wooded parks, and great spreading gardens. "Why don't you enclose some fields?" she asked.

"It would work too great a hardship on my tenants," he said. "After all, suppose everyone were like you and enclosed their lands for sheep? Where would our farm produce come from?"

She considered this. "Why, if more people enclosed, the ones who raised food could get higher prices. And anyway, my lord, everyone won't, for everyone's not like me."

He smiled. "That's very true."

The faintest frown crossed her brow. Did he think she was selfish to enclose her land? She shot him a glance from under her lashes. Here it had been a month, and although he came every day, they were almost never alone, what with Lucy always tagging along. Lord Latimer made no attempt to try to get rid of her. Quite the contrary, he was always saying, "Come, Lucy, walk with us; leave your needle." Or, "Let's ride over to Norton Conyers, I want to see the priest about a new baby; you come, too, Lucy." He is too kind to her, Katryn thought. I may be selfish, as that knave Tom Seymour says, but one can't go about never thinking of oneself! And here she had been seeing him every day, and she seemed no closer to the time when he'd propose marriage. She sighed deeply. If I fall, she thought, he'd have to hold me. She tried stumbling, and bumped against him. Correctly he took hold of her elbow, almost gingerly, she thought angrily. But she gave him a melting look.

"Thank you, my lord," she murmured. Didn't he even see the sun on her red-gold curls? Didn't he even know she was dying for love of him? They turned to start back. "Next week," he was saying, "is John's sixth birthday. I want to celebrate, and I would like you to come. And Lucy too, of course; I shall ask her myself, when we get back to the house. I didn't see her when I came. Where is she?"

"She is lying down," Katryn said. "A very slight indisposition."

"Oh, I regret to hear that," he said.

Why do you regret it so, she thought rebelliously. Why should you want Lucy when you can have me? Maybe he thinks he is too old, or too refined, like Tom Seymour says. But he's not! He's just the sort of man I want, a real gentleman and all that it implies.

They walked along in silence. When they reached the house, he said, "Please tell Lucy I send her my heartfelt regrets that she is unwell. I shall send her some fresh ale; that is good for humors. And tell her I shall be away for the next four days, and will be looking forward to seeing her and you on Saturday."

"I'll tell her," mumbled Katryn.

He mounted, and she gazed up at him longingly. He did everything as a gentleman should, even to riding and playing cards, and he ran his huge establishment like a true Englishman. He bowed from the saddle, like a prince. "Good-by, Katryn," he said, "and do not forget all my words to Lucy." He gave a wave of his hand.

Lucy! she thought. Damn Lucy! She went into the narrow hallway outside the dining hall. She could smell the apple jelly Wat was making in the kitchen; suddenly Tansfield seemed very small, tiny, compared to the huge gallery at Snape Hall, and the marble-fronted fireplace in the solar with the golden candlesticks on the mantel, and its Venetian glass. And in the midst of it he moved, truly like a prince.

She wouldn't see him for four days, then. He was going away, not saying where. That was like him, she thought. Just "I am going away," as though it were no one's business where he went or why he was going. She hadn't dared ask, either. He puts me off a bit, she thought. What will I do for four days? She could make a dress. Tomorrow, she thought, I'll ride to Richmond, and buy satin and lace; I'll tell them I'll pay next month. He always sees me in my plain day gowns; even if this is a child's birthday party, other people will be there, and I'll make a dress that will show him how fair I am. It may be my last chance this year, too. For she knew Lord Latimer had a seat in Parliament, and that he would go to London for the winter. London, she thought dreamily; I wonder if I'll ever live there. Then she pushed that thought aside. She must give Lucy Lord Latimer's message, for he would ask her later.

The color of her dress plagued her all night, so she hardly slept a wink. Should it be black? Like Nan Boleyn's? Black was so inviting. Suppose she were after Tom Seymour, what would she wear? If she chose black, she could just visualize the wicked twinkle in his eye. "Are ye trying to beguile me, wench?" he would ask. Black was too obvious; she would wait till she was safely wed to wear black, if she ever did get wed! She tossed in bed. What about white? She looked lovely in white, but her only other good dress was white, and Lord Latimer had seen her in it. Yellow was pretty and gay, but—and blue was not positive enough; it could look so washed out, those powdery blues. Then she said aloud, "By the mass, I have it!" She would pick green, a glittery, almost emerald green against her white skin and hair; and it was good luck, too, for was she not of Kendal bred? But this would not be cloth, but satin and lace, and she would cut it well away from her shoulders, but not too low in the breast—although to get him, she thought, I'd go naked, I would. But one had to remember that a man like him wouldn't like display. Anyway, she told herself, acourse I wouldn't go naked, for I'm a lady, too. What foolish thoughts I can have! I'll be proper covered up, but I shall show my shoulders and wear no jewels, no jewels at all.

On Saturday, a cool, sunny, late September day, she began her toilette early, washing and brushing her hair till it shone, fastening it high on her head. The green dress shimmered with lace and flounces; from the sea-green her white shoulders rose dazzlingly, as though she had stepped from the sea. Carefully she arranged herself on the clean blanket in the homemade litter alongside Lucy, and the jolting ride began.

Katryn hated litters, but there was no other way to go without spoiling her new dress. She sat uncomfortable and tense, her hips protesting every time the horse stepped forward. But when they began to pass through Lord Latimer's lands, she forgot her discomfort. It was all so well tended! The brush had been cleared away in the parklands, and little paths went cleanly across the forest floors beneath the sturdy high-rising oaks, which towered up into the sky like sentinels of strength. There was something quite thrilling about them, and she was tempted to stop the litter and walk for a few minutes under their great spreading cover, as though, if she did, she could encompass some of their so obvious validity. The litter dragged itself onward, and when it turned into the tree-lined drive up toward the first of the enclosed gardens, her heart began to beat fast with anticipation. It was then she noticed the bundle on Lucy's lap.

"What have you there?" she asked, somehow knowing the answer would undo her.

"A present for John," Lucy said.

"By God's most precious soul," she cried, "I forgot!"

Complete despair engulfed her. What would Lord Latimer think? "Oh, by the mass," she muttered, "however could I ha' been so dumb and blind and thoughtless? To forget a little boy," she added quickly. To think she had gone to all the trouble to go into debt for a dress, and Lucy had outdone her with a simple present. I could cry. They were passing the low hedge surrounding the rose garden and now Snape Hall itself glowered down on them, its battlements rising high as its oak forests; its new wing, faced with brick, jutting forward to greet them; its great door ajar, and my Lord Latimer himself standing on the steps, smiling.

147

He aided them from the litter. He noted Katryn's white face, and for a moment ignored Lucy. "Is aught amiss?" he asked.

"Aye," she blurted truthfully. "I will tell you, later," she added, managing a wan smile. Then her quick brain came to the rescue. "Mayhap after the refreshments I could see thee."

He nodded, a bit worried. But he saw she had brightened, and he turned from her to greet Lucy. He led them into Snape Hall and out once more into the new contrived garden, with its carefully cut yew and box, all in the shapes of various figures. He seated Katryn on a white marble bench, under the shadow of Aphrodite, and he said, "I sit you near your namesake, Katryn." His eyes rested on her brightly for a moment; it was a look she had seen many times, and it heartened her. He must love me, she thought; I'm sure he does! I can always tell!

Lord Latimer said, "She rose from the sea, the goddess."

Katryn smiled. "Thank you, my lord," she said primly. Inwardly she sighed with relief. He liked her dress, and mayhap later she would see him alone.

But during the giving of gifts, she was quiet, not wanting to call attention to herself and the fact she had no present. The children played games and bounced balls, and there was much shouting and laughter, and quarrels. Katryn tried to laugh with the others at the children. Lucy's interest amazed her. Mayhap when I have children of my own, she thought, I'll be more excited about them. Now she only wished they would end their games and go into the house for their dinner. At that moment there was a shout from one of the children, whose ball had rolled into the large silvery pond. One of the servants waded in and retrieved it from among the lily pads, but this impelled Lord Latimer to announce it was time for the various nurses and servants to take the children into the house. Katryn heaved a sigh of relief. The ladies had all drawn into small groups, and the men were gathered about a trestle table that had been set up in the garden, on which were various liquors and wines. Katryn rose, shaking out her skirts. Will he see me alone now, she wondered?

But he did not. He tended to his guests, moving among them, chatting with each one, remembering what each had brought John. She thought dully, I should not have expected he would remember, in the confusion. His manners are perfect; his mind is amazing; how can he remember? There were so many people; there must be fifty. She found herself answering questions from the other ladies about Tansfield, about her new dress and where she had bought the material. The ladies cast sly looks at her. They know I'm after my lord, the hags. There were some widows among them, much older than she but probably, from what they said, friends of Lord Latimer of long standing.

"You see Lord Latimer quite oft?" one lady inquired silkily.

"He has been most kind," Katryn said, not wanting to boast he came every day until she had a ring on her finger. "Excuse me, please," she said. She had to get away. She went into the house, and a woman servant guided her into the rooms set apart for the visiting ladies. She washed her hands, and brushed out a few curls and replaced them again. He did not come.

She thought the long dinner would never end. She ate almost nothing, and was careful to drink sparingly. John's grandmother was seated at Lord Latimer's right, and Katryn was a bit down the table. Occasionally he would glance over at her, as if wondering what made her so white and frozen. I can't help it, she thought, I feel dreadful; I am sure he loves me, but for some reason he doesn't want me to wife. Even if she did see him alone, probably naught would come of it. The cost of the dress weighed on her too. How foolish she had been!

She rose from dinner. The guests sought out the garden again; Katryn hung back a little, but she could find Lord Latimer nowhere. The ladies streamed past her, their gowns brushing at hers. Still she hung back, hopefully; then she felt his hand on her elbow. His voice said, "Come with me, Katryn."

Her heart jumped. She walked along with him silently, for she didn't know what to say. She kept her eyes straight ahead, not caring where he was taking her, while he kept glancing at her face with concern. He closed a door and they were alone.

Katryn tried to recover her voice. "What a beautiful room!" she exclaimed, for it was. A great window stretched upward to the very beamed ceiling. It must have a thousand tiny panes of glass, she thought, for the sun caught at each one of them like a jewel. Beneath the low window was a velvet padded seat, and cushions.

149

"How wonderful to be able to curl up there, and—" She turned to face him.

"And read?" he asked, coming closer to her, for she had walked across the carpeted floor to the window.

"Read?" she asked vaguely. Behind her the sun streamed in the window, lighting her hair. Her white shoulders rose from the icy-green gown. The faintest smile had touched his eyes when she had half-answered his question, but it was replaced by a sudden longing look which she caught plain. Then he looked away from her.

"Why did you wish to see me, Katryn?" he asked. "What is the matter?"

She put her hand to her breast. "The matter?" She moistened her lips. How to begin? "I had no gift for John!" She gazed at him appealingly, trying to read his expression, but his face gave her no clue.

He said only, "That should not have troubled you, my dear. It troubled me none. Why should you be so concerned over John?"

He means he knows I'm not mad over children, like Lucy, she thought, and I'll not trouble to deny it, although perhaps I should. She said, "I had a gift, my lord, and it does trouble me to have you think I do not care over him! I had a gift, and in the unsettling press of departure, I forgot it! It lies at Tansfield!" She almost believed it, and she looked stricken.

"Forgive me, Katryn," he said quickly. "I didn't mean to imply you were not thoughtful!"

"You did so imply," she said, low. "But no matter, my lord. 'Twas the matter of Lucy." She cast her eyes down, thinking rapidly. "I was undone when we left Tansfield, as I told you!"

He took a step forward. "What about Lucy?" he said. "Tell me, Katryn. Don't just stand there. Tell me!"

She said, her mind racing, "Lucy is my ward, my lord; my step-daughter by my former husband. I have her care." She stopped, biting her lip.

"I know that, Katryn," he said impatiently. "Now go on."

"Well, you do not know all about her, my lord. She is difficult and shy, and nervous oftimes, but she is much better than she used to be!"

Frowning, he looked closely at her. "She is well recovered from her former troubles. She has spoken of them."

Katryn said quickly, "Oh, aye, I know she is! But she is still my ward, and today, my lord, this morn as we were leaving, she told me she expects you to wed with her! And I thought, seeing Lucy is still very childlike, 'twas my duty to speak with you, for I do not want you to disappoint her, nay, nor break her heart. And I thought you should know, my lord." Her voice trailed off, for he was looking at her with an almost sad expression.

She listened for his reply. She had indeed done Lucy a bad turn. Did he know it? She waited, and the Lord Latimer said gently, "But I do intend to marry Lucy, Katryn, even though I've not spoke to her of it yet."

Katryn swayed. Her great eyes grew bright and gold. "Marry her?" she exclaimed incredulously. "You cannot!"

"Why not?" he asked reasonably.

"Because you cannot! Because"—she looked straight at him, and blurted the words—"I love you, my lord! *I* love you!"

"Katryn, Katryn," he said low. "Please, do not say thus!"

Her eyes blazed. She took a step toward him. "I must," she cried. "I love you! I'll die without you! And you love me! I've seen you look at me—you know you have!"

"I tried not to," he said. "Believe me, Katryn! 'Tis true I—I— How shall I put it? I don't know how to say it. But I know this. Even if I did want you, I should not marry you. You are too young."

She said incredulously, "You want me and you won't have me?" Her bright eyes grew narrow and unbelieving. "What kind of talk is that? If I were a man, and I wanted a woman—" She broke off, staring at his face.

"Exactly," he said. "So you see I am not the man for you, Katryn."

"You want me in your arms, and you won't take me?" she asked again. "When I love you so, and—" Defeat stared at her. "You love me, and you say I'm not for you?" Her eyes filled with tears. She gasped, with the sudden onrush of pure grief. "My heart is breaking."

"Don't cry, Katryn."

"I'm going to faint," she whispered. "I laced too tight, for thee!"

She gasped out the words, and he reached for her and took her in his arms. With a little sob, she put her arms around him, her head went back against his shoulder. Lord Latimer bent and kissed her. He kissed her cheek, and then her mouth. His kisses were short and almost fierce. She could feel his body tremble as he held her tight, almost like a vise. Her brain reeled. She tried to answer the kisses, but her body felt like ice. I *am* going to faint, she thought. She tried to breathe. Gradually she became aware of the passion she had roused. I did break down the reserve, but it is different than I thought. I don't feel the same as I did when Tom Seymour kissed me. But that didn't matter. He would marry her now, he would marry her! A long sigh rent her body. She leaned back in his arms, looking at him through her thick lashes. His face was set, and his eyes were closed. Slowly he opened them. The deep gray eyes looked into hers.

"I adore you, Katryn," he murmured.

"I love you, my lord," she whispered happily. Her whole body felt light and excited. Blood rushed through her veins. This man was hers, all his possessions, all his wit and grace and brilliance. And Snape Hall, and a house in London! "I am so happy," she breathed. "I am so happy I could die of joy!" She had done it! Out of defeat she had pulled victory, dragged it out. Her eyes shone; she couldn't encompass it! He was folding her close again. Obediently she raised her lips for his kiss.

Being in love is wonderful, Katryn thought. Love spilled out of her in all directions. It was showered on the inhabitants of Tansfield. It was showered on Lord Latimer's children in the form of kisses and hugs, and little presents for John, and new dresses for Margaret made from the odds and ends of the great bolts of cloth Lord Latimer sent from Richmond for his bride.

Katryn couldn't rise early enough these golden clear October days. Each morn her eyes opened onto a happy world; as if the days were russet apples in a polished bowl she couldn't wait to get her teeth into them. Ordinarily very active, she now seemed capable of enormous long hours of work. Her energies redoubled, and while her fingers sewed on her dresses and new lacy chemises and bright embroidery for her aprons, her mind flew along just as fast.

She must make amends to Lucy. It took her only a brief hour to arrive at a solution for poor Lucy, who had lost Lord Latimer. Within a day after her own betrothal, she had writ to Sir Robert Trywhit and demanded Anne's two hundred pounds back, promising him a new bride, one with a big dowry—one thousand pounds. Then she wrote to Henry Borough and told him about her plans for Lucy, and Henry wrote back quickly, pleased. He would get Lucy's dowry from Thomas. "Thomas is recovered," he wrote, "I tell you this thankfully, and I will be equally thankful that you should get Lucy a good husband, which I know Sir Robert must be if you considered him for Anne."

The matter was arranged quickly, and only Lucy cried. Katryn kissed her, and told her not to be a silly goose.

"But I never want to leave you," Lucy sobbed.

"Truly," said Katryn, looking at her, "you must eat, for thou'rt a veritable reed! And you shan't have to leave me. Sir Robert is, I'm told, an adherent of Sir Edward Seymour and is always at court, and you can live with me in London, should you choose. Anyway, Snape Hall will be your home, Lucy, I swear it! On my honor."

Lord Latimer felt guilty about Lucy too; every length of cloth he sent Katryn contained enough material for a dress for Lucy. Katryn privately thought him too generous and vastly impractical. "We can't go about wearing the same clothes, like orphans or twins," she said to Lucy. "And the colors which suit you don't suit me. You take all this yellow, for instance, and I'll take all the green." She outfitted Mistress Nell, too, and Goodie, although as Mistress Nell said, "You'll have to cover the child's face to make her look good."

"Nonsense, Mistress Nell," Katryn said crisply. "You're too hard on the child. Goodie, you be clean and neat and pleasant, and you'll have all the friends in the world."

"That's what I tell her," said Mistress Nell.

Katryn laughed, a bubbling laugh. She was dressing hastily, for she had an appointment with an agent from Richmond. With part of her returned two hundred pounds, she was buying the land adjoining Tansfield, which had previously been a nunnery. Its charter had been revoked, for the sisterhood had shrunk to six nuns and the buildings were in a bad state of disrepair. The papers were to be signed today; it was fine pasture land, and Katryn knew she had got a bargain. After she had signed the papers, she rode over to the crumbling convent with Lord Latimer, who had been present during the transaction. They walked hand in hand through the small deserted cloisters. The fall leaves rustling underfoot and the old apple trees made Katryn think of Kendal.

They sat down for a moment on the stone bench, near the chapel. "It makes me a little sad," he said, "to destroy it."

Katryn looked surprised. "Why, it's falling down."

"Aye," he said, "but think how happy must have been these walls once—what different people have stayed here, and walked these gardens, and knelt in the chapel. And now they are all gone."

"We are here," Katryn said. "And soon there will be sheep, nibbling the grass beneath these old arches, and bearing fine wool on their backs." She smiled, and drew a long contented breath.

He smiled back at her tenderly. "Let us drink to the present, for there is no past—that is your philosophy."

She frowned, digesting his words. "But I think on the future too," she said solemnly, "and how wonderful it will be!"

"I wish I were as sure as thee, my love."

"Oh, I am very, very sure," she said earnestly.

Whereupon he smiled and said, "Shall I depend on that?" He rose then, and went over and pulled the bell rope. The old bell threw out a peal of sound, echoing over the hills and the old stone building and its unused gardens. The sound died away. "The bell no longer calls the habited nuns to chapel. It makes me realize," he said, "that things endure and people do not."

Katryn waved her hand. "How silly! And you about to be wed!" she said. "It should make you think of wedding bells!"

Katryn and John Neville, Lord Latimer, were wed on the first day of November; the year was 1532. It was a small wedding, for Lord Latimer wished it intimate, with none but the very immediate families present. Will and Bess were still at Kendal, and Anne wrote a long letter saying how happy she was for Katryn, but that she was with child, and her husband feared for the long trip for her. She would see Katryn in London, later in the month. So the three maiden aunts resident at Snape Hall, and Lucy, and a few personal and favorite servants were the only witnesses in the lovely thirteenth-century chapel at Snape Hall.

But if Lord Latimer had chosen the manner of the wedding, Katryn had chosen the time. Superstitious, she thought November a fine month for weddings, and remembering her lucky color, she chose palest green velvet for her gown. The night before her wedding, on All Hallows' Eve, she came to Snape Hall with Meg and Lucy, and Wat, with Mistress Nell and Goodie in her new dress, and three of the servingmen who had come with her from Kendal a few short months before.

It was a wild night. Rain beat at the windows, and witches surely rode the scudding clouds. Even Lord Latimer agreed it was a fine night for witches. At nine he bid Katryn good night and took his leave, his kiss pressed to her forehead, his bow as correct as always. His restraint made her smile a bit, and the smile hovered on her face after he had closed the door. She looked about the lovely room.

"Much as I love and respect my lord," she said to Meg, "there is an air of dreaming about all this, as though it had happed to me afore." She frowned. This bedroom was larger than the one she had been so proud of at Gainsborough. The bed hangings were heavy damask, and they were looped back with golden ropes. A fire burned in the marble fireplace, and many candles winked on the surfaces of polished tables and gilded chairs. She laid a white hand on the arm of the one by the fire. "This must ha' come from France," she said thoughtfully. She eschewed the chair, and sat on a brocaded stool with silk tassels and watched the flames. Today Lord Latimer, with the aid of his solicitors, had settled upon her the manors of Nunmonkton and Wadsworth; she had thought at the time, with excitement, These spreading acres are mine, by deed of law. When he showed her the manors, she had been about to say she would start to enclose them. Then she stopped. Mayhap he wouldn't approve; in that case she would accomplish it before he realized it. Life is uncertain, she thought, but land is not. Kendal was lost, but someday, she vowed silently, I shall have even more land than that. All the moneys from these manors shall go into land and more land. When she raised her eyes to thank him, they shone. He looked puzzled.

"I didn't think I'd please thee so," he said. "I thought diamonds—"

"I'd rather have land, my lord," she said, with such complete straightforwardness that again he was surprised.

"Thou'rt an enigma to me, ofttimes, Katryn," he said, shaking his head. "But I do have jewels for thee."

Now, alone, she opened her jewel box and laid within it the diamond pendant he had given her. Within also was the great pearl chain and ruby cross, her two gold chains, and the old pearl cross her mother had given her. She had promised Lucy she would wear her ruby cross tomorrow; she had explained to Lord Latimer the reason why.

So the cross glittered brilliant against the green of her velvet as she knelt by Lord Latimer's side the next morning. Afterwards, coming out of the chapel into a cold November day of sun and blue skies swept clean by last night's brooming wind, she clung to her husband's arm and looked at him with pride and love. As they entered the big hall, all the inhabitants were drawn up to greet them —lines of curtsying maids and bowing servants, housekeepers, head grooms, cooks, and gardeners.

It took two hours for her to inspect Snape Hall. Rooms and gallery, floor after floor, kitchen, buttery, pantry, breweries, stables. Finally, atop the old battlements, where one could look one way across spreading parklands, another way across carefully laid out formal gardens, and yet another way into the great rectangle that housed all the shops and stores of the huge house, she and Lord Latimer were alone.

"I want you to love this as much as I do," he said.

"As much as I loved Kendal," she amended. "I shall, my lord."

"I come up here, every morn," he said, "no matter the weather. I remind myself of my heritage, and what I owe it."

She squeezed his hand. Sometimes he was so very sober. "Smile," she said gaily.

They had supper by themselves. At eight, Lord Latimer excused himself, and went to his own closet. By the time he returned, in his dressing gown, Katryn had said good night to Meg and Lucy and was in bed.

In the darkness, Lord Latimer's possession of his wife was quick and passionate, and when he slept at her side, she wondered briefly on the difference between the desires and pleasures of men and those of women. But I love him very much, she thought, and I am sure he loves me. Soon she slept too.

9

Katryn hardly had time to learn to find her way about Snape Hall before it was time to prepare to start for London. Lord Latimer was important in his native Yorkshire; he had a seat in Parliament, and he took his duties very seriously.

"I hate to leave, too," he said, "but I should be in my seat when Parliament is prorogued. For there is much that is of utmost importance to the realm."

They set forth one cold day in late November with a train of fifty. How different was it the last time I traveled down this great north road, she thought. Now bundled in furs, with gloves of Spanish leather, she had an attentive husband at her side, to say naught of all these serving people. Her eyes glittered gold, and her face was rosy with the cold. Only Lucy drooped; going forward to marriage she was full of misgivings, and Katryn had her hands full with her.

London was the third love of Katryn's life. She loved it fiercely, with partisanship, with patriotism, for certainly no city in the world could match it. She loved it with pride, because she was English, because she was young, because its streets and its populace were full proof of the excitement of living.

She loved the river, with the tall masts of its ships rising like a stripped forest; the river, with its boatmen fierce and bristling with beards, and their straight eyes as they made exorbitant charges. The day she first had courage enough to bargain and shout back, she was flushed and trembling with triumph when she stepped from the boat. She loved the fine bridge, bulging with fat stone houses and shops; and at night, the river gleamed like a moonlit pathway, flowing silently through the sleeping heart of England on its way to the sea.

Katryn loved the narrow streets, and the cries of the hawkers, and the merchants. Nowhere on those streets was drama lacking, from the sudden entrance of royalty itself to the equally sudden and ter-rifying shout of *"Clubs!"* which meant a street fight was in bloody progress.

She loved the shops. All the wonderful things that money could buy was spread before one's eyes. Greedily she eyed them, wanting all, exclaiming much; eyes shining, she surveyed the wonderful wares of London.

One could go to parties every night. One could lose thousands at the throw of a die. One could see the wonders of the world—there were real, live naked Indians on Fleet Street, and strange fish, silver in color, and monsters. Were they man-made? Tom Seymour grinned, and said he believed they were. For it had so chanced that he had taken her there, the only time she had ever been on Fleet Street.

London had coronations; she saw Nan Boleyn's. London had in-numerable processions, from wakes to weddings. London had seven prisons, and one became accustomed to the wailings from within. London had endless taverns and cookshops, bear gardens, puppet shows, all manner of entertainments, even plays; and if you went to St. Paul's to say a prayer, in the middle aisle you could buy the latest book or even meet your lover on the sly behind one of the arches.

But much of this she came to know later; the progress of Katryn's love affair with her city was slow. First she came to know her own house on the Charterhouse, with its walled gardens. The first few months of her stay in London, she was somewhat confined, for Christmas and New Year's meant staying close to home, and the weather that winter was bitter—one could actually walk across the Thames. Lucy was wed in February, the ninth of the month, the very same day that Nan Boleyn electrified a filled gallery at Whitehall by a little speech to one of her friends. Nan had come bursting out of her chamber, which opened off the long gallery, and catching sight of Wyatt as he stood talking to Ned Seymour, she had called out, "Oh, Master Wyatt, do you know that for the past three days I have had a mad desire for an apple? And do you know his Grace thinks I am with child? But I am not! I am not!"

This speech of Nan's flew about the town. At Lucy's wedding two hours later, that was all that people could discuss. "Damn Nan

Boleyn!" Katryn said fretfully, for instead of squiring the ladies and acting like gentlemen at a wedding, the men were all gathered in knots and bunches talking of what it meant to the realm. For if Nan were pregnant, then Henry might marry her—indeed he may already have married her—and to good Catholics it meant that the break with Rome was indeed fact, and to politicians it meant they would have to get along with Nan, or heads might fall.

"Vindictive little whore," one man said as Katryn passed close.

I don't care what she is, she's spoiling my wedding party for Lucy, Katryn thought, looking about her lovely gallery with dismay. At this moment, as she looked about for her husband, her eyes met those of Tom Seymour's; there was a twinkle in them, and he asked, "What do you think about it, my lady?"

"I think she worked a long time to get her man," Katryn said. "So maybe she deserves him!"

He smiled, and she did too. It was the first time she had smiled at him today. His presence had been completely unexpected; when he had first entered she had been most surprised and had shown it. No matter how hard she tried to recall his face, it was never like seeing him close. He was very tanned; she knew he had been to sea. It made his face darker than ever, and the eyes more brilliant and compelling; as they fell on her face, she got her old sense of transparency, as though he could see right through her. Could it have been seven months since they had last met? Impossible. He leaned close and kissed her, a brief little kiss on the lips, and when she raised her eyes to the dark face so near hers, she had the oddest sense that there was no one about but the two of them.

"You are surprised to see me?" he asked.

Katryn wet her lips. "Aye."

"You didn't wait, did you?" he asked, surveying her.

She couldn't think of anything to say. He didn't seem to expect her to. He just nodded, and continued. "I came because Sir Robert expects me to come. He is a close friend of Ned's, and therefore I owe him this courtesy."

"I see," she mumbled inadequately. Why am I so tongue-tied? she wondered wildly. I don't like him, I can't endure him. A brief memory of the night he had made love to her flooded her mind, and she blushed. His blue eyes were still on her, noting the blush. He bowed then and moved away to seek out Sir Robert to congratulate him.

But now, talking to him in the window embrasure, the first unsettling encounter behind her, she found she could talk more naturally. "I don't think she's a whore," she said, thinking of the six years Nan Boleyn had kept Henry at bay—for with a man like Henry, that was certainly an accomplishment.

"I don't think she is either," Tom Seymour said. "They call her that because they mislike her so intensely, and feel she has taken his Grace away from his true wife."

"Who still lives," Katryn said. "How can he wed wi' Nan?"

Tom Seymour said, "Old Warham, the Archbishop, is dead, and his Grace has appointed Cranmer to the archbishopric. As soon as Cranmer's appointment has been blessed by Rome, which will be any day now, Cranmer will be duly consecrated in the eyes of all. Then, Katryn, he can declare Henry's former marriage invalid, and his Grace will be free to wed where he pleases, still under the legal guise of a sanction from Rome."

Katryn puzzled over the words. "And is that all that will happen, then?"

"Except that Cranmer is married. From now on he'll have to carry his wife about in a box to keep her hidden." He smiled and took her hand. "Never discuss politics except with me, wench. And I mean it. There is trouble brewing. You match my example: you see I discuss this with no one, except lightly."

She said, "Are you afraid to agree? Which side are you on?" She knew Lord Latimer was set against the black-eyed Nan.

"I take no sides, because I find myself thinking differently from any of them here." He set his wine cup down, and rested his hand on the hilt of his jeweled dagger. "I must say good-by. Perhaps we shall meet again, one day."

The words jolted her. She wanted to say, "Oh, but please come again," but she couldn't, for he would misconstrue the invitation. It's only that I can truly talk with him, she thought, and— She drew a deep breath. "Good-by," she said, almost childishly, and she watched him walk away.

What Tom Seymour told her would happen, did happen. Old Archbishop Warham, eighty if he was a day, had gone from the London scene with his straight figure and thick white hair and pink face. Gone too was his opposition to Henry's new way of doing; for old Warham was a stiff Englishman who bowed his spirit to no one but God. And Henry, to do him credit, had respected him; he had waited patiently for God himself to intervene and place the Archbishop in heaven, where he surely belonged. But now in his place was a scholar, a thinking man, who had once said, "If his Grace has doubts and troubles about churchly things, let him take his case to the universities, and let thinking men bring their minds to bear on the problem."

Henry's ears had pricked up. "By the mass," he had said, "this man has the sow by the ear!" He called Bishop Cranmer to the palace and talked with him, finding his mind fluid, finding him the type of soulless intellectual who could doubt everything. To most men, black is black and white is white. To Cranmer all was gray, because he perceived too much. He was the man Henry needed, and if someday in the future Cranmer was to discover that there was something white after all, and something to die for, he learned it handsomely and paid the highest price. Like Paul, he redeemed himself; like the best hairsplitting lawyer, he married Henry and Nan Boleyn and declared Henry's former marriage illegal.

Katryn was having her portrait painted by Holbein, who was at the time residing in Chelsea at the home of Sir Thomas More. Sitting for the great artist, with his gusty humor, she would each day greet Sir Thomas, who was so kind and gentle and good. Also he was the Lord Chancellor of the realm, and Katryn felt very proud when she entered his house and spoke with him. How exciting it was to have one's picture painted, in the very house of the Lord Chancellor! Only London could offer such a happenstance, for only England could produce a lord chancellor who so loved the arts! On a spring day she had met Sir Thomas walking to and fro in his garden, and was amazed to see he wore his priest's robes.

"Why, thou'rt not wearing thy robes of office," she exclaimed.

Sir Thomas smiled. "I shall always remember thee in thy green dress," he said. "And as for my dress, what is higher office, my dear, than these robes of my priesthood? I have just come from chapel, and I cannot get the sweet songs out of my mind. So shall the angels sing, I hope, as I leave this world."

Katryn bit her lip. He meant more than he had said. "Trouble, bad trouble is brewing," Tom Seymour had told her. A shaft of fear shot through her. Had Sir Thomas resigned the lord-chancellorship because he could not sanction the King as head of the new English church? That was what Henry was founding: a new church of England. And Henry would not let Sir Thomas stand in his way.

"Sir Thomas," she whispered. "Hast thou resigned?"

"Aye, my dear," he said.

She knew he was going to bless her. She knelt, there in the garden. The crocuses were about her feet, the sunlight lay shining about Sir Thomas' head. Katryn kissed his hand. Would the King let him step out of political life, when it was a rebuff to Henry himself? The King had walked in this garden, his arm about Sir Thomas' shoulders, but everyone knew Henry could not endure a rebuff. Katryn got to her feet. Would she ever see Sir Thomas again? She went home to tell Lord Latimer what she had learned that day.

"It is time to leave the city," Lord Latimer said. He was deeply disturbed by her news, for its implications were more plain to him. But Katryn didn't want to leave London now, in the spring, with the trees budding and green peeping over garden walls, and the softness of the night air. Besides that, Anne was staying with her, and her baby was due any day. Anne was so happy. She was in attendance to Nan Boleyn and Will was a gentleman of the bedchamber, but they had small quarters and no proper house in London. So Katryn fixed up a big bedroom for her sister. Lucy was back with them, too, for her husband had gone to France on a mission with Sir Edward Seymour. And Kate Willoughby, who had wed with her duke, Suffolk, came every day to see Anne, and not only did Katryn like her much, but she felt it was certainly thrilling to have a duchess for a regular caller.

All that meant nothing to Lord Latimer, but he did agree to stay in London until Anne's baby was born. "Also, mayhap 'twould be best for me to stay a bit to see which way this wind is blowing," Lord Latimer said.

Katryn said, "If you would only push yourself forward, my lord, you could be a duke too!" He smiled. "You could!" she said. "If you would not set yourself against the new church! Why, there are lots of dukes in your family!"

"Katryn," he said coldly, "I have no intention of condoning what I feel wrong!"

For the first time dismay shook her, and some fear. "But you would not—?"

"Set myself openly against it?" he asked. "I shall act, Katryn, according to my own lights, and my own conscience."

This speech fed her fears. He was so slender, so refined; how could he battle Henry? "But you—you are not the type! You should be at court, my lord, with all your graces! You should be an ambassador, and make speeches, and be a member of the council. You have much wisdom. Think what it would be like to have men listening to what you have to say!"

"Men do listen, Katryn," he said.

"The wrong ones," she said, suddenly. "Aye, the ones who come here are the wrong ones! I've been here six months, and I know. They're the ones Henry is just tolerating. Why don't you help him found the Church of England?"

"Because I don't believe in divorcement from Rome."

"Why not?" she said angrily. "Why should we bow to the Pope? He does only what the King of Spain tells him to!"

"I've heard that argument many times," he said wearily.

"And what's wrong with it?" she asked. "It's true! Why should the King of Spain be permitted to say whether or not the King of England may have his marriage annulled? We need an heir to the throne!"

"We have an heir—the little Princess Mary, who now, God forgive her father, has been declared illegitimate."

"If the Pope had granted a divorce, she wouldn't have had to be illegitimate," Katryn cried. "Why can't you be practical?"

"I find it difficult to be practical, as you put it, in matters spiritual. Also you are shortsighted. The King of Spain will not always hold the Pope in bondage. This is not a matter of this moment, but of all time."

"You don't understand," she said.

"I do understand, perfectly," he said. "Only I cannot be expedient in matters of religion."

"Expedient or not," she cried, "you are too weak to fight the King of England! You are not able; you are not equipped."

His face was somber and his gray eyes darkened. "Ah, Katryn you have struck deeper than you know." He looked up at her as she stood before him, for she had jumped to her feet. "What you say is

164

true," he said. "And what you imply is truer. I am not the man for you."

"Oh, how you talk," she said impatiently. "What have I got to do with it?" She studied his face. His shoulders were a little bowed, as though she had inflicted a defeat on him. Annoyance sharpened her voice. "How can you be so silly?" Maybe she won, though; maybe she could push him. "If I were you," she said, "I'd go to court!" Visions floated through her mind of that dukedom. "Will you have some wine?"

He thanked her but told her no. "And we shan't discuss this further." He made his way to the door. "Good night," he said. She had followed him to the door, and he kissed her gently, tenderly—oddly too, she thought, as though he were never going to see me again. What is the matter with him? Can't we argufy a little? The door had closed, and she tossed off her cup of wine and set it down, feeling discontented. He's so gentle, he doesn't like to quarrel or fight. She sighed. "Oh, well, I'll go in and talk to Anne."

The coronation of Nan Boleyn was thrilling to Katryn. Mouth agape, she watched ladies and lords, bands of children dressed as sprites or nymphs, fountains flowing wine, musicians playing, and the exciting sight of the whole city of London on its streets.

Katryn thought it was wonderful. Lord Latimer grimly noted the number of heads which remained covered, as the new Queen passed before the critical eye of the populace. Handsome she might be, popular she would never be—that was plain. At the town cross, she was presented with a bag of gold from the city—one thousand crowns. She kept it! The city was stunned.

"Greedy whore," they said.

Katryn was thoughtful. But she agreed. "It's her city," she said to Lucy. "Certes she should have given it back, for charity or for a hospital." Suddenly she felt cheated too, like any Londoner. "I can't imagine why she didn't give it back!" she exclaimed.

"She has no love for the city," Lord Latimer said. "She is greedy, and she knows no better."

Katryn shot him a glance. Her mind was taking in a great many odds and ends these days, for she was learning about politics, about protocol. She was learning there were people to know, and people to avoid; people who were important, people who were not. She was on the edge of Henry's great struggle to reform the Church, and her quick mind absorbed all the myriad details till they came quite clear.

The summer was idyllic. On the twenty-sixth of April Anne's baby had been born, and soon after the coronation they all started north. Will Herbert gave his permission for Anne to come to Snape Hall for the summer, to get out of London and its bad humors and its possible plagues. Lucy came too, and when all had been packed from little John's hornbooks to the new cradle for Anne's little boy, who was named for his father, the long train set forth for Yorkshire.

Katryn was proud of Snape Hall. Anne thought it grand and beautiful. Lord Latimer was very busy, what with the care of his vast estates, and the journeys he made to various country estates to talk with their owners, far from London, far from Henry and interference. He was finding out about the temper of the country and the revolt brewing in Yorkshire. Each time he came back to Snape Hall, Katryn was so glad to see him she would run on flying feet to greet him; each time he returned he seemed handsomer and more distinguished. She tried to cater to his every want, from the wines he liked to the care of his precious books and the supply of hot water to which he was addicted. She embroidered shirts for him, for he always wore white linen. Meticulously, his chests were kept neat as pins, his clothes always brushed and clean, his boots shiny, and Katryn kept an eye on his manservant to see that all was done to his liking.

When he was away, she would ride over to her new manors. The hedge thorns were growing; she was enclosing the land. She saved money, and bought more sheep, and supervised the care of the flocks she had brought from Kendal. But when August came, she found she was more than anxious to get back to London.

So was Anne. Her separation from her husband was telling on her. She couldn't wait for Will Herbert to see how much his lusty son had grown. "He will be so overthrown when he sees his young Will!" On the fifteenth of August, Will wrote that Nan Boleyn had taken to her state chamber at Greenwich to await the birth of her child, and that Anne had best return. Since this event had great political implications, Lord Latimer changed his mind and packed up his whole family, and Katryn and her entourage arrived in London on the first day of September.

On the night of the seventh, Anne was at Greenwich, and Will Herbert, in the company of another courtier, Sir George Blagge, was watching the pages make up the King's bed. They plumped up straw mattresses, feeling for concealed weapons, and then laid the feather bed upon the mattresses. After that came the fine linen. Will swung about to watch his Grace's night clothes being laid before the fire to warm; meantime, in the Queen's antechamber the King himself paced back and forth—just as I did myself, Will thought.

He commanded a page to tuck a corner of the sheet in tighter; he made sure there was plenty of wood ready for the fire, and he commanded another page to rebrush the King's robe and to shake out the fur a bit. "And for God's sake, keep it back from the flames, dolthead." The fire hissed and sparked, and Will had turned to look at it when a page came scurrying in. "The Lady Herbert wishes you, sir," he said.

Will told Sir George Blagge that he was leaving. "I leave all to you, Pig," he called. Everyone, including Henry, called George Blagge "Pig."

Anne stood outside the door, and as soon as Will saw his wife he knew what was the matter.

"The Queen is delivered?" he whispered. Anne nodded. Will drew her into a bend in the hallway where there was an arch and they could be sure of not being overheard.

Anne kept glancing about her. But she spoke fast. "The child is a wench. They are afraid to tell him. None of the women want to tell him, nor the doctor. They sent me for you. The Queen is mad with grief and cries. Silently." Then Anne darted another glance about her. "She is afeared!"

"Ah," Will said only. Then he said, "Take me the way you came."

Anne breathed, "Thou'lt tell him, Will?"

"Aye," he said. "Someone must, Anne."

Henry still paced. The room was silent. He heard no longer the sound of women's voices in the chambers beyond; he heard no shrill orders, no shriek of pain. He looked toward the inner door with sudden fury when it opened, and he had a glimpse of one of the nurses, and a violet gowned girl. Then William Herbert came in at the other door, and he came toward Henry and dropped on one knee. The King raised him up.

Will said, "The Queen is delivered, your Grace, of a fine healthy daughter."

Will faced the King. Henry was taller than he, with bull-like strength in shoulders and arms, still supple and powerful. He raised one clenched fist. A word burst out from him like thunder. "I?" he bellowed. "I have a daughter? I wanted a son!"

Henry was for an instant made mad with impotent rage; the veins swelled in his thick neck; the other courtiers stood quiet, moving almost not a muscle, wondering if the King could contain his anger. But gradually the red anger left Henry's face, and he turned and strode toward his wife's chamber, brushing aside the nurses, coming into the state room where Nan Boleyn had borne a new daughter to England. Henry went past the cradle and to the side of the big bed where his wife lay back on the pillows, her face averted from him, her black hair caught back and spilling across the white pillowcases. He started to take the white hand that lay on the counterpane—and he felt the knob of the sixth finger on that hand before she drew it away hurriedly and laid the other white hand, perfect, against his chest. "I suffer more now than I did during my labor, my lord," she said. She caught her lip in her teeth.

"Do not, sweetheart," he said fiercely, gathering her against him, and she gave a little moan of both relief and pain in the oxlike grip of her king and husband. He released her, and laid her back against the pillows.

Nan Boleyn was a fighter defeated. The sparkling black eyes were dull with pain and fear and failure. "I wished for a son, more than thee, my lord," she said. She closed her eyes for a moment, as if dreaming of the past six years with all their frustrations, and all their passions, and all their ugly greed and hate. What fury had she loosed, for in that moment she knew she had reaped the whirlwind. "God have mercy on me!" she cried, opening her eyes to Henry. He was her husband now; step by step he had destroyed the Roman church in England, and men and women, for her, for this, for this child that wailed from the cradle. "I had prayed endlessly to the Virgin," she said, "and the child is born on her day. A girl! What bitter jest!" she whispered, and looking at Henry for just a second she flashed her taunting smile. "I suppose I should name her Mary," she cried. "Now you have two daughters; they might as well both be Mary!"

She is hysterical, Anne thought. Jesu, to say that to the King! Then Nan's eyes filled with tears, and she began to cry.

Henry said, "Sweetheart, sweetheart, I shall never desert thee!"

Anne drew back; she heard no more. She and Jane Seymour stood silent in the shadows, and Anne later reported to Katryn all that she had heard and that had happened.

Later in the month, the court returned to London, to Whitehall. Anne had left her baby son with her sister, and she came to Katryn's house for a week, bringing with her Jane Seymour; during that time Katryn came to know Jane Seymour well, indeed so well that she offered her the sanctuary of her own room. Lord Latimer neither approved nor disapproved.

"The state of the whole court is odd," Katryn reported to Lord Latimer. "The women say that all is in a state of flux, with aberrant gaiety like lightning in a storm—" She hesitated.

Lord Latimer said, "That was apt. You need not hunt for more words, for I apprehend you perfectly."

But Katryn went right on. "Jane says the King is moody to the extreme, and ofttimes Nan sends him into bellows of rage. Then all is made up again. But each time they quarrel or Nan teases—" She stopped then, for no one knew what the outcome would be. "Jane mislikes Nan Boleyn, whether or no she's her mistress. So I told her she could come here when it became unendurable for her. For Nan has a sharp tongue."

"That is an extreme understatement," Lord Latimer said. He was dressing to go to Parliament. He kissed her but paused at the door. "I don't know whether Jane has seen fit to divulge it to you, my dear," he said, "but rumor hath it Henry is interested in the beauteous Jane."

"By God's most precious soul!" Katryn said aloud to the empty room; she hadn't known it. But Henry had two wives already. And both living. Would Jane become the King's mistress? Was Jane already—? "By God's most precious soul!" she repeated aloud. And to think she hadn't even heard the gossip! She shook her red head and tied on her apron. "I'd best get busy," she told herself, for

Margaret had the measles and she could hear her crying in the next room.

Jane returned some weeks later and stayed two weeks. She spent most of her time sewing. Jane had little money, and she was remaking some of her gowns, using odds and ends of scraps and lace, Looking over at her bent head, Katryn couldn't believe she was anything but virgin, although by now rumors were flying thick and everyone was saying how could it be she was still a maiden at twenty-six? But her blue eyes were so guileless and her smile so sweet, although her body was strong and sinuous and she moved with the grace of a lioness. There was something oddly disturbing about Jane, as though beneath that sweetness lay a sleepy strength, of body and mind, which she would call upon when she needed or wanted something badly enough. Sometimes when she looked at Katryn, Katryn could see the same lazy determination that looked at her out of Tom Seymour's eyes.

Tom was in Hungary, the first Englishman to travel there in many a year as an official representative of the crown of England. When Katryn thought about it, she had a confused picture of that faraway land; she imagined great snowy mountains, and huge stone castles opening out room after room, and sleighs, and drawn swords, and dark deeds. What amazing adventures he was probably having!

"Do you worry about him?" she asked Jane. Although she said little—Jane never talked much—Katryn knew Jane loved her younger brother best of any person in the world.

Jane looked up in surprise. "Acourse I worry."

"Have you heard from him?" she asked, before she thought what she was saying.

"Nay," said Jane, "but his Grace has. He is in receipt of a number of letters concerning the condition of the kingdom, its intrigues, and its preparation against the Turks. That was the most important bit of news."

"Oh," said Katryn. Turks? She shivered. "When I think of all that goes on in the world, I am certainly glad I'm English."

But the women's concern was put to rest four days later when Tom Seymour walked into the house. He was a little thinner, with the lines from nose to mouth etched a bit deeper, and he had a scar running across the back of one hand.

Katryn, having flown downstairs after Jane's electrifying shout, watched him embrace Jane. He squeezed her tight. There was a love and urgency about the greeting that moved Katryn, and she wiped her eyes surreptitiously as she stood back so as not to intrude. Only when they both turned to her did she speak.

"You'll stay to dine?" He hadn't kissed her in greeting.

He shook his head. Then he said, "Get your cloak Jane; I'm meeting Ned in ten minutes at the Mitre. We barely had time for a cup of wine together last night."

"You arrived last night?" Jane cried.

"Aye, but I spent the time closeted with his Grace. I had no time to let you know. I brought back a manservant named Janos, but he doesn't know his way about the city."

"He's a Hungarian?" Katryn asked in amazement.

Tom Seymour became aware of her presence again. He grinned. "I believe he is, my lady," he said. "He has but one horn; Turks have two."

"Oh," said Katryn, "you're making mock of me."

"Why, how perceptive you have become!" he said. "Have you ever dined at the Mitre?"

She shook her head. Jane had run upstairs.

"Well, get your cloak too. You'll have the finest bird pie in the city, except mayhap at the Dagger. The Dagger's a tavern for sailors; someday I'll take you there and assault your virtue in an upstairs room. Go get your cloak; it's cold as the devil outside."

"You use the most uncouth language," said Katryn, haughtily.

"Hurry," said Tom Seymour. "Ned hates to be kept waiting."

It was the first day of winter, and the cold tingled Katryn's skin and pinked her cheeks; it hastened her step and sent the blood racing through her body. The walk was short and brisk to the Mitre. When its old oak door opened, they stepped down into a narrow room. Tom Seymour took her arm, and she sent him a dazzling smile that included the landlord and the whole room. Ned Seymour rose from the end of the long white-clothed table and waved.

Katryn was pleasantly aware that all eyes in the room followed their progress; Tom and Jane Seymour nodded and smiled at people. Flushed, Katryn sat down in the chair she was given and threw back her cloak, surveying the scene with sparkling eyes, for she had never been in one of these famous eating places before.

Tom Seymour was telling the landlord they wanted all his favorite dishes, the ones he couldn't get abroad. "The Hungarians have wonderful pastry," he told the landlord. "Veal, with sour cream—good. Meat, stewed in wines." There was a large flagon of ale set on the table, and Jane poured it into cups. The three Seymours raised their mugs, and Katryn did likewise. They drank solemnly to being together again. Then the glasses were set down, and a small silence fell. Jane sighed. "Now," she said.

Tom Seymour shook his head. "Not I first."

"You're the one who has been away," Jane reminded him.

Tom Seymour picked up his glass. Then he said, "All right. It is a country some three hundred years behind ours. It consists of a ruling class, and serfs. The river flows through the center of a beautiful and ancient city, and one side is called Pesht and the other Buda, as though we called this city Lon and Don. I stayed with a noble family which had so many servants I couldn't even begin to count them. I brought home a dozen horses; their horses are magnificent. Their women are overestimated." He raised his glass to Jane and Katryn.

"I heard this morn that you did a magnificent job," Ned said. "His Grace is pleased. You will be rewarded, Tom, probably with land in Wales or near the Border."

"How were you able to speak with them?" Katryn asked suddenly.

Ned Seymour said, "Tom speaks excellent German and French, my lady, other he wouldn't ha' been sent."

Katryn flushed, for Ned's words were in the nature of a rebuke. She said, "But what did you do on your mission?"

Ned made an exclamation, and Tom Seymour leaned across the table and put his hand over hers. "No more. This is a social dinner. We're here to enjoy ourselves."

"Oh," said Katryn. Then the bird pies were brought, the gravy bubbling through the crust. The others ate and drank and talked, and after a while Katryn forgot her momentary dislike of Ned Seymour. She began to eat too; the food was wonderful, the ale stronger than any she had ever had. But mostly she was fascinated by their conversation.

172

It was as though the whole panoply of the court and its workings were spread before her in a picture glittering with color and personalities. Not only that, but every few moments someone would stop by. Quickly she would be presented. Then the newcomer would talk a few minutes, saying how much he had missed Tom Seymour. She was amazed to see her brother, Will Parr; he came over, elegant and slim and tall, and told Tom Seymour how glad everyone was to see him back, and then he told a jest at which Katryn blushed.

"Why, Will," she said.

It was exciting to be the center of attention. From various parts of the room, men were sending her admiring glances; the landlord hovered near to make sure the food was to their liking, and all the while she was trying to listen to what was being said, and laughing at the way Tom Seymour put his forceful sentences in a language rich and racy with slang. When she looked about the room, she was aware that the two men at her table were indeed different. It is no wonder, she thought suddenly, that everyone comes over to speak with them. They were young and their laughter was rich with youth and force. And their talk ranged wide. Jane leaned over to Katryn. "They are always like this," she said.

The two men glanced at her. Ned was speaking about the rising enclosures and the hardship it was working. His black eyes grew angry. Katryn felt impelled to intervene.

"I enclosed much of Kendal!"

Ned threw her a look. "That's sheep country." He dismissed it.

"Ned, for God's sake, you've got the pig by the wrong ear," Tom Seymour said. "When it's profitable, men will do it."

"The great landlords are evading their responsibilities!"

"Half the world evades its responsibilities," Tom Seymour said. "You know that. You may be your brother's keeper, Ned, but by God, you can't be his conscience."

"Can't you?" Ned asked. "Mayhap by law you can."

"Carry that farther, and you'd be making laws against drunkards, or disease," Tom Seymour said. "Or," he said, leaning forward, "against having images in churches!"

Ned smiled, a bit sheepishly. "I'd do that too."

"You'll cure nothing," said Tom Seymour, "but I grant you, you may try it someday." He raised his mug. "To our future lord chancellor," he said to Ned, who shook his head.

Nonetheless his face took on its somber thoughtful expression, and his eyes were grave. Katryn was thrilled. It was possible indeed—given a man like Ned Seymour. It was very thrilling to think on life and what it might bring to these three people. Even Jane was caught up in it, Katryn saw, for her blue eyes were bright, and full of her dreams and her love for these two brothers of hers. She raised her mug, too. "And to our future lord admiral."

Katryn lifted her ale, and Ned, in the friendly manner he could have which was so endearing, said gravely, "Someday we may remember this meal and wonder. For if what we say comes true we shall look back with nostalgia at our youth, and if it does not we shall ponder where we went astray, or how we have changed, or what we have lost."

"One can gain by one's losses," Jane said. Tom Seymour threw her a long look, and Katryn knew he had heard the gossip and wondered if he would speak of it now.

But he did not, and she was a little disappointed. Instead he said, "Ned, I have a philosophy which says look neither too far up nor ahead. Like climbing the rigging. If you don't look to what you're doing, or if you have your eyes on the top of the mast instead of the rigging right in front of you, you're like to misstep. I have a toast I like better than Jane's, with all due respect to Jane's ambitions for me. I drink to the present, to today."

Katryn said, "Why, I think thus, too, just the way you do!" She was surprised and pleased that he had put into words what she had never tried to formulate. "I, too," she said, nodding her head at Ned. "I warrant you're impatient at the end of each day that you've not done more. But I'm not. I feel I've done as much as I can. Although—" She was thoughtful. She wished Lord Latimer would have more ambition, and go to court as these men did. But she shouldn't say that aloud. "One's ambitions one should keep to oneself," she ended very gravely.

"I never know," said Tom Seymour, just as gravely, "what is stirring in your head."

Katryn flashed him a merry smile. "You're not supposed to, sir!"

"Nonetheless, I intend that you answer me a few questions."

Ned was rising and saying he would pay for the dinner, that they were all his guests, at which Tom rose too and thanked him, adding he had an empty purse. He asked Ned to see Jane home, and it happened quickly—the two of them gone, and Katryn alone at the end of table with Tom Seymour before she had time to consider.

She said doubtfully, "I should ha' gone with Jane."

He shook his head. He was regarding her.

A little uncertain, she poured more ale from the fresh pitcher which had been set down. "Can you pay for it?" she asked.

"Aye," he said, unsmiling. But he shook his head when she offered him some. "I've had enough. Katryn, information comes to my ears, now and then. Lord Latimer is dabbling dangerously. What I hear, others hear. I want you to convey these words to your Lord Latimer. And I want you to tell him they came from me."

"You?" she echoed.

"Aye," he said, "for this message, from the enemy camp, he will trust. I am not a Cromwell, nor have I ever been associated with him or his ilk."

His words conjured up a picture of the bullet-headed minister, so adept in intrigue, now so powerful. "My lord hates Cromwell!" she whispered.

He said softly, "Why does he hate Cromwell, Katryn? Tell me."

He must know why, she thought. Yet she answered, leaning close. "He says—they say—that he will destroy every one of the monasteries and put the money in his pocket! He spies on the old nobility! He would torture a woman! They say he is Nan Boleyn's spawn and creature, set to do her evil work and draw the King away from his law-abiding subjects, who love him and who love the Roman church. They say it is a plot, of witches almost, with Nan the chief witch, and Cromwell her devil."

"Do you believe all that?" Tom Seymour asked.

She said low, "I don't know. After listening to you and your brother—"

He said, "There are other forces besides Nan, and Cromwell, for whom it is well known I hold no love. But one cannot judge the Reformation by Cromwell. Nor by Nan, although she is a deeper advocate of the New Learning than her enemies give her credit for. Ah well, the issue is much beclouded by the people involved, and by the fact, Katryn, of which you must not lose sight, that the English church was not as completely tied to Rome as the French, for instance; it always functioned more or less by itself, on this island

175

ringed by her seas; we are too independent, and we can put part of the credit where it belongs—on those seas."

"And Lord Latimer says," Katryn went on, remembering she wasn't finished, "that the Princess Mary, the King's first-born, should be reinstated!"

"Let the Princess Mary return allegiance to her father instead of putting her trust in Spain, her mother's country, and all will be well."

"But her mother has been so ill-treated!"

"She has a father too," Tom Seymour said dryly. "More than that, Katryn, she has a country. But one would never know she was English!"

She understood, quickly. This was the crime of which Mary was guilty, and for which the new party could not forgive her! Conniving with Spain!

Tom Seymour said, "I have a feeling, an inkling, from what I've seen, that we stand on the edge of a great struggle with Spain, and I mislike to see an English princess give or seek aid or comfort from the enemy. Mayhap if I think thus, one can understand how his Grace feels. I cannot talk longer, Katryn." He rose, and she rose too, he laying her cloak around her shoulders, and she gathered it tight to go out into the cold windy street. They stepped outside, and he took her arm. His eyes were narrowed against the wind and the dust it blew. "One final word, Katryn," he said. "Would you like to see Spanish helmets, here in the London streets?"

"Nay!" she cried fiercely. Her beloved London, in the hands of the Spanish!

"I wonder if you realize," he went on "how fortunate you are. Women in other countries have not a tenth of the freedom or respect that women do here."

She looked at him. Three hundred years behind, Hungarian women were, he had said. "Are the Hungarian women submissive and meek?"

He nodded absently. Then he caught her eye and threw back his head and laughed. "Aye," he said, nodding, "all one has to say is 'into bed with you, wench.' It's very convenient."

"That isn't what I meant at all," she stammered.

"It is, or was," he said, still laughing. "How did you manage to get Lord Latimer to wed with you, by the way? Storms of tears, or did you fling yourself in his honorable arms?"

"Neither," she muttered.

"It must have been both, then."

How did he guess, she wondered? She trotted along to keep up with his long steps. He noted it, and told her he was sorry to hurry her so but he had much to do, indeed even to finding a good lodging, since now he was staying with Ned at Whitehall. But all the time he was talking, she found herself thinking of the night at New Hall when he had made love to her. At her own house, she stood on the first step so her eyes met his.

"Good-by," she said, "and thank you."

He looked straight at her, in the way he had of summing her up. She wondered if he would made any kind of advance. If he would, she'd repulse it quickly, and her chin set a little as she looked at him almost defiantly. He doffed his cap. "Good-by, Katryn," he said cheerfully. He reached around her, gave her a swift pat on the backside, then turned and walked away before she could even speak. She stood on the step, her mouth open. Why, the knave, she thought, and right here in the street! She flounced up the last two steps and banged the door behind her.

She carefully repeated Tom Seymour's words and warning to Lord Latimer, who, to her surprise, showed only vague interest. For a moment, she suspected him of dissimulation. "Are you trying to mislead me, my lord?" she asked.

"Nay, indeed not, my dear," he said. But she wasn't satisfied, and an odd disquiet began to prick her.

The weather got colder, and the children, who had both just recovered from the measles, caught bad colds. Katryn resisted it but Lord Latimer did not, and on Christmas Day it seemed to Katryn half the household was sick with high fevers and terrible coughs. Jane had come, and she and Katryn spent Christmas Eve quietly together. Jane asked Katryn to read from the Bible story, and this she did, with the two children huddled at the foot of the bed, listening, till she tucked them into their own beds. Jane had talked constantly of the King and the enormous force of his physical presence, which she said Katryn couldn't understand, not coming to court. The next day brought Will Parr, and Katryn was glad to see him. Bess's father had died, a month ago, and they had taken up residence in their town house. Bess was the talk of London with her masques and dinners so soon after her father's death.

"Cromwell has his eye on the now vacant earldom of Essex. He shall probably get it, too," Will said moodily, and Katryn saw he was very disappointed. "I think it wise you know and ally yourself with the Seymours to the extent you can, Katryn. They hew a straight path, and are not suspected of double dealing with either party. There are rumors about Lord Latimer."

Will spent a great deal of time at court with Sir William, so Katryn knew he heard all the gossip. Will said plainly, "Although I serve my uncle, I do a deal, sister, more than you'd think. The office of lord chamberlain has myriad duties—endless sometimes, one thinks—from arranging for horses for visiting ambassadors to arranging state banquets. And Mother of God, that's a task! Anyway, the Seymours are forthright and you know where you stand with them. If you help Jane they won't forget it, should you need aid."

"Aid?" asked Katryn.

"Aye," said Will. "You're entertaining at supper in four days, and the list reads like the list of Katharine's and Mary's supporters."

"They are fine old names," she said. "Cannot we ha' friends?"

"If you do not intrigue," he said. "Since when, Katryn, has the Spanish ambassador, Monsieur Chapuys, been such an old friend?"

She didn't answer. Will said, as he made ready to go, "It might help if you would ask Tom Seymour to come. If you think for a minute that Cromwell doesn't know who's coming to your house next week, you're very much mistaken. You must remember he'll deal harshly with all of you once he gets a chance, and while Nan is still powerful, he is all-powerful too. No one knows how long it will last."

Did he mean Henry's marriage to Nan Boleyn? She wondered after he had gone. As she sewed, she cast glances at Jane who looked so sweet and sane, so very English, so very composed. Was Jane the key? Nonetheless, because she was afraid, she sat down that night and wrote to Tom Seymour, asking him to come and have supper with them the night of her dinner. In the morning she received his reply. It was brief. Quickly her eye went over the neat heavy writing.

My lady,

I think I have smelled out your reasons for including me. But it will not suffice. My presence would do no good, one sheep among the wolves, or the other way round if you prefer. In any other matter, I will be glad to help.

Your obedient servant,

T. Seymour

Katryn swore a little oath and cast the letter on the flames. But at the supper, each time she spoke with the Spanish ambassador she kept hearing Tom Seymour's question in her ears: "Would you like to see Spanish helmets on the London streets?" Katryn had difficulty being civil.

She kept her ears open for talk that Cromwell would consider treasonable, but she could perceive no sign of it; all seemed as usual except for an undercurrent which she could not trace. Even Jane said, when they were alone, "They do resent the Princess Mary's being declared illegitimate, don't they? I do too, truly."

Katryn said, "Jane, are you not afraid to say that aloud?"

"Of course not," Jane said. "His Grace knows exactly how I feel; I loved Queen Katharine and I served her. For years. But his Grace also knows I would not conspire." She looked at Katryn with her guileless blue eyes. Katryn smiled.

"Dear Jane," she said warmly, "no one could ever accuse you of conspiring!"

But Jane was troubled, and Katryn knew it was about Henry. The day before New Year's, she said suddenly, "Katryn, I would like to speak with you after dinner."

Katryn was dining with her husband, for Lord Latimer had retreated to his bed again with a recurrence of fever. Absently she went along to his bedroom, where the servants had set up a small table for her. Lord Latimer was propped up in bed, sipping some wine, looking thoughtful and less feverish than he had this morning. Katryn leaned over the middle of the bed to feel his forehead, resting one palm on the counterpane. Suddenly she made an exclamation of pain, and withdrew her hand; there was blood on it.

Lord Latimer, who rarely swore, was provoked into a mild oath. "I'm so very sorry, Katryn," he cried. He picked up a slender dagger, which had been lying concealed in the folds of the counter-

179

pane. "I forgot it was lying here. I'm so sorry. Does it hurt bad?"

"Nay, nay," she said, going over to wash her hand with fresh water from the pitcher. "It just startled me."

He said, "It is my New Year's gift to Monsieur Chapuys."

"That dagger?" Her eyes widened. Fear shone in them. "But that's an odd gift! Almost a message!"

His eyes evaded hers. Not at all, my dear. 'Tis just a small token."

She cried, " 'Tis just the thing Cromwell loves! He can read treason into it!"

"Nonsense," said Lord Latimer. "Sit down. Shall we eat? My appetite has improved."

Katryn couldn't eat. But she could not get him to admit the dagger was a message to the Spanish ambassador, nor could she prevail upon him not to send it. "It's got some of my blood on it already," she cried. "Do you want more? Afore you're finished that's what ye'll have!" She was trembling with frustration, and Lord Latimer grew annoyed.

"You shall leave these things to me," he said.

"But—" she began.

"I'm going to nap now," he said coldly. "You have duties, I believe."

"Aye," Katryn said dispiritedly. Many, many duties, and under Lord Latimer's eye all must be done on time, without fail. She rang for his servant, and a boy to take away the soiled plates and uneaten food. At the door his voice stopped her. "It seems to me, Katryn, that there is a great deal of uneaten food."

She said quickly, "It's not wasted. It goes into the poor box at the gate. There are so many abroad here who need it!"

"Whom you've driven here, by enclosing your lands. Do you think it sane economy to dispossess farmers and then, when they're penniless in London, to feed them?"

A vision of her neat hedged fields, the fat sheep munching against the hillside, passed through her mind. "Men should be able to get work. And food prices are high, and we need wool! I feed the poor, not because I feel guilty but because—" She stopped. His thin face was austere against the pillows. "You don't understand me!" she burst out.

"I understand—silly word—all too well. You love your sheep, and you love London. I wish you loved me half as much."

She checked the retort on her lips. I love London because it is gay and alive, she thought rebelliously, and you are not. "Why are you so mean and irritable?" she asked, quick tears springing to her eyes.

"Because I fear you don't love me," he said.

He had averted his face. The words sounded as if wrung from him. Slowly she went over to the bed and took his hand. "I'm sorry if I hurt your feelings," she said. "I do love you."

He turned his head to look into her eyes. After a moment he sighed. "Katryn," he said, "I don't deserve you. I shouldn't have married you. I've caged you."

She retorted fiercely. "I'm not caged!"

"By an older husband, children that are not yours, by many duties."

"I can handle it all!"

A little smile touched his mouth. "I love your back, Katryn," he said, "it is so straight. So straight. Symbolic."

"I warrant that's a compliment," she said. "But do go to sleep now, my lord. Acourse I love you. I'm your wife." She leaned over and kissed him, and removed a pillow from his back. She squeezed his hand and gave him a smile. "I must be off," she said, and he could hear the quick tap of her feet as she ascended the stairs outside his room to the schoolroom above.

John and Margaret were having their dinner with Father Lambert. It was Katryn's custom to sit with them while they ate, and after, to hear John recite and Margaret read the few words she had learned, and to listen to her lute. The fire burned bright, while outside rain poured down the windows. Katryn looked from one child to the other. They were round-cheeked and smiling, for all the colds they'd had. Margaret's dimples showed, and treacle ran down her chin. Katryn leaned over and wiped it off. John's eyes regarded her merrily. Katryn thought of Lord Latimer's words—"children that are not yours." But they are, she thought fiercely. And I'm so proud of them. They prosper, and he prospers, and I am taking good care of them. She kept thinking thus while Margaret finished her dinner—every bit, or no sweets—and her nurse placed her lute in her newly washed hands.

"I do believe you can start the virginals soon," Katryn said, watching her hands. "Now then, John, we'll all sing. It does Margaret good to keep time to singing."

The song was rollicking and gay, and Margaret played the chords. Then Katryn took the lute from her and strummed it with her thumb, picking out a series of running chords; then settling on her stool she said, "Now we'll sing a Border ballad, so you will come to know the songs of the North."

They listened quietly as the rain beat down. When the last note was wrung from the strings, she laid down the instrument. I am happy, she thought. Now I must go to see Jane, and find out the matter. "Tomorrow," she said, "if it's a nice day, I shall take you both on the river."

She went slowly through the empty gallery, where two men were polishing the paneling. Through the windows she could make out the sodden garden, the bare branches of bush and tree dripping; only the fat yews and the box stood sturdy and green. How dismal is winter, she thought; I wonder why I like it, the cold, the shrill biting wind. She found Jane in the solar, with a big fire blazing, the curtains drawn over the windows, and candles lighted.

Jane was at the virginals, playing a song Henry had written, a lovely haunting tune. Her expression was that of a woman lost in love. For a moment Katryn was silent. Jane played on, humming under her breath. Suddenly she broke off.

"I've asked Tom to come," she said, letting her hand fall onto the keys. Then she resumed her playing. "I have to do something, Katryn," she said, as an apology.

"Tom?" Katryn's hand went to her hair, to tuck in a curl. She glanced about the room. It looked pretty and cosy. Then a thought occurred to her. "Do you wish me to stay whilst you talk with him?"

"Aye," said Jane. "I wish you would."

Katryn was vaguely conscious of relief. She sat down behind her needlepoint screen on which she was working. She picked up the wool to put it about her neck and thought better of it; instead she coiled it in her lap, and took up her needle. Soon her hands were flashing in and out as she drew the wool through the mesh. Jane played on, and when Tom Seymour came in the doorway, she rose to her feet, almost in one motion, as though she rose to greet a challenge.

He was both booted and spurred, and drops of rain clung to his thick hair; then he came over to the fire and spread his hands to catch the warmth. He turned about to face both women, his eyes going from one to the other. "You might as well both sit." Katryn sat down obediently on one of the stools; Jane took the other. Tom Seymour dragged Lord Latimer's carved chair to the fire. "Now," he said. "Speak on." He crossed his legs at the ankles, stretching them out, and waited.

In the silence, Jane's voice came forlornly. "I don't know how to begin."

"You remind me of the time you were eight years old and threw the tankard at Ned. And hit him, too, by God." Tom Seymour smiled slightly.

This reminder had its effect on Jane, for she brought out the next sentence in a rush. "The King is making me a New Year's present, a bag of gold!" Her blue eyes grew very wide as she confessed this, and they fastened on Tom Seymour to see his expression. But Katryn could discern no visible response, he looked still thoughtful and quizzical.

He said, "Well. Well, is that all you have to say, Jane?"

Jane stammered, "What do you mean?"

He leaned forward a bit. "I mean this. The point. The truth. Have you accepted it, or have you given his Grace any reason to think it will be accepted?"

Jane shifted on her stool. "I don't think so."

He said irritably, "What kind of answer is that? By God's most precious soul, Jane! Have you accepted it?"

"Nay," she said. "But I haven't got it yet."

"God give me patience," he said. "And have you given his Grace reason to think you will accept?"

"That's what I don't know, exact, Tom," she said tearfully.

Tom Seymour swore a variety of lazy oaths. He got to his feet and stood with his back to the fire. Then he said, "Jane, will you talk, or shall I?"

"You, sir," she said, looking as meek as a kitten, Katryn thought.

Tom Seymour said slowly, "This would be laughable were not the consequences perhaps the most bitter you'd ever have to face. Let's put it bluntly: being the King's mistress is hardly the happiest position for a woman—a woman like you. A Bessie Blount, yes. A Mary Boleyn. But not you, Jane. Not you. Even as Henry's wife, you'd have difficulty, but there are two living women, two lives, between you and Henry, and I would warn you, Jane, not to set your foot on that path."

Jane said, "His Grace was bewitched by Nan!"

Tom Seymour's little smile turned down the corners of his mouth. "His Grace was like every other man," he said. "He was madly in love. Now I warrant—" his jaw set a little as he regarded her—"he tells you he needs your sweetness, he seeks the peace of your lips, the warmth of your arms, he is beleaguered on all sides, and only you can give him rest. Be generous, Jane, he says. If you love me, how can you deny me? Yield me your lips, then, just your lips. Ad infinitum."

Jane's eyes fell. Katryn had dropped the wool from her hands, and since Jane's head was bent he spoke directly to Katryn. "A man's tongue becomes increasingly facile when his—" He stopped, and even from his lounging position gave her a little bow, a nod of the head; he had a merry look to his eyes. "I'll have to guard my language, madam—when he wants to lie with a woman."

Jane lifted her head. "But I love him, Tom!"

He made a muttered exclamation. "Love, love," he said. "What is love, Jane? You to Henry will be an easy conquest, going into his arms unprotesting. Love is part respect, and his Grace will have none of it for you if you fall into his bed like a ripe plum. You may be in love, Jane, but his Grace is dallying. Anyway, you'd make a poor mistress. Your feelings will get hurt, and you'll weep and sigh. You're neither bold enough, nor sluttish enough, nor the other type—the submissive woman." He had said the last words quite calmly, looking hard at Jane, evaluating her. He paced across the room and stood by the window, pulling back the curtain to look out. Jane sat motionless, but Katryn jumped to her feet and approached Tom Seymour from behind. She came close.

"How do you know all that?" she whispered fiercely.

He turned his head slightly to look down at her. "Keep quiet," he said. "Forget you and me, for a minute. What I said has nothing to do with us."

She said, "I'll never have anything to do with you!"

His hand closed over her wrist in a crushing grip. "Oh, yes you will. Now be quiet and hold your tongue. Go and sit down."

Her eyes blazed. If Jane weren't here—! She forced herself to walk back to her stool.

Tom Seymour said, from across the room, "I'm sorry I was angry, Jane. I don't mean to belittle what you think is a deathless love for your King; I don't mean to belittle your very sweetness and generosity, which is what Henry is playing upon, and, I warrant, what he does love about you. But you are too fine. I am going to send you home."

"Home?" Jane whispered.

"Aye," he said, coming back to stand in front of her. "You go home to Wolf Hall. Rest and sleep and walk in the woods. Follow the path across the meadow to the little church. See if the pond is frozen. Listen to the madrigals at night. Sing the Norman songs that are your heritage, for you have a proud heritage. Indeed, Jane, should Henry seek to wed you, you would have to get a dispensation, for you are kin and cousin to his Grace, through a proud line. Think of the Norman blood that bred you. Stiffen your spine, and find your pride. Read and sew and do all the manner of things Mother does, as you used to. Go back to Wolf Hall and test this love you think you bear for Henry."

Jane said, "Aye. I will."

He smiled, and his blue eyes glinted. "And now for your immediate problem—the gold, which will be brought to you by one of the King's gentlemen or a messenger from his Grace."

"Will it?" asked Jane, her candid gaze upon her brother.

"Aye, most probably. 'Tis custom." He frowned down at her. "Listen carefully, Jane, and repeat my words after me. I beseech your Grace . . ."

"I beseech your Grace . . ." Jane repeated, parrotlike.

". . . I am a gentlewoman of good and honorable stock, and have no greater wealth than my honor . . ." He went on slowly, with Jane's voice coming after. ". . . For a thousand deaths"—here he flung out an arm—"I would not wish to impair it, mine honor, and if your Grace wishes to make me a present, I pray it will be when God sends me a good offer of marriage." Tom Seymour chuckled. "That last is to remind him there are other fish in the sea."

"Aye," said Katryn, nodding her head. "Aye. That's a spur."

Tom Seymour swung about to look at her. "Could you improve on my words, mistress?"

"Well," she said thoughtfully, "Jane could soften it a bit. For instance, she could go down on her knees, and bid the messenger do likewise when he reports back to his Grace. Bid the messenger fall on his knees, and then repeat, like this," said Katryn. "Say, when you go back to his Grace, I beg you kneel as I am doing, and beseech him to consider me as a gentlewoman of good stock, et cetera."

Jane stood up and looked at both of them. "You make me feel like a fool!"

"So you should," said Tom Seymour, "and I'm glad to see honest pride come up in you!"

"That's just like a brother," said Jane angrily.

"Aye, indeed it is," Tom Seymour retorted. "Now get your cloak and I'll take you back with me. In the morn, you will receive your gold from his Grace; send it back and leave for Wolf Hall."

"I should never have asked you," Jane cried. "I don't know why I did! I could have thought of it for myself!"

"You certainly could, and next time you will," Tom Seymour said. "Now go get your cloak."

"You are hateful!" Jane cried, and Katryn jumped up too and added her voice. "Pray don't be angry with me, Jane!"

At the door Jane paused. "I'm not angry with *you*, Katryn," she said pointedly. She closed the door.

Tom Seymour paced back to the window. "Women!" he said.

"Aye," said Katryn, her mind busy with Jane's problem. "And you seem to know much about them! And what of men?" she inquired, drawing a deep breath that heaved her breast. She grew haughty. "What of men?"

"God's creatures, the lords of creation."

"Oh!"

"Aye, and there's a night I remember when you wished mightily for breeks and boots." He laughed and looked pleased with himself.

"You are quite insufferable, you know," she said, aloofly, going over to her stool behind the needlepoint screen. Plucking the needle from it, she began to work. "You think you're jesting, but you truly mean it! You're so arrogant and swaggering. Look at yourself, standing there with your thumbs in your belt!"

"Look at myself?" he echoed. He dropped his hands. "What's wrong with me?"

"Don't try to smile at me like a little boy," she said loftily. "It will do you no good. Ouch!" She regarded her finger in dismay. She put it in her mouth and sucked at it.

He came toward her. He stood over her, thoughtful, and unconsciously he put his thumbs back in his belt. "I am searching for words," he said

"Pray do not bother.~

"Mother of God, Katryn," he muttered. "You can be so irritating and so obtuse."

Katryn took her finger from her mouth and clenched her hand. How irritating did he think he was? And what did obtuse mean? She looked up at him, half angry, half questioning.

"Obtuse means thick, or stupid," he said.

Her head jerked up. "I am not stupid!"

"Oh, yes you are," he said. "You are thick-headed and muddle-headed, always charging forward on the wrong path. You don't think, you act."

"Oh, have done," she cried. A big drop of blood stood on her finger, and she put it back in her mouth.

Tom Seymour scowled down at her. "You look so silly," he said, "with that finger, and all pouted up."

"Have done!" she cried again but broke off as Jane came into the room. His eyes were sharp on her as Jane rushed forward and the two women embraced. They whispered something he could not hear and, impatient, he shifted from one foot to the other, his cloak over his arm. Then they came slowly toward him, exchanged a last quick kiss. Jane went out the door.

Tom Seymour looked down at Katryn and she remembered how they had parted last time they had met. Her eyes glinted angrily and she put both hands behind her back. He leaned down and kissed her mouth, a brief warm little kiss. "Good-by," he said. Then he and Jane were gone.

Katryn walked over to the fire. I won't see Jane for a long time, she thought, and I shall miss her much. But I shall write and she promised she would write. And that means I shan't see that knave brother of hers either, and I thank God! She glanced down at her hand. Her finger was still bleeding a little, and she put it back in her mouth. She was standing in front of the mantel, and saw herself in the mirror. I do look silly, she thought with chagrin. The rain beat and rattled against the windowpanes, drops of it falling down the chimney to hiss into the fire. There was wine on the table and she went over and poured herself some. Holy Mary, I cannot endure him! Thank heaven I'll be spared his presence!

January passed slowly. Even though the King and court were in Whitehall, Lucy and Anne did not come much to Katryn's house on the Charterhouse. There were many festivities at court, even after the twelve days of Christmas had passed. Lucy had won herself a place in Nan Boleyn's court by her fidelity. She stood behind Nan, the Queen, with the white cloth in case Nan should overstuff her stomach. Anne was in constant attendance, too, because Nan could trust her. Katryn had the care of Anne's baby, and she received long letters from Jane down in the country. Jane was also lonely, although she had her family and her childhood friends.

Katryn grew restless. She wanted badly to go to court, but Lord Latimer forbade it. He did not countenance Nan Boleyn as Queen, and refused to go because he would have to pay homage to her. In February the weather was so cold that one could scarcely leave the house, or brave the icy wind that whipped over the river and through the streets. Snow lay on London's steeply sloping rooftops and on the thin ice across the river above the bridge. It was impossible to hire one of the few hackneys in the city, for the cobbles were slippery with ice, almost too treacherous for walking. Alone with her gentlewomen, who were dull as dishes, she was prisoned in her house whilst Kate and Anne disported themselves merrily in the great galleries at Whitehall.

The first day of March held no promise of spring. Katryn woke to a black sky and rain. She rose and dressed for morning prayer, and found herself violently sick. Meg thought it the fish she'd had the night previous. Will was coming to see her that afternoon, and she was afraid it was about Bess. Still, she thought, 'twill be a relief to see Will, a face from the forbidden court.

By dinner time she felt better, and received her brother at three in the solar. Will was worried and grave. He refused wine, but sat down in the chair by the fire. Katryn dismissed her women, and pulled over a cushion and sat on the floor, watching the flames with Will.

"They're about the only cheerfulness of the day," he said. He told Katryn first that Cromwell probably would be successful in snaring from Henry the vacant earldom of Essex, which Will had coveted and thought his right. "Think of our name against his—the toad," he muttered. "And I wedded to the heiress of Essex! What of my son?"

"Is Bess expecting?" Katryn asked.

"That's what I was going to tell you," he said. "She was expecting, but she got drunk two nights ago and miscarried. She's still in bed, of course. Katryn, sometimes I don't know what to do! I know I shouldn't come to you, but our uncle is very unsympathetic."

"He is?" asked Katryn, surprised.

"Aye. He tells me to give her a sound thrashing." Will raised an eyebrow and sighed. "As if that would do any good."

"Mayhap it would, Will."

He half smiled and shook his head. "You know nothing about real incontinency, either of you. I hope to God you never do. I cannot describe to you, Katryn, what it is like. She is two different people."

Katryn looked askance at him, whereupon he said, "By God, I *have* thrashed her!" He got to his feet. "Then she whimpers and whines and says she will be good, and please forgive her, and she cannot help it. 'I cannot help it, Will,' " he mimicked, in a high voice, " 'so please, you help me. Forgive me!' Then the next night, I find a leathern flask hidden in her boots in her closet! Jesu!" he said. "When she is drunk, she reviles me, you, anyone, everyone! She's like a beast! I don't know what to do, Katryn," he ended.

"Marry!" she said; she remembered Bess drunk well enough. "How oft does it happen, Will?"

"Too often," he said. "It used to be once every two weeks or so, but now it's crowding closer, and sometimes she is drunk for two days or more." Then he said, "I was overthrown by the loss of the child, Katryn. It meant much to me. She is young and strong and should have many children, and someday I hope to have an earldom to pass on to my son."

Katryn saw it was very important to him. And why not? The material advantages of marriage with Bess had ranked high; they outweighed her disabilities. Will deserved the earldom of Essex, and Cromwell might abandon it for a higher title or might lose it altogether. Gossip about the King's minister ran this way and that, and Cromwell's enemies expected to have his blood sooner or later for sure. Even Lord Latimer badly wanted that blood spilled out on Tower Green.

"Cromwell has a great many enemies," she said aloud.

"Aye, too many," Will said. "But—"

Katryn said, "Will, if Bess gets with child again, why don't you bring her to me? Especially if we're at Snape Hall. I will keep the wines and liquors from her. And watch over her health."

His brown eyes lightened and grew brighter. "Would you, Katryn? Oh, if you would—"

"Aye," she said. "I'll take the responsibility for her! And she can have Mother Nell to attend her—to bring your son into the world."

"Mother Nell!" he said. "I forgot you brought her from Kendal. Oh, how I remember her." He sighed. Then he smiled. "How's Goodie?"

Katryn laughed. "I expect she's as always. I'll be back with them soon enough. My lord wishes to leave London in April."

"April seems forever away," Will said. "Mayhap the spring will revive our spirits. In any case, Katryn, I'm grateful for your suggestion, and I shall do it, too. But now I have to return to Whitehall. The French ambasador is being feted tonight. We are very friendly with France now, you know," he said, his eyes twinkling. "I don't always understand matters of state, but his Grace is more astute than I, thank God."

"Well," said Katryn, "since we are at odds with Spain over Katharine, the Princess Dowager, and her daughter Mary, I warrant we must be friends with someone. That's only practical."

"Aye, and his Grace is both crafty and practical." He rose and kissed her good-by. He would soon be in the glitter of a thousand candles shining down on the beauty of Whitehall, the great tapestried hangings, the brilliant gowns of the women and the even more brilliant dress of the men. Katryn pictured it all in her mind. Henry himself would be there, even his caps ablaze with jewels. Think of the music that would pour from the musicians' gallery above the diners! Think of the singing, the gay rollicking songs of the day, arching up into the rafters with their lightheartedness! Think of the swarming palace, with its hundred chimneys rising squat and fat above its endless peaked roofs! What excitement must it not hold! Katryn sighed deeply, and went back to the solar and began to write to Jane. Poor Jane! She was exiled too.

The next morning she was sick again. And the next. And on the fourth day she realized what was the matter.

The realization was shattering. A fear she had not known she had, raised its head in all its ugliness. She shook with terror as she retched into the basin that Meg held. Tears streamed down her face, and sweat was over her whole body. All the pain, all the suffering she had once borne was back upon her, worse than before. Her imagination reviewed those endless days in bed; her mind tried to tell her that this time she would not be pushed down a flight of stairs, but she refused that comfort and, sick with terror, took to her bed. She had Meg draw the curtains and huddled under the quilts while she half slept and terrible dreams pursued her. Thus passed the whole of the fifth of March.

On the sixth day, Lord Latimer demanded admittance to her room. She tried to deny him entrance, for she did not want to tell him she was with child. She was ashamed of her fears, and ashamed she couldn't control them. She lay in bed and sobbed, and refused to answer his questions. Distraught, he called in a doctor.

The first sight of Dr. Huicke in his black gown and cap, and his servant trailing behind with the black bag, made Katryn cry out in alarm. Dr. Huicke motioned Lord Latimer to withdraw, and then he sat on a stool by the bed and commanded the curtains opened. There was something in his manner that gave Katryn courage. She raised slightly from her position to look at him. "Suppose you tell me, my lady, what ails thee?" he asked and took her hand.

She hadn't combed her hair for two days. She looked at him with huge eyes, golden gleams of fear shooting from them. She breathed quick, like an animal in distress. For a beautiful woman, she was certes in terror, he thought with commiseration. But it was fairly common, he knew. "Madam," he said, "are you undone because you are with child?"

"Aye," she burst out, pushing back her tangled curls. "I like to ha' died afore!" She fastened her eyes on his face, and hung onto his hand. Beads of sweat stood out on her forehead, and Dr. Huicke said kindly, "But this time you shall not, my lady. Tell me what happed before."

Katryn poured out the story, in rapid spurts. She kept eying Dr. Huicke to see if he were comprehending her, and so she went back and forth weaving a word pattern, until, though it was badly jumbled, it became like a picture to Dr. Huicke.

He smiled at her, because he was relieved. He said forcefully, "Why, madam, you've naught to fret over or worry about—nay, nor fear!" He looked so truly cheerful that she sat up straight and tried a smile.

"Mayhap you're right," she said, in a normal tone.

"Certes I'm right. You should be proud."

Proud. The word remained in her mind. She sank back on her pillows and watched him take his leave, bidding him good-by from her bed. An hour later, dressed in her prettiest gown, she confronted her husband with sparkling eyes and told him her news.

Lord Latimer was proud, too; kind and loving, he was a perfect husband, she thought, and better than she deserved. Then nothing must do but that she scribble off the exciting news to Anne and Lucy and Jane. Those messages dispatched, she sat back and waited for the recipients of her letters to arrive in person, full of flurry and congratulations.

Instead she got notes back from Lucy and Anne; their duties prevented their coming. Katryn was disappointed. She was even more disappointed when Lord Latimer told her that he thought it wise to start for Yorkshire immediately, before the child she carried grew large enough to discommode her for traveling.

She gave her consent because there was no alternative. And the next week she set forth for Snape Hall, only this time without either Lucy or Anne, for Nan Boleyn would not give her permission. "She's heard we don't countenance her, I warrant," Katryn said, and Lord Latimer agreed.

"Aye," he said. "She knows well who mislikes her. And she never forgets an injury."

But once back in Snape Hall, and after two days in bed following the long, arduous journey, Katryn forgot the Queen and her malice. Snape Hall was too far from London to concern itself with royal affairs; it existed for and by itself.

Spring came tardily. Lord Latimer had taken to going away for weeks at a time. Katryn buried herself in the enormous task of running the huge establishment, which roused her before dawn and kept her occupied until, with the rest of the household, she sat in the front pew and heard evening prayer.

Her child grew. But she herself waxed thin and white; shadows circled her eyes, and her feet and ankles hurt. As she was dressing one day, she looked down at her figure. "My little knave maketh my body quite grotesque." She held out her arm. "Look how thin I am, Meg."

Meg worried visibly; she wore her concern like her apron, and it struck some fear into Katryn. Later that night, not being able to sleep, she wrote to Jane Seymour, asking her to come stay a month at Snape Hall. Surely Jane would come! She would be of immense comfort.

When Jane's return letter arrived two weeks later, Katryn could hardly wait to open it. But it was evident after she had read the first line that Jane was not coming. She said, "Mistress Jane cannot come, Meg." She read on, turning the sheet of thick paper.

Meg stood silent. Finally she asked, "Why, madam?"

Why, indeed? thought Katryn. Because the King himself is coming to see Jane; his Grace has included Wolf Hall in his summer progresses —when Henry traveled about the land and stayed with the various families who were chosen to be honored by his presence.

Katryn laid down the letter. Henry in pursuit of Jane! What did it mean? Katryn took up Jane's letter again.

> We are nearly mad with the preparations for his Grace's visit; he will stay ten days! You can imagine, Katryn, what a state my lady mother is in, and how many orders fly out of her mouth. But everyone around is sending food, and extra beds, and candles, and all manner of things—I truly cannot tell you. And we are having the upper windows glassed, and a pavilion constructed on the lawn for eating and dancing and music. I wish very much that you could be here, for Lucy and Anne are coming."

Katryn laid down the letter. She had never felt so alone. Within her body her child stirred.

Meg said, "Madam, come upstairs and lie down. 'Tis soon time to change thy gown."

Katryn rose and let Meg lead her upstairs and unhook her gown. She washed her face and hands and was about to put on her dressing gown when she noticed the fresh blood on her shift.

Katryn climbed wearily into bed and sank back on the pillows. Meg had gone for Mistress Nell, and Katryn found herself almost in a swoon of depression and weariness. Mistress Nell was worried too, when she came in. But Katryn assured her, even in a weak voice, she had no pain, no pain whatever. Mistress Nell then told her to stay in bed and not to rise.

Katryn remained in bed a week, at the end of which time Lord Latimer came home. He sat in Katryn's room, talking late into the night, doubly distressed—for her and for his country. For it seemed that Snape Hall was within the reach of Henry's long arm after all, and that Cromwell's commissioners were already about the land. Tomorrow two of them were coming to Snape Hall to administer the oath of supremacy.

Lord Latimer said, "We must take it, you and I and all the house."

That night he drank an extra glass of wine. Early the next morn he was up, and Katryn rose and dressed too. At nine every male and female of the great house were assembled in the hall, and there they swore before Cromwell's men to honor the King as head of the English Church. Not the Pope any longer, but the King of England was the Lord's representative on earth—or at least, on English earth. Yorkshire men and women swore thus, but thought their own thoughts.

The warm days of July seemed to aid Katryn. She felt better and gained a little weight and had no more bleeding. On the ninth of July she came out into the garden to find old Lord Darcy with her husband.

"Are you two conspiring here, among the gooseberries?" she asked.

They looked guilty. She frowned at them. Katryn was fond of Lord Darcy; he was almost eighty, full of wonderful tales of the past, and lusty enough to enjoy the present. He said softly, "We were speaking of the Earl of Poverty."

Katryn had heard the name. The so-called earl went about the country masked, telling of Cromwell's iniquities. "I've heard he speaks against the King himself," Katryn said. "Do you know who he is?" She sat down on the stone bench, the men sitting on either side of her.

"Aye, indeed," said Lord Darcy. "I know he is a brave man, and one with whose words I agree, and I know that what he stands for is right, and that what he is doing is dangerous. But if you mean do I know his name, no. I do not." Then he added, "And I am happy I don't, for 'tis too fearful a secret to share."

Lord Latimer contemplated the fruit trees near them and the laden bushes. "Oh, 'tis not so dangerous as that, my lord."

"I misagree," Darcy said flatly. "Traveling about haranguing the countryside, and speaking with his peers against the oath of supremacy—the court has got wind of him, and the King will have too. And I should not envy him were his name known, for the King's wrath would surely follow him. Well, my dear, I must take my leave." He rose, and Katryn, sensing that her husband wished to have a word with him privately, bade him Godspeed and stayed in the garden whilst the two men strolled off in the direction of the stables.

After Lord Darcy rode off, Lord Latimer rejoined his wife in the garden. Katryn said idly, "I've been thinking."

Lord Latimer looked amused. "I never know what to expect when you preface your sentences with that."

"I've been thinking," said Katryn throwing him a smile, "that it is odd the Earl of Poverty has never come here."

"I do not want him here," Lord Latimer replied.

"But he has visited all the county families," she persisted, "and I cannot think who he could be, less 'tis thee."

Latimer stiffened and glanced at her with real surprise. "Katryn!" he exclaimed.

"I was jesting," she said hastily. But the idea kept nagging in her mind, and a faint fear stirred her. In the distance she heard the sound of the bells.

Latimer rose. "Supper time," he said with relief, "and I have a bitter announcement to make."

All were assembled at supper when Lord Latimer, at the head of the great table with all the household stretching down and away from him, rang his bell and rose. The head groom absently picked at his teeth with his knife whilst he waited, and Lord Latimer pointed an accusing finger at him. Then he spoke.

"Two days ago, on the seventh of this month, our former great lord chancellor, Sir Thomas More, having refused to take the oath of supremacy to his Grace, suffered a martyr's death. This night we shall have a memorial service, which you are bidden to attend, to pray for your souls and for the soul of the good Sir Thomas, and for the King. May God forgive him."

Lord Latimer sat down. The household resumed its eating. There was almost no talk, but a kind of sullen silence.

Katryn whispered to her husband. " 'Tis tragic, my lord!"

But he looked satisfied, and she wondered why. He said, in explanation, "They resent it fierce, and that is what I wish." Absently he handed his unfinished plate to his almoner, who took it gravely and went to lay Lord Latimer's uneaten scraps into the dish for the poor. Lord Latimer rose then, and assisted Katryn from the great hall.

August was a busy month, and September brought the harvest. Everyone helped, even young John, who when he knelt for Katryn's blessing at night still had straw stuck in his blond curls.

On the night of September fifteenth, Katryn began to have pain. Alarmed, Mistress Nell put her right to bed. For a week, again, she stayed there, but at the end of that time she gave birth to a premature, stillborn child. She looked once at the tiny face, touching her hand to the lifeless cheek. "He is still warm from me," she said, "still warm. My little son." She looked at Mistress Nell uncomprehending. Lord Latimer, with tears in his eyes, leaned down to take the dead child from her arms, for he was afraid suddenly that she would not let the child go.

But she did; only when Mistress Nell started to wrap the baby in the shroud did she make a move to protest. Then, like an animal deprived of its young, she gave a loud cry and started to get out of bed. Lord Latimer caught her, and she fainted dead away in his arms.

Late that night Lord Latimer sat alone in his closet, again drinking an unaccustomed extra glass of wine. He was pampering himself, he was sure, but he was getting older and the events of life were taking a heavier toll than they used to. For neither my mind, nay, nor muscle or bone has its former resilience, he thought. Tonight Katryn and I have lost our son. If that were not enough, this summer he had set himself a hard task. The despised and unworthy Cromwell must be displaced from the right hand of the King, and the nation freed from the evil that he was working against God and the people.

Lord Latimer was a sensible man. He knew well enough that to dislodge a King's minister was a hard task and one which a royal master would be inclined to regard as treason. Only too aware of what Henry would think of this unwanted interference in his affairs, Lord Latimer was also only too sure of what his God would deem just and right action on the part of a Christian gentleman. He had made the choice on the firm grounds of his deep religion and respect for the cloth, the Pope, and the ancient Catholic Church. Yorkshire was seething with revolt, and it was his clear duty to channel it into a river of protest which would drown Cromwell in its rising waters. It was for this reason that he was going to eschew London this winter and stay at home where he was needed. Plainly his place was at Snape Hall.

But when he imparted this news to Katryn, still in bed two weeks later, she turned over on her side, and although she whispered it didn't matter, that she didn't care where she lived, he felt guilty for he had been unable to think of something to rouse her from her apathy.

October began very cold. Katryn said she couldn't keep warm out of bed; so although it lacked two weeks until he usually gave orders to start the fires, he kept them burning in her room and urged her to rise and let her bed be made up as a couch, so she could get dressed and recline upon it. " 'Twill do thee good to dress, sweetheart," he said.

She shook her head. She had had a letter that morn from Jane. Listlessly she held it out for him to read. Jane wrote that she was returning to court at the King's express wish. Ned was to be with her so that none should think there was aught amiss or that there was aught improper in her position. Henry wanted her close, and he needed her. At the end of the letter she added that Nan Boleyn was with child.

Lord Latimer laid down the letter. "Rise and answer it," he said. "I wonder what it means?" His thoughts raced. The Queen with child, and Henry bringing Jane Seymour to court to be near him. How much involved was the King? He glanced down at the letter again and then noted the crest of the Dukes of Suffolk. "Why, you had a letter from Kate Willoughby."

"Aye, they came together," Katryn murmured.

"May I read it?"

She looked surprised. "Of course, my lord," she said wearily.

Kate wrote a letter as dashing as her style of dress, as plumed as her puffy sleeves, and as full of color.

God knows what will hap, [she began] and wait till you hear, what with Jane being here with us, only in separate apartments!

197

Lord Latimer read on, caught up in Kate's booming style.

I miss you truly, and so does Jane. Anne is very close to the
Queen, for Nan can trust her. You know we are not very popular with Nan, right now; she and my lord husband never did
see things together. However, my mother is here with us, and
she is most distraught over the plight of her oldest friend, the
Princess Dowager, who lies ill, and my mother has been refused
permission to visit her. Our first Queen is so afeared for her life,
that her few women cook her eggs right in her room over the
fireplace, and even the frying pans are washed right under her
eyes. She is much weaker and hears Mass five times a day, poor
soul, and she lies there in a room with bare stone walls, and they
say it smells of cooked food and incense till it sickens one. My
lord my husband is going to try to persuade his Grace to let my
lady mother visit her old friend. But you know even the Princess
Mary may not go to her mother, so no one knows where the
wind will blow. Dear Katryn, I wish I could see thee! A fine
friend is so hard to be parted from! And even though I do not
see thee, I can still hear your merry warm laugh. I will write
again, at Christmas. And pray burn this.

Lord Latimer rose, and took the letter and laid it on the flames.
"One should not mention we had a former queen by name of
Katharine, who lies ill and prisoned," he said bitterly. "Nay, she is
now a princess, and her daughter, our Princess, a bastard!"

"Marry, my lord, such vehemence makes my head ache," Katryn
said. "And I wanted to read the letter again!"

"You might forget to do as Kate says. 'Tis best burned. I want no
evidence about this house!"

She raised herself on her elbow. "They'd find naught," she said.
But she was uncertain.

Lord Latimer now threw all his wit and energy into the problem
of making his wife well again. First he made provision for Mass to
be said every day for thirty days in the Cathedral at York, for the
soul of the little boy who had not lived. For this Katryn roused herself from her bed and accompanied him to York; in the great cathedral they knelt close together, his hand clasping hers. "Cast thyself

upon the mercy of the Lord, Katryn," he said. "Pray for strength and it shall be given thee."

Tears streamed down her cheeks. When she raised her head through misty eyes, she saw the soaring nave, rising almost to heaven; the great stained-glass windows with the figure of the Virgin looked down at her through the candlelight.

"She lost her son, more bitterly than you did," Lord Latimer said.

The choir sang, the boys' voices pure and high; the crystal notes enveloped her. Images in their niches gazed down compassionately at the humans who struggled for peace.

"In the house of God you shall find rest," Lord Latimer said, and unable to answer any of his words, she bent her head and sobbed.

Yet when she rode home in the December twilight, with the sky a pale winter blue, the cold nudging her cloak and lying against her cheeks, she felt some measure of the strength she had asked for, a recurrence of pleasure stirring within, an awareness of the gladness of sights and sounds, the tasting, the smell of the business of living. When she alighted in front of the welcoming torches set in the stone of Snape Hall, she stopped to pat her horse.

She said to her husband, "You were right. I feel much recovered. But I was silly and foolish, and I shouldn't ha' needed to ask the Lord for help."

Lord Latimer smiled, a delighted smile. "Come within, sweetheart," he said, almost gaily. "We have fresh roasted ribs of beef for supper!"

He brought her a pair of little dogs, silky and smooth. At Christmas, he gave her a bird in a golden cage. He brought her these gifts on the occasions of his returns from his many trips, some short, some long. He had resumed his place in her bed, which he had forborne to occupy since her pregnancy; and although she found it difficult to respond to him, she was glad to welcome him back. And after he had lain with her, she felt content that she had received his love, for maybe it was the seed of life and she would have another child.

"I think only a barren woman knows how bitter her lot," she said one day openly to him. "I feel as though I'm being cheated. And I hate being cheated! I won't endure it!"

He said, "You're not barren, and the wine has loosened your tongue."

"The wine and Christmas Eve," she said. "I was afraid to confess it to you, when you knew how afeared I was when I first found my-self with child. But it seems a million years ago! And now I want one!" She stared into the flames, and something she had said or thought brought a forceful image into her mind; for just a moment she could see Tom Seymour plain and hear his voice: "You are thick and muddle-headed, always charging forth on the wrong path! You don't think, you act!" She bit her lip. I wonder where he is this eve. There must be a great banquet now at Greenwich, where the King always is at Christmas. She said aloud, "We should get letters soon, from Anne at least, and mayhap Jane and a Christmas message from Kate."

But Anne did not write, which was strange. Nor was there word from Jane, save for a present of a pretty sapphire ring and a brief note on which Jane had writ, "This bears my love and devotion, Katryn."

"What a dear gift," Katryn said. She kept Jane's messenger over-night; he wore the green-and-white livery of the Tudor pages and was accompanied by two servants.

Lord Latimer eyed the ring narrowly. "Do you think she is al-ready the King's mistress?"

Katryn hesitated. "It may be that his Grace gave her leave to pick from the royal household for her gifts this New Year's.

"That usually means—" Lord Latimer broke off, for he saw she was troubled and did not want to think of Jane as the expensive gift might indicate. But in truth she was thinking not of Jane, but of Tom Seymour.

What Tom Seymour was thinking he was going to make very plain. It was the night of the twenty-ninth of January, and he came quickly along one of the huge galleries at Hampton Court. He was in seaman's garb, wearing still his master's coat, his two body servants came behind, one bearing his sword, and the other, a villainous-looking fellow with one swinging golden earring, carrying the saddlebags which dripped melting snow on the big black-and-white squares of flooring. At the turn of the gallery they parted, Tom Seymour going on by himself in search of Ned.

He found Ned alone, working at his desk, his face thin and white and his dark eyes heavy with sleep. It was one o'clock. And yet, Tom Seymour knew that tonight the palace did not sleep; it quivered and stirred and was plagued by all manner of human emotions, as many and as varied as the occupants of its thousand rooms. These were troublous times, Tom Seymour thought; different, much different from the clean sweeping ocean wind and the heaving deck of the ship he had just left. He stood there in the doorway and said, "I wish to God I weren't here!"

Ned raised his head, laid down his quill. He said naught, but smiled slightly and motioned his brother to the other chair. "You look well," he offered, and waited for the outright verbal attack he knew was coming.

"You look poorly. Perhaps it is the black you wear. I gather it is mourning for Queen Katharine!"

"The Princess Dowager," Ned corrected. "Aye, she was buried today. I shall not wear this more."

Tom Seymour said, "I hear half the court was in mourning, and the other half celebrated with wine and song. You know, of course, that it is just one more thorn in Henry's side, this open discord, and that his hate of it will eventually fall crushingly upon the woman who caused it all."

"Our queen," said Ned. "The beauteous Nan."

"Tonight tragedy struck the beauteous Nan, as you call her. She was delivered of a premature, stillborn son. What did his Grace say?"

Ned raised his head. He looked as though he were trying to remember, although indeed he remembered perfectly. "His Grace said, 'I see well God does not intend to give me a male child.'"

"Is that all he said?" Tom inquired.

"He said, 'I shall deal with you when you are up and about.'"

"Comforting words to a woman who has lost a child," Tom said, not bothering to lower his voice; Ned looked at the closed door. "I hear also that Nan says she miscarried because she came into the antechamber to find Jane in the King's arms. Is that true?"

Ned said quickly, "In justice to Jane, hear this. The Duke of Norfolk came bursting into Nan's chambers this morn to blurt out his Grace had taken a terrible fall and was lying like dead—thrown from his steed. In about three minutes Henry came striding in, muddied, and Jane, alone in the antechamber, flung herself at him, crying out with joy. Just at that moment Nan burst in on them and, having seen, herself uttered a loud cry and rushed from the room screaming."

"And then she miscarried," Tom said, ending the story. "A pretty tale."

"It is perfectly true!"

"I don't doubt it's true," Tom Seymour said irritably. "But why should Jane be so accessible to fondle publicly? What are you doing, Ned? You're not watching her, or—"

"I'm not a duenna," Ned said with anger, for he had heard that was what Kate Willoughby called him, and it rankled.

"But you're the most ruthless gambler I've ever known, Ned, and it looks now as if you're gambling with lives, and the forfeit is Nan. Now that Queen Katharine is so conveniently dead, there is only one life between Jane and Henry, and that life quite expendable. All you need, Ned, is for Jane to whisper into his Grace's ear that she is with child. And then—it is not much of a gamble, is it? For what is one woman's life against the succession?" He snapped his fingers. Rising to his feet, he leaned his big brown hand on the desk and looked down at Ned's face. "By God's most precious soul, Ned, it's no gamble at all, for you've not a penny in the game!"

Ned rose too, and went over to the sideboard and poured a cup of wine, which he proffered to his brother. "I don't have a maidenhead to trade with, Tom," he said.

Tom Seymour grinned. "Does morality sit ill on me?" he asked, and said he'd changed his mind. He would have some gin. He sipped it and was thoughtful a moment. "I still don't like it, Ned. It smacks of betrayal."

Ned said mildly, "Tom, Jane loves the King, and he loves her."

"Does that make you any less of a panderer?" Tom said. "You wash your hands of the consequences?" He tossed off the gin and made a face. "I don't like the taste or smell of it, any more than I do this stuff. But this warms my belly and you don't. The carrion crow feasts on death, digging out the entrails with his beak. Thus you wait, for Nan Boleyn!"

Ned Seymour said, "It is inevitable, Tom."

Tom Seymour said slowly, "Is not divorce possible? Using the precontract Nan made with Henry Percy when they were in love?"

Ned shook his head. "Great passions have been loosed among all, and most in the King's breast." His voice was very low. "I think he wants to kill her, for his passion of love for her has changed to true hatred. You called me a crow. That was Wolsey's name for Nan— the night crow. Remember, Tom? Remember, too, she wouldn't let him alone. She wanted this—" He waved his hand, for they were at Hampton Court, the great palace that the Cardinal had built. "She compassed his death, for he didn't obtain the divorce she wanted. There are too many crimes on her soul, too much blood on her hands." He shook his head. "She cannot go free. The seeds of destruction she has sowed herself."

Tom set down his empty cup. "It grows late. Tell me honest. Is it too late to send Jane home?"

"Aye," said Ned Seymour.

"I called you a panderer. I expected honest anger; that is what I would have got a year ago. Ned, do not grow devious. Let us speak out with each other. For if we cannot, whom then shall we trust?"

"I wasn't angry, because you were partly right," Ned said.

"For God's sake, you should still resent it, openly." He held out his hand, and took Ned's in a firm grip. "I shall always tell you what I honestly feel. Good night, Ned." At the door he paused. "I preferred the days," he said slowly, "when we soldiered together." The door closed, and Ned Seymour heard the sound of his footsteps die away.

10

Rain poured down onto Snape Hall. It beat against the windows and ran cascading off the slate roofs. It was not yet dawn.

Behind closed bed curtains Anne Herbert slept. But neither the heavy curtains nor sleep could shut out from her ears the sound of Bess Parr's screams. Anne woke, full of terror and full of the dreams fed by the distant agonized cries; in her ears she could hear her own voice saying, as she had in her dream, "But there was just such a box, lying to the right of the stairway in the White Tower as we passed by."

Sitting there in bed, she put her hands over her ears; and the young girl who shared her bed, a cousin of Will's, sat up too and said, "Oh, madam, madam, what's amiss?"

Anne tried to wipe her mind free of the dream that had pursued her in these early hours of morning. What had the guard said? "But those boxes, my lady, are arrow boxes and would not be long enough for a coffin."

"They will be now," Anne had said, for Nan Boleyn's body lay there in the May sunlight on the grass at her feet, and her little dark head was lying by itself. "Help me, Lucy," she cried, and together they laid Nan's body in the arrow box there on Tower Green.

Now Anne said, "I shall never forget, never!" She swallowed. "The screams woke me, and started me adreaming of what was past. Get thee up, child, and fetch me some warmed water. I shall rise and dress and go help the Lady Latimer."

"But she said you were not to come in your condition, madam!"

"Aye," said Anne wearily, "but in truth, I cannot stay here." Clumsily she got out of bed, pushing at the curtains and feeling for her furry slippers. It was a cold morning, and gratefully she slid her arms into her velvet robe. Her baby was due soon, and she must make every effort not to take cold, or chill. She rang her bell imperatively for one of the grooms of the chamber who attended these apartments. Soon the fire would be burning bright; soon the great house would be fully awake, its hustle and bustle a reassuring comfort. "I must go help my sister," she said, "for I owe her much. What would I ha' done after the Queen's death, had she not taken me in?"

Katryn had been up most of the night, and Lucy with her. Mistress Nell, her gray hair escaping her headband, her eyes starting out of her head, was completely agitated for Bess was the worst patient Mistress Nell had ever had—"barring none, madam, none," Mistress Nell cried.

Bess screamed and kicked and struggled, so that no one could help her. She writhed on the bed; she had knocked over a table with two basins of hot water, and the floor swam where Goodie had not yet wiped it up. "Using the wrong cloth you are," Mistress Nell screamed at Goodie, who was on her knees. "Oh, my God," Mistress Nell ended, whereupon Goodie began to weep.

"Don't cry, Goodie," said Katryn warningly, "for I am losing my temper, rapid!" She rang the bell on the mantel, rang it hard and insistent, and the first groom hastening along, heard both bells at once. He knocked, and Katryn bade him enter.

Keeping his eyes from Bess, he looked straight at his mistress, as he had been rigorously taught to do. "Fetch more wood," Katryn said, "and bid the assistant housekeeper to me at once. And send a page."

"Aye, madam."

Katryn approached the bed. The guardrail had been removed, and Bess, in her blouse only, was still writhing from side to side. "The pain is constant!" Bess screamed.

"Lie still," cried Katryn, "and let Mistress Nell help you!"

Mistress Nell came close.

"The babe is coming," Bess cried. She gave a final kick with one leg, and her foot caught Mistress Nell on the temple. She reeled across the room, and then righted herself. Indeed Bess was right; her babe was born.

Mistress Nell took her scissors and cut the cord and gave the babe— "And 'tis a boy," she muttered—into the clean linen Goodie held.

Goodie took the child over to the table where the warm water was ready and sponged off the infant and gave it to Katryn, going back to the big bed to help her mother finish delivering Bess of the afterbirth. There was silence in the room, except for the little wails of the baby. Katryn kept hearing those little cries, and tears came into her eyes. What a woman's body achieved was truly a miracle. "Little red-faced mite," she whispered. She turned to throw a smile at Bess, who lay so quiet now; in a minute she would show her the child. To her horror she saw Mistress Nell sliding slowly to the floor. What was the matter? Mistress Nell was sick! She lay there on her side. Katryn, the babe in one arm, again seized her bell and rang it and rang it till the sound echoed through the house.

"We tried to tie Bess's feet, but she kicked free," Katryn said. "Mistress Nell lies more comfortable now, but she cannot speak, and she cannot move the right side of her body. Poor thing!"

Katryn sipped the wine she held. Her head throbbed. But at least Bess's room had been cleaned, and she and the baby slept, and poor Mistress Nell slept too, with Goodie curled at the foot of her bed. "I'm glad you weren't there," Kathryn ended, looking at Anne, for she was very big with child and Katryn thought the baby very low in her body, so any time now Anne could expect. Taking more wine, she wondered what they would do without Mistress Nell if it happened soon. She passed her hand over her forehead, and decided she must send for a midwife from the nearest big house.

Could it be the middle of September? Where had the spring and summer gone? Nan Boleyn had been executed the morning of May nineteenth; they said that Henry waited ahorse nearby, to hear the boom of the cannon that announced her death, and then he had ridden off to Wolf Hall to marry Jane Seymour and make her England's new queen. Anne and Lucy—who had been with Nan Boleyn in the Tower, and had seen her to the headsman's block—had come to Snape Hall. Four days later Will Parr had arrived with Bess, giving her into Katryn's care till her child was born.

Lord Latimer had hardly been home all the summer months. June, July, and August had fled past, with Katryn bearing the load of his duties and hers too. Anne had been sick. Five months with child, she could not forget the tragic death of the queen she had served. Endlessly she talked of Nan and of her spirit. " 'I shall be called Nan Sans-Tête,' " the Queen had said, in her gay and mocking manner. Then she would cry and cry, and say she was innocent! She had been accused of treason and adultery. Once she said, 'Shall I open my body, then, to prove my innocence?' "

"Don't speak of it, Anne," Katryn cried. "Pray do not!"

"The blood," Anne whispered. "Katryn, it streamed out from her severed head, and her neck! And her head, lying there with its little cap! Still on!"

"Anne, you must forget! You must! In the fall you will have to return. Will is at court."

"I cannot serve Jane," Anne said.

Katryn was silent. Then she said, "Anne, most truly, it was not Jane's fault. I think this was between Nan and the King. I would not blame Jane. And if what you say is true, Jane will need you."

"Aye, that is so," Lucy said. "Jane will need us."

The wind blew. The rain beat against the window. Anne said, "And now poor Mrs. Nell! Life is so sad, so miserable!" Her mouth puckered.

"Pray don't weep," Katryn said. "I cannot bear it. My head feels as if hammers are pounding it. And of all people to speak of life! You have two lives, right now. If you knew how I wished for a child!" She rose, and went to the door.

Anne, blinking her eyes, managed a smile, "You are right, sister."

"Take some more wine," Katryn said. "I shall be back soon, but I promised the choirmaster I'd hear the choir this morn afore he takes it to Richmond."

Katryn sat in the gallery to hear the choir; she thought the music was better here in the loft. She leaned her back against the hard wood and closed her eyes. Her mouth opened slightly as though to drink in the sound. Peace enveloped her. She did not sleep, but she seemed to float on the high pure voices.

She leaned over the gallery and waved her hand. "Perfect," she called down. She rose. "I must commend all of you, every single one! I am so proud!" And they looked well too. All their choir robes were new; they would make a fine show, both at Richmond, where they would sing in the church, and at the various great houses where they would perform. They would be gone a month. "And if Lord Latimer were here, he would commend you also. Mayhap you shall meet with your lord on your travels."

She made her way out of the chapel and down the loft steps. I wish I knew exactly where my lord was, myself, she thought. I don't like this going about the country, for 'tis trouble brewing. One would have thought, with the death of the hated queen, that matters would simmer down. Indeed not. They were worse, what with the whole county hating Cromwell and wanting his blood. One could not speak with a county man without hearing words against the King's minister. Even the bailiff grumbled about Cromwell. The bailiff . . . It would be soon time to go over the harvest figures, and the thought made her head ache. "I wish to God my lord would return," she said aloud, and entering the great hall, under the stairway, she saw Lord Latimer.

She gave a cry of delight. "Thou'rt home!" She ran forward to greet him. And what a tale she had for him! Her eyes sparkled, and she raised herself on tiptoe to give him a welcoming kiss. "Oh, but much has happed, my lord! Bess has had a son!"

"Oh?" he said. His attention seemed to be far away.

"And Mistress Nell was taken, sudden! And—"

"Katryn," he said, "this will shock you. There has been an uprising in Lincolnshire."

Katryn stared at him. "In Lincolnshire?" But that was not too near.

"Aye. Come into the winter parlor. I wish to speak with you. And Anne is there; she may as well hear, too."

Running footsteps on the stairway caused Katryn to glance past him. Lord Latimer handed his head groom a large key ring. Katryn knew what it was for—the old armory, a small round room at the foot of the ancient keep, unused now. She started to cry out, but swallowed her cry as she intercepted a warning look from her husband. He drew her along. In the winter parlor, before Anne and Lucy, he spoke but briefly.

"Lincolnshire is in revolt. Yorkshire will follow. We are ready to move, to march. Already the royal castle at Pontefract is in our hands —given over by its governor! This is a Pilgrimage of Grace, and our banners carry the five wounds of Christ. We have a motto: 'One God, one King, one Faith.' I am taking fifty men with me—

they are being armed now. We go forth with your blessing and, I hope, your love. There is not much time. I hope to be at Pontefract this eve, and the roads are muddy."

Anne sat still and stony-faced. Then she rose. "Ye may have doomed all of us to a traitor's death," she said. She brushed past Lord Latimer, and Katryn would have run after her only Lord Latimer seized her arm.

"Wait, Katryn."

She turned. She felt dazed.

"I'm leaving you a good fifty men here. And—"

Katryn cried, "Do not go! Do not go! Anne is right!"

"Anne is foolish," he said. "This is a just cause! I have worked, and spared none of myself."

Katryn said wildly, "You've been conniving against the King! All summer!" She tried to digest the fact. How could she not have suspected? How could she have been so blind? "I'm terrified," she said. "I'm terrified!"

"I am leaving you fifty or more menservants. There is naught to fear. Yorkshire men will not harm this house."

"But what o' the King's men? For they will come, surely!"

"We shall stand between you and them. And with our numbers, there's no harm possible to you. Stephen Hamerton is taking all his men!"

"The devil with Hamerton!" she cried. "He and you, and that Earl of Poverty! I wish he'd never been born! Going about the county, masked, raising tempers and inciting to revolt! He must be mad! And you must be mad to follow him! I just wish he would show his masked face here! I would—" she broke off, she stared at him in incredulous horror. "'*Twas* thee," she breathed, for he was holding a small black mask.

Under her eyes he nodded, he took the mask over to the flames and laid it upon them. Lord Latimer stood watching the flames shrivel up the mask. He spoke no word till it was completely gone to ashes. Then he turned to his wife.

"The Earl of Poverty is dead, now, and there is no further need for thee to fret." He patted her shoulder. He seemed bemused; she could not reach him. With unseeing eyes she watched him go to the door. He said, "I shall send messages, and keep you informed. Good-by."

She ran to him. "Wear your leathern cloak! My lord! Take care! Oh, for God's sake, take care!"

"I shall, Katryn. Good-by."

It had happened so quickly she couldn't believe it. She stood there in the center of the room, alone. She looked toward the fire. The mask was gone. Surely it meant death. Henry Tudor would never forgive the Earl of Poverty were his identity ever revealed. She shuddered. Maybe if the truth were known she would have to die too, as his consort. Her legs shook. The headache which had plagued her returned in vigor, pounding through her brain. She wanted to go upstairs, but she couldn't face Anne now. She sank down onto the floor and rested her head in her hands. The fire burned, but she was cold all over. A long time ago Tom Seymour had warned her, and warned Lord Latimer. Those warnings had gone unheeded, and what was to be the result? Then she realized that Lord Latimer had not yet left. A kind of duty stood her on her feet, and she went out into the big court. The men were mounted. She pulled out her bright kerchief from her savenapes pocket, and waved and waved it as Lord Latimer rode out of Snape Hall.

She had lost track of time. But when she came up the wide stairway, the sun poured onto the gallery floors and her mind registered that it must be almost time for dinner. She went to find Anne.

Anne wanted to dine privately. Katryn shook her head. "No," she said, "for the good of the house we shall take dinner in the great hall today, as though all were as usual."

"How can they be as usual, with half the men gone?" Anne cried.

"We must behave as usual," Katryn said, crisply.

She found she was hungry. She stuffed food down, even the beans which normally she didn't like. After dinner, she commanded the almoner to tell all the rest of the male servants that she wished them to remain. With four sturdy knaves, she went to the old armory, and there they picked out the least rusty of the bills and pikes. Solemnly, standing at the head of the big table, Katryn watched the clumsy arms issued. There was some talking and joking among the men; they seemed in fine humor. Dismissing the men, Katryn went back to lock up the armory.

Alone there, in the small round room, she picked out two old pikes, heavy and short and murderous. Tucking one under each arm, she went back into the new wing. Under the stairway, in the shadow of an ancient suit of armor, she leaned the first pike against the knight's gauntlet, as though it rested against his fingers. The other she took upstairs with her. Anne gave a small cry when she saw it.

"I just feel better with a weapon to hand," Katryn said, and leaned the pike on the head bedpost; against the silk flounces it looked rather grim and silly, and she smiled.

But Lucy didn't think it laughable. "Imagine someone threatening thee, right in thy chamber."

Katryn looked from Lucy to Anne. She said, "You're both over-thrown, I warrant. We should all go up to the battlements and walk—aye, even you Anne—and let the wind blow the cobwebs out of our brains. There's no sense sitting here huddled afore the fire like it was doomsday!"

But she was not so sure herself. It was good to be outside, and as she paced back and forth, the country seemed as peaceful as always. There were the customary figures in the apple orchards, small as insects from here. The sun was bright now, the September day radiant; the trees were beginning to turn, and the towering oaks of the parkland were russet against the fall skies.

"If I know aught of Lincolnshire commons," Katryn said suddenly, "they'll pull in their horns soon enough! I lived amongst them!" She paced back and forth, but her headache still plagued her. "Tonight," she said, "we shall have supper in the hall, and I shall instruct the almoner to say a prayer. Then I am going to bed. I need sleep." God knew what the next days might bring.

She slept well and deeply. The next day began as always. No one could tell from Snape Hall that there was a revolt anywhere in England. Mistress Nell was a little better; she could not speak, but Goodie had raised her to a sitting position, and by questioning, Katryn learned Mistress Nell had some feeling in her right lower arm, that she could almost wiggle her fingers. She drank a little broth.

"You'll soon ha' recovered," Katryn told her cheerfully.

Bess was remarkably cheerful this morning. The baby slept and had sipped a bit of water, and the wet nurse was with Bess. Her two women were laying out her clothes, so she could see what she had.

"Thank the Lord I'll be able to wear a fine gown again," She said. She added slyly, "You don't know what it's like to have a baby."

"You might inquire for Mistress Nell's health," Katryn said. But I'm not going to bandy words, or quarrel with her, she thought; she's not worth it. "Today we must send a messenger to Will. And I shall send Father Lambert to you, and you can discuss the details of the christening, which I think had best be here." For you're not going to get out of Snape Hall for a while, my girl, she thought, to wear your fine gowns. She glanced at the profusion of satin and lace and velvet; one white velvet cloak with white fur was delectable, and Katryn imagined it wrapped around her own figure, with the white against her red gold hair.

"I stored two other boxes, Katryn," Bess said.

"I'll ha' them sent down to you." Let her play, she thought, she's just like a child. Still, she is woman enough to have a lusty young son, and I am not.

The day continued quiet. But by mid-afternoon when they walked on the battlements, they saw the first troop of horse gallop past. After them came men marching, men with accompanying riders, orderly, with their banners waving and the arms of their lord flying bravely. They passed quickly out of sight, and they had hardly gone when another just as orderly band appeared on the now dusty road. They were singing, and their voices carried strong and firm as the old hymn they marched to. The day was darkening, and Katryn hastened down into the hall and gave orders for the gates to be closed.

The night passed without incident. It was the following day that the bands of commons began to stream past Snape Hall, and that night Katryn saw the signal fires. They burned bright, as they had done on the Border—huge fires, sending streamers of sparks into the night skies. And the night was rent with sound. The voices did not sing hymns; these voices were raucous in shouts, and screams of laughter, and yells and curses. One band beat on the closed gates of Snape Hall, shouting epithets at a Yorkshire house that would not give them food. Then they went on, leaving the women awake and trembling in their beds. Katryn rose and dressed, and went up to the top of Snape Hall, where she could see the great fires burning, calling the men to battle, summoning the county to war. More untidy groups of men went by the gates, calling out for all to join—all to join. High above, Katryn watched them as the dawning skies grew gray. In the morning light when she descended, she realized in a flash, by the complete absence of male voices, that the rest of Snape Hall's men servants had deserted. At the very time when the first band of commons had banged on the gates, she had been alone in the great house with naught but women! And she had armed them! They had gone forth to the ancient summons; they had probably deserted when the first signal fire blazed high in the night skies.

"Oh, the knaves!" she cried aloud, beating her fist on the rail. "Oh, by God's most precious soul! Oh, what shall I do?" She ran down the rest of the steps. Maybe she was wrong. She darted through the great hall, through the old door into the pantry, through the buttery. All was quiet. She flung back the door to the first kitchen. The housekeeper stood there, wiping her eyes with her apron. Two maids were bent over the fire, and Wat was coming in the other door with the four Italian gardeners, all of them talking at once.

The housekeeper sniffed aloud. "We're trying our best to light the fires, my lady, and they've taken all the bread!" Then it was true. They were alone; the men had gone.

"The sturdiest maids must carry the water and bring the wood," Katryn was saying, and the housekeeper, Mistress Bissel, nodded. "Wat can pick a few to help in the stables and wi' the stock—in fact, some of them know much about the stock anyway."

By dinnertime the women had all been allotted various tasks. Father Lambert and the almoner both made a prayer; they had helped carve. Then all sat to dinner; as Katryn, from the head of the table, looked over the bent female heads and heard only the soft sound of women's voices, she tried to push her disquiet aside.

After dinner she insisted again that Anne and Lucy come with her, to get fresh air. It was misty and damp. It was the first day of October, Katryn realized. "We shan't stay long," she told Anne, for she looked pinched and frail. Katryn was worried about her, and about Mistress Nell, but there was no question of sending for another midwife; besides, Anne had had no trouble with her first child, and Goodie was older and more experienced now. Mistress Nell had trained her well. In the distance they could hear shouts.

"There are more commons," Anne whispered.

"They can't harm you here," Katryn said, straining her eyes to see through the mist. Then suddenly she did see. The first two men were carrying the usual banner, a piece of white cloth with the five wounds of Christ on it, clumsily daubed in red. They waved it back and forth, as behind them came other men, streaming out of the mist. They were shouting and running about.

"They'll never get to York that way," Katryn said contemptuously.

They came closer, and she saw they were running through the park to Snape Hall.

"What are they waving?" Anne asked tremulously, and Katryn herself was frightened.

"We'll not let them in, Anne," she said reassuringly.

The first ones were quite close now. It was then Katryn saw what the first one carried, and she could not be mistaken. She gasped in horror. The first man was waving a man's arm. Beside her Anne screamed.

"We tore them apart with our hands," the men below were shouting. "This is what haps to Cromwell's men!"

Katryn stared down at them. There must be fifty, she thought rapidly, and each and every one of them carrying a bit of a human being.

"Give us food, we want food!" The shouts pierced the air.

Anne looked down. "One of them is carrying a head," she said, and she put her hand on Lucy's arm. "Let us go within the hall, for if I see more blood and brutality, I shall swoon."

Katryn took her arm, and led her inside. Below they could hear the pounding on the gates. If they hit the door with their bills or pikes they could break it in. She ordered Anne into the bedroom, and went down the stairs. At the foot a little knot of women and Father Lambert had already gathered.

Katryn spoke quickly. "If they pound the door in, they may be so wild as to kill. If you will come with me, Father, mayhap we can send them away. Close and bolt the doors behind me, Wat."

If I don't do it now, she thought, I shall never do it. Thank God for Father Lambert. "We shall use the postern, the side door."

She stepped out into the misty day. She felt numb. Did they see her? She raised her voice. "Yorkshiremen," she called, "I am here."

In the court, the men turned from the great doors and faced her, coming slowly closer.

"List to me," she called.

There was silence. The man who held the head took another step toward her. He held the head by the hair. Katryn moistened her lips.

"We have almost no food, for our men have taken it to provide for their march to York. We are a handful of women; our lord is in Pontefract. You must go on and not molest us. You are on a pilgrimage. Father Lambert beside me will bless you and send you on your way. List to Father Lambert."

Father Lambert started to speak. Katryn heard nothing he said. Her knees trembled, her whole body shook. "Father Lambert," she whispered, "Oh, make haste, make haste!"

He raised his hand, and the men knelt. Whilst they did so, Katryn turned to the door and went inside. Father Lambert stayed but a moment, and then he, too, was in the old narrow hall. Katryn looked at him with unseeing eyes.

"They knelt there in the court for you!" she said. "And they were carrying pieces of men!"

" 'Twas your quick thought saved us and them," he said. "For you were right! Had they broken in the doors, God knows what they might not have done! I pray the Lord will forgive me for bestowing blessings on men who have killed so wantonly. But they have been much abused. But you, my lady—you were very brave!"

She said pityingly, "Why, Father, you mistake. I was terrified." She picked up her skirts, and went ahead of him into the hall. One of the Italian gardeners was leaning on his hoe, and she had a wild desire to scream with laughter. Instead she said, "You may all go about your duties. We shall sit to supper presently."

Night fell in Windsor. Midnight struck twelve booming strokes on the huge new clock.

At two, the guards heard the sound of horsemen coming fast, and at two fifteen a frightened page scurried up and along a wide gallery past the halberdiers to summon a groom of the chamber. The groom hastened to the gentlemen of the King's chamber. He laid his hand on the shoulder of a man soundly asleep, but a man who he knew would wake on the instant and be good-humored about it.

"Sir Thomas," he said softly.

It seemed to Tom Seymour he had just fallen asleep. He raised his head and propped himself up on his elbows. "Aye, Dick?" he said low, for within the room other men slept, and one was snoring loud.

As he listened to the groom's low voice, he leaned over and shook his page, who slept on the floor beside the big bed. Indeed he reckoned it had been but an hour—for he had an uncanny sense of time —since he had been playing whist. He swung his legs out of bed, not rousing his sleeping companion. Will Herbert grunted and slept on. In the faint light Tom Seymour slipped his arms into the robe the page held. He tied the belt and found his slippers. He splashed water on his face, and his sleepy page handed him a clean linen towel. Then he brushed his hair and, thrusting hands into his pockets, left the room and emerged into the gallery.

There was light here. Torches flared against the paneled walls, and Tom Seymour squinted his eyes, much as he did against the sun playing across the vastness of blue ocean. When he saw Thomas Borough, he suppressed an oath. His eyes went to the other men and summed them up quickly: trouble.

They were muddied, their clothes were in disarray, and one sleeve hung loose from Borough's jacket. For a brief moment Tom Seymour wondered whether Borough had permanently lost the use of the arm he had so cruelly mishandled; then he saw Borough's hand, with the torn coat sleeve swinging above it, and he said, "What news?"

Did Thomas Borough recognize him? He thought not. In any case he was too distracted. "Rebellion!" he burst out. "Revolt in Lincolnshire, Yorkshire! Both counties aflame! Aye, the signal fires burn!"

"Yorkshire?" asked Tom quietly. "Begin at the beginning, man, and don't talk fast."

That voice, Thomas Borough thought. He stared at the big man in the woolen dressing gown. Memories flashed through his mind. But he did as he was told: he talked, and not too fast.

When he had finished, Tom Seymour took the paper he handed him. Taking a step to stand nearer the torch, his eyes played across the scrawled words, and he spoke their import.

"You were waylaid and taken prisoner by the rebels as you traveled to London. . . . You were made to take this oath. . . . Yorkshire wants a different oath from Cromwell's. 'One Faith, one God, one King!' You were made to swear to't, and then you were sent from the rebels at Pontefract with these terms for his Grace. 'The abbeys to be restored, no tithes from the clergy, the heretic bishops to be put aside, and villain blood' "—he smiled a little—" 'to be banished from his Grace's council.'

"Well," he said. "I see there's much to be done this night." He pointed to the groom of the chamber. "Go rouse my lord my brother, and tell him to get dressed immediately and attend his Grace. You, Lord Borough, wait here, a moment." He strode to the door from which he had just come and called, "Will! Pig! Up and into your robes." He thrust his hands back into his pockets again and waited with Borough. In a minute the two men he had called plunged out, surprised and sleepy. Tom turned, and everyone followed in his wake through the privy chamber, an anteroom, and into the chamber of the King himself. While the others waited without the door, Tom Seymour went in.

He roused the King. In the King's huge bed, a page slept. He uncurled himself, and lighted candles. Henry stirred and sat up. Tom helped him into his dressing gown, and then Henry threw his legs over the bed and sat on the edge. He straightened his night cap. His narrow piercing eyes gleamed.

"Come in, Lord Borough," Tom Seymour called.

The four men filed in, Borough looking white as death. He came forward, saw he was indeed in the presence of the King, fell on one knee, helplessly proffering the paper.

Henry stared at him through even narrower eyes. Tom Seymour said, "There has been rebellion in Yorkshire, your Grace. Lord Borough was taken and made to swear an oath, and made to bring these terms to your Grace. But Lord Borough will tell his tale himself. Speak man. His Grace awaits."

Borough began, still on his knees. As the tale poured out again, Tom Seymour stepped back and left the room.

He dressed so hastily that he returned to the King's chamber just as Borough had finished his recital and Henry was reading the terms on the crumpled paper. The King's expression, thought Tom, bodes ill for the rebels. Henry mashed the paper in his fist. He raised his

217

head and saw Tom Seymour dressed, heard the jingle of spurs. He smiled a crafty smile with cruelty in it.

"You did well, sir," he said, "for thou art dressed and ready. Summon my council! We start to deal immediately with men who dare to instruct their King in matters spiritual and temporal!"

It was a bright blue October morning, and Tom Seymour lovingly scanned the countryside on either side. How beautiful was England! This morning the mist had lain low on the meadows, gradually lifting to let the sun shine on rich wooded forests. Tiny villages nestled at the side of the road; around a bend one would come upon them, tucked next a stone mill where a stream ran merrily.

He was in command of a large troop of horse, hastily assembled. Part the King's own guard, part gentlemen and their retainers, a few professional soldiers eager for work again—in short, as many men as the Duke of Norfolk, who was in command of the royal forces, could lay his hands on in a few hours.

This was the van. And its duties were threefold: To reconnoiter and explore ahead of the more slowly traveling foot; to discover which royal castles were still in royal hands; and to engage at any point any segment of rebel troops they might encounter, to capture their leaders and bring them to the Duke.

The situation was serious, as they had known before they left London. The rebels were some thirty thousand strong, while the royal army numbered less than ten thousand. Tom Seymour studied his map; he took a pull from the flask at his elbow, swallowed his last bit of bread and cheese and washed it down with another pull from the flask. The sun was bright on his bare head, for he had pulled off his helmet. He rolled up the map carefully and gave an upward glance at the sun. He should have time to make a wide sweep ahead, drawing near to Doncaster where he had heard a large rebel force had gathered, meet his other captains in the appointed rendezvous at three, and still double back and meet the Duke of Norfolk before dark; for the foot of the army was traveling slow, stopping every five miles to dole out a groat per man for the ale upon which the English army always traveled best.

He rose. He gave a final glance at the bodies of twelve hapless rebels who had fallen into his hands this morning. They decorated the tree, swinging to and fro. They served as warnings. Outnumbered so badly, the royal forces were hoping to drive some of the rebels home by sights such as these. The cavalry, the quickest striking arm, was under orders to do as much damage as possible, and as Tom Seymour had said to himself this morn, "Mercy was not among my orders."

His servant held his horse. He was about to mount when a movement among the trees betokened the presence of a man. The nearest archer raised his bow, the arrow trembled.

"Hold there," Tom Seymour said quietly. "Let him go home and tell what he's seen. We'll ride now."

Tom Seymour galloped to the head of the line, and the small troop of horse moved off down the rutted road.

Lord Latimer had left Pontefract four days before and ridden with the main body of rebel forces south to Doncaster, where they were now in force. The town overflowed with them, and some of the difficulties of the military man were beginning to be borne in on Lord Latimer.

First, food. Second, discipline. Third, leadership.

It was late morning, and Lord Latimer had closeted himself in his chamber at the inn. He had sat alone for about an hour, and now, having succeeded in removing himself from the clatter of dissident voices of the Yorkshire gentry, he felt he could see the situation more clearly. For indeed it had become a wrangle among the men directing this Pilgrimage of Grace.

This sort of spiritual rebellion, with its worthy desire to remake king and kingdom upon the old pattern, had more than its share of difficulties. Day after day, as he sat listening to lengthy conferences on the proper way of procedure, as he heard the Archbishop of York's oily voice drone on and on, as Sir Rafe Bulmer made his bull-like interruptions, as he had heard Aske the lawyer's careful statements, judicious and portentously honest, only once in a while had there come a moment's revelation, a spark of thought. He was sure if he sat alone for a while he might rearrange those flashes of understanding so that the whole Pilgrimage would become clear.

There were too many banners. Too much division. Too many motives. And opposed to them was Henry who, God knew, was not divided but knew decisively what he wanted. On that basis alone, they would fail. Lord Latimer slapped his hand against his bony knee as he full realized his premise was correct. He shook his head sadly. Too many men opposed to one, and that one a king. That was the first fallacy; for they were not dealing with a Richard III, they were dealing with Henry VIII of England.

"I wish," Lord Latimer said aloud to the empty room, "that I had the strength to lead them onward." But he knew he had not, that ten years ago he might have but of late his energies had been draining away, and even ordinary tasks were ofttimes burdensome. He was fifty years old and his clothes fitted him loosely, and this morning an enormous weariness engulfed him. For a moment he forgot the present and mourned his own youth. For I am drifting into age, he thought and sighed deeply. Then his disciplined mind took hold once more of the problems at hand.

In point of numbers, they were strong, safe, almost invulnerable. As opposed to the King's force of about six to eight thousand men, they had thirty thousand. Their numbers alone would enable them to march to London, and justified the advice old Lord Darcy, his white beard and hair quivering with emotion, had given to Robert Aske: "Go to London," Darcy had said last night, "and treat with the King! And if he throws thee into the Tower, I shall come and rescue thee!" So secure did Lord Darcy feel of the strength of his Pilgrims. But Lord Latimer was not so sure. March on London? This meant civil war, no matter how high the ideals; blood and hatred and vengeance would be loosed, and then where would there be the ideals? This was what troubled Robert Aske himself, for lawyer that he was, he knew that while he might be speaking like a man of law, he was not obeying the law of the land as he had learned it at Gray's Inn.

The commons, unleashed now, were tigers, and there was not a man in the camp strong enough to leash them again. Perhaps Aske could; he was forceful and young. And he was honest. Lord Latimer banked on that. He rose and made his way out into the inn hall and down the narrow stairs. For he himself, as the masked Earl of Poverty, had been a big part of the spark that had kindled these fires; he had to accept that responsibility and do his best to avoid senseless slaughter, terrible reprisals, and the threat of a leaderless nation. He could not burden Aske or Darcy with a confession, for the knowledge of his identity could be only a liability to both men. But he would point out how much better it would be to try to arrange a parley with the King's forces, and see if what he had intended to accomplish in the first place could not now still be done. With honor. "We are in an impregnable position," he would say, "and we can parley and intreat with honor. We should immediately send a representative to the royal army, to treat with its leaders."

"The rebel force at Doncaster, my lord," Tom Seymour reported from his scouting mission, "are about thirty thousand strong. They mill about the town, and I warrant the townspeople will be sick of them shortly. The leaders are Stephen Hamerton," he frowned deeply, "a lawyer named Aske—a Londoner, by the way—Lord Darcy, the Archbishop of York, and Rafe Bulmer, and all of the Yorkshire gentry, sir. I warrant, most of it. They sit arguing at the inn, and the commons rove the streets." The Duke leaned his elbows on the table. Tom Seymour admired the old Duke, the hero of Flodden Field, the best soldier England had, tough as an old rooster and just as eager for the hens, he was.

"Thirty thousand men," said Norfolk softly, thinking of his own forces. He looked up at the younger man and considered him, for Norfolk's daughter Mary, the Lady Mary Howard, Duchess of Richmond, had spoken of this man. Then Norfolk gave his mind to the matter at hand. He had been empowered by Henry to deal with the rebels, should they be in too strong force to face in open battle. For what Henry needed was time. These rebel forces would disband sooner or later; their numbers would dwindle, and they would slink back to their homes, many wondering why they had buckled on sword and dagger to fight their King. Then, Henry, who was not impatient and whose army would not dwindle, could strike.

The old Duke chewed his lip. He was camped now outside Doncaster within striking distance of the rebels, in a well-fortified position on an easily defended hillside. His men were well deployed, and he did not fear attack. He chewed his lip, and said, "We shall wait till tomorrow. I believe they will send us messages, to intreat with them. We shall see what they have to say." He was about to dismiss Tom Seymour, when he added, "You have done well, sir."

"Thank you, my lord duke," Tom Seymour said. He bowed. As he started to leave the tent, he brushed against Thomas Borough. Tom Seymour frowned. He supposed Borough had been forced to join the King's forces, to prove his story of having been compelled to carry the rebel's ultimatum. Still, he didn't like Borough's presence. He hesitated, then thought better of it, and left the tent.

Thomas Borough came forward and asked leave to speak. Norfolk was drinking ale and he but nodded, wiping his lips with his handkerchief.

"My Lord," Borough said, "what of Lord Latimer? Has he joined the rebels?"

"To my knowledge, yea," Norfolk answered, his mouth full. "I warrant that he is with them at Doncaster."

"But he might not be, my lord. And he is sane and honest. We should speak with him."

Norfolk looked at Borough with some distaste, for he hardly liked suggestions, especially from strangers.

"My lord, I crave your permission to ride to Snape Hall, and if he is there, to bring him back with me!"

Norfolk could see no reason why he should accede to this request, except that he misliked Borough and would just as soon have him away. Norfolk drank more ale, wiping his mouth with his hand.

"A moment, my lord," said Borough silkily, coming closer. "I want to tell your Grace a bit of what is in my mind."

This man was sly. But so was the Duke of Norfolk. "Speak up, then," Norfolk said, bending his ear, curious, interested.

"Well, my lord," began Borough, "I present to thee an anomaly. Last month I heard Latimer say, and he said it straight to me, that the traitor unknown, the Earl of Poverty, had never called at Snape Hall. I was surprised. I asked, 'Never? when he has always sought out all the county families?' 'Never,' Latimer replied, and he was strained, my lord, and I knew he was lying. And then I thought, why, 'tis plain as a nose, he is the Earl himself, and that is why he has never come to his own dwelling places!"

The Duke was thoughtful. The story was thin. Still— He said, "You may not go now, Lord Borough. When and if the rebels deal with us, I may then give you permission, but only when we have a temporary truce." He watched him go. "I still mislike that fellow," he said to Suffolk.

At five in the morning, Katryn wakened. Beside her, Anne was stirring restlessly.

"Katryn," Anne said, "I am having a little pain once in a while. I think I am going to deliver this day, and I am glad." She managed a smile.

Katryn sat up and tried not to look worried. "I shall get dressed immediately, and we'll get the chamber readied."

"It is the eighth, is it not?"

"Aye," said Katryn, shivering, for the morning air was cold. She was thinking that Mistress Nell would not be able to help, and only she and Goodie would be present at the delivery.

"There's no need for great haste, Katryn. My pains are very slight as yet."

Nonetheless Katryn did hurry, for she was apprehensive. She sent in the housekeeper and the children's nurse, plus two maids, and they began to prepare the bed and lay out linens.

The hours passed. Ten hours passed. In Anne's room even the seconds prolonged themselves. On the bed Anne's gray eyes pleaded for help; she had been moaning softly for almost an hour.

This is the worst, Katryn thought. Of all, this is the worst—worse than that awful band of wretched commons, worse than our terrors and fears of what will happen to us and this house—this is the worst because Anne is going to die. Right here in this bed, she is going to die.

The fire burned and the candles flickered. Katryn had lost track of time; she hadn't eaten for six hours. Every nerve in her body pounded; her legs shook. Here we all are, she thought desperately, Goodie and I and Meg and Mrs. Bissell and Lucy, and we cannot help; Anne will die. Suddenly she gave a little cry and ran from the room.

"Mistress Nell!" she said. Maybe Mistress Nell, carried here in a chair! She fled down the steps to get help, her breath coming light and swift now that there was something to do that might aid Anne.

She tried to explain to Mistress Nell, carefully, while two of the gardeners lifted her from her bed and Katryn took soft blankets and tied her into a chair with huge knots in back.

"Mistress Nell. If you could see, mayhap you could tell me what to do!" She bit her lip, and tears came and she began to cry. "Anne is dying; the baby will not come! It has been hours."

She finished tying the blanket and came around the chair to look at Mistress Nell, whose face seemed more stricken than ever. Maybe I'm killing her too, Katryn thought, helplessly. Oh, God, what shall

I do? Is this right? "Mistress Nell," she cried, "if you deem aught wrong, say so, and I'll put you back in bed."

The woman shook her head. She tried to smile, a crooked smile, and Katryn signaled to the two men to pick up the chair. "Careful!" she cried.

Anne's eyes lit weakly when she saw Mistress Nell. The two men set down her chair at the foot of the bed, and Mistress Nell nodded reassuringly to Katryn. At her side Goodie took her hand, and stroked it.

"Mother, we can't—" she began.

"Hush!" Katryn said. She glanced at Anne's face, contorted as it was, and Mistress Nell looked toward Anne, and Goodie did too. Goodie screamed.

Katryn found her hand gripping Mistress Nell's chair. What she saw wasn't possible, she thought wildly; Anne was delivering a monster! Then her eyes took in the truth. Anne's baby was coming, and what she was seeing was the baby's feet!

"Holy mother of God!" she muttered. She looked at Mistress Nell, who lifted her hand as if to wave Katryn forward.

Katryn said, "I can help?" She approached the bed slowly. And Mistress Nell tried to nod.

Katryn thought, she means take hold of the baby's feet. She tried to. She laid her hand on the tiny ankle; her hand slipped. "A towel," she commanded. Her voice startled herself, it sounded so commonplace. She felt Meg lay a small linen towel in her hand. She grasped the baby's ankles gently. She said, "I am trying to help, Anne; bear hard, when you can." Gently she laid hold of the infant; Anne gave a cry, and Katryn felt the baby move. Its thighs and now its hips were in view.

"Anne!" she cried. "The baby is coming!"

Anne whispered. "The pain!"

Katryn said, "I cannot stop." She could feel herself shaking. I am killing Anne, she thought, but I must! I have to get this child from her body; it cannot stay this way, half in, half out. "Holy Mary!" she kept muttering. She grasped the infant by the hips; it was moving, its shoulder appeared. Katryn looked at Anne; she had fainted.

This can't be true, Katryn thought. I must be dreaming; this is some kind of a nightmare. Anne has fainted and the baby's head is still inside her body. She could see the tiny neck, and the outline of the child's head, pressing against the dilated skin. Frantically she turned to Mistress Nell, and back again to look at the sight. She thought, I'm going to faint too—I can't stand it. Anne will die.

Mistress Nell's eyes were starting out of her cheeks. Katryn said, "How, Mistress Nell? How?"

Mistress Nell's eyes glittered as meaningfully as she could make them. Then she opened her mouth wide, and held it open. No sound came out, but a drop of spittle ran out over her chin and dropped onto the robe.

"What do you mean?" Katryn cried. She stared at Mistress Nell. The woman's eyes looked back at her imploringly.

Then Katryn, watching her open mouth, said, "The mouth? The baby's mouth?"

Mistress Nell nodded, and her face contorted with joy. She held up her index finger.

"I can't," Katryn said. "I can't!" Even as she muttered it, she felt her index finger enter the baby's mouth. Gently she turned the head a little, so the bulge of the skull she could see was twisted toward herself. She was freeing the baby! Its nose and mouth were out, its bulge of forehead came next, and the child lay on her arm, face downward, free. Katryn stared down at it, and the baby began to cry.

"Goodie," she said, "take care of Mistress Anne!"

"You saved my life," Anne said, "and the life of my son."

Katryn tucked the quilt under her arms. She was clean washed and bandaged; her hair was brushed back again and tied with a ribbon, and although she was as white as the bed linen, she looked at peace. "Go to sleep now, Anne," she said. "The babe sleeps, and you must too."

"Thank you, Katryn," she said low.

Katryn said, "I had to hurt you so—I was so afraid! But now—"

I'll never sleep again, she thought, as she turned and tossed restlessly. She kept hearing Anne's low moans, and seeing the sight of the half-born child. She hadn't been able to eat, and a sickening nausea convulsed her stomach. She sat straight up in bed. I cannot stay here, she thought. She got up and found her robe, and tiptoed into Anne's room. Meg, sitting by the fire, put her finger to her lips.

"They both sleep sound, madam," she said, a smile on her round face. The fire flickered cheerfully, and Katryn looked about the room.

"Please try to rest, madam," Meg whispered.

Katryn looked down at the baby in the gilded cradle. The sight was almost unbelievable. She touched its hand. She looked over at the sleeping figure of her sister, thin now under the quilts, sleeping normally, one hand under her head.

Katryn bit her lip. She had gone to the chapel to give thanks, and to thank God for his help. Now she left the room and sought her bed again. She huddled under the quilts, curled up in a ball. Did she sleep? She thought later she must have, because when the messenger from Lord Latimer arrived before dawn, she cried out in terror when they roused her.

Wat was proffering her a letter, and she looked at it as though neither the letter nor Wat were real. She held out her hand for the letter and forbore opening it. Her heart was pounding. Then suddenly she couldn't endure the suspense any longer, and she tore it open and read fast.

MY DEAREST WIFE [Lord Latimer began. Her eyes skipped over the greeting, and went on],

Yesterday I was full of despair, but today I find I have succeeded beyond my wildest expectations. I shall try to arrange the news for you, simply.

Lord Latimer's measured sentences brought some calmness to Katryn.

We are some thirty thousand strong, and thus so strong we do not have to fight, which was what I had always intended and which I was afraid was going to be forgot, for there are hotheads amongst us who wanted to march on London! Lord Darcy treated with the Duke of Norfolk, who was empowered by the King to intreat with us, and all is settled and a truce declared, so there will be no more even sporadic fighting and no more blood shed. We are going to London to present our terms to the King, and I think I shall be selected because the King knows my integrity, and that I am not a man of blood or battle, and it seems that I can make it clearer that this is a religious pilgrimage with us.

If this be so, then I shall write again, but it will be after I have left for London, and thus I shall not see thee to say goodby, nor kiss thy fair cheek and mouth. But my love shall stay with thee, and I pray thy love and good wishes shall accompany me wheresoever the path taketh me. Written this night at Doncaster, the eighth of October, by the hand of your loving husband,

J. Neville

Katryn read the letter twice. Then she read it again, slow, trying to understand fully and reassure herself. But reassurance would not come. He would be alone in London save for a handful of escort. Alone, to face the King's wrath! But he seemed unafraid—he must have been promised amnesty. A truce had been declared, he had said. She wet her lips. But mayhap he wouldn't go! Mayhap they'd send another, a bolder, younger man than her soft-spoken lord. No: probably that was exactly why they would send him.

"By God's most precious soul!" she cried aloud. "Why must it be thee?" She got out of bed, grasped up her robe, then discarded it. I must get dressed, she thought, to face the day. Hastily she began to throw on her clothes without waiting for help. Mayhap another message would come soon, and in the meantime the messenger was probably in the kitchens, warming himself by the fire and having food. She would go down and question him. Rapidly she twisted up her hair, and ran down the stairs. When she reached the bottom, she heard the sound of men and horses in the court. It must be another messenger. Then probably Lord Latimer had gone to London. "I would rather ha' gone myself," she said to Wat, who was by the doors. "Open them," she commanded, and went forward.

Hours later, days later, even years later, Katryn could never remember accurately the exact series of events which followed, nor could she say when she first truly realized that it was Thomas Borough himself confronting her. By the time she reached the big doors she could see a welter of men in the courtyard, and one figure detached itself from the rest. It was a familiar figure and yet it was not. A singular feeling of dread and dismay took hold of her and she stopped in the center of the hall. Then she edged toward the staircase and took one step back up it, drawing back instinctively from the potential danger which she felt in every fiber of her body.

Memories warred in her head, her palms were damp, and a nameless horror pervaded her; and during all this time the single figure came closer, up the steps and into the dimly lit hall. As his booted legs carried him nearer and nearer, she knew who it was.

She forced herself to descend the five steps she had taken back up the stairway, as though she were coming down for the first time, and she gathered courage and her skirts in her two hands, and held both tight as she advanced toward Borough, who had now come to a stop and was surveying her. She made no form of greeting save to speak his name. "Sir Thomas," she said clearly, and her dread and distaste for him were shoved aside by the important question, What does he want, what does he want? She could feel the suspense tighten inside her. It was too much, being left alone to repulse rude commons, to run this great household, to deliver children, and now to have to deal with this horrible man whom she hated and loathed! I can't do any more, she thought wildly. She breathed fast; without knowing it she stamped her foot.

"You devil!" she spit at him. "What do you here? And what do you want?" Anger gleamed in her eyes. "Speak out your business, for I've little patience left! Aye, none, none at all!" She stood before him, her shoulders squared, and he looked a bit taken aback; she realized too that she had forgotten fear, and now she was righteously angered. She faced him, arms akimbo. "Speak!" she ordered. And because he didn't answer, she went right on. "We are a household of women." She had said that before to a group of men, speaking the words right at a man carrying another man's head. Now she had to do it again. "We are a household of women," she repeated angrily, "carrying on and working, instead of riding about the country jingling spurs. And we have naught to offer you save shelter, which you don't deserve!"

Thomas Borough stared hungrily at the golden eyes gleaming in the white drawn face. Her hair—it was the same as ever, a mass of red gold tendrils, brushed and shining. He could see the delicious rise and fall of her breast, and she drank her anger like wine. "We need not shelter," he said. "We came for your lord; you tell me he is not here."

"You knew he wasn't!" Her mouth was dry. "Of course, you knew he wasn't!"

"Of course I knew he wasn't," Borough said softly. He struck fast. "But I know who he is! Mayhap I should have called him by his proper name, the Earl of Poverty!"

Real terror seized Katryn. How did he know? How had he guessed? They would all die on the rack! Her stomach quivered. "You're still mad!" she cried. "Aye, they should chain you afore you harm yourself!"

"You cannot hurt me any more by your taunts, Katryn, you whom I loved so dearly. I would have died for you, aye, suffered for you." The words burst from him, the strength of his emotion seemed to make him tremble.

"Have ye the ague?" Katryn mocked. Her fear was so consuming that her lips were drawn back like a cornered animal.

Then Thomas Borough saw plain her fear, and saw that what he had said about Lord Latimer was true. He knew why she was afraid; she feared for herself.

But he scarcely heard what she said. His eyes devoured her; he pained himself with the memories of her—swift as a dream they went through his head, from the first time he had seen her in the great hall at Kendal, through that snowy winter, and into the spring. Katryn, Katryn! his heart had sung then, and every day was sweet pain and pleasure and the sound of her laughter and the touch of her hand. His head swam. "You should never have left me!" he cried. "Never!" He took a step toward her. And suddenly he clapped his hands together and said, "But it is not too late. For I shall save thee!"

He began to speak, then, rapidly. He said he still loved her and that was plain, now that he again feasted his eyes on her beloved face. Katryn only half heard the flood of words which tumbled from his lips. He was explaining that Lord Latimer would be executed for his crimes against the crown, and that the only way she could save herself was to depend on him; he would save her, and marry her, as they should have married those five long years ago.

"Stop! Stop!" she cried desperately. "I cannot think, even! You have done and said beastly things." He was afraid she would faint. He leaped to her side and put his arm around her.

This can't be true, she thought wildly. She stood there in the circle of his arm, and thought, this is the end of our life and all I have known, and all I have done is for naught. But I'm not going to let it happen. I'm not going to die because of Thomas Borough, and he couldn't save any of us. I'm not going to die, and neither is Anne, nor my husband; it is not for nothing I have worked and fought. Her mind raced.

"Sweetheart," he said, "you're nigh to swooning. You need a bit of wine."

"Aye," she said. "Thomas, we shall get it together, for there's none abovestairs. The men all deserted us. We have to go down even to draw beer. This way," she said. "We use a small cellar, close."

He squeezed her arm. "Katryn, please don't be afraid!"

"I'm terrified," she mumbled. Her hands shook and her knees trembled and her heart felt like ice. Her eyes looked slyly to the right, as they passed the suit of armor. There was the pike. She drew a deep shuddering breath. "Here is the door."

At her belt were her keys. She tried to fit one into the lock. Unspeaking, she handed it to Thomas. "You do 't."

"Of course," he said. "My poor, poor Katryn."

He opened the door and looked down the narrow flight of stone steps. He had no misgivings. He started down.

Katryn said, from behind him, "Thomas, do you need a light? Shall I fetch a candle or rush?" She had taken a backward step and stood outside the door.

He peered down. It was gray with light. "I think not," and he turned to look up at her.

He didn't cry out; she didn't give him time. She held the murderous pike in both hands and drove it forward at the side of his face with all the strength of shoulder and body; braced on the step, she dealt him the hardest blow she could on his right temple, and he reeled back. Katryn, who had wanted to kill, saw him fall, tumbling helplessly, bumping and thudding to the foot of the stone steps.

Still clutching the heavy pike, she ran down the steps and stood over him. He lay on his face. She raised the pike again, and then of a sudden she dropped it. She leaned against the stone wall, shaking. Then she bent over his inert figure and, pushing aside dread and horror, felt for his pulse. There was none.

She steadied herself with the pike and then leaned down and wiped the blood from it on his coat. She came back up the stairs and locked the door. She leaned the pike back where it had been, against the mailed fist of the knight in armor.

The hall was deathly silent. She looked around; no one was there. She had murdered a man, but as yet no one knew it. The cellar was not used, and no one could get down there without her key. She put the keys back onto her belt. Her legs were shaking so, she sought the nearest place to sit; she went into the winter parlor and sat down at her little desk.

"I have no time for tears," she said aloud. She forced herself to think. What would she tell Borough's men, who still waited in the court—or had Wat sent them round to the stables to get refreshment for themselves and their steeds?

"I shall have to get help," she said aloud. If Borough's men suspected foul play, they might kill her. She picked up her pen.

She wrote five words. "I am in desperate case. Katryn." She sealed the line of writing with the pink rose of Kendal and ran to the kitchens.

Tammie, the messenger from Lord Latimer, was eating. She laid down the letter in front of him. She said, "Prithee, Tammie, with all haste, take this to my lord. And if, by any chance, he has left for London, see you take this to another man, by name Thomas Seymour. Tie a white scarf to your horse. He will be fighting with the King's forces."

Tammie nodded. "There's many messages going back and forth, madam. I can get to him."

Hope surged through her, though it was so vague a hope. "Prithee, make haste!"

The sun was risen and Katryn went methodically about her duties. Anne was propped up in bed; her eyes were unclouded and she looked well. Katryn told her part of what had happened.

"That dreadful beast Thomas Borough came here to make trouble! And I sent him away, but he must ha' disappeared, Anne, for he is nowhere about. His men are eating in the hall; I told Mistress Bissell to feed them. I was afeared not to feed them. I certes hope he returns soon, and takes them away with him!"

Anne said, "Oh, Katryn, you bear so much! How did he come here?"

"I don't know," she said. "He's quite mad, you know. I think he came partly to make love to me, the beast! It was barely dawn, no one was about, and I shouldn't have been up myself had not my lord sent Tammie with a message!" Oh, if it were only true, those brave words just spoke!

She gave her sister the letter to read. Anne said she thought it sounded as though there might be no fighting, and that was well. She knew Katryn would be fretting about her lord's going to London. "But if the King has pledged his word to see John, you do not need to fret."

At dinnertime, Katryn could not bring herself to go into the hall and eat with Borough's men. The most forward of them might ask questions. The afternoon passed without incident. At supper, Borough's men were again fed and put up in the menservants' quarters. As yet they had not asked about their master, or if they had, no word of it reached Katryn. She went to bed, after having drunk ale, and at midnight she finally slept.

She wakened early to a perfect October day. At eleven, at dinner, one of Borough's men approached Wat. He was curious as to the whereabouts of Lord Borough.

Wat made noises to indicate he would seek out his mistress. He did. What shall I tell them? Katryn thought. And they here in the house —there were twenty of the rogues—and no one to oppose them. Afraid to face them herself, she sent a message with Meg to say Lord Borough had gone out walking, and that was all Lady Latimer knew of him. This would satisfy them for a while, she thought, but for how long?

At two she went up on the battlements to look out over the countryside. Her eyes scanned it hopefully, desperately. If she had help, she could say grandly, "Your lord has gone, I know not where. Now you go too!" But would they obey? This was a Yorkshire house, and these men represented the crown. They would know her lord was with the rebel forces. She paced back and forth, searching the dusty southern road. There was nothing to see save the sunny spread of land.

At three, numbed with the wind and cold, she had almost decided to go seek Borough's men and face them out. There was no other way. She was sure they would not leave if she ordered it! What else could they suspect but foul play? If they searched the hall—? Her mind refused to go any farther.

She turned to leave the parapet, for she could endure the suspense no longer. And then she saw the dust cloud that betokened riders.

Her heart lurched. She seized the edge of the parapet in both hands; the stone was cold. If it were Lord Latimer, pray he brought enough men! He would hardly expect to find royal troops quartered in his dwelling place. She leaned over, straining her eyes. She could see riders now. They were coming fast, a full gallop; she caught up her cloak and started to run down the first flight of narrow stone steps.

At the narrow slitted window she paused again to look out; they were nearer, only a mile away, a distance covered quickly, very quickly at that pace. She ran into Anne's room.

"Riders!" she exclaimed.

Anne sat up straight in bed. Then Katryn was gone again, running down the steps, crossing the hall, opening the doors. Up the graveled drive, under the russet trees came a dusty troop of horse, banners waving. The lead rider began to check his horse; even so, a great deal of gravel spurted from the hoofs as the big horse came to a sudden stop, and his rider flung himself to the ground.

I am frozen with joy, Katryn thought, as Tom Seymour, reins in one hand, came toward her. His face creased into a little smile as he put one hand under her arm.

"Hold there, lass," he said. "All is well."

The sun shone down. The wind still blew. Fifty men and their horse crowded the court. I cannot believe it, she thought. I am safe. I'm not going to have to face those knaves of Borough's; she grasped his hand tight.

"I can never repay thee," she said, and big tears stood in her eyes. "Never, Master Tom, never." He looked so big. She touched his arm; he was real. She heard him tell someone named Atkins to stable the horses and water them. In the hallway ahead of them were already gathered a group of women. Katryn felt him draw her into the hallway and heard herself telling Mistress Bissell to set out food and drink for the men. "They can help too," she added, "to bring up a barrel of beer."

Then she was in the small winter parlor, and she was speaking. "There are twenty of Thomas Borough's men here. We are alone— our men deserted! I was—I was desperate, afeared of what they might do!"

Tom Seymour asked, "Why, Katryn? And where is Lord Borough?"

"Thomas Borough is dead. I killed him. I struck him with a pike and his body is in the cellar."

"I see," said Tom Seymour gravely. He seemed thoughtful. He rubbed his hand over his chin. What will he think, she wondered? But then her knees started to shake again, and she sank down onto the cushion on the floor and put her face in her hands.

She was drinking brandy. The flask stood on the table; leather it was, with the initial S on it. Tom Seymour was washing his face and hands, splashing water, and the man who had brought the basin stood by with a clean towel. The brandy was hot and strong; it felt good, she thought gratefully, and my stomach isn't heaving any more.

When the door opened for Tom Seymour's man to bear away the used water, she could hear the sound of male voices in the distance; feet clumped along the hall. Men, she thought. A comfort and a trial. Now I have to deal with this one, the most unpredictable man I've ever known, the one I can least control. The brandy sang in her head. From her position on the floor, she had to look way up to see him. This won't do! she thought dimly, and struggled to her feet, spilling the brandy.

"That's precious," he said. "Be careful."

"I'm trying to be," she said with dignity, and went over to the window seat because she still felt she couldn't stand up properly.

He had hooked his thumbs in his belt, and was looking at her. He appeared much as she had first seen him, encased in chamois, wearing big boots. But he has changed, she thought, as I have. We're older, and he is a knight now, a baronet; she had heard one of the men call him Sir Thomas.

She said, "What are you going to do?"

"You can leave that to me," he said. "What I want is a good stout piece of canvas; lacking that, two heavy new sheets."

"New?" she asked. "Why waste new sheets on Thomas Borough?"

"You're so practical a housewife, Katryn," he said, "but I need new, heavy linen."

"You're not going to bury him now?"

"Acourse not," he said. "But I cannot send two men to go stumbling about in the night with a body, wondering where to dig his grave." She shuddered. Tom Seymour said, "You're half dead. How much sleep have you had? Give me the cellar key, and go up to your bed."

She said rebelliously, "You act like a Borderer in command of an enemy castle!" She pouted; he hadn't even said he was sorry, or he hadn't even seemed to think she was in pitiful case, as indeed she was. All she had gone through, and he didn't have wit enough to know it.

"Stop feeling sorry for yourself," he said. "Give me your keys, Katryn."

Slowly she put them in his big hand. Her white finger pointed to the cellar key in question. "Right past the suit of armor," she said.

"And now I want you to go up to bed. By yourself, this time." He pulled her to her feet. A little dizzy, she went past him and up the long stairway.

Within the curtained bed, she slept sound and deep and dreamlessly. She woke out of the deep waters of sleep like a half-drowned swimmer, coming gradually to the surface. She lay quiet within the curtained bed, trying to open her eyelids that lay so heavy. She wondered what had roused her, until she heard Meg's voice and then a man's voice. It was saying, "Sir Thomas requests the pleasure of my lady's company at supper, as soon as possible."

The door closed. Katryn sat up straight in bed. Her mind struggled with what she should wear, for she hadn't time to get into a complicated gown and this was not Whitehall, anyway. She still felt half asleep.

But she washed rapidly and dressed rapidly. With a brilliant red shawl over her shoulders, she started downstairs, and by this time her eyes were sparkling. At the foot of the steps, a man's voice greeted her. "Sir Thomas is in the small parlor, madam."

Her eyes went over to the door of the parlor, and there he was.

"I'm waiting impatiently, madam," he said, stepping aside for her to enter. Was there a twinkle in his eye? She came closer. She couldn't tell.

"Sit down, Katryn," he said.

She sat on the fat cushion, as she had before. She spread her skirt and petticoats about her and clasped her shawl over her breast. "Pray sing something for me, sir," she said. "I could hear the strumming afore."

The strings of the lute he held gave a twang. He said lazily, "The song I was trying to recall is not fit for your ears. In fact, I know few that are." He sent her a smile. "Howbeit, before supper comes, I shall sing you one of the few I know. All is done, Katryn, or will be, within the next two hours. And I shall take Borough's men back with me. I think it safer. I told them he had wandered away, and none knew where. Now I have about two hours before moonrise. I must start back then."

Katryn said, "I thank you. Without you I—" She searched his face, then looked down at her clasped hands.

"After I received your note, I went to Sir William, your uncle; he is with us. He gave me permit to come."

"I still cannot thank you," she whispered.

"What is done, is done, and I am here for a short space." His eyes met hers, he leaned forward a bit, and she thought suddenly, How truly handsome he is! At least to me he is. Knave he may be, but I would like to touch him; I would like to put my hands in that thick hair. Rapidly she cast down her eyes.

"Pray sing to me," she said.

The lute strings thrummed. His finger picked out a plaintive tune; it was vaguely familiar, like a composite of a lullaby and a love song. His voice was deep; he sang the words slowly.

> "Lady, why doth love torment you?
> Cannot I your griefs remove?

Is there none that can content you
With the sweet delights of love?

If I grieve and you can ease me
Will you still be fiercely bent?
Having wherewithal to please me,
Must I still be discontent?"

The lute string twanged. "I play by ear," Tom Seymour said in the stillness. "There's more, and most applicable."

Katryn shot him a glance. His eyes were on the strings. His voice was low, he almost spoke the words.

"If I am your faithful servant,
And my love doth still remain,
Will you think it ill-deserved,
To be favored for my pain?

All amazing beauty's wonder,
May I presume your breast to touch?
Or to feel a little under,
Will you think I do too much?"

Katryn felt the blush rising on her cheek. She glanced at him, and his eyes were on her; there was a little smile on his face.

"Once more, fairest, let me try thee,
Now my wish is fully sped.
If all night I would lie by thee,
Shall I be refused your bed?"

"The tune is very nice," Katryn said. "Let me try it."

He laughed. He handed her the lute. Katryn picked out the melody; it was sweet and plaintive. He leaned forward and caught her hand.

"Lady, why doth love torment thee?"

"You—I" she stammered. She sucked in her breath. He leaned forward and took her hand. Her eyes met his. There was no sound in the little room; it is as though we were somewhere isolated in space. We are here, together. I needed him, and he is here. Is this love? she wondered. But it is true desire, for I am dizzy with it; I want to touch him and kiss him; something aches inside of me. If I am not careful, I shall be lying on the floor like a common wench, with my blouse undone.

She tried to pull away her hand. She looked straight at him. "You said once—" she began.

His hand tightened on hers. "Forget everything I said before—except one August night in a garden."

There was a knock on the door. He released her hand slowly and got to his feet. He took hold of her waist and lifted her up. "Supper," he said.

Tom Seymour's two personal servants brought the food and Wat followed behind. They set the meats upon the sideboard, and Wat with a smile on his face and intermittent giggles shaking his shoulders, started to carve. They must have been joking with him, Katryn thought, and she smiled at Wat to see him so happy. Absently she poured water from the ewer and brought it to her guest. The trestle table was set up, and the cloth spread upon it, and Katryn bore the towel and water away. She sat on a stool opposite Tom Seymour, and spread out her napkin. She bent her head.

"Dear Lord," she said, "we thank Thee for the blessings of this day, and for Thy constant love and protection. May we be not unworthy."

She looked up at Tom Seymour. "Pray begin, sir," she said. He was eying her quizzically, a small smile on his face. He picked up the foaming tankard of cool ale Wat had poured.

"I was wondering, Katryn," he said, "just what you deemed the blessings of this day." He swallowed half the tankard, and set it down. From across the narrow table, she regarded him.

"And I warrant you mean—" She hesitated. "—that my blessings consisted of your help in—" She stopped.

"I see," he said. "Right now you're going to enjoy your supper."

"Marry, I've not enjoyed food for days! I'm thin as a rail!"

"I wouldn't say quite that," he said, looking at her critically. "But I was trying to say we are none so different as you have always claimed."

238

"I wish you wouldn't say anything at all," she said, and her lip quivered.

"Eat your supper, Katryn," he said. "Put that juicy beef into your mouth, my little one."

She did. As she chewed, she blinked back a big tear. "I couldn't help it," she said.

He laughed. Then he sobered. "Katryn, I'm as guilty as hell of many misdeeds. I don't condemn thee, sweetheart. And at the judgment bar, you're sure to get a pair of emerald wings—to match your Kendal cloth. Be of good cheer, lass, a Border wench is welcome anywhere."

Katryn giggled.

"In fact," he went on, "you're like to get emeralds long before you reach heaven. I wish I had a necklace handy, for this is the best meal I've had in many a day."

Katryn was chewing lustily herself. Food had never tasted so good. "Have ye a household?" she inquired, wiping her bread in the gravy.

He shook his head. "Not a proper one. I have two manors in Wales; they bring me fifty pounds a year. On the land is a draughty old pile called Owen Castle, where Owen Tudor took his bride. But I have the muster and command of five royal castles."

Katryn nodded. "You would suit that," she said. "How is her Grace, your sister—our Queen?"

He said, "Jane is well."

"Is she happy?" Katryn asked, curiously. "I should love to see her! You are much at court?"

He said, "I am a gentleman of the privy chamber, when I am not at sea, or undertaking my duties as constable for the castles of Lyme, Holt, Burnfield, Yale, and Chirk."

Katryn laid down her knife and looked at him. She said carefully, "Can you tell me, then, if Lord Latimer has gone to London?" She added, "You must know I sent for him first."

"He has gone, Katryn," he said.

She thought rapidly. "Could you aid us, sir?" she asked. "I mean, I fear for us, a little."

"You need not," he said unequivocally. "When I first heard the news—Yorkshire in rebellion—I thought, Jesu! what of the red-headed wench? And I made quick plans. I would go to the King and say, Look you, your Grace, let justice come to Lord Latimer if it must, but I covet the lady; let me take her to Wales, to that draughty old castle, and I vow to bounce the rebellion out of her."

Katryn said, "You didn't!" Then she asked, "But can you aid us?"

His face was impassive. She thought, He is more powerful than I realized. He is brother to the Queen, on intimate terms with his Grace. He must have much influence. But— "You also must have many importuners," she said.

He did not answer that. But he said, "Your lord is safe, Katryn. Henry has pledged his word."

She did not look at his face. Her eyes rested on his plate, and his strong brown hands. She watched him lift the tankard of ale; she drank, too. She sighed. Her stomach was full and she felt pleasantly drowsy. I would like to lie down, she thought, and stretch myself out. Again she glanced at his plate; it was almost empty. Memory struck her. The meal was almost done. After it, would he make good his threat and make love to her? Her fingers clasped around her tankard; she drank hastily. Did he think she was asking for favors before she let him kiss her? Her eyes were troubled.

"Lord Latimer is loyal to his Grace, and God-fearing," she said low.

He rose. He lifted the trestle table away from between them, setting it by the door. Then he turned. Above the open neck of his unlaced white shirt, his face seemed very dark. "Sometimes, Katryn, you anger me beyond belief. For you can imply that I could be guilty of the grossest kind of betrayal. I know that Lord Latimer is God-fearing. And no matter how much I might desire you, I would not connive against him. I would be much more apt to take the law into my own hands and kill him. You don't understand me very well, do you?"

Katryn sat motionless on her stool. "Mayhap not, sir," she said. Her heart pounded. She rose, almost with compulsion. Her whole body felt as warm as fire. Hardly knowing what she did—for what she desired was the strength of his arms around her—she set her stool to one side. Tom Seymour reached behind himself and shot the bolt on the door.

Katryn sank down onto her cushion; her legs wouldn't hold her.

The sound of the bolt echoed in the silent room. Outside the window darkness had come, the room was lit only by firelight now. Tom Seymour picked up a flat cushion from the window seat; he dropped it on the floor.

I cannot think, Katryn thought. He was sitting beside her, and she could hardly breathe. How could this happen so sudden? It was as though some mysterious force had been loosed within her. He is going to make love to me in an instant, and I am already half dead with longing for his touch. It isn't possible she thought, not possible for me to act thus. Her eyes opened wide and looked into his blue ones, her head tipped back a bit. The face she looked at was set and stern, and the blue eyes held a glitter in their depths that reached right into her very body. She tore her eyes away; the bright flat pillow lay to one side of her. She said jerkily,

"Aren't you going to sit on it?"

He shook his head. "Nay," he said. "It's for your red head."

The King was at Windsor, and thence Lord Latimer had betaken himself. He was met by Will Herbert and had dinner with him, and Will lent Lord Latimer clean linen. During dinner, Lord Latimer assured Will that Anne was well, but he did not know of the birth of Anne's second child. Will's kindness heartened Lord Latimer, who was summoning all his physical and inner strength for its interview with Henry.

Will accompanied him to the privy chamber, and thence to the King. Lord Latimer said, "Bless your kindness, Will; thou hast been a real brother to me." The thought of Will's friendliness was still in Lord Latimer's heart, warm and good, as he knelt before the King.

Henry raised him up and took him to the window seat, where they could sit together and talk in private. Lord Latimer thanked the King for speaking thus with him. He hesitated. What had seemed right in Yorkshire lost some of its force here under Henry's narrow glinting eyes.

Lord Latimer spoke gently and humbly of their love of the King —"meaning by *their*, those Yorkshire gentry and kin whom I represent, your Grace."

Henry grunted.

"They are already dispersing and going to their homes, bearing in mind your Grace's clemency and full pardon. If your Grace would see fit to come to York!" Lord Latimer went on more boldly. "They speak of never seeing your Grace. They speak of the honor of the Queen's coronation being held in York, or a free parliament there, so that your Grace could come to know what is in their hearts!"

Lord Latimer spoke full to Henry. He noted that Henry was heavier, more gross, and he received an impression of even greater will and strength and passion. The thought occurred to Lord Latimer that perhaps he had made a mistake in mentioning hearts. He was somehow sure that Henry was more interested in rebel heads on pikes than he was in the motives of God's Quarrel. Unease filled Lord Latimer.

A page brought wine, and Henry and he drank. "God bless your Grace now and forever," Lord Latimer said, and as he said it he was not afraid for himself but for the others who had joined with him. Nonetheless, Henry gave him signed pardons for a long list of friends close to Lord Latimer, and promised to come to York and hold the free parliament and to bring Jane, the Queen, with him.

Lord Latimer rode north. At York he gave into Lord Darcy's hand his pardon; he gave Robert Aske his signed royal pardon. At York the Duke of Norfolk with a spare but efficient army waited and watched.

Lord Latimer said, "Be careful, my lords, gentlemen. Be mindful that Henry is a king."

The next morning he turned his horse's head for Snape Hall. The Pilgrimage of Grace was over. The Pilgrimage on which they had set forth with such high hopes, with the banners of Christ's wounds, with the surging righteousness of God's Quarrel—it was over and the pardons signed. Why was there already a taste of defeat in Lord Latimer's mouth, gritty and unpalatable as the dust from his horse's hoofs? Lord Latimer coughed; he raised his napkin to his lips. He looked at the reddish stain with distaste and guilt. He had sacrificed too much, even his health, and he was returning to his demesne and his wife sick at heart and sick in body. He resolved to stop early that night and have a good night's sleep before he rode into the gates of Snape Hall.

He slept long and deep. But he knew it hadn't helped much. And much as he had resolved to be strong and victorious in homecoming —for, after all, had he not gone to London and presented the cause to Henry?—when he entered the hall and when he saw Katryn, a surge of weakness came over him. Although he clasped her close, he almost leaned on her sturdy shoulders. And he said, "Oh, my dear, how have I longed for home!"

11

"Thou shalt not kill," intoned Father Lambert, casting his eyes up toward heaven and over his flock in the gallery at the same time.

Katryn bent her red head. "Lord have mercy upon us," she sang, "and incline our hearts to keep this law."

She looked down at her tight-clasped hands. "Incline our hearts to keep—" Was there a ray of hope there? Could it possibly be that good men and women broke these commandments? Now that I have sinned so miserably, she thought, for the first time I understand what I am singing.

"Thou shalt not commit adultery." The words rolled out over her head.

"Lord have mercy upon us." She kept the tune. She raised her eyes and fastened them upon the image of the Savior.

Father Lambert said the tenth comandment slowly. Katryn took a deep breath before she began the response. "Lord have mercy upon us, and write all these laws in our hearts, we beseech thee."

She bent her head again and prayed fervently. "I have them writ firm, now," she ended. Father Lambert's blessing fell upon her. She rose. The rest of the household rose then, too. Maybe I'll be forgiven, she thought, making her way down the aisle. Mayhap God will forgive me. And into her mind there came unbidden, "Do not fret. Most like, when you present yourself at the judgment bar, you'll be gifted with a pair of emerald wings."

Oh, the villain! she thought, so mocking he is. But when he had said that, she had giggled. She remembered it plain. I'll not think of him, she vowed silently. But what a feeble mind I have, recalling bits and scraps of what I wish to forget. But I have an excuse, because it may be he, close to the King in London, who keeps us safe. It was cold, and she drew her shawl close about her and hastened through the hall. Yea, I am true afraid, though as yet the only blow that has fallen on this Yorkshire family is that our house in London has been given over free of rent to Lord Chancellor Audley. That is all we ha' suffered. Though Lord Darcy had been beheaded on Tower Green, and Robert Aske hung in chains high in the air in the square at York; though Stephen Hamerton and Rafe Bulmer had died, and Meg Bulmer gone screaming to her death, Snape Hall lay untouched, unharmed. But I could testify, she said to herself for the twentieth time, Nay, but my lords! Lord Latimer has not risen from his couch for these long months! How could he then conspire against his Grace? I swear to you before God that he is innocent!

But no King's deputies had come. Was it he, in London, who kept them safe? When one thought of it, and the tangle their lives were meshed in, it beggared the imagination. How strange life was. How unpredictable were the fortunes of men. How impossible that Jane Seymour was the Queen of England—and how incredible was the fact that Jane, now pregnant, was the most cherished object in the whole wide land.

How could Jane have possibly known the string of events which surely followed the happy announcement that she was quick with child? Katryn had said this to Lord Latimer. "How could Jane know that when she told the King she was with child, he would cancel his progress to York, fearing to be more than sixty miles from her side; fearing, as he said himself, that she being but a woman might be afeared by rumors blown about in his absence, and so he must not leave her!"

"He promised to come," Lord Latimer said heavily, "and when he broke his royal word, my kinsmen, my fellow Yorkshiremen, thought I had betrayed them."

"It was they who broke their word!" Katryn said, "by riding about armed and in open rebellion! After their pardon!"

"A holocaust of blood has been loosed on Yorkshire," Lord Latimer said, "and I should just as soon suffer as lie here! Aye, I should sooner die! And take my place amongst those departed dead, who marched with me on our Pilgrimage. God knows it would be easier than to be at my ease here, in torment because others suffer."

"Oh, my sweet lord," she cried. "Pray do not suffer! Thou art so good! And I do my best to comfort thee," she ended, hopelessly.

He raised himself on his pillows. "I know you do, Katryn, I know you do. It is not thy burden, and I force you to carry it. I am sorry, my wife. I am very sorry. But you must see that I led a pilgrimage to restore the Church; in good faith I set forth, and it has cost other men their lives, whilst I pay naught."

That is not true, she thought. You have paid too heavy, in health and in spirit. Look at us, for instance. We are truly wed no longer; now you sleep apart from me. Now you are a care and a child. But I cannot say that aloud, for 'twill wound you much. But you have suffered. Mayhap it is best to die. Much the best than to relinquish life, little by little. Mayhap I should choose, if I could, to die with trumpets still blowing. She looked down at her hands; they were clenched. I wonder, she thought, if such brave words will come when I too am old. She stooped over and kissed Lord Latimer's forehead, for he did not permit her to kiss his lips. He had read much about the tisique, and he said that one could hardly escape the fact that it was both contagious and hereditary. She kissed his forehead.

"I shall comfort you to the best of my ability, my lord," she said.

It was chilly in the house. She took her shawl and went up to the battlements, for the sun had come out spottily. She moved down along the parapet to the golden shining sunlight and, leaning her elbows on the rough stone carefully, looked out over the country.

How oft have I waited here, she thought? I waited at this spot the day the commons came. Here I waited for the sound of rescuing hoofbeats. Here I come for the sweep of fresh air that heartens my lungs; here I look on this so familiar land with love, the way I used to at Kendal. Strange that the more known a sight, the more beloved it becomes. Yorkshire, she thought, my poor, rugged land and fierce spirit, this winter your women hacked and almost clawed your earth to yield up the bodies of your husbands, buried so hastily in the hard, unmarked graves. Would I have been one of them if it had not been for a man whose trollop I became so willingly?

The winter and spring have passed, and the months have made it clear the way penance lies—in plain gowns, and twice daily prayers, but mostly in hard work and love for others. I am just like Mary Magdalene, she thought, lifting her red head. Now I know how she felt. And I can atone too!

246

She frowned. There was a troop of horse on the way to Snape Hall! Over the rise of the nearest hill they were, quite close. She swallowed, and the fear that had besieged her for many months now took hold again. For a wild second she thought it might be Tom Seymour himself. For a brief second she felt the last crushing embrace of his arms, the last bittersweet kiss, the whispered words, "I love you, Katryn. My darling, I love you." During the past months she had wondered whether he would send any word. He had not. So it could not be he, and the fear took sharp hold of her, strengthening and tightening until she saw the banners plain. The green and white livery!

She put her hand to her mouth. She squared her shoulders, but her heart was like stone. It had come at last—the royal summons—for the banners that waved below were Tudor. She went slowly from the battlements, down to meet the sure doom that awaited below.

All the way down to the ground floor of Snape Hall, not one single thought crossed her mind; she couldn't swallow for there was a large lump in her throat; she kept wetting her lips, but her tongue was dry. This was true nightmare, in which one moved as though arms and legs were bound by iron, as though will had left off and weights too heavy to be borne bound one's movements. There was the sound of horses in the court. At the big doors two servants waited to throw them wide. She waved her hand at them; the doors opened. In royal livery a messenger stood before her, in his hand a white letter, sealed with a crown. Katryn took it. Even if I open it, I cannot read it, she thought; but her hands did move, and she did open the letter and spread it wide. A single sheet it was, heavy, expensive. She read the few words and crumpled slowly to the floor.

"I've never swooned before," she said weakly. Meg held her head in her lap, and the King's messenger stood over the two women, concern in his eyes.

"Pray permit me to carry you, my lady," he said.

"Nay," said Katryn. She put out her hand, and rested it on the floor. Slowly she got to her feet, ignoring even Meg's outstretched hand. In her other hand was the letter. She wet her lips.

"Pray seek refreshment for you and your escort." She frowned, her brows drawing together.

The messenger hesitated. He was young and eager. "Her Grace gave me instructions I was to stay, madam, and return with thee."

"I thank her Grace," Katryn said. "And that will be well." She looked down at the letter. Summons it was, and royal, but not the kind she had expected. It was from Jane. Jane, the Queen! She could swallow now. She leaned on Meg. "I must go up to my lord," she said, "and let him read this. For her Grace has sent for me. She wishes me to be with her when she is brought to childbed."

Hampton Court had been lovingly, painstakingly, built by Cardinal Wolsey, and on the eve of his fall, he had given this great palace —his most precious possession, the brick monument to his success, the embodiment of his life's work—into Henry's hands. But that thousand-room bribe had not sufficed. It was now to Hampton Court that Katryn came, on a fine sunny September day.

On the ground floor were one hundred spacious bedrooms, intended as guest rooms by the Cardinal, who loved most to entertain, and royally. When Katryn saw the room assigned to her, she gasped. This room was a well-furnished apartment. The sideboard groaned with plate, and a silver bowl and ewer. Fine glass winked from a silver tray, and wine, sweet malmsey, made a rosy ring on the stopper of the Venetian bottle. Katryn licked the stopper, tasting the rosy drop. Her eyes gleamed.

The walls were hung with tapestry, and nymphs and satyrs chased about in a state of undress. Meg sniffed, and Goodie's eyes were astonished. "That shows you, madam," Meg said, "what kind of priest the Cardinal was!" The bed reached up to the ceiling. Katryn turned down the counterpane.

"Sheets of Rennes silk," she exclaimed, running her hand over them.

Goodie felt the silk too. Katryn said, "You may take turns sharing with me."

It had been Katryn's decision to bring Goodie, for she needed two women with her, Lord Latimer said, and Mistress Nell was not yet fully recovered. In fact, two was not many. Mistress Nell, when apprised of Katryn's decision, was amazed.

"Why, madam, you should take our prettiest, pertest maid!"

"The fairest, pertest maid will ha' sport at Snape Hall," Katryn said. "Goodie shall go."

Mistress Nell's eyes filled with tears. She kissed Katryn's hand. "Oh, madam," she said, "you are so thoughtful and kind, and 'tis what makes everyone love you!"

"Nay, Mistress Nell," Katryn said, "I was just putting myself in Goodie's place."

Goodie now looked as though she might burst momentarily. Katryn laughed. "Mind you don't get lost now, Goodie," she said. "When first you venture forth, go you with Meg, for by the mass, I'll get lost myself, I fear." She was excited too; she was shivering with excitement. Meg moved about, unpacking. Katryn watched her lay out a dress.

"My gowns are two years behind the styles." Did it matter? she asked herself thoughtfully, sitting down on the bench before the fireplace. She leaned against its padded back, pulling a cushion into place. It mattered because of the other women, but a man was not likely to distinguish between last year and this, as long as he liked the wearer.

She had a moment's respite. But soon Jane would know she had arrived, and Anne and Lucy would know. And then she would be sent for.

"I'll wear the gray," she said. It was her newest dress; in her spirit of penance she had picked this shimmering satin gray. The sleeves were plain and edged with lace, and the bodice had a soft collar of white lace. She had designed it herself. "There," she said, when she had it on. She was pleased. "It looks but simple and ladylike, does it not?"

"I warrant so, madam," said Goodie doubtfully, for she thought her mistress looked rapturously lovely. With that froth of white lace about her bosom—! Goodie said, "It is truly elegant, madam!"

"Wait till you see the others of the Queen's ladies!" Katryn said. "Just wait, Goodie." She sighed a little. Rumor had it that Jane's court was excessively fancy and bejeweled. "Jane—the Queen—" said Katryn, "always hankered for jewels. I remember when she used to buy imitation ones."

A man's step outside the door brought her back to the question that had plagued her ever since she had read Jane's letter and was still unanswered: who had sent for her? Had it been Jane, or Tom Seymour?

She sat down again on the bench. Much as she tried to tell herself to not even think on him, she had dreamed about him more than she admitted to herself. It has been ten months gone now, she thought, with never a word. He has ridden off from me as he must have from many other women, and this is what I find difficult to face. I have lost my self-respect, in his eyes. When I meet him, if he gaze at me with negligent eyes and think, Oh, this is another of the lights-o'-love I've had and pleasured with, I shall die of shame! She stared at the empty fireplace, and her heart was beating unaccountably fast. When he sees me, he will surely remember me as he saw me last! No, not last, for then I was clutched fierce in his arms—ay, he almost broke my ribs; I had a big black bruise on my left side where he hugged me. Oh, by the mass, if he is here, what shall I say to him? And if he is not here, where is he then? And if I redden like a schoolgirl—? Sometimes I wish to high heaven I should never lay eyes on the knave again. She rose. There were more footsteps outside. "Anne!" she cried as the door opened. "Oh, Lucy! Anne!"

With Anne on one side and Lucy on the other, and two maids-in-waiting coming behind, Katryn slowly made her way up the three wide stairways past long galleries that joined various wings of the great palace to the chambers of the Queen.

"Her Grace has taken to her great chamber," Anne was saying, "to await the birth of her child. 'Tis custom."

"A full month before?" Katryn whispered, so the maid wouldn't hear her question.

Lucy nodded. "Aye, she becomes restless already."

"I don't wonder," Katryn whispered back.

"At least, it being but September, the casements can be open and fresh air let into her room. And you will be another breath of it, Katryn. She has spoke of you much, and oft."

"How extremely kind," Katryn murmured, thinking that then indeed it must have been Jane only who sent for her. She entered the privy chamber of the Queen. A beautiful woman was standing within. Katryn almost preceded her into the Queen's room, but Lucy laid a hand on her arm.

"Her Grace the Duchess of Richmond," Lucy said. "The Lady Latimer."

Katryn curtsied. Mary Howard inclined her head a trifle, sweeping by with her train. Katryn entered the room in her wake, and then she stood and stared.

The whole room seemed to be awash with bejeweled and fair women and girls. There must be a million creamy pearls here, Katryn thought. Within these walls each maid-in-waiting wore a girdle of more than one hundred and fifty pearls, and this was just the beginning. Katryn fingered her ruby cross. Then she saw Jane. She went quickly forward and gave her a deep curtsy. Jane lifted her up, and threw her arms about her neck.

"Oh, Katryn, Katryn!" she cried. "How I have longed to see thee!"

Jane emptied the room of most of its occupants. Two maids-in-waiting remained, sewing in the corner, and seeing to Jane's requests. Anne sat at her lute and played softly. Katryn and Jane sat in the window seat; they talked low.

"Do you remember?" Jane asked. "Do you remember dining at the Mitre?"

"Acourse," Katryn said. Did Jane remember the afternoon when her brother had sent her home to Wolf Hall? She didn't dare ask. She wanted to ask Jane what it was like to be queen. This question, too, she forbore from asking. "You are happy, your Grace?" she asked.

Jane said, "I am happy now that you are here."

Katryn said, "Can it be, Jane, that you cannot trust some? Or that you—?" She stopped.

"Have enemies?" Jane whispered. "Aye."

"In thy condition?" Katryn asked incredulously.

"Because of it," Jane whispered back. "Oh, Katryn, the jealousy that exists! And there are even some—I know there are some who pray for misadventure to me and to my child!" She moved a bit clumsily. "He stirs, all the time now."

Katryn noted the word he. "Your little knave."

Jane nodded. "If I should give birth to a daughter, I think I should die."

She was afraid, Katryn decided, afraid of Henry. She said, "Jane, put these silly fears aside, and trust thee to God and the Holy Virgin. You can do naught, yourself. Hold thy head high. If you have a daughter, you shall be proud! You will have more children!"

Jane bit her lip. Her face was very pale and a spot of color burned bright in her cheeks. "I knew you would be good for me, Katryn. But you see, his Grace thinks thus too. Put our trust in God, and if God should not let me bear a son, then his Grace will think we are being punished!"

Katryn was silent. So Jane and Henry were guilty of the same crime as she and Tom. She looked at Jane. Within her body stirred the unborn child on which the fate of a nation might hang. The succession! Powerful, pregnant word, as pregnant as Jane's womb. Katryn wondered what Jane would say if she blurted that she was guilty of breaking the same commandment. Instead she said, "Jane, you must try to say to his Grace that the ways of the Lord are inscrutable."

"I have tried," Jane whispered. "But thou knowest his Grace deems himself the Lord's representative on earth. He studied much theology, Katryn. All during his childhood he was groomed for the church, and his fund of knowledge is truly inexhaustible."

"He is our most wise and gracious king," Katryn said. "And the Lord will bless you and him, I know it. I have an inner feeling all will be well with your child."

"You do, Katryn?" Jane asked.

"Aye, I truly do," Katryn said. "For some reason I am sure you will bear a son. And speaking of males," she said, "how is that villainous brother of yours by name of Tom?"

Jane laughed. "He is well, I hope. He is in Calais."

"Calais?" Katryn repeated, not knowing whether to be glad or sorry. But she was conscious of distinct irritation. Away, was he?

"He is being readied to be master of ordnance, his Grace told me. But Calais must be fortified for the winter months, and Tom is seeing to its garrison, its weapons, et cetera. He returns soon."

How soon? she wondered.

"I am trying to get him wed," Jane said.

"Wed?" Katryn repeated. Her eyes grew golden. One should face the fact that Tom Seymour could probably wed any woman in England. One should face the fact that she, Katryn, should forget him. What was Jane saying?

"I know you must be weary. We shall sup soon here, for you know I do not leave this chamber. Then you may retire, Katryn, but prithee wait on me tomorrow, in the morn, early."

Katryn smiled. Jane's quality of imperiousness had increased, and why not? "I am most proud to be thy good friend," Katryn said.

Katryn's duties were much harder than she had expected. Her duty was Jane—Jane confined to one room, Jane worried and big with child, Jane besieged by doubt and by the great figure of Henry looming above her, waiting, waiting for her to bring forth an heir to the throne.

On Jane Seymour rested Henry's vindication. Should she not bear him his son, then was not the ghost of Nan Boleyn ready to laugh and laugh and laugh till the ghosts that already thronged Hampton Court would join in to mock him?

Twice a day chapel was held in Jane's room. Now that September was nearing a close, the weather took a turn for the worse. A northeast storm beat in from the sea—keeping sailors away, Jane said fretfully; for she longed for Tom Seymour and said so daily. The rain and wind kept the chamber from being properly aired, and the room grew stale till one day Katryn ordered a great applewood fire built, and Jane placed in the big bed, and the windows thrown open. The other ladies grumbled, and Katryn ordered them from the room. After half an hour, Jane's face looked refreshed.

"You see," said Katryn. "I was right. 'Tis not yet winter, and no harm can befall from fall air. Every day, twice, mayhap after chapel, I shall air this chamber to keep out foul humors."

The meals were the best part of the days. Jane had a fondness for quail; they arrived at the palace literally by the hundreds. The meals were intimate and gay; to keep them so Katryn let the wines flow free, until finally the jokes and jests would fly from unfettered lips and Jane would at last laugh. Henry came sometimes, and always came at chapel time to kneel with Jane and pray. This was too great an event to be treated with aught but the utmost seriousness and solemnity; much prayer, more tears, and a great deal of spilled blood waited on its outcome. Jane grew more and more restless; fits of sobbing took her, and again the ladies would be ordered from the room. At least ten times a day she would suddenly cry, "I've not felt my little knave!"

Katryn became accustomed to this. A few minutes would pass, and then Jane's child would move and the crisis would pass for another hour. Katryn grew pale too. She slept in Jane's room now, constantly close. October came. It was the first day of the month, and Katryn had been at Hampton Court three weeks. In the arduousness of caring for Jane, she forgot her own problems. Seeing the morass of intricate intrigue and the weight of terrible responsibility that rested on Jane's swollen body, she was appalled.

One night Jane gasped, "If I hadn't lain with him afore marriage, I wouldn't be so afraid! Katryn, I lost our first child!"

Katryn said, "Pray then, Jane. Pray!"

"You pray for me," Jane said. "You pray too!"

I am not good either, Katryn thought. In the light of a flickering candle, on the hearth sconces by the side of Jane's great bed, she knelt. "Bless thy servants, O Lord," she said. Jane rolled over and grasped her hand; tears dripped down on those clasped hands. "Bless thy weak frail clay and bless the bed that shall bring forth a son to England."

There was silence. Then Jane said, "Katryn, I saw the face of the Virgin, plain. Right here."

Katryn took her hand. "Sleep now, Jane," she said. "Sleep."

The next day Tom Seymour came back to Hampton Court.

He came by river. Leaning back against the gunwales of his boat, sleepy—for it had been a miserable voyage—he untangled his long legs, then stepped out onto the stones of the wharf and walked under the archway leading to one of the courts. It was a misty, cold day. The court was deserted. Past the first arch, in the nearest garden, Katryn walked back and forth, her cloak held tight against the damp. On a golden leash at her side trotted Jane's precious white poodle, which Tom had brought her four months before from France. Behind her, almost in the same way, trotted one of the maids-in-waiting, a young woman Katryn cared little for.

"She's almost a tart," Katryn had said to Jane.

"Aye," said Jane, "but she is gay, and if she is naughty the men about appreciate her. Even I watch her antics with them and laugh."

What was her name? Katryn wondered. "Isabella," she said, remembering, "you can take yourself off. 'Tis beginning to rain, and there's no need for you to get wet."

Isabella said politely, "My lady, I can walk the poodle."

"I prefer it," said Katryn. She was speaking the truth. The last two days she had taken to walking Jane's dog herself to get outside, for sometimes within the chamber she felt stifled. "I shall take another turn about."

She proceeded at a brisk pace. The misty rain felt fine; it is good for one's complexion, she thought, it is good for my hair. She passed the yew garden and went down past a row of young chestnuts. Nan Boleyn must have had these planted, she thought, and now they are growing straight and strong, and she is not here. It made her remember what Lord Latimer had said, a long time ago in the deserted convent garden. "Things endure; people do not."

She pushed away the thought. After all, she was but twenty-four. Jane *was* a trifle old for a first child; she must be nearing thirty-four, because she was the eldest, older than Ned, and older of course than Tom. At this moment, with his name in her mind, she came through the archway into the small stone court and heard his voice. She stopped. The dog stopped with a jerk, and looked about patiently at her. She could not be mistaken! Although low in pitch, it was his voice, with a hint of laughter and his lazy drawl.

"No, sweetheart," the voice was saying, "it grieves me, but I can spare neither the time nor my codware for you this afternoon. Maybe later."

Katryn jerked at the leash. She ran forward, around a stone pillar. Indeed, there he was! And with Isabella crushed in his arms, his mouth on hers.

"Sir Thomas Seymour!" Katryn's voice shook. He has placed a dagger in my heart, she thought, as Tom Seymour swung quickly about, setting Isabella to one side, almost lazily, negligently, like a toy. But how could he? Her lips quivered and she looked into his blue eyes. It had been so long, so many months, and then to meet like this!

For an endless second their eyes held. Then he reached for her hand; she felt his fingers, tight and strong. His eyes were glittering and intense. He gripped her hand tighter; it was the hand that held the leash, and as though it recalled him to the present and the gray place where he and Katryn stood, he took the leash from Katryn's fingers.

He said slowly, "Isabella, take the dog. And tell my sister, the Queen, that I shall wait upon her in an hour."

Katryn backed away but the stone wall was behind her; he took a long step and imprisoned her against the stone, blocking her way with his arm. I'm not going to look at him, she thought, casting down her eyes.

He said, "I am feasting my eyes. When did you come here, sweetheart?"

She didn't look at him. "Two weeks ago."

"The devil take those damned storms, darling. I would ha' been here long ago. I didn't know you were coming."

So he hadn't had a hand in sending for her. She stared at his wide shoulders. She didn't answer.

He said, conversationally, "It all comes of your having been deprived at an early age of a stern father. You know the old adage: never spare the rod; for while cherishing marreth sons, it utterly destroyeth daughters."

"Oh," said Katryn furiously.

"Before you are utterly destroyed, I should take a hand and give you a sound thrashing," he went on. "When would you like it administered?"

"Never!" she cried. "And pray do not lay a finger on me!"

He frowned. "I jest, sweetheart." He put his hand under her chin and tipped her face up. "You are more deeply distressed than I thought," he said. "I am in bad grace, am I not? But Isabella means naught to me. I couldn't write to you. I am in an entirely helpless position where you are concerned, and if you think I like it, you are much mistaken."

"And if you think I like remembering what was betwixt us, you are much mistook!" she flashed. I'm going to cry, she thought.

His face set. "I see." His eyes were sharp on her face, studying.

"Don't even look at me," she said. "And don't take me in your arms! I couldn't bear to follow that little tart!"

For a moment there was a deep silence.

He said, almost casually, "I had hoped our meeting would be other than it has been. I had hoped much. So you did not wish to remember, did you? And I don't know from what you have said whether you are a silly selfish child or a woman capable of love. Now go on up to Jane. I shall follow you presently."

Katryn stood silent.

"Go!" he ordered, and stood there, uncompromising, as she went slowly away from him.

Her head ached. It ached violently, and the laughter and songs and the wine made it worse.

It was a very gay supper. Jane was happy and smiling in the midst of this select company, with Lucy and Anne, and Will Herbert, and Ned and Tom Seymour, who had brought a few gentlemen with him. Katryn sat on a stool before the fire. Anne and Will were over on the window seat, and the rest of the company still sat at table, with the wine flagons full and the fruit gleaming in the silver bowl and the sweetmeats piled on two silver trays. The servants had gone. Jane sat in her huge, carved chair with three pretty maids-in-waiting hovering over her.

"Pray extinguish some of the candles," Jane commanded. "Then we can sing by the firelight."

The maids hastened about, and the room grew shadowy, and yet full of the lovely glow of firewood in the big hearth. From her stool Katryn watched Tom Seymour, for he was not looking at her. He had paid her very little mind, hardly any save for the brief welcoming kiss, which had been mainly for Jane's benefit, Katryn decided. Jane would have thought it odd they didn't greet each other in the usual manner. Then he had been closeted with Jane alone for more than an hour.

Tonight, for some reason, she was conscious that she was an outsider. Her dress wasn't quite in style, her jewels few compared to the magnificent glittering diamonds that winked from the Duchess of Richmond's white hands when she laid them caressingly on Tom Seymour's arm.

"You play for us, sir," she said. "A sailor's song."

"I?" asked Tom Seymour. "How much wine has filtered down the ladies' throats?" He took up the lute Katryn handed to him. This time he did look at her, and a flash of memory went through her. Do I love him, she thought stupidly? My head aches so, and he is

257

angry with me. I feel dead inside, and I wish I were at home with my poor sick lord. That is where I belong. Katryn took a big gulp of wine. He was dressed in black-and-white striped velvet. In the half-dark, he looked like the Italian paintings she had seen, the Continental courtiers. One of the maids-in-waiting sat at his feet, the Duchess of Richmond leaned close, too close—why, if he moves his arm he will touch her breast, Katryn thought. The firelight flickered over his dark face, just as his eyes played over her once in a while. Faithless he is, a knave, a scoundrel, and I knew it from the beginning. But to see it, to witness it—it is too much, and I cannot endure it. And with all this was Jane, who, as each day passed, grew more and more fearful. Last night she had prayed the whole night and sobbed endlessly and cried till there were no more tears left in her eyes; nay, Katryn thought, she couldn't have a drop of water in her body, so deep had she been wrung.

"I have sinned," Jane cried, "and the Lord will punish me!"

Now that her time was near, she was gripped with terror. But, that night, even after she slept, Katryn, shaken, lay awake at her side, lying quiet in the bed so as not to disturb the heavy unmoving body of her Queen.

This is my Queen—Jane, Jane who is now deathly afraid. O Lord have mercy on her! she prayed. Let her bear a son, let her be happy, pray let her be happy! I won't think on Tom Seymour, she vowed, I will not, I shall not! She closed her eyes and plainly she heard his voice, as close as though he were lying beside her singing a silly ditty; "And I will take a special care of rumplin' of your gown, O!"

Am I asleep, she wondered? The voice changed, and he was saying, as he had said the second day he had been home, "Katryn, at the risk of annoying you, I am going to warn you. You are making enemies. The lady-in-waiting Anne Stanhope, who was Jane's closest friend, is jealous and angry. Be careful. You are running Hampton Court like Snape Hall. There are some who resent it."

"I am taking care of Jane!"

"Aye, and I am grateful. But use care and caution if you would not stir up the twin dogs of malice and envy. I am told you even insist on arranging the flowers."

"Baa," said Katryn. "You sound just like a black-faced sheep!"

Their accents warred. Tom Seymour pronounced flowers without the w, slurring the whole word, and Katryn's a's came out like o's.

"Block-faced!" he mocked.

"Flahrs," she shot back. She glanced about. Were people looking? She essayed a smile. "Thank you for your solicitude, sir," she said. "I'll treasure it, you may be sure!"

"You had best heed it," he said. "You make it difficult for me to help you, Katryn."

The waking dream persisted. She was sitting on the window seat after dinner that day, when Tom Seymour took his place beside her, turning toward her a little. If he leaned nearer, she thought, I would be in his arms.

"This is a peculiar kind of agony," he said low. "Or do I fail to judge it correct? Anyway, at the risk of a rebuff—and damn it, I don't go about pursuing women!—will you meet me this afternoon in the garden?"

She said, her eyes triumphant, "Nay!"

"I see," he said. "What a proper little wench you are! But devil take me if I don't remember you with your petticoats up about your waist and your breasts bare."

"Oh!" she gasped. She looked full at him, and his blue eyes were glittering and full of knowing. "You devil, you taunting devil!" His eyes held hers; he was so very close. "If you think my guilt has not cost me hour after hour of sleepless nights!" she cried, under her breath.

"I might be able to match you in that," he said, "but maybe for a different reason."

"You jest, and make fun," she said. "But I'll not be one of your lights-o'-love; I'll not! I'll not have you look at me, and think there's a wench I've had enough of." She stopped. What had she said?

He was still frowning, black brows drawn, regarding her with intent and curious gaze.

"I've said too much," she said low. "And so have you." Unspeaking lips uttered no secrets.

Katryn stirred in the big bed. She opened her eyes. Had she heard a noise? Had Jane wakened? Then out of the darkness she heard Jane's voice. "Katryn," she cried. "Katryn! I have pain! My time is upon me!"

12

It was night. The presence-chamber stretched vast and polished and tapestried. Crosses and images were within the room, and about the bier twenty-four tapers burned, bearing light aloft on their slender height.

At the foot of the bier, Katryn kept her nightly watch, her red head covered with a white pleated kerchief, her body gowned completely in black. This was the final night of her vigil, for tomorrow Jane's body would be removed to the chapel. The wages of sin was death.

Jane! Katryn thought. Oh Jane! If I could only have helped, only have aided thee! I stood helpless and watched tragedy enfold thee! Jane who was so brave, and whose hours of seemingly unending labor had brought forth a son for England, a little boy named Edward, who kicked and cried in his cradle this very night.

The palace slept. Its occupants moved black-clad. Its King was gone, withdrawn to Windsor in grief, leaving behind the mortal remains of his wife and Queen and the mother of his son.

Katryn shifted her position on her stool; her legs and arms and back were stiff, for every night she had maintained the watch on Jane's coffin. Stay with the dead till they depart. Leave them not alone in darkness; light twenty-four candles to dispel the night; see how merrily they burn! And let the men not enter here. As women bring life into the world, let them then be present at the gates of death.

Katryn closed her eyes. I cannot pray, she thought; no more can I pray, and all Jane's and my prayers were unanswered. They never ascended to heaven! Here on earth we walk alone, tonight I am sure of it. Jane did not think so. And Jane wished to be buried in the old faith. I mind me the night she quarreled with Ned, till I had to send him from the room. "You're too much for her," I cried, "aye, and you too, Sir Thomas! Big argufying men, and with your laughing and talking."

Tom Seymour had looked boyishly abashed. "I thought we cheered her," he said getting to his feet.

"What her Grace needs is some solitude and some solicitude," she said firmly, and Tom Seymour looked at her uncomprehending.

"Solitude?"

Katryn heaved a big sigh. "Aye," she said. "You don't understand, and this chamber always bulges with people."

Now Katryn looked over at Anne, on her stool. Past Anne was Lucy's white-kerchiefed head, and past Lucy was Anne Stanhope. Her head was bent. She mislikes me much, Katryn thought. I have made an enemy; Tom Seymour was right. But what did it matter? Except her mother had always said, "Never, never, Katryn, make an enemy." She drew a long breath. Well, soon she would be going to Snape Hall; all the boxes were packed, and tonight was her last night in the great palace of Hampton Court. She stared at Anne Stanhope's white kerchief, and white swam before her eyes. Jane, lying on a state pallet, swathed in five ells of whitest lawn, wearing red velvet, covered with jewels, wearing her crown, all asea in the white lawn as it fell about the pallet and onto the floor. There she had rested last Sunday night, Jane with Henry beside her—Henry the proud father—Henry who at last had a male heir to the throne of England.

White . . . Tom Seymour dressed in white velvet, attending at the christening whilst Jane waited in the state chamber. Her little son was borne to the chapel here at Hampton Court, and all the greatest nobles in England attended him, paying homage to their new prince. Katryn closed her eyes and saw the proud procession coming back from the chapel, and remembered how she had advanced to meet Tom Seymour and taken from his arms the three-year-old Elizabeth, the Lady Elizabeth, daughter to Nan Boleyn. Sleepy and fretful had the child been, for it was after midnight.

Midnight.

Katryn took the child, and gave her to her nurse. But by the time the company had dispersed, color burned in Jane's face higher than the red velvet of her royal robes.

Childbed fever, the doctors said. Fever and pain and thirst—and death.

"God bless you, Jane," Katryn whispered, under her breath. Soon it would be midnight, and her hours of vigil past. She heard the first chime of the clock, the first of the coming twelve strokes. "God bless you, Jane." She laid her hand on the edge of the coffin. She rose. She stood with head bent. The Lord had not heeded Jane, and he certes should have! "Lord," she said, not aloud, "you should make her a saint!"

Katryn blinked back her tears as she thought of Jane in heaven. How beautiful she must be! She stood stiffly. Then slowly, with no backward glance, she left the presence-chamber, and the candles burning, and the long bier, and the silent, seated figures of the other women.

The long gallery was dimly lit. The palace, which had been so unfamiliar, was now part of her life, and she set her foot on the top step of the twelve-foot-wide stairway and placed her hand on the carved rail, only partly conscious of the great tapestries, the brilliant colors of the paint, the angels leaning from the ceilings. Up the stairway came a man dressed in black.

They met at the rail. Katryn looked at his face, almost at a level with her own. How wickedly handsome he was, she thought distantly, and I am leaving him. She looked into the blue eyes. Arrogance and breeding was stamped on the dark features. The clock was still striking, but time had stopped.

"Master Tom," she said low, and gave him her hand.

He took it gently. After a moment he said, "That old greeting, from your lips, moves me, Katryn. How much happier we were!"

She nodded wordlessly. Then she said, "What tragedy strikes within these walls!"

Tom Seymour looked at her close. "Whenever there are a few hundreds of people gathered under one roof, Katryn, you will find all extremes of living." He frowned, his thoughts obviously going on. "Do you remember what Ned said the day we dined at the Mitre? If I recall correct, his words were: 'Someday we shall look back, and wonder where we went astray, or how we have changed or what we did wrong.' "

Katryn said, "Jane felt she had sinned."

Tom Seymour said, "We all are sinners."

Katryn was silent, remembering. The three of them, together, so vital. Now Jane had left them. The triumvirate was no longer. Change . . . To resist was to try to hold the floodgates with one's bare hands. To face life one had indeed to be strong, to stand straight, to have faith, to have courage. To love.

"Learning about living is very difficult," she said, and Tom Seymour squeezed her hand and smiled at her.

"Sweetheart," he said, "your words make me realize why I love you. Thou'rt a sturdy little wench, with such capable little hands." He turned her hand over; he looked down at it.

Katryn tried to think straight. "I love you," he had said. Did he know what he was saying? she wondered. How could he not? She swallowed.

"Katryn, as for Jane's request that you look after Edward—you know of course that the appointments to Edward's train have already been made, and you are not amongst them."

Katryn said, "I was torn two ways! I should not leave my lord, for you know he is ill. Snape Hall needs me—aye, and my children there, e'en Bess's little boy Will. How would they do without me there in Yorkshire? And I could not bring my lord with me!"

"Nay," he shook his head. "Lord Latimer is in disfavor; there would be no question of his accompanying you. I was greatly tempted, Katryn. One request from me to his Grace would have made you a gentlewoman in Edward's household, husbandless, where I could pursue my dastardly aims. I am letting you go, Katryn."

"I—" she began.

"Say nothing," he said. "Good-by."

" 'Twas her last request, from her dying lips," Katryn faltered. " 'Prithee, care for my son, my little boy.' " Her eyes filled with tears.

Tom Seymour said, "Listen, Katryn. Edward is but two weeks old. He shall need you more later than he does now, and now he is surrounded as much as an infant can be with love and thought and kindness. Later—" He broke off.

When is later? she thought. What will the months ahead bring?

"Good-by," he had said. "Good-by."

Below her the stairway shimmered down, down, in the faint light. For the last time, she thought, I see him close.

"Good-by," she whispered. She put her hand on the side of his face. His arms went around her and she clasped his dark head close to her black-covered breast. Under her palm the feel of his thick hair was inexpressibly dear. How could a moment of parting be such poignant happiness?

He set her away from him. "Good-by," she said tremulously. Then she put her hand back on the carved railing and slowly went down the great long staircase of Hampton Court.

BOOK TWO

13

The wind was contrary. It blew gustily from the north-north-west, and the ship's uneven pitching brought Tom Seymour out of his cabin and up on deck, fastening his leather coat tight against the December wind. Indeed, this was no sailing weather. The *Sweepstakes* dipped and shuddered and then held firm. Tom Seymour paced the deck to keep warm. Although he was quite sure his crew could bring the *Sweepstakes* into port, still this was tricky business with the wind so gusty; and so he paced back and forth while the shores of England came close.

He was making for Southampton, and the winter sunlight touched the Dover cliffs with brief white fire; then the sun went under the clouds, and the gray day and the gray sea closed down on ships and men again. It reminded him of the day he had brought Anne of Cleves, the King's bride, from France four years before; and as he remembered that royal cargo a brief smile touched his lips. He swore, aloud, and rubbed his gloved hand against his cheek. He had known when he saw the lady that Henry would never have her, and he had been right. "I'd as soon bed a mare," Henry had said, and got his divorce as promptly as possible.

He remembered his own dismay when he had first seen Anne of Cleves. She bore no resemblance at all to the portrait Holbein had sent of her. So while her impatient bridegroom waited in London, Tom Seymour entertained Anne of Cleves in Calais till the winter storm that had blown up should subside. "Although," he said to Southampton, who was there to entertain and greet Henry's German bride, "it might be best for us to set sail and pitch her overboard."

Southampton grinned. He was trying to teach Anne to play cent, which the King enjoyed, and he found it difficult, for he knew no

German and Anne no English. Tom Seymour used to have to absent himself from the chamber in which they played, as Anne's horse-faced ladies watched, because the situation became so hilarious to him that he could not control his laughter. "I thank God every day," he said to Southampton, "that you have to entertain her and I have only to sail the ship. I'll wager you a hundred crowns his Grace won't lie with her."

"Done," said Southampton, but he had to forfeit the money after a long, merry talk with the Queen's attendants some two months later.

During the voyage across to England, all the Germans, men and women, had been seasick, Tom remembered, and it was a sorry bunch they had landed in England. When Anne received Henry's gift of sables, and then Henry himself, she was still green and shaken. And Henry, who had come down by barge to meet her at Rochester, recoiled. He lumbered into the room where Southampton and Tom Seymour were lounging.

"Do you gentlemen think she is like to her picture?" he asked.

Tom grinned. "Your Grace," he said, bowing, "he couldn't very well ha' painted her naked."

Now Anne was comfortably installed in various residences, including a house in London; she loved England, and Henry had asked Parliament to naturalize her, and she took precedence over every other lady in the land save for the King's two daughters. She would probably send Tom a home-baked gift for Christmas—some puddings and some blackberry preserves, delivered to his door with a nice note. He could imagine her in her kitchens herself, up to the elbows in flour, humming happily.

He turned from the rail. The sail above his head was slatting a bit, and he shouted an order and squinted upward to watch the trim. In an hour he should be stepping ashore.

In London, he went direct to the house that had been his for three years now; for in lieu of services rendered to the crown, Henry had given over to him the former palace of the Bishops of Durham, a commodious, old-fashioned town house set in the part of the city Tom Seymour loved, the Inns of the Court. Renamed Seymour Place, it welcomed him home.

In the study, he deposited safely his maps and charts and the confidential reports for Henry; then he mounted the wide stairway, passed through the gallery, down by guest bedrooms to his own big room in the front of the house. From within came the murmur of men's voices. He stepped into the room. It was paneled, and a huge fire burned on the hearth, its light gleaming on the great oak sideboard and chests, and on the carved oak bedstead with its plain, dark, damask hangings. Tom Seymour sank down into his chair, already drawn before the fire, stretched out booted legs to have the footgear removed, and sighed with some pleasure. The thick Moorish carpet he had picked up on one of his voyages felt soft and warm beneath his feet. He had an hour's respite; he could have a bathe, and a half hour's nap before he should seek out the King. He leaned his dark head back against the chair back and closed his eyes.

When he opened them again, the room was less crowded; only Fowler, his favorite gentleman, and his barber were within. Fowler said, "I have commanded hot water to be brought."

Tom Seymour closed his eyes again; but when the door opened, it was not a man but a woman, and in some surprise he surveyed her thoughtfully. His was mainly a household of men, and— He leaned his chin on his hand, sitting straighter now, and watched as she laid down towels on the bench. She started for the door when his voice stopped her.

"Hold there a moment, wench."

She came to a full stop.

"Turn and face me," he ordered, puzzled. How had she been introduced into Seymour Place? Young and fair and lusty she was; his black brows drawn slightly, he evaluated her and her presence here.

He said, "You may answer me a few questions."

It took him two minutes to elicit the information that she was the youngest daughter of one of the Earl of Surrey's bailiffs, thus probably placed here apurpose. He thought briefly on Surrey and the powerful family he represented, the Howards. The Howards could not be other than bitter that the Seymours had presented England with an heir. Edward was five. That little prince—Tom Seymour's nephew—stood square between the Howards and their pretensions.

Tom's barber, half French, could restrain his Gallic temper no longer. He advanced on the girl, razorstrop in hand.

"Miserable wench!" he cried. "Do you think to spy, then? I'll beat you for this!"

The girl flung herself at Tom Seymour and grasped his knees. "I haven't spied, my lord!"

Tom glanced up at the vengeful face of his barber. Obviously he knew this wench well; probably he had already seduced her. Tom laughed. Surrey may have thought to beguile him with this girl, but one of his household had beaten him to her. Tom Seymour looked at his barber.

"Why, you villain, François," he said. "I believe you have already introduced her to your manly talents." He placed his hand on the girl's shoulder. "Rise up. You shan't be punished, unless it be that I hand over François to you as husband. That should be punishment enough."

"Get out," François cried, waving his strop.

Tom Seymour closed his eyes again, and leaned back his head. He was thinking that this was a clumsy trick on Surrey's part and deserved payment in coin. And it would not be long in coming, for he should meet Surrey tonight, at supper. He rose and began to take off his shirt.

The Earl of Surrey at that moment lay face down on his bed in Hampton Court; having chased his gentlemen out of his bedroom, he was alone.

He knew very well he should not stay here at court; he was far better off in the country, striding the hills and meadows, writing or reading. But his ambitions pushed him, and he could never forget that he ought to be able to quarter the royal arms on his standards. Some day he would, by God, he swore into his pillow, for according to the laws of birth and nature, he was endowed more heavily than any of these clods with whom he had to deal, and he included Henry himself.

These were dangerous thoughts, but he was sure they were safe if he kept them to himself. His family's career had been fraught both with success and tragic failure, and in the last year the Howards had offered another queen to Henry, and she had betrayed both Henry and them. After Henry's quick divorce from Anne of Cleves, the Howards threw into Henry's path Surrey's eighteen-year-old cousin, Catherine.

Catherine had been brought up by the old Duchess of Norfolk, her grandmother; she slept in a big room with other giggling girls, and supervision was delightfully lacking. Into this bower of unguarded femininity, the young men of the household crept at night, laden with spoils from the pantry. They lay on the beds together and ate and drank.

Catherine shared her bed with Joan Bulmer. Joan had already known a lover, and Cat Howard, sleek and soft as a kitten and as amoral as her nickname, quickly discovered that midnight raids on her ardent body were the sweetest pleasure of all.

Her first lover was a young man by name of Manox, whom the old Duchess had discovered caressing her whilst he taught her the spinnet; the old Duchess cuffed her soundly and sent her to bed. She was fourteen then. Next came Francis Derham, a young kin of the Norfolk family. With him Cat fell in love, and this affair stretched into her seventeenth year. The Duchess, warned by gossip, descended on her chamber one night and found them together. The Duchess cuffed Derham this time, and aimed a blow at wild Joan Bulmer, who stood tremblingly by. The Duchess then sent Catherine to court.

But now the King saw her, and within two days he was calling her his rose without a thorn. She was small, with a full and perfect figure, and she dressed in the French manner, her little corset worn so tight at the waist that her high, round breasts strained at her bodice, and Henry could keep neither eyes nor hands from them. Openly he caressed her. On July twenty-eighth he married her; it was the day he sent Cromwell to his death. As he remembered this, Surrey shuddered.

Catherine loved to give. She gave away Henry's gifts to her with bursts of generosity; she showered favors on her own family and the Howards prospered. To Joan Bulmer, who was still with her, she gave the little dog Henry had brought her one morning; she passed on jewels to her ladies. To Henry himself she gave her warm sensuous body, and she created a gay amoral court. Cat Howard loved to eat and drink and make love; she waxed plumper and richer and her bodices grew tighter; she blossomed like the rose, overflowing the confines of her gowns; and as long as she gave away trinkets but kept herself for Henry, all went well.

"But there is no rose without a thorn," Surrey said; "we should have been warned." The old Duchess had whispered to him once, "Well, she cannot be tried for what happened *afore* she was wed." Surrey had assured the King that Catherine's virtue was spotless. Then her past rose to haunt her. Derham appeared and demanded a sinecure at court, and Catherine, frightened, made him a gentlman of her chamber. The ring of old friends around her soon became a temptation. Catherine Howard was tried for treason and infidelity, and she went to her death bravely. On Tower Green, before the headsman, she cried her last words, "Good people, I never sought to harm the King!" She sobbed aloud. Then she knelt, like her cousin Nan Boleyn, and her little head rolled over three times before it reached the bottom of the straw basket.

Surrey had reproached his father. "We never should ha' placed her in Henry's grasp!"

Norfolk was wild with rage. That this could happen to him! That he, the most cunning of them all, should be surrounded by this family of ninnies, who gave away all that was valuable for a few caresses in bed. He could not believe it. He had disposed of Cromwell, married Henry to Catherine, and sat back to reap the rewards. But through the folly of Henry's rose, because of the folly of a stupid girl who gave away all, he, Norfolk, had lost too.

Henry had retired and cried over Catherine Howard. He was stupefied that she could have betrayed him. This big hulking man was hurt to the quick.

Now it was six months later and, as Surrey said cynically to his father, "His Grace's tears have dried."

It was no use thinking and regretting the past. The fault had lain in Catherine herself, who was too generous. It was her generous sensuality which had aroused the King; it was her very nature which had betrayed her. It was over and done. Surrey sat up and clenched his hands. His own sister—it was best to face it—was kin to Catherine Howard in every way, except she was capable of the Howard malice. She, Mary, wanted Tom Seymour, dark-faced devil that he was. "God!" Surrey swore aloud. That there could be such defection in their ranks! He sat up on his bed. He agreed with his father: all the Howard women were fools—beautiful but fools. Two of them, Nan Boleyn and Cat Howard, had wed with Henry and driven him to despair and murder. Mary his sister had wed with the King's bastard son; now she was a widow. But the upstart Seymours had managed to intrude themselves, and now, instead of two female princesses needing good English husbands, there was a young prince with two swarthy, towering uncles to do battle for him should aught befall the massive King himself. The struggle betwixt Howard and Seymour was fought with deadly intensity; for kingdoms were at stake here, and Edward Tudor, five years of age, was frail. Surrey pushed that aside; the thorn in his flesh now was Mary, who wanted Tom Seymour as a husband.

"I've a huge dowry," she cried.

Surrey had tried to be calm. "Mary," he said, "Seymour has a deal of money himself, but even if he didn't, I doubt if you could bribe him. He is—let's give the devil his due—not inclined to value money. That is, he thinks he can get it if he wants it. He is the kind of man who thinks he can have anything he desires if he desires it bad enough."

"I offer him the finest name in England!"

"Ah, yea," he said. That was true. Even Tom Seymour should be impressed by the name of Howard. And was it possible that Mary might beguile him, might win him over, might cement an alliance? He frowned. Did she have wit enough? Or would it be that she would succumb to his policies, and instead of gaining his allegiance, they would lose hers? He eyed her sharply. She was his sister, and he was inclined to think she was cleverer than either of his two cousins, even though Nan Boleyn had been witty enough. But there was in all of them that streak of headstrong, unpredictable excitement that drove them to unseasoned deeds. Surrey was sharp enough to wonder whether he was guilty of it himself. An alliance between his sister and Tom Seymour? It might not go amiss. Mayhap it was worth a trial. He seized his sister by the arm. "But guard your virtue," he said with sarcasm, "you are the widowed Duchess of Richmond! Remember it!"

She had left him, and now he sprawled full length on his bed; he realized that supper must be over. He should leave this room and go out. Anyway, he was in no mood to think longer; his moods changed of a sudden. He strode to the door, picking up two of his gentlemen from his privy chamber, and went out into the gallery with them at his heels.

In the gallery the women were grouped around the Princess Mary. The women sat demurely at one end of the long gallery sewing and chattering, their musical instruments laid aside. The men were gathered about Henry, who stood with his back to the great fire, almost under the huge overhanging mantel, feet well astraddle. As Surrey approached, there was a roar of laughter from the whole group, and he guessed someone had just told the King a joke. The ladies looked over to the men, and the Princess Mary pursed her lips and grew white. She couldn't have heard it, Surrey thought; she merely disapproves of men's laughter.

He crossed the inlaid floor. The court was cheerless. They had all thanked Catherine for the gaiety she had created. All her women were young, and the night's festivities ended in lovemaking. There had been no end to the dancing, the wines, the laughter, the titillation occasioned by a new face and a pair of sparkling eyes and firm young flesh eager for a man's caresses. Surrey walked slowly over to the group of gallants around Henry.

Henry was saying to Tom Seymour, about Princess Mary, "I don't believe that Lady Mary would even understand your words." The King was glad to have Tom Seymour back, for he was a man after his own heart. And Henry, who trusted no one, trusted Tom Seymour because he was sure it was to Seymour's interest to protect Edward. Now Henry noted that Tom Seymour had seen the tall, suave Earl of Surrey approaching, and that there was a glint in Tom Seymour's eyes; as a master politician, Henry Tudor liked to see two powerful factions at court wrangle and fight. If one of them became too powerful—well then, he could always step in himself and even the odds with an execution on Tower Green. Surrey was getting too big for the boots he wore, too. Henry, feet planted very wide, settled his jeweled cap and waited with some pleasure, for his just now court was excessively dull.

As Surrey approached, Tom Seymour stepped forward from the circle of men, watching. Even across the room the women fell silent, and the two men met face to face. Tom Seymour's voice was low but it carried.

"I've been wanting to see you, Surrey," he said. "Here!"

Surrey instinctively reached out and caught the shiny object tossed at him. He glanced down at the gold coin, as Tom Seymour said, "Is it enough?" His voice was genial. "I've never had a man pimp for me afore, but I must admit you're clever at it. You should make it your profession."

Surrey grew white and tense, and his eyes burned. He clutched the coin, and almost threw it to the floor; then he didn't know what to do with it, for it would be too childish to throw it. He stood there helplessly enraged. Tom Seymour smirked his wicked smile, and Surrey put his hand to his dagger. It took that long for Anne Herbert to cross the floor, seemingly unhurried, to put herself between the two men.

"Why, Tom," she said, in her clear sweet voice. She lifted her face for a kiss, which Tom Seymour bestowed on her lips.

He whispered, "Are you putting your frail female body between two angry men?" She gave him a dimpled smile. Aloud he said, "You look well and happy, Anne."

"Oh, I am," she said. "Very happy. And I ha' good cause. After these many years away"—she almost said "in exile," but bit off the words—"my dearest sister Katryn is back in London."

Katryn wakened early. She could hear the sound of Lord Latimer's coughing, and she rose and went to him.

It was still dark, although the house was stirring; there were kitchen noises, and noises from Bess's boys' room—Katryn supposed they were wrestling in the big bed. She could hear the servants tramping up the stairs with wood for the fire.

Lord Latimer was sitting up in bed, his cap awry, holding his hands to his chest and trying to check the paroxysm of coughing. She found him a clean napkin and poured him some wine from the flagon which stood by the window so it would keep cool. He drank gratefully, and finally patted her hand and managed a smile. He sucked breath into his mouth and said, "Good morning, my dear. What time is it?"

"Very early," she replied. She was lighting the candles on the mantel.

"I roused you," he said regretfully, but she shook her head. In the light he could see her better, and he peered at her and settled his cap. "You're so fair, even sleepy and mussed," he said. Her hand went to her uncombed hair, and she tied her robe more securely. Lord Latimer motioned to her, and she went over to the bed and sat on the edge of it and he took her hand. He ran his fingers up and down her white middle finger. "Such beautiful hands," he said, and kissed it.

She leaned over and kissed the side of his cheek. "Good morning," she said.

He lay back against the pillows, and she rose and pulled them into a more comfortable position and straightened his bed, settling the quilt. He suffered these ministrations impatiently and, when she was done, patted the bed again. "Sit a moment. Stop fussing."

"I wasn't fussing," she said, and laughed, for between them were many small memories and knowledges of each other; he often teased her about her abilities as a nurse, and she twitted him often as being her most fretting patient. "Worse than a woman in childbed," she would say.

"Sit you here, Nurse Nightrobe," he said. "I shall not eat a morsel unless you do."

"I wish you would eat this morning," she said, after a moment's silence, whilst he held one hand and stroked the other, leaning back with his eyes closed, having his fill of her nearness. He sighed and asked her why he should eat.

"Because Bishop Latimer is coming this morning to preach, and you know how much you enjoy it."

He nodded. He was not averse to Hugh Latimer, or even to Archbishop Cranmer, feeling that they were men in the tradition of Sir Thomas More, who had carried their thoughts into the New Church, forsaking the old. He himself would never forsake the Church, but during his illness he had read widely and deeply on theology, and he was content to have the New Learning broached to him. He found much good in it. "As I grow older and sicker," he said, "I find my passions leaving me." He gave her a small deprecatory smile. "And my processes of logical thinking replacing emotion. Except, my dear"—he raised himself on one elbow—"my love for thee."

Katryn bit her lip and leaned over to kiss him. He lay back against the pillows again, and was quiet, and so was she, and this interlude gave her time to contrast the woman last evening with the one who sat now alongside her husband's bed, and it seemed quite incredible;

she could not reconcile it. Last night she had dreamed of Tom Seymour.

It had been a week since she had seen him. He knew she was here in London, but seven days and seven nights had passed, and he had not come. And this absence was an unspoken message, she knew, as though across the steep-pitched roofs that separated the two houses, along the busy daytime streets and alleys, and along their sleeping loneliness at night, his absence spoke clearer than words. But what was he saying by it? It had been five long years since she had heard his voice, and she couldn't recapture it. But the words, what were they? "I have forgot you Katryn, and what is between us is over. Did you think it would not be?"

Damn him! she thought furiously. Here am I, a woman grown, amooning about a man. Here am I, with a huge household to run, with Bess's two boys and Bess herself, with Margaret to get a good husband for soon, and John in Oxford, home now; and my husband, and my maids, and my new position—attained in two months with no influence whatsoever—as London's favorite hostess. She didn't herself know quite how she had done the last. Kate Willoughby said it was because she was a saint, and good for London. Lord Latimer said it was because for five years she had immersed herself in the welfare of others, and that a wealth of charm and kindness and warmth showered from her smile.

Tom Seymour had seen none of her new gowns. He had not laid eyes on her, and it had been merest chance that she had seen him, for he had passed by her as she listened to the preaching at St. Paul's Cross a week ago. Just one week ago he had gone riding by, and the thick press of men and women about the Cross had been diverted.

"The next lord admiral," the man next her said.

Tom Seymour waved his hand in greeting to the crowd. Men smiled and waved back, and called to him. The preacher had stopped talking a moment, and the man next her spoke again. "Those are well-armed knaves with him—see them, madam? But even alone I warrant his enemies wouldn't lay hands on him!"

Katryn raised herself on tiptoe and waved. An instant's vision of him were he to recognize her in the crowd went through her mind. How exciting it would be! He would rein in, and leap down from his horse, and— He was riding on. Disappointment and irritation filled her. It was the beginning of a week of wondering. His face intruded itself at the oddest times—when she was helping Margaret with a gown, or hearing the boys' lessons, or going over the lists of necessaries with the housekeeper. It intruded into the sermons she listened to, and into her sleep and into her dreams. After all these years, she thought, and I considered myself grown to woman's estate, putting aside love and romance, being a mother as best I can, and a wife and a sheep farmer, getting my pleasure not from a man's kiss but the beauty of a spring day; getting my love not from a man like Tom Seymour but from the sweet kiss of a child. Foregoing and being denied a man to lie with and children to bear, I have done the best I could.

Thoughts plagued her. Alone in bed at night, she was plagued by memory. Last night she had risen and sat by the dying fire wrapped in her robe, and had drunk wine while Meg fretted until Katryn finally told her to be quiet. She had drunk too much, and then had sat at her mirror in the light of two candles and studied her face and unbound hair. The eyes she looked into gleamed with their gold sparks, and the wine loosened her inside till she felt as if she were composed only of warmth and passion.

What would it be like to be Tom Seymour's mistress? She visioned herself sweeping into Whitehall on his arm, holding her head high and haughty and giving back stare for stare. She smiled at herself in the mirror. Then she had another glass of wine and got into bed.

"Oh, by the mass!" she said aloud, so forcefully that Lord Latimer jumped. Katryn looked at him guiltily.

"It will probably snow today," she said, as if to explain her profanity. "And I must go ready myself."

She dressed in a green woolen gown with a white collar.

She hurried, for nine o'clock came quickly. At half past eight the cart of the town's leading vintner arrived, with two hogsheads of French wine, a gift from Ned Seymour. Pleased, Katryn knew he would come then today.

Her gallery filled. The Bishop arrived, and then, ten minutes before the hour, a carriage drew up. Out of it, Ned Seymour clambered, then his wife, clumsy with child, and Mary, the Duchess of Richmond. Alongside of them, Tom Seymour dismounted, and took the Duchess' arm. From the top of the stairway, where she stood to greet her guests at the threshold to the long gallery, Katryn saw him coming toward her.

She felt numb. Now that he was here at last, she couldn't swallow, and she was afraid she would do something foolish, like forgetting her name. And it was a sickening reality that he had brought a woman with him. Were the good gossips right about Tom Seymour and Mary Howard? Was he going to wed with her? His progress up the stairway was slow, impeded by Ned's wife, who took one step at a time, her cloak swinging to reveal her heavy proportion. "She must be carrying twins," Katryn thought jealously. "I've never liked her and she's never liked me since the very beginning, when she was Anne Stanhope and hated me for coming between Jane Seymour and her. No, she has never liked me, and long long ago Tom Seymour told me to be careful. I shall try to be." She made her voice very warm.

"My lady," she said, and took Anne's hand. It was big and heavy like her body. Katryn drew her forward, and told one of Lord Latimer's young cousins to find Lady Hertford a stool immediately. Then she greeted Ned, thanking him for the wine.

Katryn steeled herself. To the Duchess of Richmond she had to curtsy. Her foot slipped, and she righted herself hastily, looking up to see Tom Seymour's blue eyes resting on her with a hint of laughter in their depths. He saw that slip, she thought, he never misses anything; he's just the same as always—the villain.

He towered over her, and he leaned down and kissed her lips, a brief brush of the mouth. For a second he regarded her. He said, "I perceive we have a new fashion in London, Katryn." His eyes went over the rest of the company briefly, noting the faces. He seemed unhurried, he bowed to several of the nearest men, and then he settled the Duchess on a stool next to Ned's wife. Katryn threw a hasty glance about. Most of the women were already seated, but the men continued to stand.

Tom Seymour said to the Duchess, "I prefer standing, Mary. I mislike stools." Then frowning slightly, he said to Katryn, "Tell me. Who is that young gentleman talking with the Bishop?"

Katryn understood that the young man in question was the only man in the room he didn't know. "That is John Cheke," she said. "My boys'—Bess's boys'—" she corrected, "their tutor. He was at

Oxford, but Stephen Gardiner disapproved of his teaching Greek. Master Cheke was without a sinecure then, and I took him in."

Tom Seymour looked hard at the young man in question. "Excuse me, Katryn," he said, and Katryn watched him go over to the Bishop and John Cheke. Why is he interested, she thought? And he had acted as though—as though— She couldn't put her finger on it. As though they had never been separated for five years, and yet as though they had.

Katryn turned to greet another arrival, this time the Lady Frances Grey and her precocious daughter Jane. It was almost the hour for the Bishop to begin. Katryn saw Tom Seymour leave John Cheke; he came over to her side just before she sat down.

"I would like to speak with you later," he said. Then he stepped back, leaning slightly against the wall with his arms folded, and the Bishop began. Tom Seymour obediently bowed his dark head. Katryn bent her red one. Out of the corner of her eye she could see his polished-calf high boots. She closed her eyes.

She tried to listen to the sermon, but it was well nigh impossible. She was too conscious of Tom Seymour's presence, and she couldn't help darting glances at him every once in a while. He seemed intent on the Bishop's words. But his eyes would flick over the rest of the company in the closely packed gallery, as though he were summing up who was here and who was not. Today even the Lady Anne of Cleves was here. The Lady Frances Grey was the King's niece, his sister's child. "I perceive a new fashion in London, Katryn," he had said. He acted rather as though he were surveying it, to see why it had happened. Katryn remembered her first days in London, opening the big house.

Then after a week, after she had listened to the sermons at St. Paul's, she had sought out Miles Coverdale. "My lord, Lord Latimer, lies ill," she had said, "and cannot leave his house. Would you come thither some day to preach, sir, to give him and our house your wise counsel?" Miles Coverdale had come, and Katryn had invited Anne and Lucy and Kate Willoughby to come too. That had been in October. Now, in December, Miles Coverdale was coming each week, and on Christmas Eve at twelve, he was coming and so, thought Katryn, was half the court.

Guests continued to arrive, but the two most powerful men in the room were Tom and Ned Seymour. Ned Seymour was the Earl of Hertford now, and a privy councilor on his way to the lord chancellorship they had talked about eight years ago at the Mitre. Tom Seymour was master of the ordnance and vice-admiral of the Navy. Jane's death had not impeded their ambitious progress, as their enemies had said it would. Katryn knew her gallery was full of their adherents, too. Tom Seymour has almost a proprietary air, she thought angrily, as though I were putting on a show for his and his friends' benefit.

Bishop Latimer was famous for his sermons. His exhortations rolled thunderously over the heads of his listeners, for he believed the words of God were even mightier than these noble names. But would he never end? Katryn thought. Today I cannot listen. Suddenly the Bishop began to pray, and gratefully Katryn bent her head.

The Bishop's voice ended. Lord Latimer rose unsteadily from his chair to thank him. Katryn looked over at him; leaning on his cane on one side, his favorite manservant supporting his other arm, his smile flashed out genuine and sweet. Of all Englishmen, she thought, he epitomizes the real gentleman, all the word implies. With Lord Latimer honor and courage and learning were combined with what the Bishop said was sweet charity of soul. She moved swiftly to his side.

Lord Latimer bestowed his most winning smile on his wife. It enveloped her, enabling her to stand beside him sure and unafraid. She realized of a sudden that his presence had helped her immeasurably and that the triumph she had garnered so quickly from London was partly due to him—not only to his innate charm but also to the fact that his presence gave her the last bit of assurance she had needed to face the brilliant figures that had thronged her gallery for the past six weeks. And it was even more remarkable when one considered that Lord Latimer never stayed at these gatherings. Soon he would leave, after speaking with but a handful of his guests. Ruefully, and making light of his sickness, he would ask them to excuse him and his infirmities.

"I should much enjoy speaking of the Bishop's wise words with you, my lady," he was saying to Anne of Cleves. " 'Tis but misfortune that I must meditate on them alone, and at rest."

Anne of Cleves stood looking after his departing figure. "Your lord," she said to Katryn, "is an endearing man."

Katryn smiled, her eyes watching his progress to the door. She knew Tom Seymour was standing to one side of her. She felt his presence physically. She turned and met his eyes. Wordlessly, the past was reviewed; in a glance all that was between them was summed up; in one long look five years was taken account of and reckoned. What had happened? Five years of living, five years of learning at sometimes bitter cost, five years of getting up each morn to face the new day, to welcome it, to rail at it, to be afraid, and to hurl the challenge back.

She stood straight. Anne of Cleves had moved away. "You wished to speak with me?" she asked evenly.

From the window seat where they sat, Katryn could see over the garden wall into the gardens of the Charterhouse, unkept now and lonely. The man beside her was partly responsible; certes his brother Ned would take pleasure in dismantling the monasteries stone by stone with his bare hands, so deep was his feeling for the New Church. She had been amazed to see the ruins of the religious houses within London itself. The state of the realm, she thought, is as disordered as my mind right now, with old feuds being waged and religious quarrels sundering families and, above all of that, the threat of a boy king; for what would hap if the King died? A boy prince, five years old, who would look to his two uncles for help. Katryn shot a glance at Tom Seymour. Difficult it was to separate the man from the political figure; now with Tom Seymour's blue eyes on her, she rallied her forces. "I perceive a new fashion in London," he had said. One would think he would be proud of her! Why not? She had come unheralded and without friends at court, not as rich as many. Why, he should ha' seen her house!—neglected, used without license by a friend of the chancellor. Much was missing, even more broken and worn! Hadn't she come to this big city, with a sick husband—and look what she had done! She ran her red tongue over her lips. Ned had sent wine. Did that mean the Seymours had arrogantly set their seal of approval on her, for gathering the court to hear the Protestant preachers? Were they planning to use her salon for a political rallying place? Tom Seymour raised his black eyebrows.

"Certainly you expected me to come and investigate what has become London's most popular gathering place?"

"I don't need your approval."

"You're going to receive it anyway," he said. "For possibly without realizing what you've done, Katryn, you've moved into our circle. Willy-nilly, you are one of us; willy-nilly, you've espoused the cause of which Ned is the spearhead." He sent her a quick smile. "I attribute your success to various circumstances." He slurred the word till she hardly understood it, but the soft accent invoked memories with a rush.

"You," she said, "are the head of your party too."

He shook his head. "I am a soldier, sailor."

"You are the watchdog, the guardian." The blue eyes surveyed her lazily, with a glitter in their depths. What was he thinking? Then his other sentence occurred to her. "And to what do you attribute my success, as you put it?"

"Don't challenge me, Katryn," he said. "There are a variety of reasons, outside of your so obvious charm. I remind myself what Master Coverdale must have thought when you said, 'Pray come to my house, sir.'" He cast his eyes up to heaven and simpered. Katryn giggled.

"Go on," she said.

"Well, in the first place, there's no queen at court. The Princess Mary tries to be less grim than her nature intended, but 'tis most difficult for her to forget and forgive her former injuries. Secondly, you are a fresh new face. How old are you, Katryn?"

She shot him a glance. "Twenty-eight."

"Somehow you have lost a year along the way," he said, "and you don't need to pout. I can count. Do you want a little advice?"

"Aye," said Katryn, annoyed.

"You don't of course," he said, and laughed. "But your dress is so plain. You should be more elegant to reign over London. I see I am receiving a stormy look. But you should wear satin or velvet, with fur." He threw out his hands. "My God, I don't know exactly what I mean."

"I warrant you mean my gowns aren't low-cut enough," she said furiously. "How dare you criticize my clothes? I set a fashion with this white collar!"

He glanced about the room. "Is that where they're all coming from?"

"I have made it fashionable to be a learned lady, too!"

"God help us," said Tom Seymour. "Ned would approve. Look

at Mary Howard, Katryn, see her clothes." He watched out of the corner of his eye while she looked over at the Duchess, who was gowned in velvet with a great gleam of diamonds at her white throat. Katryn's eyes blazed with gold fury; she was so angry she couldn't speak. Tom Seymour grinned wickedly. "I know you want to give the impression of children at your knee, waiting for your sweet motherly kiss and admonitions. But unless I have been sadly misinformed—"

"Oh, how you talk! What a great jest!"

He laughed. "Nonetheless, Katryn, the white collars may beguile the Bishops and the clergy, but in fact they already have beguiled them, for in all probability the Bishop would be here if you looked like a horse. But now you will have to deal with the gallants of the court. I suggest you wear more artful and female clothes. What's the matter? Have you spent all your money on white collars?"

Katryn bit her lip. "I ha' bought many clothes."

"Well, don't fret. I'll send you material you can preen your feathers on." His eyes were on Bess's boys across the room, with Margaret Neville. "I have been watching them for some time, Katryn," he said, "and they are certainly fine-looking and well-behaved boys. How old are they?"

"Almost five and almost six," she said. "But I cannot accept—" Her voice trailed off and she looked at him worriedly.

He smiled. " 'Tis not a bribe, Katryn. To welcome you into our ranks, so to speak, I shall be glad to help you any way I can."

He is speaking as the leader of a political faction, she thought. Were I Anne, he would speak just that way. She met his eyes; he is speaking the truth, and her heart felt as though it would stop. He's not interested in me any more, she thought. No, it's not possible! She drew a deep breath, and her heart was now beating fast as she tried to listen to what he was saying.

"Is there any favor I can do for you?" he was asking. "Who is that pretty woman now with the boys, Katryn?"

"The lady is Cat Strickland, my cousin," she said. "She has just been widowed. I brought her to London wi' me. I know what it is like, to be left alone and widowed, and spend the winter way up in the North in a great lonely castle." He couldn't be interested in Cat. She was older than he was. I am full of fancies, Katryn thought.

She looked up at him, for he had risen and was standing over her in his usual attitude, his thumbs hooked in his belt, his eyes amused and slightly mocking.

Tom Seymour asked, "Would you like me to bring a few of my roistering friends to help this Cat pass her lonely hours?"

Katryn didn't trust any of his roistering friends, as he put it. She said crisply, "I warrant the Lady Borough will be a match for your wolfish friends!"

"The Lady Borough?" he asked.

"Aye," she whispered. Could he hear, as she did, her own voice saying: "Thomas Borough is dead. I killed him. His body is in the cellar." Katryn rose. She stood straight, squaring her shoulders. I'm not ashamed, she thought proudly; I did wrong, but I had to. She said defiantly, "Cat was wed second to Henry Borough. Henry died last year, out hunting as did his father!"

Tom Seymour looked into her eyes for a long moment. His expression was somber, almost brooding. "That was a long time ago, Katryn," he said.

"Aye, very long," she agreed swiftly, as if to say that she was done with it too, all of it was past and he too, he was part of the past and she was done with him! Her mind raced. How could she see him again? Would he call here? She blurted, "One favor I do ask! I should like to see our prince, the little Edward!" They would have to ride down, and mayhap together. I cannot stop myself, she thought. I want to see him again, even if he doesn't suspect it. Tom Seymour was hesitating.

"I ride down to Hatfield once a week, when I'm home," he was saying, slowly.

"A long time ago," she said, "Jane asked me a favor."

He studied her. "Aye," he conceded.

A long time ago. Five years ago. They had said good-by at the top of the stairway outside Jane's presence-chamber, in the low light of candles at midnight. Did he remember? Five years ago she had not tried to stop the tears when she had thought of Jane. Now, had they both forgot Jane and her last whispered wishes from them, the living? Tom Seymour's face looked drawn.

"How complete is death," he said. "But if you wish it, you may come with me. I shall send you word." He turned away then. Was he going to say good-by? But no, he was correctly going to make the rounds of her gallery, speaking to all he knew, and he was taking Mary Howard with him. A blind wave of anger passed over her;

she squashed it ruthlessly, and turned to bestow a dazzling smile on the Lady Grey and her sober and studious little Jane. I'm not even going to look at him, she thought, nor that milk-faced Duchess; I cannot bear it. I shall not see those limpid eyes and the daughter of the Howards with her proud airs, and her velvet gowns. I shall stay right here, and bid my guests good-by as I always do.

Would he never leave? Most of the guests had gone, and he still stood talking with Lady Frances, and her little Jane looked excited and alive, her eyes fastened on his face. Then slowly the four of them came toward her, and Frances and Jane said good-by. Katryn leaned down and kissed the child, for she was fond of her, she was so appealingly small and honest. Then she turned her eyes onto Tom Seymour, almost without wanting to. Their hands touched. Then Katryn curtsied to the Duchess. This time she didn't slip. She rose again, just in time to see the eyes of Mary Howard turn to Tom Seymour before she took his arm to descend the steps.

Katryn stood rooted to the floor. She gasped, for there was no mistaking that warm glance. Katryn kept seeing it as she watched their descending figures. She couldn't be mistook. Not she. Her face was white. So that was the reason for his disinterest. He had a mistress like he had described to Jane so many years ago, beautiful, assured, with a touch of boldness. And what a sly triumph, to have brought so neatly to heel and into his bed the daughter of his rivals! Did it amuse him? Her hands clenched. John Cheke's face swam unseeing before her. He said "Madam?"

"I'm all right," she muttered, and brushed past him and went down the gallery to her own chambers. Her withdrawing room was silent and lonely. Weakly she leaned against the door, her body shivering, in the grip of an anger she had never known she could possess.

The material arrived the next morning, and for a moment she wouldn't touch it, but looked at it lying on her chest. Then with swift hands she flipped over the bolt of fine, lustrous, green velvet to see how much there was. There was much too much. And he had overbought the pale green satin, too, and there was an extra ten yards of silver lace, so fine spun she knew it must come from Brussels. She stared at the profusion of gleaming satin. He didn't know how much to buy; there was some small comfort in that he hadn't gone about buying women dresses before. And he hadn't forgotten. Even with Mary Howard's kisses warm on his lips, he must have been out early this morning. But I won't think of it today, she vowed desperately, for I've not slept all night. She began to fold up the velvet. Lord Latimer stood in the doorway, leaning on his stick, and she flushed guiltily.

"Lovely, lovely, my dear," he was saying, absently. "Do you have a little time for me?"

"Aye, my lord," she said, with some diffidence. "Is aught amiss?"

"Nay, but I summoned my solicitor this morn, and I wish you to join us, for I'm making my will."

She stiffened. She dropped the material. "Your will?"

"I thought it a ripe good time to set things aright," Lord Latimer said mildly.

"I hate wills," said Katryn with vehemence. Oh, how frail he looked, leaning on his stick! She ran over to his side and took his other arm. "And you came down the hall alone," she scolded.

Lord Latimer hesitated. Then with a sigh he leaned his hand on her shoulder. "Come, Katryn."

But he insisted she precede him into his study. How typical of him! If he were dying, he would do all the small courtesies. She bit her lip hard, and hardly saw Master Baines rising to greet her. She hardly saw Lord Latimer's room and his desk, with his theology books stacked neatly on the side of his table and the rest of the table covered with papers, even perched on top of the sand bowl. She sat down on one of the stools because Lord Latimer told her to. She folded her hands on her lap and waited.

"Now," said Lord Latimer, for it was his belief that solicitors talked too long and too much, and he wished to take this conversation into his own hands. "First of all, I don't expect to die in London." He smiled at Katryn reassuringly. "I don't expect to die this winter, you see, my love, so do not fret. Thus I wish to be buried in the south side of the Church of Well, in Yorkshire." He watched the solicitor write busily, and he went on, "And the master of the hospital and the vicar of the church to receive all rents and profits from the parsonage of Askham Richard in the city. But if I should die in London, I wish to be buried in St. Paul's." He threw a little glance at Katryn. She seemed still reassured, and the lawyer wrote on. "When I wed with Lady Latimer," he said to Master Baines, "I settled on her the manors of Wadsworth and Nunmonkton, and two other estates in Warwickshire—the papers are here. At my death, I wish her to receive the manors of Cumberton and Hamerton. Both goodly properties, my dear, as you can see by these papers here." He passed them over to Katryn, who shook her head. He frowned and ordered her to read them whilst he went on with his will.

John was to receive, of course, Snape Hall itself. Margaret had two manors and a dowry of a thousand pounds. There were bequests to Oxford and to various churches, and small bequests to his body servants and the household, which, as he said, had served him well and faithfully. When it was finished Lord Latimer looked at Katryn gravely. "Do you think I've decided fairly and well?" he asked. He looked so weary her heart ached for him.

"Aye, my lord," she said. "No one could have made a fairer nor more generously Christian will. Thou hast remembered all."

He put his hand to his head, and rubbed his temple. Again he looked at the notes he had made. "I keep thinking," he said apologetically to Master Baines, "that there is someone or something that I've forgot, and I should not want to leave anything uncompleted."

Katryn said, "It is all here," and Master Baines, seeing his client obviously exhausted, dipped his pen, and called to his assistant who was sitting against the wall half asleep.

"After all, my lord," he said, "your lordship may add to this; I am at your call. My assistant and another member of the household should witness your signatures, and then all will be dispatched." He smiled heartily and wished his lordship long life, as he did always, inwardy wondering how long it would be before he would be called to have this will proved. "But it is an excellent will," he said, patting it; the papers were all in order and there would be no scrambling about for gold, and no need for dealing with usurers.

Katryn put Lord Latimer to bed. She fed him mulled wine and the almond wafers he loved so much. She read to him. When she had done, he looked at peace and rested, his eyes half closed. "You sleep now, my lord," she said. "I'll ha' the house quiet for thee. And you didn't need to make a will! I'm going to take care of you as I have these five years gone past."

Lord Latimer opened his eyes; he looked amused. "You have convinced me, sweetheart," he said.

Katryn tiptoed from the room.

The next day it began to snow, in honor of the season. Katryn came back to her house to find the first flakes clinging to the pine branches that decorated her doorway, and the lamplight shone on them like fairlyland.

The household went to bed early and the snow continued to fall. At four the whole household assembled to hear early morning prayer. Katryn had asked the eminent John Parkhurst to be with them, and he read the story of the birth of Christ and then blessed the kneeling household. The morning was cold and dark.

But by noon the sun was out on the white rooftops of the city. And at eleven, when Katryn's guests came to hear Miles Coverdale, the stars were bright in a blue-black winter sky. It was Christmas Eve. Outside her house, the lamps burned and carriages crunched on the snow, and within, great massed candelabra and pine and ivy spelled the season as much as the servants' smiling greetings.

"Merry Christmas!"

Miles Coverdale read from the Bible. "Aye, though ye speak with the tongues of men and angels, and have not love . . ."

At midnight it was time to celebrate. The Christmas carols—surely there is no lovelier music, Katryn thought, some so solemn, some so jolly. There were great barrels of oysters, and beer to be drunk. She had never seen her gallery and chamber of state so crowded. Now that the Seymours had set their seal of approval on her house, everyone was here. How brilliant was the gathering, from the Lord Chancellor to the French ambassador! How cultivated, how witty, how purposeful are these men and women, and what an age do we live in! How it shines with so many facets, like a jewel. Her eyes found Tom Seymour; he is the epitome of it, she thought.

He was saying to the French ambassador, "I sincerely believe every man has the right to read the Bible in his mother tongue, and not hear it mumbled in Latin. What can it mean, thus?"

"But—" said the Frenchman, and broke off.

Tom Seymour smiled. "But I bow to your French superiority in many artful endeavors, and I agree with you they are vastly important."

The Frenchman laughed. Tom Seymour turned to Katryn. In the mill of people, he drew her a bit aside. He said, "I go to Hatfield the day after tomorrow. I go alone. Do you wish to come?"

To see the little prince, she thought, Jane's Edward. "Alone?" she echoed. "I may not bring Anne or—"

He shook his head. "You go on my terms or not at all."

She was silent. What did he mean? It was like an ultimatum, and no quarter given.

"I want no clacketing women along," he said. "I wish to see Edward myself. He is surrounded by petticoats already."

"But it is not—"

"Proper?" He scowled at her. "The devil with it then, Katryn."

"I'll go. When?"

"Eight," he said. "Eight o'clock. And be ready."

It was a frosty morning, full of pale sunlight. The last trace of the snow had disappeared into last night's fog. The small troop of horse, ten strong, were in neat dark livery with the Seymour crest on their jackets. Ten years ago the man who now helped her into the saddle of a blooded mare had worn such a badge himself. The badge was gone, but not the air of reckless adventure; even though this morning the blue eyes regarded her gravely, the thought of riding to Hatfield with him was somehow as exciting as riding forth to battle.

The faces of her escort were young. Their eyes followed their master, and she knew she was receiving hard and evaluating stares. Tom Seymour himself was preoccupied. He was adjusting the stirrups for her.

"It that right?" he asked.

Katryn nodded and was about to speak but he cut her short. "I expect to set a fairly hard pace, so if you cannot keep up, shout."

"Aye, m'lord," she said meekly, because that was what his men called him, and he shot her a glance of some surprise.

"Well, well," he said, looking up at her in the saddle.

"They are very well armed," Katryn said.

"We avoid trouble that way."

She watched him covertly as he mounted. I'm so happy, she thought, hugging her joy to herself. Now today, for this ride, I can wipe my mind clear of thought. When I am with him, I can live by sense and sight and sound.

They left the city behind and the pace increased. The wind blew sharp on her cheeks, but her body was deliciously warm and the horse she rode had a fine steady gallop. A sense of freedom enveloped her. For these few hours she could ride by his side, and there was a oneness about it even to the steady beat of the horses' hoofs. Riding together, unspeaking, knowing his presence, was briefly to relive the vibrant youth that sometimes she thought she had lain aside. Here, in the open country, was release from the trivialities that plagued her days. To exchange the known for the unknown made life more sweet, more forceful.

She was proud of riding well, and she knew that he had picked this smaller animal just for her, for the Border horses her father had first taught her to ride were small. Memories of her childhood flashed through her mind. The ride would end, but until it did, she could savor it down to the last last minute. Until he lifted her down from the saddle in front of the ornate stone of Hatfield House, she drank deep of the cup that had been bestowed on her today in some incomprehensible fashion. She relished the clasp of his gloved hands, and the ease with which he lifted her from the saddle. But there was no time for words, for the great carved doors of Hatfield House were opening.

The hallway and staircase within were celebrated. The stairway was of polished and carved oak, thick, with solid balustrades almost half a foot wide. It was a double stairway, its two arms meeting on a heavy carved balcony. And halfway down that huge staircase, dwarfed by its ponderousness, stood two small figures, hesitating, looking down. A small boy of five, and behind him a slender blue-eyed girl. There was in their attitude eagerness, and there was in their size appeal.

Katryn's fingers tightened on Tom Seymour's hand. He looked at her. He said low, "Spill me no tears, Katryn. No tears!"

Edward looked like Jane. Jane's solemn thoughtful eyes gazed at Katryn from Edward. Edward was saying, pointing to the books on the floor under the window, "I put them there, madam, to look out to see who was coming. Of course," he added very solemnly, just like his mother, "there is no Bible there. I wouldn't stand on the Bible."

No tears, Katryn thought, desperately. She blinked her eyes rapidly. Tom Seymour had made good his threat and had sent away the women; Edward's nurse, Mother Jackson, Elizabeth's Mistress Ashley, even the servants were banished, and the four of them ate dinner together before the fire. From her stool Katryn could see out the window to the slopes of pasture land; it looked lonely and cold, like the life of the two children here at Hatfield House.

There was no need for her to make conversation; Tom Seymour led it, drawing the two children to talk, and gradually Katryn relaxed herself, for whatever strain there had been at first was disappearing. She had time to note that Edward's appetite was poor, and she thought the food served him too rich, full of wine sauces. And there were sweets right on the table, but when Edward reached for one, his uncle's long arm shot out and removed the plate. Elizabeth smiled.

"I had a bad dream last night," Edward was saying.

"Everyone does, at times," Tom Seymour said.

"Even you?" asked Edward.

"Even I," said Tom Seymour ruefully, shooting a glance at Katryn, and both children followed the look and smiled.

Elizabeth's glances were admiring. Slyly she watched Katryn, her quick observant eyes on her manners and her dress. Elizabeth looked from Tom Seymour to Katryn many times. "Sir Thomas never brought a lady afore, madam," she said.

"I am glad he brought you, madam," Edward said. "I expect you have boys and girls at home."

"Aye, I do," Katryn said.

"My age?" asked Edward.

"Your age, and one a year older, and one fourteen, and a girl twelve."

"I warrant that is very gay," Edward said.

"Oh, they have to study and work, too," Katryn said.

, Tom Seymour rose and lifted back the table. He put more logs on the fire. When he was done, Katryn brought him some water and he washed his hands. "Now we'll open the presents," he said.

This is their holiday celebration, Katryn thought. Just the two of us. But the children were happy. They sat before the fire opening their presents, Edward entranced with the toy soldiers and the white-sailed ship. Katryn had brought cards. She cleared off the table herself with Elizabeth's help, and they drew it close again to the hearth, making a circle of warmth and turning their backs to the big room. They taught Edward a simple game.

The afternoon was upon them and it was time to go. It wrung Katryn's heart to see how both children swallowed their disappointment when Tom Seymour finally stood up, and said that he must leave them. "I'll be here before seven days have passed," he said, patting Edward's shoulder and passing his hand over Elizabeth's head.

"Will you bring the Lady Latimer?" Elizabeth asked.

She wants me, Katryn thought, but, femalelike, she is also a bit curious about me.

"If I come, and of course I should like to," she said, "is there anything I can bring you?"

"Oh, no thank you," Elizabeth said. "But we should like you to come."

Edward nodded solemnly. "We should like it if you would come, madam," he repeated. "We should like it very much, Bess and I."

Tom Seymour said nothing as they mounted. It was two o'clock.

The afternoon was colder, too, and the sun had disappeared. After an hour, Katryn found the pace tiring. And she couldn't rid her head of the image of the two children she had left behind. Brow furrowed, she rode on, and her legs and back and arms began to ache. He probably will not stop though, she thought, and I shall not ask. She was startled when he leaned down from the big horse so close to her and put one hand over the reins. She checked her pace; up ahead were houses and a village, and most probably an inn. Gratefully she slowed her horse.

In the innyard, he lifted her from the saddle. "There is a small parlor here, most like empty, where we can sit for a few minutes and talk," he said, ushering her through a long narrow room. He was preoccupied and grave, paying the landlord and commanding wine to be brought. Katryn loosened her cloak and sat down on an unpadded bench. He pulled a stool up to the round table and leaned his elbows on it, regarding her. The wine came; he poured it, and said they didn't need a fire. The door closed.

Katryn sipped the wine. From the next room came the sound of men's voices; they seemed very far away. Katryn avoided Tom Seymour's eyes.

"I thought they liked me," she said, almost defensively.

"In fact they did," he said in his deep drawl, startlingly near. We are alone for the first time, she thought. She could lean across the table and touch his big ungloved hand. *In loco parentis,*" he murmured, and then, "We managed to give them a taste of what ordinary children have—two parents."

"I understood your Latin, sir," Katryn said. "I was well trained in my childhood, with two tutors and a singing and music teacher, for my mother had been brought up that way. And second, I've been reading and studying with my lord for the past five years."

"Is that what you have been doing, Katryn? What else?"

Katryn's mouth was dry and she took another sip of wine. "Well, then I have a few estates, and I managed them, and on certain seasons I would go to them and stay a few weeks to see all was well."

"Like a progress?" Tom Seymour asked.

"I hunt and play cards and run my household."

He said, "I noted when you told Edward about your family you did not say they were not your own children. Are you ashamed of that, Katryn?"

Was it a taunt? Her eyes blazed. " 'Tis God's will."

"I'm not trying to argufy with you," he said. "I'm trying to find out what you think and feel and want. But no matter. I observed you, riding away from Hatfield, and I was mindful of your old trouble, hurling yourself at a new scheme without proper planning. I could see the wheels turning inside your red head. You have seen Edward. You have seen Bess. You feel sorry for them. You see the need for action, so willy-nilly you plunge ahead. But let me tell you something, there is nothing to be done. Nothing!"

She clenched her hands. "There must be!"

He shook his head. "Katryn, even if you could get yourself appointed to a post with Edward's household, what would you be able to change? That lonely dwelling? Where's the man who could bring what's needed to those two children? The women there adore Edward. They spoil him, of course. It is unnatural to be born a prince, in any case. You would like to pick up Edward and bring him home with you. That would be wonderful—and quite impossible. Even if your lord weren't ill, it would be quite impossible."

"Jane said—" she began.

"Jane couldn't see the future! And you think you knew Jane's miseries? You didn't know them all by a great part! Anyway, every woman in the country—aye, and every man—wants Edward. You keep your hands off, Katryn, I'm warning you!" He rose. "Finish your wine," he added, picking up his cloak.

Katryn rose too. "I don't want the wine," she muttered. Then she cried, "Why are you so angry, and cruel?"

"I am neither," he said. "I mean to be emphatic, and I mean you to obey me."

"Obey you?" She couldn't speak for a moment. "There are times when I hate and despise you, so much that I—" She broke off. What had she said? Why did her feelings for him trap her into such admissions? She picked up her cloak and tried to put it over her shoulders. She looked up at his face.

"You cannot rule me, Katryn," he said evenly. "Come now. I am having an early supper with some friends."

"But—but—" she said, trying to fasten her cloak and think how to persuade him to take her with him next week, both at the same time, "but you will take me next week? The children want me!"

They were in the doorway, and he looked down at her. "And what *I* want?" he asked. "What of that?" He paused. "I should accede in better grace, since you have me in a vise. If the weather is clement, I'll take you."

14

The King had spent Christmas as usual at Greenwich, and then, toward the end of January, restless, he had moved back to London and Whitehall. And on the first of the month, Candlemas Eve, he had invited fifty of the fairest maidens in the land to a huge banquet. A thousand candles burned in the Gothic banqueting hall that he had built for Jane, and from the head of his great table Henry ate steadily through course after course and surveyed the flower of English womanhood before him.

Henry was not given to dalliance, as was his rival Francis I of France. Henry knew that the seed of his loins was far too precious to be bestowed on an errant miss of playful morals; instead it should be nurtured between the flanks of a fine fair woman, fit to bear a child to England. His cap on the side of his head and his narrow eyes resting on the faces and figures of the women he had summoned, he finally finished his meal, wiped his mouth, washed his hands, and leaned back in his great chair. The seat alongside him was empty.

Widowed by the sword, as Surrey had said, now he found his tears had dried. He was but fifty-one. Although tonight his leg pained him, he could feel the stirring of his blood; watching him close, Sir George Blagge suppressed a smile; for, as he said to Tom Seymour later, "Were his Grace a stallion, one could have heard him neigh like a trumpet."

Henry watched. There was Southampton's niece, a pretty thing of twenty. She simpered before him, trembling. Henry patted his dog's head, and sipped his wine.

Kate Willoughby was bewitching tonight in white satin. Two sons were hers, too, proving her worth. But she was wed to Henry's oldest friend. Regretfully, Henry laid aside thoughts of Kate Willoughby, Duchess of Suffolk.

Mary Howard, Duchess of Richmond, swam before his vision. Twenty-two she was, or thereabouts, and undeniably a beauty, with a white, white skin and eyes of cornflower-blue. Her hair was black. But she had been wed to Henry's bastard son, the child of his passion for Bessie Blount when he was young and overflowing with his manhood. Henry was afraid of wedding with the widow of his blood kin. God frowned on such marriages. Henry's eyes went past Mary Howard.

There was a woman speaking with Will Knyvet, about twenty feet away she was, generously formed, with a gay manner and sparkling eyes. Will Knyvet, good friend to Tom Seymour, was well known for his ability to pick a female companion. Henry said to George Blagge, "Pig, who is that speaking with Will?"

George Blagge crinkled his eyes. "Oh," he said. "Why that is the Lady Borough, born Strickland, your Grace, and cousin to the Lady Latimer. She is staying with Lady Latimer in the city; she is a widow."

Henry stared at Cat Strickland. Then he shook his head. She looked lovely, but a bit old; she must be thirty-eight or so, he thought. But— Aloud he said, "The Lady Latimer's cousin?"

Blagge nodded and Henry was silent. The Lady Latimer . . . Her name recently had been coupled with Tom Seymour, for he had taken her down to Hatfield three times. Edward adored her, as Henry had been told. Even the Princess Mary liked her, and had been present at her chamber-of-state last week to hear Gardiner preach. Henry remembered Lord Latimer well. The Lady Latimer had a reputation of going to chapel daily; probably she was a motherly sort.

"She is Mistress Herbert's sister, is she not?" Henry asked to refresh his memory, which truly never forgot a single scrap of information which came his way.

"The Lady Latimer is here tonight, your Grace," Blagge said. "She was accompanied by her cousin. She is within that circle over there; Ned Seymour is betwixt your Grace and her."

Henry turned. At that moment Ned stepped aside to speak with his countess and to guide her from the floor.

"There," said Blagge. "There she is, your Grace. In the pale green gown."

Henry looked. He looked and chewed at his lip. His hand set down his wineglass. She had red hair. Her shoulders rose sloping and white from pale green satin that did not cover the edge of her curving white breast. Henry's hands would span her waist. He picked up his wineglass again. Her antecedents were perfect; she was descended from the great Lancastrian duke, John of Gaunt; her great-grandmother had been a Beaufort. Henry sipped his wine; he cleared his throat. Then he commanded George Blagge to bring the Lady Latimer to him.

The chair beside him in which Henry's queens had sat had been removed, and Katryn sat on a brocaded stool, her gown falling gracefully on each side of her till she looked like a flower. She was turned just a trifle sideways to the King. Before her Henry had placed a tall goblet of gold with jewels around the lip, and full of wine. Henry's big dog yawned at her feet, and before her eyes in blinding brilliance spread the whole scene of the hall, filled with color. Over her head in the gallery, the musicians played. But close to her, very close, was the King.

He had been reminding her of her forebears, speaking with such full knowledge that she could but gasp.

"Why, that your Grace should know! 'Tis a true father that knows his children," she said, smiling, looking into his eyes.

They devoured her. Katryn sucked in her breath. And amazement was suddenly hers. The King was looking at her in a way no woman could mistake. But she was not free! She had laced tight, and she felt she couldn't breathe. She raised the heavy goblet. I must keep my hand from trembling, she thought; I surely must. He must perceive no schoolgirl symptoms. And I must listen. What was he saying?

"I am told, madam, that my son is fond of you."

"It has been my rarest privilege, your Grace," she replied, "to see our prince, and—" She hesitated, then she said clearly: "—and her Grace, the Lady Elizabeth."

Henry's eyes glinted. So she had mettle, did she? In her way, she had flung a challenge at him. He placed his huge hand on her bare shoulder. He cared little whether his court saw him openly caress a woman. His fingers felt the bare skin and reached across the sweet curve of breast. He looked into her eyes beneath those level brows; they were almost gold, with a dancing light in the depths in which a man could drown. He saw the tip of her pink tongue as she ran it over her lower lip.

"Your Grace," she said, "prithee—!"

Henry withdrew his hand. His eyes are fierce on me, she thought. I must say something. "I am a woman wed, your Grace." Carefully she lifted her wine again.

Henry nodded his massive head. But her lord was very ill. Mayhap there would not be so long to wait. "I shall send my physician to Lord Latimer on the morrow," he said. He would send Dr. Huicke, and he could report back to his master.

"Your Grace is so kind," Katryn murmured. She felt suddenly cold with fear. It raced through her like an icy wind. The King . . . What had the French princess said, when she heard Henry was widowed? They said she had laughed, and said she'd wed with him had she two heads! Katryn swallowed. But Lord Latimer stood betwixt her and Henry. Her hands were damp. Alongside of one white hand on the tablecloth was Henry's hand, thick and clumsy with power. That hand covered hers as he spoke.

"I remember you at Edward's birth. You gave him unto me, and I would not touch him—nay, I did not dare—but touched my finger to his tiny hand. Then you laid him in his cradle and I knelt to look at him."

Katryn's fear disappeared. True was the scene; she would never forget it. Such was the homage Henry had paid the small morsel of life Jane had borne for him. The scene was so plain. She whispered, "And later, your Grace, Jane asked me to look after Edward. 'Take care of my prince, my little son. . . .'" Katryn's words trailed off. Henry was looking at her full.

"You are a good woman," he said. He was smiling. Was this the will of God?

Katryn's head whirled and her legs felt weak. Had she drunk too much wine there at table with the King? "Anne," she whispered. "I was terrified!"

"Be quiet," said Anne. "Cat has gone home with Will. And a servant of the Seymour's just arrived, Katryn; Ned is lending you his carriage."

"Why, that is good of him," she said.

"I shall accompany you to 't," Anne said. She raised her hand, and two maids-in-waiting appeared. They took the two sisters' trains, and the four of them went down the stairway, under the arch of the Gothic hall—the arch that had the initials *H* and *J* carved in them. Out in the court were more initials. *H* and *A*. Katryn kissed Anne good night. Then she got into the carriage with the Seymour crest on its door.

It was very unusual to go unaccompanied. She felt a little strange and lonely, but there were two liveried men up front. The carriage jolted along, and she was alone with her thoughts. Surely she would not become Henry's mistress. Such a thing was unthinkable, and she would never in the world consider it. Women who slept with men for a few jewels were fools, and in any case the stakes were higher than a diamond or two, a manor or two. She frowned. Am I thinking clearer with all that wine, or am I thinking foolish? Anyway, mayhap I can persuade him to let me take care of Edward. A few caresses, properly protested, and a few smiles. The carriage lurched, then stopped. Katryn sat forward in the seat, drawing her cloak close, feeling the fur tickle her chin. Then the door opened.

She screamed. A hand with a towel went over her mouth. She struggled, and the other door opened and powerful hands pushed her back against the seat. A voice said, "Pray do not struggle, madam! This has been well planned. You are in no danger!"

The towel was over her mouth. She choked. It was removed then, and the voice continued hastily. "His lordship does not know we've used his carriage, madam. It has been borrowed by the Admiral. You are in no danger, madam. You are being taken to Seymour Place."

She couldn't speak. She couldn't believe it. "No!" she cried.

"Aye, madam, by the mass, we swear it!"

The carriage was moving again. She could see no faces in the blackness. "You are abducting me!" she cried.

"Please do not cry out, madam," the voice said, "for I am under strict orders not to hurt you. Very strict orders. Nor to touch you save with hands wrapped in linen."

Katryn could see the white towel he held up. She lay back against the seat. "I am going to faint," she thought. Why has he done this, why? I still don't believe it. She could feel her knees shaking.

"I shan't believe you," she said, suddenly angry, "till I see Seymour Place! Why, what's to prevent you two rogues lying your heads off?" She sat up straight as the carriage jolted to a stop.

One door opened. One man got out first. Correctly he held out his hand and Katryn took it. There was a single torch burning against a solid stone wall, and in its light she could see plain the badge of Sir Thomas Seymour embroidered on the tunic. Her eyes widened. So it was true! She tipped her head back to look up; the stone wall stretched upward endlessly. She knew this was a huge dwelling, for it was the palace of the see of Durham in the old days. And in front of her was a small door.

"This is a private entrance, madam," her escort said. He took the torch from its bracket, and went ahead of her. Behind—to see I don't escape, she thought angrily—came his fellow. They climbed two flights of stairs, then a wooden door opened.

There was light here, and Katryn stepped into this room hastily, looking about, hunting for the man who had dared to waylay her and bring her here. She breathed rapidly as her eyes searched the big empty room. What was that fellow saying?

"You are in the Lord Admiral's room, madam. Pray wait here, for my lord may be detained."

"May be detained?" she cried. Anger left her speechless. And she had spoken to the empty air; the men had disappeared, and she heard the sound of the bolt being thrown. She was a prisoner here, in Tom Seymour's chamber.

For ten minutes Katryn paced the room. Then suddenly feeling her legs wouldn't hold her, she sank down into his large chair before the fire. But after she had sat there for one minute, curiosity stood her on her feet again, and she went over to his chest and opened it. It was very neat, and it smelled clean with fresh herbs. The carpet was beautiful; she leaned down and touched it with her fingers. So soft it was! She avoided the bed. She saw only it was a big old-fashioned bedstead of carved oak with heavy curtains. There was an intricate clock on the mantel; its hands stood at twelve. On the polished sideboard was wine and glasses and a bowl of fruit. She picked up an apple and bit into it. I want no more wine, she thought, but I am hungry. If he doesn't come by the time I finish eating this apple, I've a mind to bang on the doors and rouse the whole house. She tiptoed over to the door. She put her ear against it and listened. She was sure there was a man standing without it. "By God's most precious soul!" she said. He would probably station one of his knaves out there to see she behaved. She finished the apple, and turned and threw it into the fire. Then she heard footsteps.

Katryn retreated slowly from the door. There was a murmur of low voices outside, and then it opened, giving her a brief glimpse of the hallway without, and Tom Seymour stepped into the room, shutting the door quickly behind him.

"Good evening, Katryn," he said evenly. "I am so sorry I have kept you waiting. But perhaps it is just as well, for an hour ago I should have been only too pleased to wring your pretty neck." He laid down the cloak he was carrying, while Katryn slowly backed away from him. Never in her life had she faced real male anger, and she knew she was facing it now. The words he had delivered meant nothing; he was trying to conceal it by this even flow of words. He stood by the chest.

"I also hope you were not physically hurt. If you have been, say so, and since I am in the mood for murder, I'll avenge you before—" He broke off and came toward her. Katryn, rooted to the rug, watched him with huge eyes. He came very close.

"I wasn't harmed," she cried.

Tom Seymour reached out long arms. She felt him lift her; she put her head back against his shoulder. Slowly she opened her eyes to look up at his face.

He carried her over to the bed and laid her on it. He looked down at her. "Did you allow the King open caresses to gain your own ends about Edward?"

"Aye," she said. She sighed deeply. He was jealous. She was fiercely glad.

"You disregarded my warning. Did it occur to you that his Grace is looking for neither a lady for Edward nor a mistress for himself, but a wife?"

"I cannot think," she cried, "when you look at me like that!"

"I'm going to take you home tomorrow morning at six o'clock," he said grimly. "And if we're lucky, you, please God, will be carrying a child."

The February dawn was gray with winter's cold, but the room was cheerful with firelight. Katryn saw by the clock that it was but five, so there was an hour left. She had come to know that Tom Seymour meant exactly what he said, and he would take her home at six. But an hour could hold a wonderful lot of living.

She could hear him splashing water. Then he came from behind the screen, in shirt and hose, and stood by the bed. She smiled at him sleepily. If he touches me, she thought, and starts to kiss me, I shall break into a thousand pieces and tell him I adore him, which he certainly does not deserve. He finished drying his hands and said, "Even though you think you are barren, you must admit we fought fiercely against the odds last night." His grin was infectious and she couldn't keep from smiling, even though she felt her cheeks grow pink. He went on. "You don't seem a bit undone by the thought of an illegitimate child."

She said, "I have a good husband, and what would a wench do without a good husband if she were entangled with you? Knave that you are, to have escaped so long the honorable bonds of matrimony. You are very spoiled, you know," she continued, putting her hands behind her head.

"You don't spoil me very often," he said.

"I know," Katryn said, "and when I do, I part regret it, for it seems as if you've scored a victory you don't deserve."

"Maybe a Pyrrhic victory," he said lazily.

She bit her lip. A Pyrrhic victory, she thought. It means I won too. He chuckled and sat down on the edge of the bed and hugged her. "True, I don't deserve you, sweetheart," he said in her ear. "If you were free—"

"If I were free—" The words stopped and she sighed. She held him close, her hand against his rough cheek, for he had not shaved yet. The fire crackled. "If I could only stay with you," she whispered.

"This must be what marriage is for," he said, "that we should not have to part in the dawn."

303

If only I could stay with him! If only I might be living here at Seymour Place with him. I shall pretend I am. For the rest of the hour, I shall put away all else. I shall watch him shave and finish dressing just as though it were every morning of my life. She sighed happily, and ran her fingers through the dark thick hair of the head against her breast. What calamitous misfortune, she thought, to love a knave like this one. But it was true.

An hour later, at six fifteen precisely, Dr. Huicke came out of Lord Latimer's chamber and, diverted by the sound of a carriage, went to the top of the big stairway to look down. He was anxious to see Lord Latimer's wife, and perhaps this was she returning. The doors opened, and in the gray light he saw two figures. They merged, the lady disappearing into a sweep of cloak and a deep embrace. Dr. Huicke stepped back hastily and tiptoed away, but he could hardly be mistaken; surely he knew that figure well, and surely the Lady Latimer's lover was Sir Thomas Seymour. Dr. Huicke waited in the shadow of Lord Latimer's door; he had been up most of the night with his lordship, for he had been sent here at ten the previous night. Katryn came toward him, head bent a little, her hair in some disarray as though the last passionate kisses and caresses had disarranged her hair, as it had left warmth in her eyes and a sweet moistness on the lips; she was unutterably lovely, Dr. Huicke thought suddenly. How could he confront her with the news he had? But he stepped forward.

Katryn saw him then, coming from the shadow with his black gown and flat black cap, like the crow of death. She gasped. From within Lord Latimer's room came then the sound of coughing. She took a step toward the door and then paused, afraid to open it.

"I am Dr. Huicke, madam," he said hastily, taking her arm.

She looked at him, uncomprehending.

"I ha' been sent this past night by his Grace."

Katryn remembered. She had forgotten the King. But Dr. Huicke's presence betokened Henry's presence, looming in the distance. Dr. Huicke felt it too.

"My Lord Latimer—" she said, taking his hand. Then she stopped; she could not ask.

"Your lord is very ill, madam," Dr. Huicke said. "He was taken last night with hemorrhage."

Katryn swayed. I cannot tell her now, Dr. Huicke thought, that her lord will not live upward of three weeks or so, and mayhap not that long. I shall let her see him; he is weak but at peace. I shall take her within his chamber.

"Your lord lies more comfortable now," he said trying to smile. She looked frozen. In his mind's eye Dr. Huicke saw the figure of the King. Against that he saw the lithe, poised strength of Sir Thomas Seymour, and between them this half-fainting woman whose husband was dying. "Oh, madam," he said, and he put his arm around her, "I have taken a solemn oath!" Do I sound like a silly owl, he wondered? How could he make her understand that from this instant he would do all in his power for her? "I shall never forsake you by word or deed, madam," he said, "nay, nor divulge what my eyes may have seen. You can trust me, madam, I swear it, to the end of my days! Now come with me and see thy lord; he is ill and needs thee."

Dr. Huicke, as one of the King's physicians, was permitted two servants, and as Henry had instructed, he sent one of them to Hampton Court to report on the state of Lord Latimer's health. Henry was well pleased with the news he received, but he was far from pleased at the rumors which were rife in the palace. Upon finishing dressing, he sent for Sir Thomas Seymour, and he waited for him alone, behind his table, his furred mantle close about him, his leg propped up on a cushion. When his brother-in-law came, Henry observed him closely. Six feet three he stood, the same height as Henry, but almost twenty years separated their ages, and Henry knew had he been lucky he would have had a son like this one.

Henry did not minimize this subject's worth. The women of England had produced this type of man—the Surreys, the Wyatts, the Seymours—keen men, gifted with the pen and the sword, gifted with daring and recklessness. They could ride till they reeled in the saddle; they could sail the fine new ships and lead an army into battle. Beds did not know them, unless there was a woman within. They seized on life, and they would bring glory to England; her flag they would carry to the farthest parts of the globe; they would spread their lovely mother tongue far, and farther. They would bring France to her knees for him, conquer Scotland.

Henry said, "Last night you were closeted with Sir Henry Wallop prior to his mission to Flanders."

"Aye, your Grace," said Tom Seymour easily.

Henry was silent a moment. Then he said, "It has come to our ears that the Lady Latimer has been receiving advances from you."

The answer was the same as before, only given with a shade more force. "Aye, your Grace. That is true."

Henry's narrow eyes met his subject's blue ones. For just a moment in the silent room there beat a new note, tense. So it was true. I am taking his woman, Henry thought. For this I can send him to his death—easily, a hundred years ago. Were this then, I would have, and he—what might he have done? Drawn that long dagger at his side? The knuckles on his hands showed white. But we are sensible modern men, and I shall give him a chance. If he refuse, then—well, it should be impossible to refuse.

Henry said, "I have changed my mind, sir. You shall accompany —nay, lead—the mission to Flanders, and take over your duties as master of the ordnance. Find me ordnance for the army, which you know is to be sent to France in early spring, scarce two months from now. Tell me, Tom, how old are you?"

"Thirty-three, your Grace," Tom Seymour said.

"You shall be placed second in command of the army, and I am sure you will fulfill your duties well."

"I thank your Grace," said Tom Seymour. No visible change of expression was in him; Henry felt a flicker of pleasure at his calm. This was a breed of man in which a king could take pride. No heroics, like the silly French.

"You shall leave with Sir Henry," the King said. "After my council meeting I shall speak to you further."

"Aye, your Grace," said Tom Seymour. He backed from the room. Outside, he paused for a moment, his head bent; then he straightened and walked swiftly down the long gallery, his stride even and long as always.

15

It was a typical March afternoon, rainy and with a whistling wind. The solicitors had gone, the house was quiet, and Anne, moving almost without sound, poured Katryn another cup of wine and brought it to her.

Katryn was reclining on a pallet with a curved back, and a bright cover was thrown over her legs. But she was dressed in black, and Anne thought her very wan and pale.

Lord Latimer's funeral had been two weeks ago; today the will had been proved. Katryn said, "The last link with him seems to have been cut today!" She sat up straight, drawing her legs up under her. He had said, wry and sweet to the end, "You will be better off without me, sweetheart." But she was not!

She drew a deep breath. The quietness of the house oppressed her. Bess's boys were with their mother, and Margaret was in her room. John moved silently about the big house. "I feel so alone," she said low.

Both women were silent. Lucy watched them both, keeping her thoughts to herself; she had laid down her needle, and now her long hands played with the bright wool. The silence deepened. Then Katryn, leaning forward, asked a single question.

"Was little Cat Howard guilty of infidelity, the crime for which she died?"

Lucy glanced at Anne. Anne's gray eyes were steady and kind. "No, Katryn, she was not," she said.

Lucy took up her sewing again. Finally she spoke. "She was alone in her room a few times; she had an unwise waiting-lady; she was heedless and generous and her friends were light."

"All that the people around you do reflects on you," Anne said.

Katryn shivered. She drew the bright cover up around her hips.
I am so alone, she thought. My lord is dead and my lover is gone,
gone without a word, and today I know I am not carrying a child.
He was right; the child would have saved me. And I think he would
have married me. If he were here now— But he was in Flanders; he
had arrived there three weeks ago, the day of Lord Latimer's death.
He had presented himself to the Queen Regent, and they said she
was so charmed with him that she would not excuse him, as he asked,
to seek a change of dress, but insisted he ride alongside her to noon
mass. Fate had played a nasty trick. If she were with child—! Instead
of that, he was being plied with the festivities of a foreign court,
and she was left alone to deal with Henry VIII of England.

Her eyes flashed, and Anne leaning forward, said quietly, "Katryn,
never mention another man's name, even to me or Lucy."

Katryn stared. Had she been so transparent? How much did Anne
know? She questioned her with her eyes, and Anne shook her head.
"We shall not discuss it," she said, but her voice trembled.

Lucy rose. On the small lectern was an open Bible. "I shall read,"
Lucy said.

Anne watched her. Lucy was too upset to look for a particular
passage. Instead she began to read from the open page. She read
slowly, and Katryn found her eyes filling with tears. This was one
of Lord Latimer's favorite readings. "So that which of you," Lucy
read, "having intent to build a tower, sitteth not down first, and
counteth the cost, whether he have sufficient to finish it?"

Katryn blinked back the tears. Lucy stopped, and Katryn could
hear a deep, drawling voice: "I mind me of your old trouble, hurling
yourself at a scheme without proper planning."

Katryn threw back the cover and rose to her feet. Suppose she
hadn't planned? Was she more to blame than he was? Never a word
of good-by, and he enjoying the flavor and wines and women of
Continental Flanders! Anyway, it was done, and somehow they had
done it together. I shall have to manage it, she thought fiercely.
Maybe no other woman could handle Henry Tudor, but I must!
I am not going to die on Tower Green—not I! Her eyes were narrow and golden. "I am not going to leave this house, for I'm in
mourning," she said. "My lord lies in his grave but a scant two
weeks. I am undone with sorrow, unable to face the world,

positively weak and frail, a poor widow who wishes only to be alone with her grief!"

Henry Tudor could be either devious or forthright, depending on the action the circumstances warranted. Besides that, there were so many weapons to his hand that it was simply a matter of picking and choosing. So he decided to confer on Will Parr the vacant earldom of Essex which Will wanted; he knew he would please Katryn Parr. More than that, the investiture was solemn and full of pageantry, and so it was an occasion to which she would want to come.

Katryn did come. But she had gained three weeks, very neatly, for it was now the first week in April. It was a beautiful sunny day, with breezes that wafted the sweet smell of cut grass and the fresh earth, redolent from yesterday's rain. She did not leave off her black gowns, but came in full mourning even to a black velvet cloak. Henry, who did not care for black, was nevertheless fascinated by the sight of that red-gold head against the boldness of the black. He let her return to her house on the Charterhouse. Then, the second week in April, he sent for her to come to court.

This summons could not be disobeyed. John had gone back to Oxford, but Margaret was with her, and Bess's two boys; so what with the servants there was quite a number in her train. Henry waited exactly two weeks before he made his wishes known to her.

It was the first of May, Henry's favorite day of the year. It seemed fitting that he propose marriage with the lady of his choice on that day. After the tournament, he sat with Katryn in the garden. She was still wearing her black because the obvious mourning seemed to provide a kind of armor, the protection left over from Lord Latimer, and also because she had never been able to flout the rules too openly. It wouldn't be right, she told herself, not to wear black!

The garden was pretty and they sat on a bench at the edge of the bowling green where the Princess played at bowls with some of her ladies and gentlemen. Katryn could see Anne and Lucy, and their presence was reassuring. But while Katryn was in black, Henry was glittering with color and jewels, fully as bright as the peacock who swished his tail up the garden path ahead of them.

Henry said, watching the sun on her hair, "Your apartments are too small. I should wish you to use the suite at the top of the gallery stairs." He waited.

Katryn said, "But your Grace, I—" She stopped. "They were Jane's!"

"Aye," said Henry. "And I am asking you thus, my sweet Kate, to be my wife."

Katryn was unprepared. She hadn't believed Tom Seymour completely. She hadn't thought it possible for the King to propose to make her his wife so soon. Even though he was in love with her, she had expected first a proposal of a different sort. She blurted, "By the mass! 'Twere better, I think, to be your mistress rather than your wife!"

Then she realized what she had said. Her face paled. "Oh, I am going to faint," she whispered. "Oh, your Grace, 'tis too soon! And my poor lord in his grave but a scant eight weeks!"

His eyes were on her, and she could perceive plainly that he was truly in love. Men, kings or no, are very transparent, she thought, her mind racing. She clasped her hands in her lap. Surely no woman had responded to Henry with such a sentence! What a mistake she had made, and how she must try to control her tongue! It came of being at court so seldom. I am still a north-country wench, she thought, ready to speak my mind bluntly, not enough used to dissembling, and I must learn. Certes Nan Boleyn begged Henry to wife with her, and Jane was eager; Anne of Cleves had been discarded, and little Cat Howard had been overthrown by the privilege. Katryn sat on the bench, feeling as though she must be floating into a world where there were no rules she knew. She wondered whether she should cast herself down before the King but, mindful of the rest of the company about her, decided she would look like a foolish figure on her knees before Henry in the garden. She laid her hand over Henry's and lifted it, placing her lips on his knuckles. "As a woman and as a loyal subject, my love for your Grace will be forever, and you have done me too much honor. I am overthrown." She fastened her eyes on his face, looking as appealingly at him as she knew how, and wondered if she sounded silly. But men in love were apt to believe the veriest nonsense; thank God that was true, she thought, for Henry was still looking at her with a bemused expression.

"My sweet Kate," he muttered, squeezing her hand.

"My heart is fluttering," she informed Henry. Indeed it was.

Surely this was not possible—she to be queen! But they could not be wed for months, and mayhap he would tire of her before that. One might well pray God he did before marriage, for what if it happened after? "My lord," she said softly, "we should attend chapel this night."

Henry put his arm around her. She was young and warm and delicious, and she looked fruitful. Look at her breasts and hips! he told himself with both desire and sudden need. Quickly he seized her and kissed her, running his tongue over her warm mouth; he felt her tremble in his arms. Her eyes were closed.

Katryn was shivering with fear and distaste. She felt him release her, and she opened her eyes, looked about, and there was the garden. Clasping her hands in her lap, she sat still and small in her black gown, her head bent. The Lord help me, she prayed to herself, for today on this instant my heart is breaking. Instead of my black-haired knave, I must wed wi' the King. Where is he, my true love? I'd just as soon die, right now. She raised her eyes to Henry, and he looked into them, fathomless and golden and glittering with unshed tears. "I love you, my lord," she lied, "but prithee give me a bit of time." If he hate me for it or misbelieve my love for him, it cannot be helped. By God's most precious soul, it cannot be helped, for I cannot, cannot, wed with him now.

Jane's big beautiful apartments had lain unused for a number of years, for Henry had been loath to put Cat Howard in them. Now their casements were opened and the tapestries taken down and aired, and the bed fitted with new mattresses. The dust flew. In two days Henry could take Katryn up the three long flights of stairs into the gallery and thence to the queenly apartments.

Slowly Katryn ascended the stairs. Memories were sharp upon her. Who would ha' thought five years ago, when she ascended them for the first time, that Jane would die and she would be forced to take her place? Katryn wished passionately she loved Henry as Jane had done. Love is the key, she thought; it unlocks all doors.

Katryn seemed a small figure beside Henry, even though she was of middle height and too voluptuous in figure to be frail. Her eyes under the level dark brows glanced this way and that. Here was the great presence-chamber, with the queen's chair and the brocaded window seat. Next, through carved ornate doors with massive golden handles, was the queen's closet. This had been Katryn's favorite room, and she looked about. It had fine windows over the river, looking out past the gardens. It was fairly small, being but twenty by thirty feet, finely proportioned, gracious. Its marble flooring in black and white, and its pale gray tapestries were reflected in its mirrors and its marble fireplace. The ceiling was painted in frescoes.

Henry preceded her into the privy chamber, and thence to the fourth room, the bedchamber.

"I remember it so perfectly, my lord," Katryn said low.

"It is fitting that you be here," Henry said; indeed he wouldn't have bestowed the chambers on her had he not thought so. There was something sweet and compelling about her reluctance toward him. Her fidelity to her dead lord touched him. He put aside the thought he might have a rival for her heart. The pursuer, even a kingly one, likes a bit of flight in the hunted, and Henry was not mocked nor taunted by it as he had been by Nan. This woman was entirely different, capable of boldness, as when she'd said frankly she would rather be his mistress. But deep in the core of her, Henry sensed something else: the true unfathomable female, her secrets buried deep; not a mocking sprite but a woman who could bestow much, when she was ready. She drew away from him with such slow grace she drew him after her.

"I cannot have these apartments redecorated for you," Henry said. "The war with France is too costly."

She looked at him with her golden eyes. "They are lovely, my lord, and I could wish for naught else, save perhaps some lengths of material for new cushions. Red, for instance, would be an accent in the queen's closet."

"The royal wardrobe," said Henry, "is at your disposal."

She gave him a small smile. All that material! The idea of it stirred the imagination. Laces and intricate cut-velvet mixed with the gleam of satin. And what priceless furs! She smiled, the small smile of delight she could have, and Henry was relieved.

"What a true wench you are, my Kate," he said, heartily.

"I love cloth," Katryn said, and went over to the window seat in the closet to look out again.

For a long minute Henry stood watching her black figure. Then he approached her. He said, "I cannot wait too long, my sweet."

Katryn looked up at him, the heavy face. His great chest swelled. He needs me, she thought; surely he does! He limped a little. A faint pity stirred her. Men, she thought, they rule the world, and so they need their women's comfort even more. "When then, my lord?" she asked, tipping her head back to look up at him.

Henry placed his hands on her shoulders. "July," he said, "and early in the month."

"Stuff the towel into your mouth if you're going to cry," Anne said.

"What would I do without her?" Katryn thought miserably.

"If Ned's wife should know you were in your chamber weeping, it might mean your pretty little head," Anne said cruelly.

Katryn blinked. She sat up on her bed.

"You're going to be a queen, and you have to behave like one," Anne said. "Or I'll be putting your body in an arrow box like Nan Boleyn's—that is, if I don't suffer along with you! Like Lady Rochford with Cat Howard!"

Katryn put her hands over her mouth.

"After all," said Anne, "why should you moon over a man, even if he be dead and gone? For a week," she went on inexorably, "you have mourned a man—your dear dead lord, no doubt. But shall I tell you a bit of gossip that came to Will's ears this noon? Sir Thomas Seymour has the fairest lady in Flanders as his favorite leman."

Katryn stared at her stonily.

Anne leaned over and shook her. "Forget all save that you shall be Queen!"

Katryn slid off her bed. There was a lovely marble table with a huge Venetian mirror. In front of it was a brocaded stool. She sat down. Behind her Anne took up the brush and began to brush her tangled hair. It is the middle of May, Katryn thought dully, and I have six weeks, for his Grace insists we be wed the first week in July. I am going to be the queen, and when Tom Seymour returns he must kneel to me!

Her image in the glass looked back at her. I am going to be queen. I am going to be pampered and covered with jewels. I am going to have so many servants I cannot count them—nay, nor remember their names. I am going to have five royal manors, mine for the rest of my life; the King said so to me yesternight. I shall take precedence over every lady in the land, and no one may enter a room before me. I am going to be queen!

I am going to hold my husband firm, no matter whether no woman ever did it before. There are many ways, and none of them shall I overlook. And I am going to be good, like my poor dead lord taught me to be—to love all, rich and poor, enemy and friend, little children. The children! Edward, five years old! How could it be possible she had forgotten? In my mooning over one man, I forgot Jane's little prince, and that nine-year-old motherless princess with the splendid eyes. Even poor Mary—poor thing—aweeping and tremulous, wanting a husband and never getting one, wanting someone to love her and who ever will?

Had the clock struck? She rose from her stool. "Fetch me my new robe, Anne," she said, "and summon Lucy and Meg, for the Lady Mary has asked I receive her this afternoon. And I think there should be flowers about this room. Since his Grace has explained to me that I cannot have it redecorated because of our war wi' France, we should fill it full of flowers and find some fine vases."

"Indeed," said Anne softly.

"I must set aside my grief," Katryn said, "and learn to be gay again." So he had already a favorite woman? She closed her eyes. I should have known better than to think he truly loved me. I must learn to be a queen now, at all costs I must learn. And I have six weeks to learn it. I am dying inside because he is so faithless, because he has deserted me! But I shall be brave and worthy to be England's queen. I shall pour out the love he does not need onto those who do, for I know what heartbreak is now. In this sweetness of May, the gentle beauty of spring, the heady stirring of living things, I now as a woman shall make amends to the dead husband I was unfaithful to. If I suffer, I shall understand others better. Here I am, and look how lovely I look; how could he treat me thus? Were he here now, what should I say to him? Mayhap he would go down on one knee and put his arms around me and say would I forgive him? I would cry and say how could he treat me thus?

But maybe he would not say anything at all, but come striding in and expect kiss for kiss and me in bed with him in five minutes! "Oh!" she said aloud, outraged at the image. If he came walking in now, I should look right past him. Surely no woman ever had more grief from one man! And he deserves nothing at my hands but blows! She paced up and down her room. These chamber walls had been Jane's; they echoed to the sound of his laughter, his lazy drawl, his booted feet. But I shall surely banish them, she thought fiercely. Banish them and bury them. She put her hands to her hair.

"Pray pour me some wine, Anne," she asked. She glanced at the clock. It was time for the Princess Mary.

The princess was twenty-seven years old. She was slight and pinched, and her brown eyes were watery from too many tears, Katryn thought. She had now an allowance, but she was inept even in that, spending far too much on her gambling, and then not having enough left over to pay her servants. Mary accepted a cup of wine, and in her hesitant voice, her eyes on Katryn's beauty, admitted she had come to ask Katryn to employ an old servant whom she could no longer pay.

"A Mistress Barbara," Mary said. "And I so mislike to see her leave me! And what should she do, poor thing, if I turn her out?" The Princess' eyes filled with tears, which did not overflow, but she blew her nose and blinked and said she was troubled today with toothache.

Katryn thought, Oh, how miserable are both of us! Mary who wants a husband, and I who have a faithless lover! Such is the destiny of women. She put her arms around Mary and hugged her. "Acourse I'll take her, your Mistress Barbara," Katryn whispered.

"Oh, madam," cried Mary, undone by the hug, for it had been years since anyone had shown her such affection. She smelt Katryn's perfume, and for a moment they clung to each other. Katryn brought out a lacy handkerchief and delicately wiped her eyes, and Mistress Barbara, who had been standing listening, as unobstrusive as possible by the door, where Mary had left her alongside of Meg, was also undone by this kindness, for it moved her deeply. She could not remember when any of Henry's queens had actually hugged the Princess. She came forward and cast herself down on her knees, and picked up the heavy satin of Katryn's gown.

"I swear I shall serve you, madam, to my death!" Katryn looked down at her kneeling figure. She was kissing the hem of Katryn's robe. "My lifelong devotion will be yours, madam. You are a saint!"

Katryn leaned down, in a flurry of satin and lace, her unbound hair tumbling about her shoulders. She lifted Mistress Barbara up.

"A saint?" she cried. What would Mistress Barbara think if she knew that she had lain naked in her lover's arms, dizzy with delight under his kisses, while her poor husband was coughing up his life's blood? She put her hand to her breast.

Mistress Barbara cried, "You are so fair, madam!"

Katryn drew a deep breath. The little clock struck again. "By the mass," she said, " 'tis almost time for supper! In twenty minutes his Grace will expect me!"

16

The day dawned hot, and the reddish sun streaked the sky with color, touched the silver river, and then slanted down with summer's heat upon the endless roofs of Hampton Court. Its plain brick façade shimmered under perfect weather.

The ceremony was set for afternoon. Two days before, the Archbishop had granted the license, as he would to any other couple in England, their names being signed to the petition. And for the first time in many a year, it was done open and honestly.

Katryn's sense of what was proper both amused and pleased Henry. Quietly she assumed her woman's prerogative to be wed the way she wished. It made him chuckle, but he was proud of it, none the less.

"And since we've both been wed afore," Katryn said thoughtfully, "we should most like be wed in one of my chambers, since that's where I live now, and thus I think it should be in the queen's closet. I shall fill the room with flowers, and we should entertain our closest friends after, and you, my lord, should be attended, as well as I. So pray pick the men you wish."

Henry grinned. "As you say, my love." Oh, but it was good to be able to rely on a woman who knew how things should be done! "Mock as men do," he said, "we bow to your practicality."

"I think also," said Katryn frowning, "that the Princesses Mary and Elizabeth should be present; they can attend me."

Henry pursed his lips. "Aye, then," he agreed.

"A wedding is a fine solemn thing, and all concerned should be invited, our close relatives and friends."

"Aye," said Henry, meekly. He picked Ned Seymour to attend him personally, and invited the Lord Chancellor and the Keeper of the Seal and five others of his favorite gentlemen.

Katryn looked up from the list she was compiling, to make sure the room would not be too crowded. "Your niece," she said, "the Lady Margaret Douglas. I almost forgot her! By the mass, how thoughtless!"

Henry smiled. He touched her red-gold hair tenderly. He looked over her shoulder at the list. Her writing was beautiful and slanting. "Have you put my name down, my sweet?" he asked.

Katryn giggled. Her husband-to-be had a nice sense of humor, wry at times. She lifted the hand that lay on the table and laid it against her cheek and kissed it. "I want to make you happy, my lord," she said.

The Bishop of Winchester was to perform the ceremony. Bishop Gardiner was a member of the privy council, and close to Henry. Katryn liked him much less than she liked the other divines in London, but she didn't demur at Henry's choice because she didn't want to offend him. Gardiner could hardly be called a papist, but he leaned toward suppressing the new books, and he was always hunting for heresy, and he had quite a few deaths on his hands. He gobbled poor reformers mercilessly, sometimes having them burned, like the Spanish.

Still, there was not a man in the palace who did not have blood of some kind on his hands. England had seen seventy thousand executed in this reign, and Katryn found it hard to reconcile the big hulking man who smiled at her with the red-eyed monarch who had signed too many death warrants. I shall get to know him better, of course, she thought. A husband, king or no, has no secrets from his wife. Sooner or later, I shall know them all. But a man, thank God, never knows, and 'tis well he does not, for he would never understand.

The sun rose higher and stood directly over the palace, so that the sundials winked and looked back blankly. Katryn ate no dinner at all. She had spent hours on her dress. Once again she had chosen green for Kendal; it meant good fortune. At ten minutes of two her door opened, and her procession of women began.

First the two princesses, Elizabeth's face solemn and white and full of excitement that she should be here at all. Gratitude entered Elizabeth's heart at that moment and never left it. With her walked her half sister Mary, gowned in ivory satin, with a pair of winking ruby bracelets that Katryn had given her previous to the ceremony. She had had a gift for everyone, she thought, and no two had been more pleased and excited than the two princesses, whom no one ever paid any mind.

They walked first, and Katryn was conscious of real pride in them. After them came Lucy, and Margaret Douglas and Lady Frances, the King's nieces. Then Katryn stood in the doorway with Anne at her side, Anne carrying a great mass of flowers. Slowly they approached the King and behind Katryn, bearing her train, came the little Lady Jane Grey, seven years old and shaking with the excitement of participation in this great event.

The Bishop was magnificent, but not more so than Henry, who wore his kingly robes. Even his hands glittered with jewels. In front of the Bishop, he and Katryn knelt.

When I rise I shall be the Queen, Katryn thought, listening to Henry's responses. She shot him a glance and caught the Bishop looking at her. Why, he's looking down the front of my dress! she thought, and began to repeat after him. Why, I cannot believe it! she thought, even while she said aloud, "Till death us depart. Amen."

Henry lifted her hand, and placed upon it the heavy nuptial ring. Then the royal couple rose. Katryn turned. The company knelt. I am the Queen, she thought dizzily, the Queen of England.

No man was a happier bridegroom than Henry Tudor. More than that, he was at the height of his own political power and acumen, the reins firm in his hands, and all that he had learned from his famous ministers, Wolsey and Cromwell, was in his heart and mind—and they were dead. Beware the lion who knows his strength.

The war in France was proceeding apace. It would be a long war, and he knew it well. He had made a temporary alliance with Spain; now that the Princess Mary was reinstated at court, he could feign smiles and let Charles of Spain help him in the humbling of France—even if it meant abandoning Cleves; for the Emperor Charles, with Henry's approval, was fighting in Germany while Henry fought in France. Let each eat well, while the other keeps hands off.

The King of Scots had died last year, leaving an infant queen, Mary, Queen of Scotland and the Isles. Six months old she was now, and Henry wanted her as bride to Edward. Thus the policy of uniting the two nations should come to happy fruition. Henry had sent Ned Seymour to make war on the Scots, who were as recalcitrant as always. Now, however, an uneasy peace existed, and the little Mary was betrothed to Edward.

And Henry loved summer. In the summer he made progresses to various country seats of the great nobility. This was a fine cheap holiday, too, for the nobles thus honored by the royal presence paid for the finding and board of the King's train. All the countryside turned out to greet their monarch, and great hunts were arranged, and Henry shone expansively.

This summer Henry had a new wife. If he looked out his windows now he would see her, sitting in her barge with the two princesses and holding little Edward. Henry leaned his elbows on the sill. The barge slowly pulled to the water steps. Edward was laughing on Katryn's lap. She held him tight. How fitting, thought Henry, for my son to sit cradled on those lovely white thighs which shall receive me this night.

Below him, Katryn set Edward down and took his hand and stepped from the barge. Her ladies and the princesses and the children clustered around her, and their gay voices and laughter floated up to him. They had been on a picnic down the river, and soon they would proceed to chapel, their voices hushed. They disappeared from Henry's sight, and only the servants, carrying woven hampers, were left to unload and stagger into the palace with cushions, lutes, and a forgotten shawl.

In her chamber Katryn retired behind her screen, her ladies departed, and she was alone save for Meg and Mistress Barbara. This was one of Katryn's favorite times of the day. For in truth, she thought, I am so surrounded by people I can never be alone and rearrange myself, as the French might put it. Oh, and the weather was still so delightfully warm, when one could be naked and have a bath without freezing to death—at least on the side away from the fire.

Naked she stood in the tub, and while Meg washed her she could think. Katryn was thinking about Joan Bellingham, for whom she had sent to be one of her maids of honor. It had been so good to see Joan! She had never wed, and the rest of the manor house at

Burneside overflowed with children and their parents; Hugo had seven, Joan said. Katryn looked down at Meg's bent head. It might ha' been her! She might still be living there, with seven children. I wonder if I would have; still I would have liked to have seven! Imagine! All in a row, kneeling to say their prayers at night! She sighed, and absently took the end of the towel to dry the back of her neck where the curls were pinned up. If I could only have one child, she thought passionately, looking down at her body. He would come into the world a red-headed prince of the realm, a lusty little knave with a nation at his feet. And yet, Katryn thought, even a virgin would know that ofttimes the King's ardor did not result in completion. It was a worrisome thought. Here at Windsor was a palace full of children, and none of them hers!

All the children were still with her, and even though she could not always have Edward with her, she had planned not to send him back to Hatfield until after his birthday. Then she would take him there herself and make that house more livable; she had all sorts of plans for it. Children could not always be with their parents. But most of the time they could be, and when they were not, she would see they had a fine comfortable dwelling that meant home. I will stay at Hatfield a few weeks myself, she decided.

She had already advanced the name of John Cheke to be Edward's principal tutor. He had resumed his post at Oxford, but she had invited him to Ampthill for Edward's birthday; he would bring John down with him and the King could meet him.

While Meg wrapped her in a big towel and Mistress Barbara knelt to dry her feet, Katryn looked unseeingly over her head. Joan was tonic. She was glad she had thought of bringing her to court, not only because she was literally buried alive in Westmorland, but because, unlike everyone else, she had no favors to ask. Even Anne, acting for Ned Seymour, had come this morn before the picnic to report that a man named Marbeck had been arrested by Gardiner.

Katryn wiggled her toes. Damn Gardiner, he was already testing her. He probably knew very well that she had patronized Marbeck, for he wrote music and Katryn had known him. A month ago he had sent her his Latin Concordat, having forsaken his music for a semireligious treatise. I shall have to speak with my lord about it this eve, she thought, and I must use care, for I cannot push too hard and I have succeeded in doing much already. Witness the fact that

Elizabeth is with me. Elizabeth reminded Henry of her mother, Nan, and he could not forgive her for being her mother's child. But as they got to know each other better—? One found it hard to predict, for they had similar traits, Henry and Bess, and they might clash.

The sun already was beginning to sink. Tonight she and Henry were to have a late supper together. She must, then, speak about Marbeck, other he would go to a fiery death; and it was a point of honor, too, for she must show now how much influence she had. I think I can win Marbeck's liberty for him, and mayhap Gardiner will let well enough alone and leave me alone. I'd never trust him though—a divine who peers down into a woman's dress! Her eyes snapped.

She wore a new evening gown, and had the table placed in the window embrasure; with its white cloth, and its two chairs, and its high-piled fruit, it looked very inviting.

By the time Henry finished eating it was time to light the candles. The servants had been dismissed. Henry leaned back in his chair, looking massive behind the great footed dish that Katryn had piled with grapes. He held a huge bunch of them in his hands.

Katryn said, "Anne told me this morn that Marbeck, whose music you enjoy so much, has been arrested for this Concordat. It would please me much, my lord, if you'd read it yourself and see if you find heresy in 't, for I confess I do not, although I'm not as wise as you, acourse. I warrant I have a rather simple mind."

Henry frowned. But he took the bound paper she handed him, leaning forward a little to place the writing under the candlelight. His fingers were stained purple. He read on, flipping the pages.

Katryn rose and poured water into a silver ewer and brought it to him. Absently he laid his hand in it, and just as absently let her dry his hand while he read. Katryn bore away the water; it looked purplish red, and she emptied it quickly.

When she came back to the table, Henry was shaking his big head. But he was smiling. "Alas, poor Marbeck!" he said. "He should stick to his music! But it would be well for his accusers if they employed their time no worse."

Katryn knew this meant reprieve. She knew too that Henry would not forget; he forgot nothing, ever. In the morn then, Marbeck would go free. Justice had been done. Sometimes, thought Katryn, right prevails. She reached out her hand to him and smiled. Soon he would want to go to bed. "Holy Mary," she prayed inwardly, "let me have a child."

The weather continued warm and pleasant. Edward looked better than he ever had, he was sunburned. When Katryn's train set out for Ampthill, all were in high spirits, so much so that all the ladies rode and Katryn's litter came jolting behind empty. Still Katryn was glad she had brought it, for no sooner was the royal party settled at Ampthill than Mary sent word she was taken ill suddenly on her way to Woodstock from Grafton, where she had been staying. Katryn sent the litter right away, with orders to bring Mary to her so she could be properly looked after.

Mary arrived at noon the next day, feverish and sick. Katryn put her right to bed and kept Edward away from her, even though he was fond of Mary. The King was hunting. He spent his days hunting at Ampthill.

Katryn had planned a big birthday party for Edward on the twelfth of the month. The day was fine and the October sun bright. Katryn had invited the gentry from all about, and it was a wonderful party; it reminded Katryn of John Neville's sixth birthday party, and so the memories were sharp on her. How worried and unhappy she had been that day in her fine new dress and without a present for little John! There was John now, placing Edward on his pony. And here she was, sitting on the still green lawn on a heaped mass of cushions in a beautiful new velvet dress, and around her throat a heavy and precious diamond chain; every once in a while her fingers touched it to feel its cold, smooth-cut beauty.

But that night it began to rain. Henry came home wet and limping. Edward began to sneeze and snivel, and Mary got worse. The next day Henry's leg began to swell. Muttering, he was ahorse early despite it, but when he came home in the afternoon, he could hardly stand on it when he dismounted. Nonetheless, he would not go to bed. He despised bed. He stumped into Katryn's chambers; worried, she set him in a big chair and propped the offending limb up on a stool with cushions. Supper was served. The rain continued to fall, over England and over France, where English armies were fighting; the spell of bad fall weather had begun.

It beat against the window panes and rattled into the chimney. But the food Katryn served was good and hearty and Henry seemed to be enjoying it. Suddenly Katryn glanced over at Edward. He was having a queasy spell, she could tell by one look. In a moment his dinner would come up.

She jumped up, and at that moment Edward uttered a loud cry of despair, for he had been trying to ignore the warnings from his stomach. Henry tried to move quickly and succeeded in bumping his leg against the table, whereupon he shouted an oath that made the room rumble. Edward was quickly sick. Katryn scooped him up in her arms and ran from the room, leaving Henry swaying on one foot, grasping the table for support. His leg felt like a running fire of agony. His red eye fell on Elizabeth. "I'm not only cursed with this leg," he muttered, "but with sickly children!"

Elizabeth looked up at her huge father. "I'm not sick," she pointed out.

"No," Henry growled. "Not you, you're like to your mother, thin and sinewy and much too quick wi' your tongue!"

Elizabeth said, "At least I'm strong!"

"Aye," growled the King, fury mounting in him rapidly at her impudence. "Aye, you have her devil's spirit and body!" He struck his hand on the table and the plates jumped; and so did Katryn, coming back into the room to say that Edward felt better and she was going in to him to say good night and hear his prayers. She never got out the word prayers, for Henry had risen to his feet, again maddened with rage.

Henry at this time was about the waist fifty-four inches, and his chest measurement was a mighty fifty-seven. Swaying a bit, for his leg would not hold him, and his eyes just as red with anger as his brain, he raised his hand, whilst Elizabeth stood waiting, almost with contempt, thus speaking more words than she could have aloud.

"Elizabeth," Katryn snapped. "How dare you? Kneel down and beg your father's forgiveness!" She pushed at the child, knowing instant humiliation was the only way for her to find royal forgiveness.

Elizabeth did not move. Henry's great chest swelled. Katryn raised her own hand and slapped Elizabeth neatly.

The girl slipped to the floor, her head bent. Wordless, she remained there, and terrified that Henry would fall, Katryn seized her shoulder and pulled her to her feet.

"Run for aid," she said.

Elizabeth flew on her thin legs. Henry was still swaying back and forth, his face and eyes red as fire and contorted. Katryn slid the heavy chair under him. "Pray sit," she implored.

She hardly knew later how they got Henry to bed. But when the leg was uncovered she almost fainted. It was swollen twice its size, and an angry redness reached in fiery fingers down almost to his ankle. "We'll have to lance it, your Grace," Dr. Huicke said.

"I never wish to see the whore's whelp again," Henry roared from his pillow.

Katryn trembled. On her knees beside the bed, she was watching Dr. Huicke lance the big boil. Pus and blood burst out. Dr. Huicke's voice was calm.

"When it begins to drain, madam, 'twill ease his Grace. We will keep hot cloths on it, madam, as hot as his Grace can endure."

Katryn thought, I am going to be sick or faint, and I cannot. He'll never forgive me if I desert him, I know he won't. She stayed on her knees beside the bed, taking the cloths a page handed her, laying them gently on her husband's leg.

After an hour, she had time to ask for a cushion for her knees. They were completely numb. But Henry was in less pain. He was even able to reach out his hand and lay it on her head.

"Thou'rt kind and gentle, my sweet," he muttered.

"You're so brave, my lord," she whispered, wanting to cry for he was brave. How could he have possibly ridden today with this leg? He ignored pain until it felled him. When the knives had been thrust into him, he had not even winced but set his huge jowl and scowled. No wonder, thought Katryn, he was bitterly disappointed in Edward, Edward who was frail and whose physique frustrated Henry until he couldn't endure the sight of it. Katryn now realized that Edward's health was of paramount importance to his relations with his father, and she would have to see that he was not indulged or allowed to stay up late, or served rich, sickening foods so that he wouldn't eat his good red meat.

Her knees ached; she had been here two hours. She laid another cloth on Henry's leg. He was almost asleep. She looked at his face and he opened his eyes. "Send Elizabeth away," he muttered. It was Katryn's first taste of his implacability.

She found it difficult to explain to Elizabeth. Not that the child demurred; she set her jaw much the way her father did and her long eyes were obviously concealing. How can I explain to a girl that her father doesn't wish her about him; yet she has lived with this hurt ever since her birth. Poor child! What might it not do to her later? How can she trust? Katryn laid her hand over Elizabeth's; the child was in bed, lying still and rigid. The candle flickered; the wind sighed outside, yet with enough force to announce the hint of winter.

"My dear," said Katryn, "there is much sadness in life." She wiped her eyes, and Elizabeth stared up at her. "You have sadness early. Perhaps it will prepare you better, as princesses should be prepared. Have patience, Elizabeth, have patience." She looked at Elizabeth's white face and thought suddenly, This child is very keen; perhaps she could profit by plain speech such as I'd use to an older girl. "I am a barren woman, Elizabeth," she said, biting her lip. Her curls fell over her shoulders and her hand pressed to her breast in a gesture already familiar to Elizabeth. "Can you think how I long— nay yearn, nay pray—for a child of mine own? It has been denied me, my own child and its love, and thus you are denied another love. But be of good cheer, for only thus—and I firmly believe it— only with good stout heart can you be made worthy of what you most desire! Why didn't you get down on your knees tonight afore your father, as I commanded?"

"I could not," Elizabeth whispered.

"Never say could not or cannot," Katryn said irritably. "Lord, how I despise those words! And from you! Now go to sleep. We shall speak further in the morn; pray the sun shines! The world looks much better in the morn. Sleep, Elizabeth, and remember you are England's princess and England loves thee. Aye, at this very moment there will be prayers for thee ascending from even unlettered lips to the gates of heaven. Surely God will hear, and surely it should bring thee comfort. Maybe," Katryn added, looking down at her face, "it has comforted thee already; I shall blow out the candle," she added. "God bless thee and the saints keep thee."

It was cold in the hall. It will soon be winter, she thought, winter, and our armies fight in France. The wind howled suddenly. Was he outside now, lying rolled in his blanket, or was he in his tent, laughing and dicing with his officers? She scurried into her rooms and was soon surrounded by her anxious women.

As soon as Henry was well enough to be up, the court moved back to Hampton Court, a long train of three hundred with Katryn and Henry at its head. Much, much was on Katryn's mind, so that she waved her scarf and smiled her dazzling smile, only half knowing what she did.

The Christmas season would soon be upon them, but until then Edward would go back to Hatfield, and it was imperative she set a watch on his women and see that her orders were not disobeyed. "E'en though there's ice upon the pail, he shall drink milk!" she said. "And eat beef and eggs and bread! And no wines!" Mistress Ashley would report to her. "I want him five pounds heavier by New Year's!"

She could see Ned Seymour ahead of her. She frowned slightly. She was drawing nearer and closer to the Seymour party, of necessity. The Howards hated her truly and resented bitterly her influence with Henry. It wouldn't matter to them whether or not I have influence, she told herself, they just cannot bear to see anyone not their kin close to the King. They'd like to see me dead. Imagine! I who have done naught to them! What had Jane said? "I am afloat in a sea of envy and malice!" It was true too, Katryn thought.

Her face was troubled. Anne, alongside her in the litter, laid her hand over hers. "Smile, my sweet sister," she said, in her gentle voice.

Katryn threw out a smile, first to one side and then the other. "London," she said, aloud. "Ah, London!" Well, if no one at court loved her, the city did. Heads were uncovered, and greeting shouts filled the air. No wonder princes are distrustful of their nobility; I know just how my lord the King feels now! Her mouth opened in some surprise. They're like to wolves about the lion—aye, and who could trust them? Even Ned Seymour—do I truly trust him? And I cannot abide Dudley. But I must mask my feelings, mask them well; and yet who is there to trust?

Little Jane Grey bore the candle before her as Katryn retired early. Within her room, she blessed the child, and suddenly her heart was filled. The children love me, she thought, all my foster children I ha' gathered close about me. Tomorrow they start their lessons with John Cheke, and him I do trust! Him I trust much, although Gardiner will never forgive me for his appointment. Well, damn Gardiner! 'Tis the children and their welfare that is most important! And maybe if I am a good woman, the Lord will bless *me* with a child!

"Summon me Master Parkhurst," she said to Anne. "I would pray and commune with him this eve."

November came quickly. On the fourth there was a battle in France and news reached England the next day. It ran wild over the palace, and it reached Katryn via Anne, who came on running feet, white-faced. Nevertheless her voice was calm. "There is a rumor being blown about the palace, and how much credence you can put in 't, I don't know."

Katryn looked up. She was at her desk, and Master Buckler, her secretary, suspended his writing.

Anne's eyes were warning her. Fear clutched at her heart. She stared at Anne, trying to drag out from her eyes what was amiss, trying to think ahead to what Anne would say.

"Speak, Anne!"

" 'Tis naught but rumor, yet I thought you should hear it from my lips," Anne said, almost coldly, as though Katryn should begin to understand and turn her heart to stone and make no sound—nay, nor feel naught. " 'Tis that we ha' fought a big battle in France, and fought it successfully, but that they say—" Anne hesitated. "—that Sir Thomas Seymour has been killed!"

Then I have died too, Katryn thought. 'Tis true I feel nothing. Dead? Ah, but it was not possible! Not he!

"Impossible, Anne!" she cried. She staggered to her feet, pushing back her desk, and turned to face the door. There was movement and noise outside. Men's voices. Suddenly her knees trembled. What foolishness had she thought? What crazy foolishness! He was mere mortal man. Certes he could die, and mayhap in pain, alone, at night on the hard ground. Her knees sagged. "Lord help me," she whispered. Anne seized her arm. She raised her eyes, and it was Ned Seymour in the doorway, expostulating. Katryn even heard part of his words.

"But I must see the Queen's Grace. Pray announce me."

She waved her hand. Master Buckler went to the door. Katryn looked across at Ned, Ned so like and yet so unlike. I shall never see him again, she thought—never, never. And I shall never be truly alive again. It must be true, for Ned himself was here to tell her. He came close. Wordless she looked up at him and extended her hand. Ned was grave, his face looked leaner and more ascetic; his eyes burned.

"My lord," Katryn said low. "Thy brother?"

"My brother?" He studied her; suddenly his eye lighted. Katryn took a backward step, her senses alert. Was it not Tom? But Ned Seymour had seen—plain—the depth of her distress. She clenched her hands.

"My brother," he said, "successfully took command of the force in France and led it to victory, pursuing the French far into the night. He did this because Henry Wallop was taken acutely ill, and bestowed command on Tom. What had you heard, your Grace?"

"Then it was Wallop!" Her eyes gleamed. They thrust gold sparks at Ned. Had he discovered her secret? Well, let him try to make something of it! "I heard Sir Thomas, your brother, had been killed. Naturally, my lord, the Lady Anne and Master Buckler and myself were much distressed that England should lose such a fine soldier on the field of battle. We were much distressed, my lord, and your news fills us with gladness, except that we shall pray for Sir Henry. We shall go immediately to chapel, and we shall give thanks for our victory."

But that night she dreamed. Dudley was facing her, with his hard light eyes; he was reading, but not looking at the paper; he knew those words by heart. Maybe he had even writ them into law! "So if any man should know of any acts of indiscretion of the Queen, even prior to her marriage, it is his solemn duty to make it known, and a crime of treason to conceal it!"

Katryn sank down on her chair. "Ah, to be a queen and to be treated thus!"

Her accusers smiled. She was being led away. Her Tower room was small. She cast herself down on her knees and began to pray. Only instead of the Lord, she was asking Tom Seymour for help. Then Meg leaned over her. "He is dead, madam," she said.

Katryn screamed, and the strangled noises she made in her sleep roused Meg and Mistress Barbara.

"She dreams," cried Mistress Barbara in horror and pity. "Madam, madam," she cried. She touched Katryn's shoulder and Katryn, suddenly awake, sat up in bed.

"Oh, oh!" she sobbed, looking at both women, looking about the room in sudden terror, and in sudden relief also. "I had a nightmare," she breathed and put her hands over her face. She began to cry.

She refused their ministrations. She buried herself in the big bed, lying on her stomach, burrowing close into the comfort and solid warmth, hugging her body tight, as though she hid from all there under the coverlets and the blankets, between the silken sheets. Over her head Mistress Barbara's eyes met Meg's. "So I have seen the Lady Mary," she whispered. "Aye, and our poor departed Queen Katharine. So have I seen the terror that comes by night."

Katryn didn't hear her words. In the darkness induced by the coverlet, she cried soundlessly, knowing that while her body was safe, her mind was distracted by fear. Why had she not recognized before the awful danger in which she stood? Loving one man and wed to the King! That was treason, pure and simple.

Till those false rumors undid me, she thought, I'd kept it a secret. By God's most precious soul! She rolled over and sat up in bed. Pushing her hair back, she surveyed her two women.

"Pray bring me a bit of wine." She wiped her eyes. "I dreamt I was in the Tower," she whispered.

Mistress Barbara almost dropped the wine. "I was right," she said to Meg. She carried the wine to the bed.

Katryn took it and drank.

Mistress Barbara said, "Madam, you have naught to fear. 'Twas just a dream!"

"Hold your tongue," Katryn said. "You foolish woman!" The huge room was full of shadows, like the shadows that lurked in her husband's head, that big round head with its fringe of hair sticking out from under a golden cap. I am wed to a monster, she thought wildly. Aye, God knows what evil lies prisoned in his heart. A nasty rage, an unconcern, the will to kill—what names can be put to it? He himself does not know whence his deepest malice comes.

She gathered the shawl close about her. "Yes, 'Twas a mere dream!" But she knew that, dream that it was, it would come again.

Katryn brought Edward and Mary to Greenwich for Christmas, but Henry would not permit Elizabeth to join them. In fact, Katryn did not yet dare to ask him; she was waiting for a word, a sign, that he had relented, and she knew that before that sign came she would only anger her husband if she spoke of the matter. So she bided her time, trying not to think too much of the lonely child at Hatfield House. She sent Elizabeth more presents than the child had ever received. "Albeit much *is* necessary clothing," she told her women; for it would not do for Henry to think she disapproved his order, or that she was trying to circumvent him, or that she was showing royal kindness where Henry did not wish it shown.

On New Year's morn, she sat in a new robe at the foot of her bed, the bedrail having been removed. There the lords and ladies came to present their gifts on bended knee. Katryn's eyes sparkled. "I'll never be poor again," she thought. "Never! Such riches as are mine!"

She gave herself up to the purely childish joy of receiving—not only gift after gift, but the homage that was due her. And so many people sent gifts! Even some of the divines at the colleges, and long, long lists of people that she couldn't remember doing a favor for. But I must have, she thought, or else they want one. I'll soon know!

Henry was in splendid humor. The armies were wintering in France. Tom Seymour had fortified captured Douay and was resting there, waiting for spring. Henry was waiting for spring too, for he intended to go to France himself to lead his own troops and to finish off this battle and ensure himself the city of Boulogne.

January was very cold. Katryn kept the children with her, and what with Edward and Bess's boys, and little Jane Grey and Margaret, the schoolroom was cheerful and gay with sunlight and children's voices. Katryn found herself getting into the habit of going up there. In this vast palace, it was somehow reassuring to hear a young voice recite. There, one morning with Mary, she turned over the quill in her hand. Her brow puckered.

"I think I'll write a book," she said.

Mary looked amazed. Her watery eyes gleamed with admiration. "I wish I could ever do such a thing, madam."

Katryn hunted for words and ideas. Mary didn't have an original thought, she was sure, poor thing. "But I know what you could do, Mary," Katryn exclaimed. "You could translate! Why, your Latin is so good! You could translate—" she hunted again in her mind— "the paraphrases of Erasmus, for instance! And not only that, but when you're done I'll have it published for you!"

She was quite close to Mary. Katryn didn't realize how much she had done till one morn, at greeting, Mary called her "my lady mother." Katryn gave her a little kiss. Why, she's turning human! she thought, squeezing Mary's hand; there's a lesson to be learned here, certes.

Neither Mary nor Katryn had had a new gown in quite a while, for all moneys went into the war with France. But now the King had said that each could order a new dress. The reason was that the new alliance with Spain meant a special envoy, and on the seventeenth of February Katryn was to receive the Duke of Nejara.

Katryn kept exclaiming over her gown. The brocade was shimmering, and over it she wore an open robe of cloth of gold, and her little girdle was cloth of gold too. Her train was two yards long. She managed it neatly with a little flip of the hips which Ned's wife watched with envy. Princess and Queen, surrounded by their ladies, were trying on their new-finished gowns on the fifteenth of February, when word reached them that some of the men had arrived home from France. There was much excitement, a flurry of talk; their gallant warriors were home victorious. Among them was Sir Thomas Seymour.

So it was that the audience for the Duke of Nejara was also a welcome-home for the men who had fought in France, and the Queen's presence-chamber was crowded. Katryn's guard glittered in their red satin breeches. The trumpets blew a flourish, the great gold doors were flung wide, and with Anne bearing her train, Katryn began her slow walk toward her chair at the far end of the room.

The lords and ladies and the soldiers and the visitors bowed low as she passed. Is he here? she was thinking. She smiled down upon the bent and uncovered heads; and then as she passed so close she could have put her hand on that thick, dark hair, she felt herself shiver with excitement. To see him at last! To hear his voice! When she turned to face the company and to have her train laid to one side so she could sit, her face and eyes were radiant. He would be standing looking at her, but for some reason she postponed finding him, as though she would fully savor the moment afore she saw him.

The Spanish duke was tall and thin, and looked, she thought, a bit like Ned. I wonder why all Spaniards look as though they had suffered intensely. They can't all ha' been racked. Mary had that way, too. She glanced up at her, but today Mary looked alive and eager; her Spanish was rippling off her tongue, as she and the Spanish duke talked.

The hum of conversation filled the room as the men and women spoke among themselves, awaiting their turns to go up and speak with the Queen, to plead a cause, to present a younger son or daughter, to beg a favor, or to cite a wrong. No matter what the occasion, there was always some who snatched a moment to beg a favor. All the time her eyes were resting on the man who stood about twenty feet away.

Katryn answered automatically. Her heart beat fast, and her mouth was quite dry, and she tried to quiet her tumult by telling herself it was just that his presence was exciting after so long a time. For he wouldn't have changed. And God knew what he would say.

Once long ago she had thought of being Queen. She remembered perfectly. In the garden maze at New Hall, after Will's wedding. How silly I was, she thought, to want him to kneel to me. And yet today he will. A little delighted smile began to tug at the corners of her mouth.

He was coming close to her. There was no one about her chair save Anne, and Lucy to one side. He was as wickedly dashing as always, and as bold as the pirate and brigand he truly was. Oh, the knave, and he is kneeling down on one knee and my hand is in his.

The brown fingers were strong over hers. His lips brushed the back of her hand. I would like to touch his head, she thought. Her voice was low.

"Welcome home, Sir Thomas," she said, and as he straightened and stood before her, her eyes followed his face, and her head tipped to look up at him. "It is a pleasure, my lord," she continued, "for us to congratulate you and to have your presence amongst us!"

"Thank you, madam," he said gravely. "But I cannot conceive our mere return would bring such a smile of delight to your lips. Is your Grace eating sweetmeats, under cover?"

333

Katryn's eyes flashed. "The homage you do us is a true comfort, sir."

Tom Seymour smiled. He bowed and backed away. Katryn felt cold. The joy that had been hers for just a moment faded. How wide, how deep, how fathomless and unbridgeable was the gulf between them! This small exchange itself was dangerous, for he had read her eyes and had known she was pleased to have him kneel. She had provoked a response which only Anne and Lucy could hear: "Is your Grace eating sweetmeats?" Had she looked so titillated, as though she sucked a forbidden fruit? I shall have to be careful, she thought, and so shall he, or my nightmare will be no nightmare suffered amid silken sheets, but suffered indeed in the pale morning sun as it rises and dispels the mists outside the Tower walls! Still, he will be careful; I can depend on him. She sighed and devoted herself to the task of trying to talk to the duke, while Mary interposed Spanish, until she finally had to say, "Prithee, Mary, speak English!"

Katryn didn't see Tom Seymour again for more than two weeks. She knew he had gone down to Wolf Hall, and that he was returning to London for a few days before he made a trip to the Border, for he was the Warden for Wales. Henry had given him land and manors and castles in Wales because he felt that a strong man was needed on the Border; so instead of comfortable demesnes in Kent or Suffork, Tom Seymour had vast lands and rude tenantry and a great garrison at Owen Castle. But as Henry knew, he was popular in the Border, and it was said that he could raise ten thousand men to his banner should he wish it; and since the Tudor himself came from Wales, he was pleased with the result. Only the Howards and Dudley fretted that so much potential power should accrue into one man's hands and those the hard hands of Sir Thomas Seymour.

Thus it was a cold day in early March when the Lord Admiral, booted and spurred, came into the schoolroom to bid Edward goodby. He stood in the doorway, bigger than life. Katryn dropped her quill, and the children all cried out with delighted greetings; John Cheke hastened forward, and even Mary looked pleased.

"They are so pleased to have you here, my lord," John Cheke said.

Tom Seymour's eyes rested fondly on Edward. He patted the top of his head. "The little rascal is always pleased when he can stop reciting. Is 't not so, my prince?"

Edward started to deny it. Then he smiled, a little boy's smile. Poor prince, Katryn thought, no one ever jokes with him.

"When you are a bit older," Tom Seymour said, "I shall take you with me. I start for Wales and the Border this morn."

Edward looked as though he would choke with excitement. He imagined himself riding alongside this towering strong uncle of his.

"I shall look forward to 't," he said.

Tom Seymour grinned. "Spoken like a true prince," he said. His eyes turned to Katryn. He looked down at the table before him. "What is this, your Grace?"

"I'm writing a book," Katryn said, with great dignity.

"Ah?" He leaned over, putting his hand on the pages, reading swiftly. Katryn followed his eyes.

So that if they be women married, they learn to be obedient to their husbands, and to learn of their husbands, at home. Also that they wear such apparel as becometh both holiness, and becoming and pretty, with soberness, though; not being accusers nor detractors, not given to too much eating, or drinking. To teach, honest things they have learned, to love their husbands, and to love their children, and to be discreet and housewifely.

"I see," he said gravely, "that your Grace is giving the world the benefit of the wisdom you've acquired during your long life, and your many years. Thirty-two, is it not?"

"Indeed not!" Katryn quivered.

He chuckled, and John Cheke couldn't help smiling.

"And what is the title of this book, your Grace?"

"Is 't not an odd thing," said Katryn, "but immediate anyone knows I'm writing a book they ask what the title is. I have a title. I am going to call it *The Lamentations of a Sinner*."

At this Tom Seymour looked perfectly amazed. Then he threw back his head and began to laugh. He laughed till he had to wipe away the tears from his eyes. The children laughed too, and John Cheke pressed his hand to his mouth. His eyes met Tom Seymour's and both went off again into gales of laughter.

Katryn had risen to her feet. Why, how can they laugh so! she wondered angrily. The knaves! They think just because I'm a woman I know naught! She cried, "What is funny? I know a deal about sin!"

Tom Seymour was gradually subsiding. "You do?" he asked.

Edward said solemnly, "I truly don't think you do, madam."

"Oh!" said Katryn outraged. "I'm going to name it that, no matter what," she said.

"You do, madam. You do. 'Tis a captivating title, and everyone will read it."

Katryn tossed her head.

Tom Seymour bowed low. "Forgive me, madam," he said. "I'm a rude knave." He set off his cap and knelt and took her hand. "A rude knave, and unfit to have the grace of thy presence. I was laughing, your Grace, because you aren't a sinner at all. You're our beautiful fairest Queen. Is it not so, Edward?"

He kissed Katryn's hand and rose. Her eyes followed him to the door. I love him, she thought; dangerous or no, I adore him, and the day is suddenly black because he is going away. With a sigh she picked up her pen and began to write.

17

Henry was going to war. During the spring, whilst his leg troubled him, the royal armourers built and hammered him a new suit of armour, big enough for two ordinary men, and his ship was fitted with sails of cloth of gold. The troops had gone, many men had already died; his ally Charles of Spain and his enemy Francis of France were warily ready too, circling and cautious. None of them were fiery youths any longer; now with age they maneuvered and deceived each other. But Henry, who knew Charles might make separate peace—that haunting fear of allies—wanted a piece of France, namely Boulogne, and the final humbling of France had begun. Europe could rot with corpses and England would pay dear, but a place in the sun came high and Henry knew his countrymen were ready to pay it.

He sat at his table and wrote. "Thus first, touching on the Queen's Highness, the King's Majesty hath resolved that the Queen's Highness shall be Regent in his Grace's absence."

Katryn said, "Your confidence in me touches me deep, my lord." Henry's narrow eyes regarded her sharply. He told her then the name of the men he had empowered to attend her, to be resident in her court. Ned Seymour, first, the Earl of Hertford. Next Cranmer, who liked and respected her. Next her sturdy, honest uncle, Lord Parr. Then Wriothesley and Gardiner, who didn't like their queen. Henry watched her face as she heard the names. Katryn knew what Henry was doing. He was following closely his old policy of the balance of power. "Let the two factions fight, and let thee, Katryn, keep peace; or let them destroy each other; and find a new face to supplant them and take over their duties." She nodded her head. "You've learned well, and much," the King conceded, "for such a fair woman." He was thinking he had had good fortune before, when he had left another Katharine as regent while he fought with France long ago in the very flower of his hot youth. Left at home, Katharine of Aragon had met with aplomb and dispatch the threat of the Scots descending into England, and it had been the old Duke of Norfolk who had inflicted on them a bloody defeat on Flodden Field and paved the way for the uneasy peace which had prevailed so long. This time Katryn would not have to worry about the Scots, for Henry had carefully made war on them before going to France and this time, much older, he was leaving behind him a nation tamed, or almost tamed to the Tudor yoke. So it had to be, by God, or things should not prosper. God had given Henry power, God had given it to his son, and God would give it to his daughters if aught should hap to Edward. But any man who tried to interfere with God would find Henry to deal with first. Henry rubbed his leg and wiped his brow. It was July seventh and hot. He would be traveling down to Dover soon, for he intended to sail for France on the fourteenth. And here in England, Katryn would gather up the royal children and keep her court, and England would be happy and safe with the queen she loved.

"I shall expect to take the field from Calais toward the end of July," he said, "and to have my victory soon after." Two days later he was hoisted into his armor, and Katryn waved her long green scarf from the window. The King was gone, and she was Katryn Parr, Regent of England.

How fair she looks today, Anne thought, and how much sweet peace must be hers as she drinks the cup of freedom from fear. Anne felt it too. Will had gone with Henry to bear his headpiece and spear. But certainly, Anne thought, no one at court could fail to have felt Henry's increasing grasp of power, and no one was free of fear of the great lion who sat so unwieldy and grim upon England's throne. She went over by Katryn's chair.

Katryn was writing slowly. Her brow was furrowed. "O Almighty King and Lord of Hosts," she wrote, "we most humbly beseech Thee to turn the hearts of our enemies toward peace. Or else grant, O Lord, that with small effusion of blood, we may to Thy glory obtain victory, and so, with our hearts and minds, we praise Thee who reigneth, world without end, Amen." She dipped her pen. "Katryn," she wrote, "the Queen Regent. K. P."

The last bold stroke ended. She sanded the parchment and handed it to Anne to give to John Parkhurst, who stood at the window talking to Lucy.

"I wish this proclamation and prayer for our King and soldiers to be said in every church in the land." She rose. Henry had not said she could not have Elizabeth. Manlike, he had avoided the subject; so, womanlike, she knew he had at last come to relent a bit. She pondered her husband. He knew she wanted Elizabeth. Surely by not speaking of her, he had given the sign that she might have the princess with her this summer. He might even smile when she told him how she had reasoned. "Master Buckler," she said thoughtfully, drawing her long scarf through her fingers, "pray thee write to Mistress Ashley, and ask the Lady Elizabeth to join us at Chelsea the end of this week."

Anne stiffened, but held her tongue. They would soon be going to chapel. There, thought Anne, I shall pray not only for victory, but also I shall pray to the Lord to help the Queen's Grace, my dearest sister, to have a care, have a care.

But that was difficult for Katryn. The present was too compelling.

She made Hampton Court her headquarters. There, after the privy council met in the early hours of the morn, she would receive Ned Seymour, who reported to her what had happened.

Ned, champion of causes, found Katryn a willing listener and a sympathetic one. Protestants went free from Gardiner's charges of heresy, and poor men found redress against their grievances. Occasionally Lord Parr would shoot Katryn a warning look from under his gray brows; other times he would speak out, saying a "Nay, nay, your Grace!"

Katryn would then try to listen to both, and when she decided in favor of her uncle, Ned's wife would tighten her face. Even during her hours of audience, with a poor petitioner kneeling at her feet or a titled lady begging a favor for son or niece or daughter, she could feel the Countess' eyes on her. She hates me, Katryn thought. Well, let her!

Every two weeks, she would escape London and set forth for a country house, or one of her dower houses. She traveled to Hanworth, to Chelsea, to Windsor. Katryn loved Windsor, lying on the river with its beautiful trees and great gardens. She spent time, too, with her army of bailiffs, for property after property, manor houses and manor lands were hers, and her deed box was as full as the locked coffers of gold and jewels. I am very wealthy, she thought; mayhap I am the wealthiest woman in England—I, poor Katryn Parr, who carted sheep from Kendal to start a flock.

New deeds and new purchases were added to her lands all the time. Henry, in a gesture, would hand over convent lands, laughing at her eagerness to own the land and calling her "my hedge-thorn wench." She was enclosing Fausterne, a royal manor deeded to her. When Ned learned of it, he remonstrated. This time she did not give in. "All our tenants prosper," she said sharply, using the royal *we*.

Ned winced. He knew it meant that farmers would be sent from the land. This morning he had forbidden enclosure to a wine merchant from the city who had bought land. "There are free farmers on those acres," he could hear himself saying. "Why do you want the land, to enclose it?"

The merchant looked at Ned with amazement and annoyance. Everyone wanted land; it was the fever of the times, and everyone was buying. No sooner did a London merchant prosper than he bought land from the nobility who wished to sell, or had to sell to keep up the magnificence at court Henry demanded. "Why do I want land?" he echoed.

"Aye," Ned snapped. "Why not let be, and let the poor farmers rest?"

"That is impossible, my lord," the merchant said coldly.

Katryn too was angry when Ned said she had no right to enclose. "Are ye mad, my lord?" she asked. "These are mine own lands, part of crown lands!"

"The crown owes a duty to its people," Ned said.

Katryn said, "Dare you speak thus to me? Such temerity, my lord! Think you to remind me, the Queen, of duty!" She rose to her feet. "Your audience is ended!"

It was not the first time they had had a clash, but it was the most serious one. Gardiner, who had been present, pursed his lips and waited.

But a greater danger made its appearance that first day of September and both Ned and Katryn forgot their quarrel, for the plague was reported in London. Hastily Katryn gathered up her household and all the children; the royal train and the court set out for Oking. No sooner was she there, and the royal flag flying from the pole, than she issued a proclamation. "No person who has been with either an infected person, or household, could come to court except under the Queen's indignation, and under further punishment at her pleasure!" She signed her name.

An anxious week passed. The royal children were examined daily. The council and court functioned as best they could away from London, and, as no plague appeared at Oking and no member of the court succumbed to it, the palace took on a holiday air. Edward had never looked better. Elizabeth was growing so fast Katryn could scarcely keep her in clothes, which suited Elizabeth, who, had the Tudor love for clothes and ornament and who now had more new gowns than ever. Thus at the end of the week Katryn could write Henry that all was well, and the imminent danger past. When she had finished her writing and laid aside her pen, couriers were announced with letters from the King.

Katryn was in her big bed, for the September night was cool. She took the letter, and she could imagine him writing in his tent, with the gay flags waving atop, and Will Herbert pacing and waiting for Henry to finish.

At the closing up of these, our letters today [Henry wrote], the Castle before named is at our command. This day, the eighth of September, we begin three batteries and have three more at our command going. No more to you at this time, sweetheart, for lack of time and occupation of business, saving we pray you to give in our name our hearty blessings to all our children, and recommendations to our cousin Margaret, and the rest of the ladies and gentlemen, and to our council. Written with the hand of your loving husband.

And then the heavy signature, Henry R.

Katryn leaned back against the pillows. So he had sent his blessings to *all* his children. That meant he condoned her taking in Elizabeth. She summoned the three children and read them their father's greeting. They all smiled and then eyed her thoughtfully. Their feelings are mixed about the King, she thought, and rightly so, as are mine. Great king he may be, but who would willingly have him as parent or husband? Jesu, soon he shall be back! Then she pushed away the thought. Now it was so pleasant at Oking.

"What a lovely month September is," she said, looking about

her crowded room; for besides her ladies, Ned and her uncle and Gardiner were with her, and John Parkhurst. She was thinking she was glad they had all been driven down here. Then she reminded herself that was indeed a selfish thought. *I must make amends, for what would the Lord think of me?* Aloud she said, "Master Parkhurst, let us have an evening prayer now, but not only for the welfare of our lords and husbands abroad, but for our great and precious city of London and the souls dwelling there."

One by one the lights went out in the palace. Flags flew on the battlement to show the royal family was in residence; the two hundred and fifty ladies and gentlemen and members of the council and yeomen of the guard slept. In France there was war; here in England was peace.

On September 18, Henry entered Boulogne, his prize and his price of peace for France. The next day, the news having been hurried to England, Katryn sat at her table and issued an order that a public thanksgiving be offered up to Almighty God in all towns and villages in England. Her secretary copied it and couriers set forth posthaste for all corners of the country. She sat back after her signature and looked down at it. Katryn, the Queen. She rubbed her finger over the sand, and shook it off. She knew Henry would waste no time getting home. Probably he'd be in England by the first of the month. She looked over to Elizabeth, who was standing at the window. She rose and went to the window. "It is truly wondrous news, isn't it?" she asked.

"Glorious," Elizabeth replied.

Katryn looked at her; there was something different about her. "Marry, Bess, you ha' dyed your hair!"

Elizabeth turned a little, and the sun glinted on her red curls. Katryn smiled to herself, for it was almost exactly her own shade. She put her arm around Elizabeth and squeezed her tight. "It's most becoming," she said. "I only hope it suits the new length of velvet I purchased for you and Mary."

A trumpet blew in the distance. In the court around by the front wings, even from this distance could be heard the sound of horses. It meant Ned was on his way back to London, Ned and others of the council. On this morning, when the news of victory in France had come, and when Henry would soon be returning, she and Elizabeth were talking about clothes. How inconsequential! But it were far, far safer and more prudent to have the mind occupied with clothes than with aught else, from another man to one's religious tenets. Being a woman was essentially simple, she thought. Love and honor one's husband, and love and take care of one's children, as she had written in her book. From now on, she resolved, I shall do that; but in the meantime, 'twill be two weeks almost afore Henry comes home.

The wind blew gently. The sun shone bright. Katryn leaned her elbows on the window sill, looking out the casement. "What a beautiful, fair day!" she exclaimed, with satisfaction. "I think I shall ride out today. Wilt thou come, Elizabeth?"

Henry came home in triumph on the first of October. Contrary to the hopes of his ill-wishers, he had withstood the campaign well, and although his leg was bothering him, Katryn found him his hearty gay self and quite amorous. This planted the hope in her mind that she might conceive a child, and what joy to have such a gift for New Year's! During December she went much to the chapel by herself. One time, opening the door of the royal pew, she found Henry himself there, kneeling as best he could with his bad leg; he looked like a great square bit of velvet and fur against the dark wood of the pew.

"I did not expect, my lord—" Katryn began.

He raised his great head; it seemed firmly affixed to his body without the benefit of a neck at all, and his heavy jowls rested on his fur collar where the jewels of his chain glittered.

"I come to pray for a child," Katryn began again.

His narrow eyes fixed her, and there was a gleam of truculence in their depths. Oh, by the mass, she thought rapidly, I've reminded him of his first wife, who always spent her days on her knees praying to conceive! Marry, marry, my wench, what quadruple trouble is yours, to have a husband with so many previous wives! Surely women's minds are apt to run the same, and the things I say unwitting remind him of what he wishes to forget!

But she knelt beside him, hoping she looked sweet and fair and desirable and that her perfume pleased him. Had she put too much on? She could smell it herself faintly. *I am supposed to think about God, and here I am wondering about perfume, but it might mean my head!* She tried to pray, but she was too conscious of Henry, and the most she could manage was the Lord's Prayer, which she said automatically with an aside to the Lord to forgive her since she had much on her mind and such a difficult husband. *Had she imagined that look of truculence? Nay, she had not!* Her heart beat fast. Henry rose to his feet, and she rose too. *His beard is so sparse,* she thought rapidly. *What if it's his fault we've no children?* She wet her lips. *If he read the thoughts in her head he'd have it off her body in a trice. Oh, Jesu!* she said to herself, smiling sweetly at Henry. *He's been so marvelously pleasant, how can he change so quick? And this is what happened afore!*

"My lord," she said, hoping her voice didn't shake. But he smiled not and strode off, leaving her clinging to Anne's arm. Slowly she made her way from the chapel. In her own rooms, she found Lord Parr waiting to speak with her. She was so glad to see his grizzled friendly face that she almost didn't hear what he told her, after she had kissed him and told him how much even the sight of him cheered her.

"I'm afraid I can no longer be about with thee, and no longer be of much use to thee, my dear," he said.

Katryn made an exclamation of denial.

"Aye, and I have told his Grace. I ha' resigned as lord chamberlain, Katryn. I can no longer carry out my myriad duties. I am sorry, my dear."

She pressed him into a chair. Somewhat reluctantly he sat. Stumpy and broad and indomitable, he never sat in the Queen's presence, and Katryn could see of a sudden that indeed he was much older, he had failed in the last few months. She had been with him so much she hadn't noted it. Distress and concern shone on her face.

"Pray don't fret, your Grace," he said, almost irritably. "Thou'lt do well without me. Thou'lt find you're a sturdy wench and can make your own way, as ye ha' proved. By the mass," he growled, "cannot a man grow old a bit without his womenfolk afretting and asighin', like as you're already crying over my grave?"

Anne giggled and brought him a cup of wine. She proffered him a plate of rosy apples, and he took one, biting in sharply and wiping the juice from his chin. "Nay, nay," he said, "I'm just old."

Anne sank down upon a fat cushion before the hearth, with the pretty painted screen between her and the flames; but Katryn stood, as if she needed to stand, for this was a blow. Acourse, she thought rapidly, I cannot tell him it's a blow, for then he would fret and to no end.

"It is that we shall miss thee much," she said. "Thou'rt a true friend to us."

He scowled, looking up from the half-eaten apple. Lord Parr always made short work of anything he did. "You have many true friends, Katryn."

"I expect so," said Katryn.

"Aye, betray none of them. You know well what we hold most dear on the Border—a man's honor, a man's word."

"Aye," said Katryn.

Lord Parr heaved himself to his feet, tossed the apple core into the fireplace, and lifted his glass of wine. "I drink your health, your Grace. And remember from whence you came."

Katryn kissed him. Into her mind unbidden came the picture of Kendal Castle, rugged and challenging against the hill and the gray skies. Will I ever see it, or this dear man my uncle again? she wondered. Then she lifted her head. Acourse I will! "Good-by, my uncle," she said. "Thank you with all our hearts, for all the love and care thou hast bestowed on us. We are eternally in thy debt!"

"I count the two of thee amongst my blessings," Lord Parr said. Then he paused. "You have done much, Katryn. Much."

Katryn opened her mouth to speak, but he waved his hand at her in his old manner, as if to say he wanted no further words from her; he was through with words, and wished to have done with them and this parting. At the door he bowed. "There's a bad storm outside," he said, and was gone.

" 'Tis the twenty-ninth of November," Katryn said aloud. "I should have urged him to stay until Christmas. Mayhap he will."

The wind howled suddenly. Katryn said, "I think I shall walk out, Anne."

Anne went to the window. "I don't believe that the weather is clement enough, your Grace."

"Nonsense," said Katryn. "To be sure, 'tis raining and windy, but—"

Anne drew her to the window. "There are three trees down in this part of the gardens."

Katryn said angrily, "By God's most precious soul!" Why, they were big, beautiful trees, and how pathetic they looked on the garden grass, felled thus in a stroke by the elements. I pray God, she thought, that the sturdy oaken masts of the flagship *Salamander* will better withstand those elemental thrusts of wind. If he can weather the storms at sea, surely I can weather them at home.

Katryn began to worry over Henry's health. They went down to Greenwich for Christmas, and, in a good mood about the season plus his victory over the French, Henry ate well and waxed fatter. He was keeping the French on tenterhooks, refusing to negotiate, refusing to make peace, holding on tight to Boulogne, keeping a winter army in France, and ordering Tom Seymour to keep the sea lanes open, to refortify and revictual Boulogne even through the winter, which had thus been done and the French fleet driven into its various harbors. When Henry thought of it, his eyes twinkled and his jaws chewed faster; he meditated on his new Defensive League, and alliance of nations of which England should be the leader. For this, he refused the advances of the French, for he was in a strong position now abroad, and his country, his small country, should have her high place in the sun.

Meanwhile he fortified the seacoast. Docks and harbors were now protected by sullen-mounted cannon, and especially fine new ships. Henry had a love for ships. Endlessly, on the drawing board, he studied them, and he could plainly picture them spreading their canvas to the wind, leaning on it, flying the bright red standard of St. George. Life was good, if it weren't for his damned leg.

On the twenty-fourth, the day before Christmas, he appeared before Parliament, to explain briefly his policies with France and the need for subsidies for the coastal defense of England and for the Navy. He spoke of Scotland, and the happy prospect of young Edward having to bride the lovely Mary, Queen of Scots, an infant yet. Rich with promise was this alliance! Then he spoke of the succession.

No English king had ever taken the succession into his hands as Henry was doing. But the men of law nodded their heads, for it was legal; all of Gray's Inn deemed it legal. And the English could understand it was of prime importance not only to Henry but to the realm. A great deal of Henry's pride in his country and country-men had seeped through from great noble to rudest commoner; their King had made their nation one to be reckoned with, and they fully understood his concern for their welfare when he left them.

First, then, the young Prince Edward, son of Jane Seymour, his loving queen; and after Edward, the children, male or female, of his beloved queen, Katryn Parr. And after—his voice did not falter—the Princess Mary. Henry made no mention of Mary's mother; he had no wish to. And after Mary, Elizabeth.

Henry prorogued Parliament then. It was Christmas Eve. He went by barge to Greenwich to rejoin his wife.

Christmas Eve. Katryn knew what Henry had told Parliament, for he had told her about the succession the night before. And it caused her disquiet. Here I am, second on his list—nay, he men-tioned no other wife and queen but me and Jane! After Edward, issues from his Grace and me! Jesu, what do I have inside me any-way? A useless, empty womb! Alone except for Mistress Barbara and Meg, she hurled her glass into the fireplace. "By the mass!" she cried. "By God's most precious soul! Why should I be cheated?"

Again she began to understand Jane's disquiet. And the fears Jane had confessed she felt after she had lost her first child, and the long months betwixt when each succeeding four weeks told her she could not expect a child. Katryn bent down and picked up the pieces of the wine glass thoughtfully. Henry, the big man, fell violently in love; then he looked to his new love for an heir.

Maybe the long years of his youth, when he had hoped so much and seen those hopes dashed, had made an imprint so deep one could not reckon it normally. Time after time had fate snatched from Henry the fruit of union, the real proof of man's immortality. Look what I am doing, he must have said to God on his knees, look what I am doing and who then shall do it after me? Look at what I am building! Where is the sturdy troop of sons I should have to build after me, to repair the walls and see them unbreached? Where? I have loved my wife, before God I have been almost faithful! And if I sinned, I did it unwitting, for men of God told me it was right to wed with my brother's widow!

Oh, those words must have sharpened his anger with her! No wonder he hated her in the end! I can see him so plain, Katryn thought; of all men he cannot be crossed—nay, by God nor man, nor most especially by woman! I shall be the same reproach to him that Katharine of Aragon was, poor woman, with her robes of St. Francis dripping from underneath her fine court gown!

"I have tried so hard to be properly fit," she said aloud. "Certes I am highbred enough to bring a prince to England! I am strong and sturdy, never sick! And I have loved my King and husband."

She cast down her eyes from Mistress Barbara's, her heavy lashes falling against her cheek. Could it be, she wondered, that it's because I hanker for another man? Was she to be condemned because the image of a dark-faced man—rogue and pirate that he was—intruded into her dreams? How to still the restless heart? I truly cannot abide him. It is true what I said before: he deserves nothing but blows at my hands! And he doesn't love me. Never, never shall I be sure of him! Why, look how he left me in Lincoln. How he has mocked me! and flaunted his infidelities right afore my very eyes! She clenched her hands. Anne was right! She was a fool to cry over a man, moon over him. I shall pray, for I do not know whom else to ask for help but God. From now on, for the rest of my natural days, I shall attend chapel twice daily, I swear it. And I have found, when I'm dissatisfied with aught, that I should list my blessings, and certes all my faithful women are amongst them. And tomorrow Cat is being wed to Will Knyvet, a rakish friend of Tom Seymour's! aye, if he thought for one moment he was going to seduce her, he wasn't reckoning wi' me! It will be a lovely wedding, too, on Christmas Day.

Katryn went to the window. Outside the snow was falling gently. She pulled the curtains aside. How beautiful was the white world, how marvelously beautiful! How good it was to drink it in. Pressing her nose against the pane, she could smell the fresh cold air. It tingled. Her senses raced. Certainly, this new year coming would be the best one in her whole whole life!

It continued to snow during January. And the festivities at court picked up in tempo, for Henry was entertaining many foreign missions, cementing his European Defensive League. From the portly Van der Delft, to the lean Spanish duke, the court glittered.

Katryn kept her vow. Twice a day she retired to chapel, her prayer book clasped between her jeweled hands, its little marker made of velvet sewn with pearls. That January saw Anne diffidently announce she was adding a panel to her gowns; her new baby was expected in May.

"May?" said Katryn softly. Even the name was beautiful. Her eyes filled suddenly with tears. "I am so glad for thee, Anne," she whispered.

Anne must understand, she thought as the tears streamed down her face. Anne hugged her and she was crying too. "Oh, Katryn, Katryn," she was saying, "pray do not weep!"

"I cannot help it," Katryn said. "It is just that I am so glad for thee, and I think how very wonderful it must be! How very wonderful to have one's own little baby!"

Anne drew a long breath, she essayed a shaky smile. "Oh, your Grace," she whispered. Was there compassion in Anne's voice? Was there pity? Oh, never! Why, she was healthy and strong, and surely soon, any time, she too would have a baby! Surely she needed no one's tears. Still, Anne hadn't told her about the baby till she had been forced to. Anne had known then that her own condition would be a constant reminder to Katryn.

But her court was young. And as January hurried into February, and March gobbled up its first weeks, it seemed to Katryn that every other one of her ladies was pregnant. Worse than that, Henry fell ill.

On the third of March he took to his huge bed, coughing and sneezing like a spouting whale. The whole bed heaved when he sneezed, his cap sat awry on his bald head, and his fever rose as high as the mound of handkerchiefs piled on his table. That day Katryn came back to her chambers to find her ladies in a high state of chattering excitement because Ned's wife had been delivered of another son, and it was their second boy and they were going to call the child Ned; they had named their first boy Edward, too! Interposed with this they queried Katryn about the King's health. It was Cat Strickland, now Kynvet, who was talking the most. She was waxing very plump. Why, she's going to have a baby too, Katryn thought suddenly. By the mass, she was wed only three months, and already—

"And can you imagine, your Grace, naming her second son the same as the first? I wonder what they'll name their third?" Cat's eyes were as round as her little belly.

"Be quiet," Katryn said sharply. "And all of you leave us!"

Later that night she went back to Henry, who hated bed and was restless and uncomfortable. She played cards with him, careful to let him win, careful also not to touch his sore leg, for they played on his counterpane, smoothed out rosily under the bright playing cards. But he had heard about Ned's second son. The King too remarked on the giving of the same name. Still, Henry said, he could understand it. Suppose aught happened to the first child? But Ned, Henry said, was a lucky man. He shot Katryn a look under his brows. Had she thought of a present?

"Aye," mumbled Katryn. "Poison for his Countess."

Henry chuckled. He chewed his lip, and played a card. Recklessly Katryn won it. Recklessly she almost said—blurted out—how much she longed for a child. Then she stopped. It would never do to make such a confession of weakness. Henry might think she had lost hope! The next card she played deliberately to let Henry win.

"Oh," she exclaimed prettily. "Thou art so quick, my lord. I can never hope to win from thee." Best make him forget Ned's wife and her ability to whelp like the bitch she was. Katryn poured Henry some more wine, placed a fresh handkerchief to his hand, and began to shuffle the cards again.

By the twenty-second of March, Henry was still convalescing, but trouble was brewing in France. The Defensive League was put to its first test, and many messages flew back and forth, and envoys arrived. Sometimes Katryn entertained them first, speaking with them for a while; then she would report to Henry, and sometimes he would see them himself in his bedchamber. April was sweet and mild. That meant the French might strike soon, and Tom Seymour was given command of the fleet as both nations refitted their ships for the coming test. He had not been in England all winter. But Henry insisted on reviewing the fleet and this he did, traveling down to Portsmouth, and taking Katryn with him, and Elizabeth, who was starry-eyed with excitement. Two days later Tom Seymour defeated the French in a decisive sea battle, and Henry and London and England rejoiced. The final insult had been placed upon their ancient enemy, and Henry's eyes gleamed like a beady shoat's. What was his good brother Francis thinking now!

But Henry could not resist summer. He went down to Guildford and every day saw him out hunting. His leg was sore, but he endured it until August, when he came back to London and Hampton Court, his brief holiday over, and business was resumed.

Politics occupied him incessantly. He was carefully calculating when to resume negotiations with the French, drafting a humbling treaty which would keep Boulogne in English hands. Meanwhile he fought with his bankers and Parliament for money, for even more fortifications were going up on the coast, and the new ships were building on the ways, and under his guidance the officers of the Royal Navy were growing apace. Similarly, Henry attended every council meeting, and the council met at eight in the morning. He reviewed every decision of the Star Chamber, stepping in when he saw a chance for crown revenue, or the ghost of it. And he kept his small hands on the affairs of the Church, steering a neat middle course between the mounting waves of dissent that Catholic and Protestant were creating between them. Henry at the helm of the ship of state had never worked so incessantly not with such single-mindedness of purpose; and, except for England's mounting debt, her head was kept into the wind and she swept on, throwing long billows of white foam regally to each side as Henry's royal ermine swept a path to each side of his immense figure.

In the fall, while Anne held at her breast her infant daughter, and while Cat Strickland bore a big son, Katryn held her own audiences, dealing out the favors that would please Henry, and dealing out some that would please her. Ned Seymour was often in her chambers. Church business brought him there, for Katryn had become as much an arbiter as Henry, and Henry seemed content to let her deal in his stead. Yet here was where the greatest bitterness lay. And then one day Gardiner had the temerity to arrest Sir George Blagge on heresy charges.

Sir George, an old bedfellow of Henry's and one of the gentlemen of his chamber, was thrown into the Tower, and Henry knew naught of it. Katryn ordered his release, through Ned, and sent Sir George to apprise Henry what had happened to him.

"Pig," Henry said, when Sir George appeared white-faced.

"Jesus, your Grace," muttered that gentleman. "I'd be roast pig by now, were it not for her Grace's intervention!"

Henry waved away his explanations that he was not guilty and the charges trumped up. He cared little to hear about it. Deliberately he was permitting Gardiner and Ned to feud. Let their followers suffer, but he was glad Sir George had not, himself.

Gardiner was furious too. "Her Grace interferes with your Majesty!"

What a clumsy sentence, Henry thought, scowling at him.

Gardiner went on. "She's a barren woman, your Grace, and you should set her aside and—" He paused. Marry again? He looked at the towering figure of his king, for Henry was standing by the window, looking out at the fall colors. "The Lady Willoughby?" Gardiner went on softly. "A fair widow, now."

Henry frowned. His old friend Suffolk had died. True, the beauteous Kate, who had borne two strapping sons, was now a widow. "Stick to your churchly endeavors, my good bishop," he said tartly, "and let other men worry over more earthly affairs."

Left alone, he stared moodily out the window. Was his queen barren? It had been almost three years now. And no issue.

Fortune favored Katryn. The French were coming around to Henry's terms. Winter approached and Parliament convened; Henry spoke. The first snow fell, and the French gave in. Envoys arrived, meek. Their main mission was to set a date to speak of peace. Henry made them wait. He wished to enjoy Christmas. Let them come then on January second. He would then be ready to listen. He, the victor, would listen. He passed his hand over his sparse reddish beard and smiled down at the little Frenchman. January the second then.

He called Katryn in to speak with her, and they talked long about the French, and how they should be received. Henry wanted to impress them. "Redecorate all thy apartments, my sweet Kate," he said expansively. "Everything. You should have a new wardrobe also, and the princesses."

He hasn't given me much time, Katryn thought. She flew into a frenzy of activity, and long processions of merchants came aknocking on her chamber doors, followed by trains of their own servants bearing goods. Katryn weighed colors and costs, paint and gilding, new ornaments, new hangings. And when she was done and the gowns were ready and the great rooms newly painted and freshly hung, she led Henry in and he was pleased. A man with a good eye to color, he went from room to room, exclaiming with pride. He squeezed her, enveloping her in a huge hug.

"Their eyes will bulge," he roared. He looked down at her. "And you—my fair queen!"

He was so pleased he sent for his jeweler. That night, he displayed before her eyes an array of gems. Great huge diamonds swinging on an intricate chain. An emerald pin for the shoulder of one of her gowns. A pair, for each wrist, of blazing ruby and diamond bracelets. He kissed her. "These are thine, my own," he said. "Thy very own. They are not crown jewels. Put them in thy little box." Then he whispered something bawdy. Katryn blushed, and later tried to return his ardor with as much fire as she could summon. Good King Hal, she thought, under his kisses. This is the best side of him. And then, even though he was making love to her, her mind flew to what Anne of Cleves had said about her three years ago: "A fine burden Katryn Parr has taken upon herself!" Katryn shut her eyes. I hope I conceive, her mind murmured, while her arms held Henry tight.

Because of the weather, the French did not arrive until the second week of January, and after consulting with Katryn, Henry permitted Edward to meet them at Hounslow Heath. Edward had never looked better and his solemnity had given way a bit; although Henry did not know whether to attribute it to Katryn or to John Cheke, he was inclined to allow that each had helped Edward enormously. So it was a proud father who saw his son ride forth to greet the principal French envoy, the Admiral d'Annebaut, and his attending train.

With this beginning, the next weeks took on a high flavor for Henry, who saw his demands met and acceded to with grace. He kept Boulogne, and the French signed. His queen had arranged festivities which Henry was sure truly dazzled the sophisticated erstwhile enemy; his court had never been so brilliant, and Katryn's ladies were beautiful and witty and charming. Gallons of fine wine were consumed, and all manner of delicacies which kept Henry munching after everyone else had finished. When it was all over, he had never been more content, except that it had all cost a deal of money. The golden flow he had had when he was young had, like his own youth, disappeared so quickly!

And yet another blow fell. Not only did the old ulcer flare up again, but the long dormant one in his left leg began to swell and pain and thrust its long red fingers down into his calf. Infuriated at his own disability, Henry blustered, but his doctors cornered him, much as hunters advance on a bull stag in the nets, and drove him into bed.

So the King conducted business from his pillow. He needed money. He fretted. Gardiner slyly put forth a plan. Since the monasteries had almost all been confiscated already, their wealth used up by Henry in prodigal fashion, what about the great universities and the immense grants and endowments that they held? What about them?

The first whisper of this brought the chancellor of Cambridge up to London to see his old pupil John Cheke. On their knees they pleaded their case before Katryn.

"If the universities become crown possessions, madam," Sir Sidney Smith cried, his voice shaking with passion, "if we are then subservient to the crown, then our culture is dead and Cambridge shall be no more!"

John Cheke murmured, "Hear, hear, madam, prithee!"

"I hear both of thee," Katryn said.

" 'Tis for the good of thy country," Smith cried. "Do it for England!"

Katryn held her little gold pomander to her nose. The room was silent. She looked down at Sir Sidney's bent gray head. Ah, how men suffered over their ideals! "Rise, both of you, and let me think," she said. Sir Sidney reminded her of Lord Latimer. So would he have pled, she knew. "Pray take a chair, Sir Sidney," she said, "and you shall be served some wine."

One of her maids moved swiftly to bring the chancellor wine. "Independence is a very valuable thing," she said, remembering how on the Border gentry and nobles alike had resisted the encroachment of the crown. "I shall do my very best," she said gravely.

Henry's leg hurt him badly, and the next night she spent by his bedside applying the poultices and fomentations, feeding him wine, reading to him, and singing him to sleep. Before she sang to him, she told him what had happened two days ago, and how Sir Sidney had come to beg her to speak to her lord about Cambridge. Henry lay back, a huge mound on his huge bed, and the quilts moved convulsively; she trembled with fear, for she did not know whether he would be furiously angry with her. Unaccountably he was not. The King said, "He is right, and so art thou, sweetheart. And I shall take over and re-endow Cardinal College myself." Wolsey had founded it.

"Oh, my lord," she cried, "thou art as wise as Moses! I cannot ever but be amazed at thee—thou art the finest King England ever had!" Tears of relief stood in her eyes, and Henry saw them. "Why dost thou weep?" he asked.

"Because thou art so good and kind to me," she said, and kissed his hand.

"Nay, thou art an angel," he muttered. "Edward loves thee, and Mary loves thee, and I love thee."

He has not mentioned Elizabeth, she thought, the bright-eyed, now bright-haired, daughter of the passion of his middle years; but she is more like to him than any of the rest.

The following week, with Henry still confined to his chambers and on a blustery February day—the fourteenth it was—Katryn's little book was published. She held it in her hands proudly. It was bound in red velvet stamped with a gold crown. She turned the pages lovingly. One hundred and twenty pages; of course, they were small, but was not the print beautiful? The ladies were very excited.

Lucy said, "All the women in the kingdom should read it, madam! What wondrous advice is contained here!"

"Being a woman is very important," Katryn said, "and we have almost nothing writ about it. And I take no credit, Lucy. Most of the advice I have writ about was given me by my mother." She looked over to Anne. "I hope she would be proud of it, Anne," she said diffidently.

Anne smiled, her warm, sweet smile. Why, she is almost exactly like our mother, Katryn thought. I never noted it afore! And I am not at all like Anne, so maybe I am certes not what my mother intended me to be. Aloud she said to Mary, "We shall ha' your translation published this month, too, Mary. And we shall all be very very proud of thee."

But Bishop Gardiner distrusted mightily this upflare of writing and intellectualism in women of the court. Erasmus, indeed! And the Queen devoted three long paragraphs, five pages, to a dissertation on why the clergy shouldn't marry! He read it to Henry, who was still confined to bed. "Are we to be instructed by women, then, your Grace?"

Henry grunted. The Bishop retired, muttering.

The following day at dinner, Katryn's usual circle of ladies and gentlemen were joined by both the Seymours, Ned to thank Katryn for what she had done for the universities, which were close to his heart, he said, and Tom Seymour to make a courtesy call on the Queen, for Henry had summoned him briefly to London to confer upon him the supreme command of the fleet. After greetings had been disposed of, Katryn, who had been surprised to see him, was endeavoring to keep from noting him at all. But the trouble was she had seated Ned and Tom on either side of the Princess Mary, and the Princess Mary always sat opposite her at table; for Katryn felt that was her proper place as the eldest princess of the realm. So there he was, right opposite her almost, and saying he had enjoyed her book very much, madam.

"Thank you," said Katryn woodenly.

Ned said, "But I misagree with you, your Grace, about the clergy not marrying. It almost smacks of papistry!"

Katryn's eyes snapped. Tom Seymour laid down his knife. He said, "I think, Ned, that her Grace, being a woman and knowing the frailties of her sex, believes divines should not be troubled by them. After all, think on the misery they bring."

I'm not going to answer either one of them, she thought. "Pray tell us the latest gossip, sir," she said sweetly.

There was a real tidbit of gossip, too, that had not yet reached the ladies' ears. Last night the Earl of Surrey had got himself drunk and, in his roistering about the town, had broken a couple of windows and a couple of heads. This morning, on being apprised of his deeds by the startled victims who had come to complain in the Star Chamber, the council had ordered Surrey, noble blood notwithstanding, to pay the damages and repent his actions in the Fleet. So thither he had been removed by four stalwart yeomen of the guard, and there he was now, cooling his heels in a common prison. Ned thought it disgraceful, but Katryn could see Tom Seymour thought it a joke. Henry was vastly annoyed, Ned said, and that pleased him because it put disgrace on the Howards, although he didn't say that aloud.

Katryn tried to eat. Tom Seymour is putting away as much food, she thought, as the first time I met him and sat thus, opposite him; he looks at me the same way he did that night so long ago, as though he could tell what I was thinking. Anyway, he was paying her no mind now, but talking with the Princess, telling her about Spain; for he had lately been there, and he had brought her orange and lemon trees. She was pleased and explained she would keep them in their tubs till the weather was milder, and then she would set them out in a sunny place against a wall so the north winds would be kept from them.

The meal ended. Perversely Katryn wished it hadn't. The sun had come out, and sunlight flooded into the long windows. She went over to them gratefully, and then he was beside her. For a moment they were alone out of earshot. She glanced up at him. What was he going to say? He had maneuvered this neatly, but there would not be much time. I am never alone, she thought fiercely. Never!

He was saying now, "Katryn, I've only a second. Long ago I warned thee. You are running Hampton Court like Snape Hall. But it is not; nor is Henry Lord Latimer. Do not forget, your Grace, ever, that Henry is King." He bowed over her hand. "It's been my great pleasure, your Grace."

He was gone. Katryn turned her back on the company. The sound of the closing door still echoed in her ears. He means, she thought, that I have a difficult time thinking of Mary as a princess; I am apt to treat her just like Margaret. And I run the great palace as I might have run Snape Hall, for did I not say in my book that a woman should never neglect the housewifely arts? But think on the pleasure it brings to all within the household. Aye, as a bird makes a nest, so should a woman make her house comfortable for all within it, even to servants, so that all are happy and loved. And worst—am I treating Henry like a husband? How can I help it? But Tom's words echoed in her ears. "Do not forget, your Grace, ever, that Henry is King!"

Ned was bowing over her hand. "Madam," he was saying, "you know how deeply I felt about the universities. Now Bishop Gardiner is attempting to suppress further translation of the Scriptures. If you could speak with his Grace—" His brown eyes questioned her.

"M'lord," she said, with truth, "methinks you ask much."

Ned's gaze could be compelling, as it was now. Like a hawk fixing its prey, she thought, almost exactly like my fiercest hawk! She shivered. True, he stands by me, but would he be at my side were I in deep trouble? Nay, for he could not! I shall have no help from anyone!

"Prithee, madam," Ned said, "think on it, and let us always ponder our true duty to God."

Anger flared in Katryn. "We always ponder our duty to God, m'lord! And we need no instruction!"

"Forgive me, madam," Ned said. His voice was as silky as his beard, she thought; somehow, on this instant I don't trust him, for he thinks he knows all and knows everyone's duty! That is a dangerous thing to think, surely—that we could speak for others, or know exactly what they should do! He takes too much upon himself; he'll bury himself under it, he will, if he's not heedful. Oh, I should pay no mind to either of the Seymours—and I would not except I have become, willy-nilly, as Tom Seymour said, one of their party.

"My lord," she said, softly, " 'tis a tragic thing for friends to quarrel. If, then, we misagree, let us keep it free from—" She hunted for a word. Malice? Nay, she meant not that. "From aught else but misagreement," Katryn ended. I do not want to offend him needlessly. She gave him her hand. "God keep thee, my lord."

Katryn was still thinking deeply about her encounter with the Seymours late that afternoon, when Anne came in and said that the Duchess of Richmond was without and wanted a private audience with the Queen.

"Private?" asked Katryn, puzzled.

"Aye, she insists, and she is much undone."

Katryn nodded her head. "Bid her enter, then." The ladies laid aside sewing; they were still laughing over Katryn's last remark, for someone had said that the gossips had it that Dr. Huicke beat his wife. Katryn rose to his defense, immediately.

"He is the best doctor in the palace," she said, "so mayhap it would be better for all of them to beat their wives!"

The ladies now had all departed, and Anne ushered in the Duchess of Richmond, who flung herself at Katryn's feet.

In some consternation, Katryn looked down at her dark head. True, her brother Surrey was in gaol, but certainly she could not be so upset about that, for all knew there was little love lost between brother and sister. Katryn said, "Prithee, Mary, have you such troubles?"

Mary Howard raised her face. She bit at her lip, and then pulled over a cushion and sat thus, at Katryn's feet, trying to compose herself.

"Madam," she blurted, "I have just come from my lord my brother and there in his cell he told me to cajole and lie with the King, to get us favors!" She bent her head, and stared at the floor.

These astonishing words made Katryn cry out, "What?" She rose to her feet.

"Aye," said Mary Howard, stubbornly, as if to blurt out the truth and have done with it, no matter what. "He said the King would not marry me because I'd been wed to his son Richard, but he said I could—"

"Be silent!" cried Katryn, raising her hand. "Why, how do you dare repeat such words to me, the Queen! Why, I could have your head off your body for that, for what you've said is treason!"

Mary Howard sat up straight; her eyes were dry. "I came to tell thee, your Grace, to confess and thus prove my innocence."

Katryn gasped. " 'Tis treason on your brother's part! And are you then willing to tell me of it?"

"Aye," said Mary Howard.

"By God's most precious soul!" Katryn muttered. Brother against sister; such hatreds loosed! It was wicked. "D'ye realize," she asked, "that it is your own blood which would be spilled?" She stared at Mary Howard. What words, what bitter anger had preceded this quarrel? She tried to reconstruct the scene there in Surrey's cell. And swiftly Katryn could perceive the reason—there was only one who could drive Mary Howard to this pass: Tom Seymour.

At this moment, she cried, "Help me, madam!"

"Help you?" whispered Katryn, looking down at her. Aye, she is more beautiful than I, for her face is perfect. "Help you? What kind of help, madam? Help," she said very low, "with your lover?"

Mary Howard bent her head. She put her hands over her face. "Aye, madam."

"You've said much," Katryn muttered, and turned aside. I can hardly speak, she thought, my heart is beating so fast. If I look at her, I shall strike her! To come to me, of all people! To tell me that first she is advised to seduce my husband, and second that— I cannot think it, even. Thank God he has gone! What if she threw herself at him and twined those fair arms around his legs as he stood above her, as I am standing? She is capable of it too, the— Her brain refused to think of any name bad enough.

She said, "What you have told me has discomposed me entirely, madam! That there is such wickedness in the world! I gather that your family, your brother and even your father, have not offered you as wife to Sir Thomas Seymour because he might refuse to marry his mistress! So they urge you to try your talents on his Grace! Dry your tears, madam! Second you will stay here with me. You will attend me and take your place as a lady-in-waiting."

Katryn was still standing over Mary Howard, looking down at her bent head. 'Tis good she can't see my face; I'll have to compose it ere she looks up. For if she thinks she'll see either her lover or my husband she is mad. From now on, I'll not have her out of sight! She can pine and yearn for her lover's kisses! Her eyes gleamed. And he! Let him try to get her out of my clutches! He'll not see her in his bed for many a night. She drew a deep breath. "Pray rise, madam," she said crisply. "Get thee to the door, and bid my ladies enter. Then you may retire behind the screen and wash your face."

Katryn sat down in her chair again and watched Mary Howard do as she was told. Then she flung a final word. "And do not dream, madam, that I permit dalliance! My ladies are virtuous and God-fearing, and so shall you be!"

But later that night, as she lay in bed watching Mary Howard draw the lovely shining satin bed curtains and pile the satin quilt into neat folds so that Katryn or one of the ladies could pull it up easily should she need it during the night, Katryn wondered how she could bear the sight of her always about. I cannot endure it, she thought, sulkily, for each time I lay my eyes on her I think on him. His mistress! Oh, was ever a woman brought to such a pass as this! I shall never forgive him for this. Oh, to speak with him for five minutes! What should I not say! But he is probably sound asleep. And I—I shan't sleep a wink. Angrily she sat straight up in bed.

"Do not put out the candles," she snapped. "Instead, madam, you may read to me." She settled herself among the silk sheets. If I'm not going to sleep, she'll not sleep either. She raised guileless eyes. "What a nice voice you have, Mary," she said.

The next day one could smell spring in the air. It was most exciting, this first breath of spring; one could smell it and feel it and savor it. As soon as morning chapel and her morning audiences were over, she would go out into the garden, and she found herself waiting anxiously for the end of her audience. Her last petitioner was a young woman named Anne Askew. Lucy explained that she had been driven from her home by her husband. Anne knelt at Katryn's feet.

"I have nowhere else to come, your Grace," she whispered. She reminded Katryn that her father, Master Askew, was a poor reformer who had received a small grant of land in Kendal from the Queen; he was old and infirm, and Katryn had given him a bit of land for his last years.

"I cannot give you a place with me," Katryn said kindly. "But I shall see what can be done for you, if you ha' no living."

"I shall pray for thee, your Grace," she said, and curtsied deep. Kate Willoughby found her rather exceptional, she told Katryn later. "She has visions," Kate said. She would go into a trance and tell about seeing Christ.

Katryn didn't believe in visions, but a great many people did, and soon some of the ladies were going to see her and paying her little moneys and bringing her gifts of clothes. This came to the ears of Bishop Gardiner, and it was just what he was waiting for. He arrested Anne Askew, for was it not against the law to have visions and speak about messages from Jesus? It was hertical, it was un-godly, it was treasonable! He took her to the Tower; he knew he had a weapon against the Queen if he used it aright.

Gardiner took his young victim into the torture chambers, where, deep into the night with rushlights flickering, they pulled her young naked body on the rack. But she told him nothing. Not a word against the Queen escaped her lips, not a word against the Queen's women who had come to hear her visions. The next day, Gardiner consigned Anne Askew's racked body to the flames for heresy.

Katryn sent for Ned. They could not stop the execution, but they could shorten her suffering. Ned ordered a charge of gun powder placed in the pyre, and the blast could be heard plain in Whitehall, telling the ladies with Katryn that Anne Askew had gone quickly to her death.

It had all happened so quickly. That was the terrifying part of it, Katryn thought. A scant four weeks ago Anne Askew had knelt in this very room, and Katryn had been kind to her. Katryn couldn't eat; her head throbbed. In real misery, she sent for Dr. Huicke. Lucy read the Bible and prayed for the soul of the young woman who had suffered so. Katryn was white-faced and drawn; Gardiner undoubtedly wished it were she.

And indeed he did. At that moment he was closeted with Henry, a Henry who had been suddenly taken ill again. Both legs were swelling and his whole body was hot with fever. God, I am rotting away, Henry told himself. I can smell the putrefying flesh!

He had insisted on being dressed that morning. He had staggered over to his big chair, and received members of his council. And he had refused the use of the block and tackle to get to that chair; he leaned on the arms of his gentlemen. At this juncture in the after-noon, Gardiner requested an audience. He and Henry were alone.

Gardiner came swiftly to the point, telling Henry about the heretical Anne Askew and her visions, and how she spoke with Jesus and then gathered Katryn's ladies about to tell them so they could report to the Queen what the Lord had said! This surely was heresy!

Henry gritted his great face in pain. Gardiner went on fingering his cross. "Heresy is growing apace." Everyone was reading the Bible, God's word, and argufying about it and debasing it, as it necessarily must be debased if all could bandy about the Lord's word. He asked Henry to suppress the new translation of the Scriptures.

Gardiner went on. He said that Anne Askew had not implicated the Queen, but all knew she condoned the girl and her visions and had interfered in the manner of her death. Not only that, but there were whispers, Gardiner said, about the Queen's virtue, and that she had lain with other men afore her marriage, one of them Sir Thomas Seymour. One could see how she led on the French envoys, and it was rumored she had been alone with one of them. "And now I hear that she has asked your Grace not to forbid the translation of the Scriptures."

Henry muttered, "Ah, in my old age, to be instructed by my wife!"

"She laughs and calls you Moses, among her women," Gardiner said. "Your Grace knows not what she does. She is barren; she brings naught to your Grace save to try to instruct on what should be done, and now, to interfere in such a matter as this heretic's death and to interdict your Grace when it comes to this new translation! It should be suppressed and so should she!"

Henry's red eyes gleamed with rage. He heard "She laughs and calls you Moses!" Distorted images flattened and elongated themselves in his brain; he sobbed aloud with a sudden thrust of pain through his leg; he looked almost insane, his face contorted with rage, and Gardiner had a sudden fleeting fear that this was a two-edged sword he was using.

"I am asking for a warrant to investigate the Queen's Grace, and Lady Anne, her sister, and Lady Lucy Trywhit," Gardiner mumbled, thrusting the warrant in his hand at the writhing King.

Henry took the pen and, seizing the quill in his fist, with his whole hand around it, he rose to his feet, leaning on the table. The great *H* was scrawled, and then Henry, with a loud trumpet of rage, fell to the floor. Terrified, Gardiner ran to the door, shouting for help.

About ten minutes later Gardiner emerged into the long gallery at Whitehall. It was deserted. He hastened on, for as yet no one knew of the warrant he carried, and he wanted no one to know it. He was anxious to return to his house at Winchester and lay his plans. The Queen could be arrested the day after tomorrow, and he would have to summon at least forty of the guard, and prepare his warrant, writing it carefully, and listing even more carefully all the charges of which she could be guilty. He walked quickly along and had almost reached the end of the gallery, when he noticed someone coming.

It was Dr. Huicke, responding to Katryn's summons. The two men went by each other, the Bishop's gown swinging, one hand at his cross, his precious paper in his voluminous sleeve. He made a kind of greeting gesture to Dr. Huicke, and unbeknownst to him the paper slipped from his sleeve. He hastened on, and Dr. Huicke leaned down and picked up the paper. For a second he started to call out to the Bishop, but knowing the man and distrusting him greatly, Dr. Huicke stepped behind a screen and opened it. His eye ran quickly and incredulously over what purported to be a warrant for the Queen's arrest and investigation of her sister and Lucy Trywhit. He checked a muttered oath and tried to think past the furious anger that gripped him. He knew that the discovery of the warrant was vital; also was it vital that Gardiner not be aware of its perusal by him. Dr. Huicke dropped it behind the screen, pushing it out toward the gallery with his slipper so Gardiner would think it had lain there undiscovered. Settling his flat cap, he hastened on. In one minute the Bishop reappeared, his eyes darting this way and that. The gallery was deserted, and there lay his warrant. Hastily he retrieved it and left the palace with it safe in his sleeve again.

Dr. Huicke went straight to Katryn, finding her on her bed with eyes closed and cold compresses on her pounding head. When she heard him, she lifted her hand in a small greeting and in the same gesture took away the linen cloth. She smiled at him.

Dear Lord! he thought. Dear Jesus! How am I to tell her? Was she then to tread the same path as the others, and to enter the Tower by Traitor's Gate on the river by royal barge, as though Henry were a gentleman to the last? Was she to enter where the lacy patterns of the wrought-iron gate threw bluish shadows on stones always damp? Dr. Huicke met her eyes. Could she save herself? He leaned close.

"Dear Lord, madam," he whispered, "this day I ha' discovered a dreadful thing! A terrible plot!"

Katryn's face changed. A stab of pain went through her head. "What plot?" she asked. She raised herself on her elbow. Of course, it could be no plot against her.

Dr. Huicke had no choice but the truth, and quickly, for God knew how much time they had. "I passed Bishop Gardiner in the gallery. He was carrying a warrant for thy arrest and investigation! He dropped it, and I read it unbeknownst to him."

The words swirled around her in a cloud, almost pressing against her physically, as if she could actually feel the terror right against her skin and in her bones. She uttered a loud cry. Anne turned from her place by the fire and Mistress Barbara started forward, but Dr. Huicke, horror stricken that she might give away their secret, turned and waved them back, at the same time laying his hands on Katryn's shoulders and forcing her back against her velvet cushions.

"Quiet, for God's sake!" he implored. She was shivering under his hands, he felt it plainly.

"No one must know but you and I." He almost shook her, when he saw there was full sanity in her eyes, full realization, and he need not be afraid. He saw anger in those eyes, too, and oddly enough it made his heart race, for it was honest anger and it sent a shaft of courage through him, and pride. Her face was set.

"Is Anne—the Lady Herbert—on the warrant?" she whispered, inclining her red-gold head toward the seated figure of her sister fifteen feet away.

"Aye, and the Lady Lucy," Dr. Huicke whispered back.

Katryn pushed aside his hands. She stood, there by her bed, her dressing gown falling in soft folds to her slippered feet in their heelless slippers. "By God's most precious soul," she was saying, clearly. "I ha' killed a man once, and I could kill Gardiner too—aye, with my two hands!" She raised them up before her. She looked toward the fireplace at the heavy poker. She didn't see Anne's startled face, nor did she hear Mistress Barbara's gasp.

Quickly Dr. Huicke poured a little wine into a cup, and quickly he added an opiate. He thrust it at her. "Drink," he commanded.

Katryn took the cup. She swallowed off the draught, set down the cup, and then, very slowly, she realized what he had done.

"You ha' drugged me!"

"Aye," he said, his voice trembling. "Your Grace needed it!"

She threw the cup at him. "I did not! I must think, and you have drugged me!" Like an avenging angel she raised her hand. Anne cried out and Dr. Huicke dropped to one knee before his Queen.

"Madam," he cried. "I did not give thee much!"

365

Katryn stared down at him. But how much? her brain wondered. Yet it was still but afternoon. Her brain raced. Gardiner—he would not act today, pray God he wouldn't! She went over to her bed. She sat down and lay back against the pillows. There was Anne bending over her. She had to save Anne too, dear sweet Anne, and her faithful Lucy. A warrant for Anne's arrest! Anger swirled up again; she was almost choking with it.

"But I must think," she said. Through that door was Henry. That was one mistake Gardiner had made! Never had a queen been arrested under Henry's eyes. Always before his queen had been taken away to never, never see her husband again. "I'm going to go to sleep," she said aloud. Her eyes were closing. But you must not sleep long, she told herself. Remember, you must not sleep long.

The great clock that Henry had had made six years ago chimed ten. It echoed over the silent palace as it struck its deep tones. Katryn opened her eyes.

The room looked as always. It was in muted colors, with petit-point wool hangings of rosy tones. The fire burned lazily on the hearth, and Meg and Mistress Barbara dozed on their stools by the fire. How long have I slept then? she wondered, and reckoned it must be four hours at least. Probably Dr. Huicke still waited without, prey to fear and distress. Her eyes opened wider.

Anne lay alongside of her, sleeping lightly, for when Katryn said, "Prithee, Anne, bring me water," Anne sat right up.

Ten o'clock, thought Katryn and everyone must be asleep this night. She permitted Anne to wash her face and brush her hair. She said nothing. She must save Anne, she must save Lucy.

"A little powder," she commanded, not paying attention to Anne's look of bewilderment. She used rouge for her mouth, and she applied perfume, and when she studied herself in the glass she was satisfied. She lay back on the bed a moment.

It was perfectly true, she told herself, this is the only way. For those other two queens of Henry's had had the misfortune never to be near him after he had signed away their lives. She, Katryn, was very near! She braced herself, for her body still felt incapable of response. Then she opened her lips and let out a loud terrified cry. She repeated it, long and high.

Meg jumped to her feet, and Mistress Barbara screamed, "Merciful God! Merciful God!"

Katryn screamed again. The door burst open and Dr. Huicke flew into the room, as Katryn continued to scream and cry out in terrible anguish, sobbing wildly and writhing on the big bed.

The palace awoke. A terrified page ran for Lucy, pounding down the halls. The women's chambers came awake with a sudden uproar, as the startling screams from the Queen's chambers persisted and grew worse.

In the King's rooms his gentlemen dashed down the halls, fearing a physical attack on the Queen. And Henry, stirring on his huge bed, sat straight up himself as he heard his wife's first loud cry of anguish.

"By Saint Mary," he shouted, struggling to a sitting position. His leg still hurt but it was not afire any longer, and sleep had refreshed him. Katryn screamed again, and Henry shouted in his bellowing tones again. "By Saint Mary, what devilment is afoot? What haps? To me, knaves, dolts!" He continued to shout for help, for his leg was useless, and he writhed to the side of the bed. His pages and gentlemen heard him and came dashing back, except the ones who had already reached the Queen. Those were milling about the closed door, along with the gentlewomen of the court. Within the Queen's chamber the cries still came unabated.

Henry bellowed even louder. "A chair, a chair!" he roared, for he couldn't walk. It took three of his gentlemen to get Henry into the chair.

"Carry me!"

Will Herbert and Blagge staggered under the load of both Henry and the chair. The connecting door between the two chambers was flung open, and they bore their burden slowly into Katryn's room; as they did so, Katryn sank back upon her pillows and gave one last long shuddering sob. Through her half-closed eyes and the tears glittering on her lashes, she saw Henry being borne toward her, his cap awry, his eyes bloodshot, his big face honestly concerned, as impatiently he bore his infirmity, for she knew too well he hated to be carried. She rose from her bed, clutching her gown close. Will and Blagge set down the chair and Katryn flung herself at Henry's feet, careful to lay her head against his good leg. She began to cry.

"My lord, my lord," she sobbed.

"Leave us," commanded Henry to the entourage. "By God, leave us!"

The company melted away. The doors closed. Henry looked down at the curly red-gold head pressed against his knee. He touched her hair, feeling its silkiness. "For God's sake, darling," he said lower, "what happed?"

"I had a nightmare," she whispered. "A nightmare," she repeated, raising her face to look up at him. "I have had it before." She drew a long shuddering breath, and lifted her hand to put on his, as if to reassure herself it was truly he.

"A nightmare?" Henry asked.

"I dreamed you tired of me," she whispered, looking at him with melting eyes. She touched his hand and arm, tilted her head back further to look at him. "I dreamed you tired of me and wanted me no longer, and I was sick with grief and misery and I was like to end my life!" She believed all this suddenly, and her eyes filled with genuine tears. "I dreamed—and I was all lost without thee, my lord!"

The candles flickered over her face and her white shoulders, and Henry leaned forward a bit and his hand went to her bare shoulder.

"I shall die if you do not love me, my lord!" she said. "Oh, what have I done? Roused the palace, and screamed and cried, but I couldn't help it, my lord! I was so undone and filled with grief, and it seemed so real, and I was so miserable! I cried out for thee! And you came! Good my lord, pray you forgive me, but I am only a woman—and I had to see thee!" She stopped. Then knowing she must put this question, she whispered it: "Have I offended thee?"

"My sweet Kate," he said, squeezing her shoulder.

"And you have been so sick, my lord, and then to come to me." She bit her lip and her eyes filled with tears again. Through them she saw Henry's big face, and he looked almost abashed, as though he were wondering if he had started this. My God, Katryn thought, does he remember what he did this afternoon? Or is it like a cloudy memory? She blinked away the tears. "Holy Mother of God," she whispered, "I have got you out of your bed, my lord, and affrighted thee, but thou knowest—you could see plain—I was beside myself with terror and fear! How if you deserted me? I should die!"

"My sweet wife," Henry said. He squeezed her shoulder again. What had he done this afternoon? He searched his mind and felt there the flicker of remembrance. He scowled deeply. His eyes were bloodshot. Once more he looked down at the kneeling figure of his wife. This was enough revenge, Henry thought. He said it simply, and Katryn knew she had succeeded.

"I love thee, Kate," he said.

Somehow Katryn was sure the danger was past. Never completely past, for no one could say what was deep in Henry's heart, but this was victory and it was very heady. By a woman's methods had Henry been defeated, and that creature Gardiner!

Katryn was eating breakfast, and she relished her plain beef. She was hungry. Her mind flew to that scene between her and Mary Howard, who waited upon her now. I hope to God that she doesn't learn too much from me, else I'll have to send her away. But would Tom Seymour respond to floods of tears? She frowned. Then she wiped her mind clear of his image. She was still wed to Henry, by the mercy of God and her own wit and those old-fashioned women's weapons that women were like to forget. She was very pleased with herself, and she sent word to Henry that she was much recovered, due to his kindness.

Henry was better and sitting with the privy council, so the rest of that May day Katryn spent in sorting out clothes, thinking, for she pretended her illness of yesternight kept her in her chambers.

At six, with little Lady Jane Grey bearing the candles before her and Anne coming behind bearing her train, she sought out Henry. She sat on a stool at his feet, and Anne and Jane Grey sat by the fire.

"Thou art recovered, my Kate," Henry said, almost fondly.

"Last night thy visit rejoiced and revived me," she said.

Katryn sat before Henry, her close little white cap set tight on her curls, and when he looked down at her he could see the sweet lines of her face and the alluring tininess of her waist and the beautiful swell of her breast as she seemed to have difficulty drawing her breath.

She clasped her hands in her lap and cast her eyes down. "I am but a woman—" She hesitated. "With all the imperfections natural to my sex," she added, and raised her eyes to Henry. "I never meant to quarrel with thee, my lord. In all matters of doubt and difficulty, I refer myself to your Grace's better judgment. As my lord and head, from thee shall I learn." She stopped, going carefully, for she knew she must explain that she knew she had essayed too much, in the matter of disagreeing with him about that translation.

Henry said, "That's not so, by Saint Mary! Ye are a doctor, Kate, to instruct us!"

She glanced at him. He didn't truly mean it; he thought he did. Men thought they wanted to be argufied with, but they misliked the worst end of an argument. "Indeed," she said earnestly, "if your Grace hath so conceived me, my meaning has been mistaken; for I have always held it is preposterous for a woman to instruct her lord."

"So?" Henry asked.

"Aye," she said vigourously. "And if I have ever differed with your Grace on religion, it was partly to obtain information on nice points and sometimes because I perceived that, in talking, your Grace, were better able to pass away the pain and weariness of your leg—" She paused. "Which emboldened me to the hope of profiting by your Majesty's learned discourse." She sighed, and caught her breath, for indeed she had difficulty breathing, she was laced so tight. And this is all true, she thought; I'm not so foolish and silly a woman as to nag and quarrel with my lord.

"And is it so, sweetheart?" Henry asked, indulgently. She was wearing the great black opal he had given her; it lay between her breasts invitingly, like his badge upon her, and she had just assured him that she held his every word as better judgment than hers.

"We are perfect friends, Kate," he said.

Katryn kept hearing her own words to Henry: "I should die if you deserted me." And that, my girl, is truer than you think, she told herself. At least Henry is convinced I'd die of grief; but there are others who know different, and I among them. So she decided against telling even Anne or Lucy that their names were on the warrant, for as yet no one but herself and the loyal Dr. Huicke knew that she had been informed of the warrant, and thus had taken steps to obvert it.

The following morning was beautiful. Katryn and her ladies sought the garden, and Henry, looking out the windows, perceived them there, and decided to join her.

No one could be sweeter, he thought. His leg pained him, and since they were seated on a wide bench, she told him to sit sideways and put his leg up on her lap. Henry did as he was told, and smiled and laid his stick against the bench and drank in the warm air. Katryn's footman brought him some wine. At that moment Gardiner appeared at the far end of the garden with forty of the guard.

Henry moved convulsively. He remembered signing the warrant; he remembered the pain in his leg, and his fever. He remembered Gardiner had played upon his emotions. Henry staggered to his feet, throwing the wine cup in the direction of the Bishop, even though he could not possibly have hit him at this distance. His hand fumbled for his stick, and he seized it and got to his feet. Even though his leg would hardly hold him, he deigned not to use the stick but waved it as a threatening club. Gardiner stopped dead in his tracks, and the forty guardsmen did likewise; they all literally trembled with fear. No one could be sure what the King might do or order in a rage. The ladies and gentlemen in the garden stood transfixed.

Still waving the heavy stick as though it were a toy, Henry bellowed at Gardiner. "Fool! Beast! Knave!" His face was empurpled with rage; he hobbled forward and Gardiner reeled back into the arms of his guardsmen. "Get hence!" Henry roared. "We shall never receive you again!"

Henry was panting. His eyes still glittering with rage, he hobbled back to Katryn, muttering and pounding his stick on the ground. Katryn didn't dare speak. Gardiner was gone, and the others of the court were endeavoring to behave as though nothing had happened. Henry continued to mutter as he sat down again. "We shall never forgive him," he said with violence, and Katryn knew he was struggling with the desire to have Gardiner thrown into the Tower but that the political animal within him was fighting the rage.

Katryn's lips were sealed. She couldn't tell Henry she knew why he was so angry, that Gardiner had betrayed him into an act which he now regretted. But now in the bright, harsh sun Katryn saw that he was not well; he was ill. How ill? she wondered suddenly. He was so heavy and huge he gave the impression of great strength for all his grossness, but was it not true that the eyes were too bloodshot, and the flesh sagging, and his leg–! Pity suddenly filled her. "Prithee, my lord, put up thy leg on my lap."

Henry grunted. With difficulty he and Katryn laid his leg across her lap. He could hardly breathe, she saw, with the exertion of his anger.

Katryn's eyes glinted with anger too. "That fool—he has upset thee!"

Henry growled, "You little know how evil he deserves grace at thy hands!"

I know only too well, she thought, but I must not say it.

Henry's great jaw was set. He didn't want Gardiner's head, because he didn't want lives unless they interfered with the throne. "After dinner," he muttered, "we shall summon the council and strike Gardiner's name from it!" He banged the ground with his stick, "And he shall never be received again nor permitted to come to court!"

Henry kept his word. Katryn had thus disposed of her fiercest enemy, or rather the one through whom the others could strike. It is incredible, she thought, watching her face in the glass as Anne brushed her hair, why anyone would want me dead! Do they think I have that much influence on Henry, or whom do they want to put in my place? For certainly someone would take my place. Henry cannot live without a mate, and in that way I understand him perfectly. Or might they think he is getting too old to care? They could not be more wrong, for I have a notion that during the coming months—that is when he will need me most.

She brought the children within the bosom of the family for the summer. It is time, she thought, now that Henry is ill, for us to be a family again; royal or not, we should still be a family. In July, for half the month, he suffered from colic, and his doctors tried to get him to bed and tried to restrict his diet; this was as difficult, Katryn thought, as trying to teach Latin to a bull elephant. He roared from his bed, when she got him into it, that he wanted meat, by Saint Mary, and wine! He liked gin; he would sip it and say it put fire in his liver, though God knows, Katryn thought, what truly is in his liver or inside his great huge stomach. Dr. Huicke and she conferred. "You see, madam," Dr. Huicke said, "he has abused his vitals for years!"

But by July twentieth, Henry was tired of being ill, and in spite of his leg he insisted on going hunting, and every day he was up early and sitting with his privy council.

His irascibility increased, and now it was well known that only the Queen could assuage him. Coming swiftly to his summons, or those of his gentlemen, Katryn would appear at his chamber door; and at the sight, Henry would soften a bit and, when she came to his side, place his hand in her red-gold curls and sigh. He was quite unpredictable. He would send word that he wished to attend mass, and Katryn would dress and be ready. Instead a grim-faced Will Herbert would arrive. "Your Highness, his Grace has gone out into the garden; he sits there alone!"

She would find him brooding, staring at the grass. Good will and a kind of love flowed from Katryn to her ailing, aging husband. The fire which would have destroyed her had been extinguished under floods of her own tears and protestations of love some months ago.

"Kate," he said, low. "My sweet wife. Thou camest to me."

He laid his hand over hers. "I have so much to do, Kate. So much. Where would they all be without me? What should happen?"

"But you are here, my lord."

"Ah," said Henry, and sighed. On those occasions music would appease him. Music, Henry's oldest and purest love. Katryn played all the songs he had written, and saw to it that his masses were played; as he listened, his big head resting back against the wood of the royal pew, sheltered from other eyes, his own would grow moist as the music he had written in his youth comforted him in his age. How sweet had been his youth! Surely there was much to be remembered that was good and honest and clean, and his ideals as shining as a Crusader's sword. He is not all bad, Katryn thought, sitting quiet alongside him, occasionally holding his hand. They exchanged a smile. He has done so much, and God knows he is brave!

But by September, Henry felt better and began his annual progress with Katryn by his side, and he consented to take Elizabeth. On the fourth they were at Oatlands, hunting with stags and bloodhounds, and Katryn in a new hunting dress felt that life was good and exciting, and Henry was much better. She ate venison that night till she could eat no more, and so did Henry. But at Guildford, on the eighth of the month, Henry caught cold. Mumbling, he retired to bed, and yet again it was impossible to keep him there. Katryn thought his doctors were worse off than he, for Dr. Linacre was so upset from looking after Henry that everyone knew he had to take potions to sleep a wink. Only Dr. Huicke remained as calm as always.

In October Henry decided to go to Windsor. But he was restless. Katryn, coming in one day to find him in a rage, suggested Westminster, for the baths. They would refresh her lord. Henry assented, but she could keep him there only eight days; then he wanted to go back to Oatlands for the hunting.

The winter had begun. Cold seeped in through the windows; cold and damp began the winter, as only London can be damp and cold. The stones of Hampton Court, regardless of Wolsey's intricate system of conduits, sweated and froze. The river filled with ice, and the gentlemen of the court were making wagers that this winter, if it kept so cold, they would be able to ride horseback across the Thames, as Jane and Tom Seymour had done many years ago.

"Do you remember that winter, Anne?" Will Herbert asked.

Katryn was not listening. Henry had been taken ill again, very ill. She was putting on her cloak to walk through the icy halls. That night she would spend all night on her knees beside his bed, applying the poultices. Anne threw her a look of compassion, and Katryn frowned. It was her duty, and she was perfectly prepared to do it, she thought; why should Anne be sorry for her? But there was no use trying to explain to Anne. Henry was her husband and he was sick, and truly, Katryn thought, there is no one but me to care, no one. He has sacrificed all in his effort to rule; he is no longer human to his court. Only I am left, only I—a woman whom he almost destroyed—am left to stay by his bed and care for him. This then is surely what God intended when he made me marry Henry. God, as Kate Willoughby says, is truly a marvelous man.

Her eyes found Kate. "Pray attend me, and see me to his Grace," she said. She went swiftly down the hall. In sickness and in health, thought Katryn, as she walked ahead of Kate. "Till death us depart—and surely soon, it will be death."

Henry made his will. Four days after the night he had been so sick, he called Katryn to him. Propped up in bed, with both legs now inflamed he spoke in a voice more high and squeaky than usual. "I have instructed, my dear sweet wife," he said from his pillow, with the candles flickering and the winter wind sighing, "that all my people are to treat thee with all the respect they showed when I was living. For the rest of your life, you shall have apartments set aside in each of our royal palaces, and all homage must be done thee. So have I instructed!" His eyes gleamed. Let them try to disobey. I shall come down from heaven and destroy them.

He truly does not think he is going to die, she thought. He believes his will as strong as God's! He is sure he will always be Henry Rex, bold as life, immortal—the King of England forever!

She fed him wine. She played softly on the virginals. That night he slept well . . .

It was December. The cold had deepened. Ice was on the Thames. Katryn had sent Edward down to Hatfield, but Elizabeth and Mary and Jane Grey were with her. Two days before Christmas, Katryn sent again for Edward to join them, and Henry climbed out of bed, for he was going to speak before Parliament and prorogue that body on this day.

He had talked with her long the night before. He had spoken of the enmities and hatreds that abounded, and how wrong and ungodly they were; his eyes had become moist. Now, half-sick, he towered over her and she kissed his check. She asked if her secretary Buckler could attend and hear him speak.

It was a dark day. Within the great walls, hundreds of candles were lighted. A hush fell as the King entered, Henry in red velvet and ermine, concealing his limp, huge and towering—Henry, the King.

His voice rang forth as he surveyed his Parliament. He drew a deep breath and solemnly began, each word spaced as though he wrenched them from the depths of his great body, speaking as though he would forever take care of them, always love them, all of them, even though at times he, their monarch, must be harsh.

One by one the words came out. "Of such small qualities as

God has imbued me, I render to His Goodness my most humble thanks!"

The galleries sighed. Henry leaned on the lectern. In a more normal voice he thanked Parliament for the subsidies they had granted him, for the chantries, the hospitals, the universities; he touched on the worth of all these, his endeavors for the realm. He thanked them for the money for the war with France. He paused. Then he began again.

"Now since I find such kindness on your part, I cannot choose but to love and favor you, and for your defense my treasure shall never be hindered, nay, nor my person never unadventured."

Silence deepened through the halls of Parliament. Henry raised his hand. "But, I see that charity and concord is not amongst you. St. Paul says charity is gentle, charity is not envious, charity is not proud. Behold then, what love and charity is amongst you, when one calleth the other heretic and Anabaptist, papist, hypocrite, and Pharisee! Are these the signs of fraternal love?"

Henry surveyed his Parliament, his people. In this moment, and he might never have another, his love encompassed them, he was sure, coming straight from heaven, straight from God through his appointed sovereign. His small eyes swept Parliament for the last time. His voice commanded them, as it had for thirty-eight long years. "Love, dread, and serve God," he said. The hall was deathly silent. "To the which I, as your supreme head and sovereign lord, do exhort and require you!"

Tears stood in Buckler's eyes, and he stumbled home and told the Queen that the King had been moving, magnificent, and had spoken so true. There was a solemnity about it that pervaded all, Buckler whispered. "It was as though a father had bid us good-by." He knelt and kissed the hem of Katryn's gown. "God bless his Grace and thee, madam."

She blinked back the tears herself. "Nor my person unadventured." He had spoke true; he should not be up and about at all. Since the twentieth he had been ill, he had constant fever; it shone in his eyes and rasped his voice; he must have been swaying with fever and fatigue when he said those words.

On the first of the new year, she put him to bed again. He wanted to receive Van der Delft, the Imperial ambassador from Spain. Katryn saw him first, and told him to be quick.

Henry told Van der Delft heavily, "We have always tried to be honest."

By the tenth, he was very ill and both legs were inflamed. The ulcers would have to be cauterized, Dr. Linacre said.

The huge King closed his eyes and set his great jowls against the agony of the flaming irons. He spit out oaths, not against the pain but against the stench. The windows could not be opened because of the bitter cold. And now the temper of the court was imperceptibly changing, as the palace waited for Henry to die.

Only Katryn was unaware of what was happening, of the eddies and the undercurrents. She knew well enough that Ned Seymour went about more drawn and haggard and intense than ever. Dudley, whose name she had ever despised, slunk through the halls, as though to make himself inconspicuous lest all see plain the attitude of the vulture waiting not so patiently for his victim to die. Tom Seymour returned.

"Their feast awaits them," he said to Will Herbert. "They see it in the distance. Power, power, power." He had talked for more than an hour with the King, and Henry, his bloodshot eyes slanted and still sharp, made him a privy councilor and one of the executors of his will, bestowing also upon him the office of Lord High Admiral of England. Henry worked every day on his will and the naming of the council.

First the succession: Edward, then Mary, then Elizabeth. And after Elizabeth little Lady Jane Grey, his grandniece. Oh, what frail buttresses for a great country and a great King! Nervously Henry contemplated the prospects for a young prince. He should have had four or five grown sons by now! Henry shouted an oath and called for help; he would be up and dressed, and meet his council!

Katryn did not demur. It made no difference now. The King would do as he wished; thrusting aside mortal wounds, he was Henry. Staggering, he attended the council meeting, and when he returned to his bed, fears and dreams plagued him. He saw Edward, alone and defenseless save for the Seymours. Could they handle the Howards and their pretensions? In the dead of night, he made up his mind. Both Surrey and his father, the old Duke of Norfolk, were arrested.

The news burst like an organ peal into the chambers of the Queen. Both Surrey and the old Duke his father! Eyes turned on Mary Howard, who pursed her lips. She went to Ned Seymour, and told him she would be willing to testify against her brother, repeating what she had told Katryn—that he had advised her to be Henry's "Madam du Temps" and curry favor for the Howards. The day was the seventeenth of January, and Katryn thought her own blood no less icy than that of the proud Earl of Surrey who died on Tower Hill that morn. Later that day, in the antechamber of the King, she came face to face with Tom Seymour.

Katryn was prey to so many emotions she could not look at him. Neither could she speak. She set her white teeth together; what kind of work had he just accomplished! She raised her eyes to his face and saw there a blaze of anger in his eyes; his face was taut with it and he made no attempt to hide it. She stepped back.

"Once before," he muttered, coming closer to her, "I seem to remember telling you that you can anger me beyond belief! For you can imply that I could be guilty of the grossest kind of betrayal! I added then, that you don't understand me very well!"

"Aye, and I don't wish to!" She could feel herself trembling. "Seek out your milk-faced mistress, for I've sent her from me!"

Imperceptibly his face changed. Even his body seemed more relaxed. He will mock at me now, I know he will!

"Are you giving me orders, then, madam?"

"Orders?" Katryn repeated. By the mass, she thought rapidly, 'tis soon he who will be giving them! It is soon he who will be so powerful, what with the wardenship of the Borders and the Navy in his hands! She tossed her head. "Oh, I don't apprehend you!"

"I think you apprehend me perfect," he said, almost negligently. "I shall always give you credit for wit and practicality, and seeing where your bread is buttered." He smiled down at her—that mocking smile she hated so much. What was he saying?

"But mayhap, madam, you should eschew butter, for to tell you true, I mislike plump women."

"Oh!" cried Katryn. She turned and walked away. I cannot endure it, she thought, seeking her own chamber. No, I cannot, and I know what ails me! Only too well. For soon I shall be free, and I am desperately afraid he will not ask me to marry him! Nay, he will not! He will be at liberty to seek me out, and then what shall I do with him? Never, never, have I been able to handle him aright! But this time I will!

There was not much time left. Henry could not now leave his bed but lay propped up on great cushions, his chest laboring. He wanted to see Mary.

Katryn brought her into her father's sickroom. He motioned her to the bed. He talked in broken sentences.

"I am sorry," he said to her, "that I did not arrange a marriage for you. I was prevented," he added, "by fortune, or by misfortune, whichever you deem it."

Mary began to cry.

"I pray thee, my daughter, to be good to thy brother, for he is so little yet."

A sob burst from Mary's lips. Henry waved her away. He couldn't endure her weeping.

Henry turned his massive head to look at his wife. "My odor," he muttered. "Do not stay." Katryn put her hand over his. His eyes were closed, but his mouth lay open and he was breathing noisily. Sudden horror took her. The sweet and sickening stench of rotting flesh was almost unendurable.

She swallowed, with difficulty, feeling that she would swoon and fall to the floor. The candles had been lighted; they swam before her eyes in myriad dots of flickering light. The curtains were closed, but outside the January night was deeply cold and it was snowing. Snow beat against the glass in flurries. Within, on his huge bed, Henry was dying. Death was in the room, and death was at the bedstead.

Katryn shut her eyes and opened them again. Now Henry's eyes were partly open. Did he see her? She leaned close. "Thou shouldst see a man of God, my lord," she whispered.

Henry quivered. "Cranmer," he breathed. "But not yet."

He would postpone death, Katryn thought wildly. He will not have it yet, like a cup of wine thrust aside to be tasted later.

"Not yet," Henry muttered. "I will sleep a little, and then, as I feel myself—" He stopped. Katryn waited. Then he said, "I shall advise on the matter."

His eyes closed again. She felt Dr. Huicke lift her to her feet. He is dying, she thought. She lifted the inert hand, and tears suddenly found their way into her eyes. She kissed his hand. "The Lord keep thee," she whispered. Dr. Huicke led her to the door; slowly it opened, and she stepped out of Henry's room.

Katryn leaned back against the door, shaken, and Dr. Huicke steadied her. She paid no attention to the gentlemen in this outer room, the antechamber, the gentlemen who were waiting for news. She hardly saw them.

"How long?" she whispered.

Dr. Huicke said, "He cannot live the night, madam."

"It is now ten," Katryn said, putting her hand to her temple.

"Madam!" Dr. Huicke said, catching her arm again.

"Nay, I am able," she said. "Go back to the bedside." Dr. Huicke obeyed her, as she looked about the room. She faced the gentlemen of the court; for here, within this room, were most of the council that Henry had appointed. The reins, which hung slack now in the useless hands of a dying monarch, were waiting to be taken up.

She squared her shoulders, and faced them. There were Anne and Lucy, to escort her back to her own apartments. Her eyes went past them and found Tom Seymour. He looked back at her, his face impassive. I wonder what he meant the other day, she thought—was it five days ago? Did he mean he was going to wed with Mary Howard, because after she had admitted that she loved him in court, any gentleman should? She looked away from him to Ned.

Ned was booted and spurred. He is ready to ride out and fetch Edward, she thought; aye, as soon as he receives word from the doctors, he will ride through the snowy night to Hatfield and kneel before Edward and bring him back to claim his kingdom. Little Edward. What had Henry said to Mary? "Prithee be good to thy brother, he is so little yet."

Katryn allowed Dudley to kiss her hand, and he murmured something—she didn't hear it and it didn't matter. I am the Queen, she thought; aye, for the next hours, or maybe minutes, while Henry still breathes, I am his Queen! And after that—what had he said? "I have ordered all my people to treat you as though I were still alive!"

For some reason her breath came fast. There were so many of

them, and God knew that Wriothesley, for instance, had always disliked her, to say nothing of the slippery Dudley whom she couldn't abide nor trust. These men—and into whose hands would the greatest power fall? Today was the twenty-sixth. The room seemed suddenly shadowy. Like my future, she thought. Am I dreaming, or am I standing here outside the King's door and he dying. But I am still the Queen, and I shall be, too, until I die. The Dowager Queen, and no one—no one but Edward himself shall outrank me!

She raised her hand and beckoned to Anne. Lucy picked up the candle, and Katryn threw a long glance about the room. For just a second her eyes found Tom Seymour's and for just a second she read encouragement. Why he understands what I am thinking! she thought, I believe he does. And her eyes gleamed. And I am not even going to speak to any of them; there is no need, I can do as I please! Let them bow, let them realize the Queen is amongst them, passing through from her husband's room. She held her head high, acknowledging none of the ceremony as they bowed and with bent heads stood back and away to let her pass.

At one in the morning Dr. Huicke came to tell her that the King was dead. Katryn wept, then. Why? she wondered, for the tears sprang unbidden to her eyes. I weep, she thought, because he didn't want to die. I weep because I tried my best to give him as much love and care as I could. I weep because this is the end, and it is tragic, for he cannot now right the wrongs, and he was guilty of so much. I weep because he suffered so. And I weep because I am alone. 'Tis so easy to forget the bad and remember now the good in him. But was not that fortunate? That one remembered the best? She frowned and looked over at Anne. Ned Seymour would be on his way to Hatfield and to Edward. Here in the palace, Tom Seymour would be on guard and alert. Weariness assailed her. I must sleep, she thought, for myriad tasks await me in the morn, even to the readying of my mourning gowns. It was so cold. The windows shook suddenly. Her bed was ready for her. But in the morning maybe the sun would be bright upon the new fallen snow. She sighed deeply.

The King was dead. It was true. Anne and Lucy were looking to her. But I am too weary, she thought; I am going to bed. "Whatever is to be done," she said, "will wait upon the morrow."

81

It was early morning. Katryn paced back and forth, back and forth, her gown, black as ebony, swinging away from her black shoes to show a glimpse of black hose. Over her shining hair she had drawn her sable hood, for though it was the second of March and thirty-four days had passed since Henry's death, it was still bitter cold, as though a reluctant winter was never going to take its leave.

Was it possible it had been only two and a half weeks since Henry had been laid beneath the stones of the chapel at Windsor, buried beside Jane as he had wished? And only a week since Edward had been crowned? Poor little Edward had got sick at his coronation, just as he had that night when Henry had been so enraged by Elizabeth.

They had taken Edward from her! When she thought of it, her hands clenched.

Her mind reviewed the weeks. If she closed her eyes, she could still see the chapel here at Westminster with the royal casket, and still hear Norroy's voice calling out from the choir door, loud and high, in a sing-song, echoing voice, "Of your charity . . . pray for the soul of . . . the high and mighty prince, our late sovereign . . . lord and king Henry the Eighth . . ."

Katryn had prayed. At her side the black-gowned Elizabeth had prayed. Little Jane Grey had been absent, for her father had come and taken her away. A warning, thought Katryn, of what was to come, although I didn't know it at the time. I should have prayed for myself, she thought, for suddenly now I am beginning to see what small account I have become. A widow. It hardly mattered that Gardiner still began his prayers before little Edward, the King, with the words, "And I commend to God, Katryn, the Queen Dowager."

Katryn turned to the fire, and spread out her hands. The little

Lady Jane Grey had been taken from her, and so quickly. The child had cried. I almost cried myself, Katryn thought, and I should have, only it was the day that the fearful story about Henry's corpse was being whispered. She shuddered when she thought of it. For Jane Grey's father, coming up from Sion, told her the King's casket had rested there the night before within the outside walls, a stop for Henry's earthly remains as he was being borne to Windsor. And the casket, broken somehow by the jolting ride, leaked out Henry's blood. During the night, stray dogs had got within the broken walls, and had licked it up. "The first plumber we summoned to repair the casket fled in terror," Grey said. At least Henry was now decently laid to rest under the stones of the chapel at Windsor.

The flood of letters of condolence had all been answered. Her desk was bare today, completely bare; the last letters had come, and the few she wanted to save, like Edward's careful Latin one, put away. Edward's letter began, "*Caterina Regina, cara mater,*" and it ended like a premonition, "*Vale, Regina venerata.*" Farewell! Katryn thought. I had been so sure I would have his care, and so, poor little boy, had he. But all my protests went for naught; it availed naught that I have been the only mother he has ever known. The two younger children have been taken away, and I warrant my life is over.

Edward is a king. For all his nine years and three months, he is a king. The colors of the coronation swam before her eyes. From her royal box, clad in her black, she had looked down on Edward. The crown had been fashioned smaller for him, but it was still far too big. It had wobbled on his head as his elder uncle had been made Duke of Somerset. Already men were forgetting Ned's former title and he was called Somerset all the time. And I cannot, nay, do not dare think of Edward's other uncle; yet even if I deny the image, I can see it plain, as he knelt before the new King to receive the barony to which, Katryn knew, he was surely entitled. "Rise, Lord Seymour," Edward had said, and Katryn could see again the easy grace with which Tom Seymour had risen, now Baron Seymour of Sudeley.

I cannot think of him, she vowed. I, a widow! and yet it has been as though my heart, freed from the bonds of matrimony I never wanted, has now fastened itself on him. He is my heart's desire, she thought despairingly, and yet from him, nothing—nothing but the briefest letter of condolence. Brief, courteous, and cold. Her hand clenched.

She and Elizabeth had gone to the jousting which Edward had decreed to celebrate his coronation. Edward had named Tom Seymour as principal challenger for the crown. In glittering armor he had borne Edward's colors victoriously. Katryn caught her breath when she thought of it. The huge horse, the leveled lance—how the sun had shone on them! The galleries were hoarse with cheering, and all Katryn had seen was the gay scarf that he wore. Whose was it?

She had only seen him once again. He had come with Ned and two other lords of the council. They had come to tell her she could not have Edward's care.

I tried to be calm, she thought. Mayhap I protested too much! And if I did, it mattered nothing to him, for it was betwixt the two of us the battle was fought. It was he who answered me. In various ways he told me no. The tables are turned now; it is he who has the power to say me nay.

Whose scarf had he been wearing? Was it Mary Howard's, his beautiful mistress, whose father he had released immediately from the Tower the day after Henry's death? Had that paid his debt to her, or would he wed with her? I'll die, Katryn thought, if that happens I'll die.

The sound of music from the virginals in the far part of her privy chamber momentarily distracted her. Lucy was playing a plaintive love song. Katryn spoke out. "Prithee, stop, Lucy!"

Lucy's hands fell from the keys. Anne laid down her sewing. Katryn went over to the sideboard and poured herself a glass of wine, thinking as she did so that this was the third glass she had drunk. Guiltily she sipped it, and Anne said, "You should retire to Hanworth, your Grace."

"Withdraw?" Katryn asked. She bit her lip and set down the wine. Dowager queens did retire; they moved out of the active orbit of the court. Her great eyes searched Anne's face. Was Anne thinking to spare her the small indignities that might be coming? Like yesterday, when the Chamberlain had come to tell her that the allowance for breakfast could no longer be continued her, even though the meat for her women's meal had cost the crown only eighty pounds per annum. She had pointed to the low cost, but it had still been denied. She picked up the wine again and went over to the window. There below her in the court were horses and carts and baggage. She stared. The court was moving, and she the Queen had not even been informed! They were taking Edward away, only a week after he had been crowned. Probably they were going to Hampton Court.

Feet without the door startled her. She barely saw one of her gentlemen ushers, but she heard his words plain. "The Lord Admiral, your Highness."

Katryn took a step forward. He had come! But—but most probably only to tell her the court was moving. She heard her voice say, "Pray bid my lord enter." She raised her eyes; he was in the doorway and her heart was pounding—like the silly foolish wench I have become, she thought. I am as hot as fire all over. Her hood fell back, framing her red-gold head in the black sable. She pressed one hand to her breast, the other she extended. For a second she felt his lips on her hand, brushing; he bowed and then straightened, and she looked up into the blue eyes, hesitating to see what was in them. They were bright and merry, with the hint of wariness.

"I've brought you a letter from Edward, madam," he said.

"Thank you," Katryn mumbled. So that was his reason. "We thank you," she said stiffly.

"Today his Majesty moves to Hampton Court," Tom Seymour went on. He said nothing further. In the room Lucy shifted her feet, for she and Anne were both standing, since their Queen was.

"You are taking him away," Katryn whispered. Then she blurted, "Why did you not apprise me afore?"

Tom Seymour frowned slightly, black brows drawn and heavy. Katryn took a step toward him, so they stood very close. "Why did you not tell me?" she whispered.

He didn't answer immediately, and when he did she hardly heard him, for of a sudden his eyes held a message that was unmistakable. He said, "But I know naught of your plans, Katryn."

He had used her name. "My plans?"

"Aye," he said shortly. His eyes were suddenly narrow and his voice decisive. "Will you dismiss your women, madam?"

Katryn took a step back.

"There is something I would say privately," Tom Seymour said. And now he took matters into his own hands, and went toward the door and held it open.

Anne went toward it obediently. Lucy hesitated, fluttering a bit. Katryn summoned her dignity. "Pray leave me, Lucy, Anne," she said, striving for calm. The door closed on them; she truly couldn't believe it; she and Tom Seymour were alone for the first time in long long years. By all the saints, she thought desperately, I don't know what to say! I am as undone as the veriest virgin maid. I must think, she told herself, I am the Queen.

She tightened her fingers on Edward's letter. "Pray excuse me, my lord," she said, "whilst I read Edward's words to me." She sank down on a stool before the fire, broke the seal, and read the first line.

"My lady mother," Edward wrote, "when I could see you, I did not have to write." Suddenly Katryn's eyes filled with tears. She could not read any more. That awful woman Anne Stanhope, Ned's wife, having Edward's care! "I think of Edward as my little boy," she whispered, "as Jane said."

Through her tears, she saw he had come close. He was standing over her, she could see his polished boots and the silver spurs. Think how wonderful it would have been if she could have taken Jane's place! Then she could have stood alongside both him and Ned to help bring up Edward. Instead—she was battling them both. I am so alone, she thought. A tear dropped onto Edward's letter, and she wiped it off with her finger. Katryn sniffed. There was a handkerchief extended in his brown hand. She took it and blew her nose.

Over her head his voice sounded. "But I am not extending any sympathy, Katryn. The custody of a nine-year-old prince is a grim business, and one for which you are entirely unfitted."

The tone of the sentence, the use of her name, made her struggle to her feet. "And you and Ned are fitted?" she flashed.

He raised one eyebrow. "I pray to God we are."

There was silence. It was maybe true. Maybe it was too big a job for a woman. Tom Seymour said, "When Elizabeth Woodville had the custody of her two sons, they were both murdered."

Katryn sniffed. I must think, she told herself. She blew her nose again, determinedly.

"But that was a long time ago," she answered. Still— She glanced up at him. I could hardly get my fingers around the heavy-hilted dagger he wears, she thought. Maybe is he right. "Oh," she said, "I wish to God that I had been born—" She stopped. He was smiling. He remembers when I said that afore, she thought. He remembers perfectly. "Of course I am older now, and I know I don't want to be a man, heaven forbid! But I am so alone," she said. "I need a—"

"Finish your sentences, Katryn," he said. "You need a man?"

Her voice was sullen. She turned away. "Aye!" She flung the word at him. I don't care what he thinks, that's exactly what I do need: a good strong man to wage my battles. Here I am, all alone, a woman fighting a whole council. Aye, they will probably want to take Elizabeth from me next!

"You have had so much experience," he was saying in his lazy drawl, "that you should have no difficulty. You come well recommended, I should say. Marriage by this time must be an art with you. Against you, I should be the veriest novice."

What does he mean? Is he thinking of wedding? An icy cold fear enveloped her. She looked at him.

"Are you thinking of getting married?" she whispered.

"I am almost forty and am not yet married," he said. "But surely there must be compensations. I might have overlooked them." He was mocking at her again; he was never serious, except the times when she didn't recognize it. "I should put the question to you," he said. "And you already answered it. I was going to ask were you thinking of marrying then, since you've confessed to me openly you need a man. Do you have someone in mind?"

"No!" said Katryn furiously. But, she thought, I'd wed with Ned if I could, since I cannot have the man I love. What difference does it make?

"You can't have Ned," he said. Katryn gasped. How had he guessed? "And Dudley is tightly knotted, and Will Herbert, and Knyvet, and—I believe, your Highness, there's truly no one for you to marry save me."

"You look just as pleased with yourself as always!" Katryn cried despairingly.

"Of course," he went on, as if he hadn't heard her, "there are others, to be sure. I must have forgot some hapless male." He frowned thoughtfully, but his eyes were sharp on her, even though she had averted her face and was looking into the fire. "There's my vice admiral, for instance," he said, "Sir Edward Clinton. He has much to recommend him."

Her eyes were narrow and golden, and she raised them suddenly to Tom Seymour; for he had laid his hands on her shoulders and had turned her to face him. His hands hurt, and he had that devilish look to his face.

"You little devil," he said, almost incredulous. "You were in truth considering Clinton!"

"I was not!" She denied it. "Acourse I wasn't!" Oh, why, she thought, did he trap me into that? He would never understand it is just because I cannot have him. Suddenly—and she didn't know whether it was because he was holding her or because he was so close or because she yearned only to have his arms around her— she gave a little cry and put her arms around him, turning her face into his chest. Marry, this is heaven, she thought. She could feel his arms around her.

He made no effort to kiss her. He held her against him. "I suggest," Tom Seymour said, over her head, "that you take my first hint and marry me, Katryn."

Katryn, whose eyes were closed, blinked and shut her eyes again. She couldn't have heard aright. It wasn't possible, of course; he didn't mean it. Slowly she raised her head, and just as slowly he set her back from him, looking down.

"Is it so great a shock?"

"Aye," whispered Katryn. "Marry you, my lord?" Her heart was pounding. It was true! He was actually asking her to marry him. Out of the whole kingdom, from the whole court, he was asking her! "Sweetheart—" she breathed, looking at his face. It was as darkly handsome and impassive as ever. She didn't understand. I never comprehend him, she thought wildly. "I am undone," she said honestly. "Acourse, we must wait," she floundered. "Two years?"

He raised an eyebrow. "Two years, Katryn? But I had in mind not so long a wait."

Katryn shivered.

"His Grace waited a brief three months, I remember."

Was ever a woman proposed to like this! "But I am the Queen," she faltered. "And the will, Henry's will, has mentioned heirs from my body."

"I know every word in Henry's will," Tom Seymour said. "I was one of the executors."

"Queens are supposed to wait, to make sure," Katryn faltered.

"Nonsense," said Tom Seymour. "You know perfectly well Henry couldn't have an heir."

Her eyes fell from his.

"I suggest you stop being childish, Katryn. We are no longer in the first flush of youth. You have had three husbands and you have, briefly, been my mistress. One of the reasons I kept my sanity during your marriage to Henry was that he was impotent. Did you think for a moment I forgot you? What do you think I felt when the King lumbered into your chamber?" He swore, low. Katryn stared at him. Her heart raced. Oh, Lord, Lord, she thought, heaven be thanked for giving me a man like this one. "And I may not stray unless you cease to please me. And I have definitely decided on marriage. I discovered the law is on my side. For instance, the Duke of Norfolk brought Bess Holland right into his house."

Katryn's eyes grew wide with horror. He might! "I'll not marry you! Nay, I'll not!" She averted her face. "I'll wed another!"

He turned her to face him and tipped up her head, his fingers under her chin. "Clinton? Hadn't you better pick a man who at least is not my subordinate? I'll have him hanged."

"You're laughing at me," she whispered. She was suddenly seized with panic. Suppose he rescinded his offer? It would be just like him. She said hastily, "I'll wed with you, my lord." She raised her eyes to his face. "Whenever you wish," she whispered.

"A long time ago," Tom Seymour said, "I let you put me off, because you said you were in love with another man."

"I thought I was," Katryn said. "Only later I knew it was you, always you, as long as I live."

His blue eyes were narrow and glittering. Will he say he loves me, she wondered? But he does. Now it is so blindingly clear. All these years he has stood by me. It was he who rescued me from Thomas Borough, he who answered my call for help at Snape Hill, he who tried to wrest me from Henry. I mustn't cry, she thought.

"We'll be wed now," he said. "Now. This morn. Call Dr. Parkhurst. And we must have witnesses to make it legal. Call Lucy and Anne."

Was she hearing aright? Was it her voice saying, "Not Lucy and

Anne, my lord. They'd be undone. Lucy would faint and scream. We shall have as witnesses my two women, Meg and Mistress Barbara." The room swam before her eyes. This was fearful scandal. The past wrapped her for a moment. She could hear her own voice, saying to Lord Latimer, "Why if I were a man, and I wanted a woman—" She hadn't finished the sentence. Tom Seymour had. We are just the same, she thought, in some ways we are just the same.

"I love you," she said. "I adore you. But we must keep this secret, for 'tis a scandal which would rock London."

He had walked over to her table and had rung her little bell. He moves with the grace of an animal, she thought. He was saying, "I commend you, my little one. In the midst of emotion you can keep your head. For a while we must keep this secret—you are right." The door was opening. "Mistress Barbara, you are to fetch Dr. Parkhurst here, immediately."

The fire crackled in the grate. The wind blew at the windows. And within the room Master Parkhurst repeated the old, old words. On her knees, Katryn clasped Tom Seymour's hand. She looked down at her hand in his. Thank heaven I wore no ring this morn, for he has one for me, a nuptial ring. It is his way of saying he loves me; he planned this, it was no accident. She looked down at her hand in his, at the wide gold band, through shimmering tears. She blinked hastily.

Dr. Parkhurst blessed them. Then Tom Seymour lifted her to her feet. He kissed her, a brush of the lips. "Go to Chelsea, Katryn," he said, very low. "Chelsea. I'll come by the garden. This night."

Katryn's royal manor house of Chelsea was new. Henry had built it, using the new ideas, and it was turreted and castellated and many-windowed, with an entrance like a Gothic arch between two chimney turrets. Its walled gardens along the river boasted a ᶠsh pond, and every room had a fireplace. Katryn loved it; it was one of her favorite dwelling places, and she had never ceased to be overjoyed that Henry had bestowed it on her. And it was very near to London.

There was a village near by. From the village an old footpath crossed the fields, bare now, and crossed a narrow stone bridge called Blandel's bridge; but it was a lonely way from the village to the royal manor and men had been waylaid at the bridge, where the path made a sharp turn. So the villagers called it Bloody Bridge, and that was the way Tom Seymour would come by night, alone.

She had arrived at Chelsea in the afternoon, with a train of one hundred ladies and gentlemen, musicians, servants, grooms, her two chaplains, and the Lady Elizabeth, who had her own smaller train, including Master Parry, her bookkeeper, Mistress Ashley, her personal woman, and her tutors. Elizabeth was glad to be at Chelsea, for she thought it friendly and cosy, and it seemed like home.

Tom Seymour came always at night. Sometimes he was very late, and it would be one o'clock in the morning before she would hear his step on the outside stair rising from the garden. Sometimes he came for a late supper, some nights he came not at all.

The first night he had not come until ten o'clock, and she had waited in a fever of impatience. Early she dismissed her women; the March night was cold and clear, and the fire burned bright in the hearth in the silent room. The reality of the events of the day, his unexpected presence that morn, the hasty marriage, her quick removal to Chelsea to await the night hours, all blurred together and became as nothing before the thought that soon he would be here, in this very room. Katryn waited breathlessly; she sat like a statue, hardly moving, so she would hear the muffled hoofbeat, or the careful squeak of the garden gate, or the muffled light tread on the outside stair.

Her little mantel clock struck ten, and as its sound died away, she heard indeed a step on the stairway. The door opened with a rush of cold air and closed. Katryn felt his arms enfold her tight. She felt his kiss, and hot tears squeezed themselves through her lashes.

"It has been so long," she whispered.

He hugged her. "I'm held quick and good with words," he said, "but, sweetheart, they fail me now."

Words truly don't fail him, thought Katryn, but they do me, for there are no words for this, this happiness, this belonging. No words at all; I am helpless to express it.

She wore her wedding ring around her neck, on a thin gold chain. She could not leave off her mourning; each day she dressed in her filmy black, and each night she doffed it gratefully for a silk or satin robe. She had sent to London for materials, for lace and furs and velvets, for she knew it would offend Tom Seymour to see her mourning for Henry.

During her days, Katryn attended chapel, but heard no word of the sermon, since she was recounting to herself all that had happened the night before. Elizabeth had never won so consistently at cards. She teased Katryn. Once, when they were walking in the garden, it began to rain. "Why, madam," Elizabeth said, "it's raining, and I don't believe you even noted it!" Flurried, Katryn caught her cloak tight, and fled into the house.

He left her before dawn, roused by Meg's knock, and it was always still dark. Vividly Katryn imagined the lonely ride, past Bloody Bridge, but when she spoke of it he waved his big hand. At seven she ate, knowing he was dressed and eating too, either at court or at Seymour Place. At eight the privy council met, and at eleven, when she dined, she knew he was dining too in the council dining room, and she knew that next he would go to the big room with the stars on the ceiling where the council heard complaints in the manner of a court of law.

"After the meeting is over," he said, "I snatch a cup of wine, and hie myself to the Tower."

He works as hard as Henry did, she thought. He had established a board of the Admiralty in the short weeks since Henry's death. And he had commandeered a room in the White Tower, where the board met. "I cannot possibly do as was done before me," he said. "I need the advice of others, and our expanding Navy makes it mandatory, this Admiralty board." It was one of his favorite projects and she knew he was proud of it. Then, if all went smooth, as darkness fell he rode down to Chelsea.

With Meg and Mistress Barbara's connivance, she always had food for him. She knew she couldn't have kept this marriage secret without their help, and they worried over his food just as I do, she thought gratefully. They always fussed over the cheese, and made sure the beef was rare enough.

The three women in this conspiracy strove to do all they could for the care and comfort of their lord. " 'Tis such a dreadful ride, madam," Mistress Barbara would say, anxiously scanning the deepening dusk; and when rain beat against the window panes, she would be just as upset as Katryn. On those evenings Mistress Barbara would take the dripping cloak he handed her with concern; she would have hot wine ready.

"I never catch cold, Mistress Barbara," he would say. "I am rather healthy."

"Aye, that you are, my lord." Mistress Barbara eyed him with pride.

"They are as proud of you as I am," Katryn said. She looked at him lovingly. He was lounging in her chair before the fire. His wet boots stood on the hearth; he was wearing but shirt and hose, and against his white shirt his face was as dark as always. "It is March thirteenth," Katryn said, "and we've been wed nine days."

"A lifetime, it seems," he said, his eyes twinkling. "March thirteenth, and today we made Ned the Lord Protector of the realm. Eight of us signed the warrant, including Edward, of course. And Dudley, although he signed at the bottom, and I expect him to sneak into the archives some night and cut off his name. There's nothing I'd like better than to run a length of steel through him."

The words rolled around in Katryn's head. Think of all that has happened to him today, she thought. Of course I know I cannot share his life in London—now not at all, and later, when what I've done is laid before the world in all its shocking haste, I can still share only a part. Probably when he speaks before the council he forgets me entirely. Men always do. And with him there is the sea too.

"Ned, the Lord Protector?" she whispered.

He gave her a brief look from underneath his black brows. "Aye, the lord-chancellorship was not enough. The position not strong enough."

"Acourse it wasn't," she said. Again she looked at him. He and Ned are trying to do what Henry, with all his inherited power, his iron will, his ruthless strength, his very kingship, had tried to do. Katryn looked at the big brown hand lying on the white cover of her chair. He will be equal to it, she thought fiercely.

"Come here, sweetheart."

Katryn rose from her stool, and he reached for her, pulling her down beside him. "Don't fret when I tell you this," he whispered.

He's going away, she thought. After a brief nine days he's going away.

"Don't fret," he repeated in her ear. "It's a long story, but I find myself suddenly hot with love for you, so I'll make it brief. Katryn, I sail in two weeks for the Scillys."

Katryn cried. "In two weeks?"

"Aye, we are endeavoring to get on better terms with the French, trying to undo Henry's mad policy concerning Boulogne. We want to made a trade. Hands off in Scotland, and they get Boulogne back. Anyway, the French have complained about the Channel pirates, operating from the Scillys and Lundy."

Katryn said, "But why can't some one else go? You are the lord admiral, and a privy councilor, now!"

He looked amused and kissed her. "Don't wriggle," he said. "I've made these pirates my business since I first had a command. They know me. I can sail right in there, and they won't fire a shot. I want to talk to them, and principally their leader, Thompson of Calais. He calls himself that." He laughed. "What a thorough rogue he is. He'd think you a pretty piece of booty too, just as I do."

"I warrant you feel a kinship with them," Katryn said.

"I would have made a splendid pirate," he said. "And just imagine yourself falling into my bloodstained hands, as indeed you have done, you fortunate wench."

"Oh!" cried Katryn.

"Oh," he mocked. "And whilst I am gone, I wish you to come out of retirement and betake yourself to Marlborough, your palace there. In these times of instability, it will be good to see the Dowager Queen, and her court, and the princesses."

"I would rather stay here," Katryn protested.

"Don't gainsay me," he said. "It is best you travel about, and it is my wish."

I've never been ordered like this in my whole life, she thought. Never.

"Stop kissing me," Katryn cried. "I can't think!"

"You don't have to think. I've two weeks left to make love to you. Then you go to Marlborough, and I'll go to sea."

Katryn felt herself lifted in his arms. He was so strong. I always knew this would happen, she thought. He will leave me. But he is worth it.

By the middle of April, Katryn was established at Marlborough Palace, her dower palace. Anne had been glad to see her remove there, and Lucy too. The six weeks they had spent at Chelsea were long for Katryn to spend in one place, and Anne found herself puzzled by Katryn's behavior. All were glad to see little Jane Grey again; Tom Seymour had effected her return. Even Elizabeth had shown her emotion, and squeezed Jane and called her fondly a silly goose for crying. Katryn looks so happy, Anne thought; I've never seen her look like this. Even in her mourning, she is radiant. Look how she laughs!

I am happy too, Anne thought, for my husband is here, if only briefly. Will was a member of the privy council, and in the excitement and duties of a new reign, Ned the Regent had forbidden any member of the council to be absent from London more than two days. But Will and Cat's husband, Will Knyvet, and some of their gentlemen had ridden down for Saturday and Sunday; and how marvellous, Anne thought, that this April day is so warm and sweet. Will had been made the Earl of Pembroke; yesterday Edward had conferred the title, and when Katryn was told of it, it reminded her of the night in the garden at New Hall, that summer night so many years ago.

"Tom prophesied it," she said, unthinking.

Will Herbert looked surprised. She had never used his first name to him before. Then he said, "I miss him. Although, truth to tell, we saw little of him in London at night. We haven't had a game of whist; I taxed him about a new mistress and he laughed."

Katryn's face went white. A new mistress!

"Who is it, Will?" Anne asked.

He shook his head at her. "What a question? I could not tell you in any case, even if I would."

Katryn's face now turned pink. Why, it is I, she thought, I, the Queen. She carefully wrapped her black scarf about her shoulders. She missed him so much. Her thoughts drifted. After he made love to her, she would lie in his arms and they would talk, low, while the whispered words they had waited so long to say were said. "But you must sleep, sweetheart," she would say, and his answer was always the same.

"Someday I'll be forever asleep. What is sleep?"

"But you must," Katryn would repeat.

Then he turned her over on her stomach the way she liked to sleep. He put one arm around her. Thus deep in the featherbed, with his body half-covering hers and the weight of his leg across hers, she would sleep. Katryn sighed again. Even thinking about him is heaven, she thought, and then she bit her lip to keep from smiling. Her eyes sparkled. What would Will think if she suddenly told him with whom Tom Seymour spent his nights?

Katryn shot a look at Anne. She sobered. The men were talking of London and the unrest there. Now that Henry's heavy hand was no longer lying on the land, license was abroad, priests were being openly mocked on the streets, and churches despoiled. Every noble wanted something from Edward, or the new regime. Ned was harried, to be sure, but oft, Will said, he will go over the heads of the conservative members of the privy council, and seek advice only from those he knows agree with him.

I know exactly what he means, Katryn thought. The whole state of the realm is like water flowing too fast over a broken dam, and that dam had been Henry. "Do you know I have here to my hand a letter from my brother, Will Parr, and do you know what he is thinking of doing? Divorcing his wife!" Katryn brought out these astonishing words, and her eyes were wide and gold. A fine state the nation must be in if men suddenly thought they could get divorces!

Will Herbert was inclined to smile.

"That exemplifies the state of the realm," Katryn said. "I wrote and told him it was a royal prerogative only."

"He is a marquis, now," Will Herbert pointed out.

"Aye," said Katryn. It was true. Will had been made Marquis of Northampton. It was a title Henry never would have granted, and so Katryn looked a bit askance on it. "All is proceeding much too fast," she said. She suddenly saw what Tom Seymour meant. "All is in an extraordinary state of flux. We shall remove to Windsor tomorrow," she announced.

Will Herbert spoke again of Tom Seymour. "Tom is no chapel-goer and handy with a weapon, but he is much the steadiest of the lot. He is clear-sighted and forthright. Practically, he knows a good deal about the Continent, having been there so much. We miss him in the council meeting; i' fact, we often held the meetings at Seymour Place, big barn that it is."

"Is it?" Katryn asked, leaning forward.

"Aye, it looks like a man's dwelling," Will said.

Katryn folded her hands together tightly. I can hardly wait. To dwell there with him! Scandal it will be, but we can surmount it!

At Windsor, a week later, all were proud and glad to see the Queen and the royal train. Katryn held morning audiences, she heard petitions, she dispensed favors and food to the poor. Her two chaplains preached twice daily, and all were invited to attend chapel. Thus April passed.

There was no word from Tom Seymour. Every morn when she awakened she would lie and dream of him, wakening too, in his narrow bunk. When it rained, she would imagine slanting decks, slippery with water and foam; when the sun shone, she could imagine plain the lift and swell of blue seas under the prow of the *Salamander*, and the white, white canvas spread to the wind.

On the first of May, she allowed her maids and gentlemen the usual celebration. "It was Henry's most favorite day," she announced. "How better to celebrate than the way we always have? But without the tournaments, acourse."

The palace was then filled with greens and laughter from before dawn. Katryn walked in the gardens, the most beautiful in the world, she thought. Windsor Castle, the favorite dwelling place of English kings. Here the past balances the uneasy present; here the royal flag flies on this May morn as it has flown for so many many years past. She watched Elizabeth with pride.

"You shall be here many years after I am gone," she said, and Elizabeth looked at her from those bright eyes.

"Do you so think, madam?"

"Aye, I do," said Katryn. "You're a fine daughter to England."

When she left Windsor, it was the middle of May. She was afraid to stay longer for fear Tom Seymour would return. So she arrived at Chelsea on the sixteenth, and the same day a courier came with letters.

Katryn's hands shook. He was home then! The letter was written from Baynard's Castle, from Anne and Will's London house. Then Anne had seen him, for she had gone back to London to be with Will.

"I had supper tonight with my new sister and brother," Tom Seymour wrote. "I am glad to be back, as you might guess. But as I write this, it is twelve of the clock, and impossible for me to ride down, sweetheart. So good night, and tomorrow I shall be with thee, no matter what. Written by the hand of him whom you have bound to love, honor and, in all lawful things, obey."

Katryn raised her eyes from the letter. She could see the twinkle in his eyes as he wrote that closing! Oh, he is just the same. How can I possibly wait till tonight?

He came at nine. Tears stood in Katryn's eyes. And Tom Seymour, his eyes alight in a deeply tanned face, held her off to look at her.

"Why, sweetheart," he said. "I do truly believe you have missed me!"

The next night he came right after dark for a late supper, and Katryn kept glancing at him as she ate, almost dizzy with happiness. He was so close across the narrow table. She watched him eat, lovingly. He was hungry, and he talked as he ate.

"I was telling you about the pirates," he said, "and only Ned knows this tale. The French are trying to circumvent us in Scotland and prevent Edward's eventual marriage to the little Queen of Scots. We hold over the French, Boulogne, and now the additional weapon of the Channel pirates, for I have made a kind of covenant with them."

"And they will honor it?" Katryn asked.

"They will honor it," he said wryly. He saw for a moment the face of Thompson of Calais, and heard his own voice, "Monsieur Thompson"—for Thompson pretended to be French—"if you break your word to me, I'll see you hanging from your own yardarm." Thompson had grinned.

"And then," Tom went on, "I told him I had been lately wed and was anxious to return to the loving arms of my wife. So from his pocket he brought forth, as I'm doing now, this present for you. Green for Kendal."

Across the table he handed her an emerald chain the like of which Katryn had never even dreamed of. Her eyes opened wide. "By the mass!" she said, astounded.

"It probably was stolen from a Spanish grandee," he said.

Katryn held it in her hand. He smiled, a little. "Sweetheart, you know me for a natural pirate, but I told him I could not accept it."

"But then—how—?" She looked at it incredulously.

"It was early in the evening," Tom Seymour said. "And there is not much diversion to be had in the Scillys. So we diced. Put it on. So from now on, you can hide your petty knaveries behind my very large ones."

Did the pirate Thompson of Calais look a bit like to the man across from her now? Probably he did. Tom Seymour had rolled up the sleeves of his white shirt. Down the powerful right forearm ran a long jagged scar. As she watched he picked up his dagger, speared a disjointed leg of fowl, and offered it to her. She shook her head slowly.

"No thank you, my lord," she said. She lifted the chain and put it around her neck. The stones were smooth and warm from his pocket.

"I should like you to be able to wear that openly," he said.

"I should, too," Katryn said.

"And your ring," he added.

Katryn nodded, her eyes big.

"Soon," he said. "Soon we should make our marriage public. There is no reason to wait much longer. Even though I am used to this, you are not."

His eyes glittered, and Katryn said, "Oh, you knave!"

He grinned. "Someone is sure to see me, sooner or later. The only person about whose opinion I give a tinker's damn is Edward. I want to apprise him myself. What are you thinking about? You are looking at me as if I had committed some frightful sin."

Katryn said, "Were there women on those islands?"

"Oh, indeed. A spirited breed, hot-blooded, responding well to brutality and force."

Katryn's mouth flew open.

He leaned back in his chair. "Mayhap it would ha' been kinder of me not to have wed with you. I can be very difficult. You in truth know little of me, Katryn. Sometimes I drink. Heavily. When I do, I am apt to be rough on women. Now tonight, I think I'll forego these sweets and have brandy."

"I don't apprehend you," Katryn said. "You're jesting."

"You're trying to decide whether I'm jesting or not. But I wasn't jesting about the brandy."

Katryn sat straight.

"Fetch it, please." He was wiping off the slender dagger with his napkin, and uncertainly Katryn rose and went over to the sideboard. She poured a small amount of the liquor into a silver cup. He was watching. "Fill it up," he said, getting to his feet.

While she was doing that Tom Seymour drew his shirt over his head and threw it on the stool he had vacated. Katryn came forward and extended the brimming cup. He took it, his blue eyes merry and full of laughter.

"You big brute," said Katryn, "you're teasing me!"

"Partly," he said. He drank the brandy, quickly set down the cup, and snuffed the candles on the table. Katryn, backing away from him, looked at him standing there, his powerful torso naked, and the dagger thrust through his belt.

"You look truly like a pirate," Katryn said, with dignity, "and I'm not sure I like being in a room with one."

He came toward her. "No? But I think, your Grace, you will like going to bed with one."

The next night he was abstracted and paced the room. Katryn was afraid some one would hear him, not only his voice but the heavy man's tread. But she said nothing.

"I'm conscious of increasing friction with Ned," he said. "He wants to make a Protestant nation of Scotland. Instead of an alliance, with its Queen and Edward betrothed, we must wage a church battle. Ned calls this our 'Godly Cause.' You know what the Scots call it, in their inimitable way? 'The Rough Wooing!' There'll be war by August if Ned pursues this path."

"War?" Katryn breathed.

He nodded, scowling.

"You will go?" Katryn took a step forward.

"Of course," he said. "We want this alliance, and we want the little Queen. It is the fruition of Henry's policy concerning our two nations, and I'm convinced it is a good one. Ned is too. Your late husband, my love, wouldn't have cared if the Scots worshiped toadstools, as long as we wed the two children." He sighed. "Ned already has a name for our new nation. Great Britain. I said, that's a fine title, Ned, but how if we write the book first?"

"Was this in the council?" Katryn asked.

"Aye."

"I warrant a many of them laughed."

"They did," he said.

Katryn giggled. Then she sobered. "But 'tis thou who'll fight the war!"

He shook his head. "Not only I, sweetheart. Ned's a good and ruthless soldier. He'll command the land forces."

He had flung himself down on the bed. "Today sweetheart, I spoke to Edward about my getting myself wed. He said I certes should. I asked him whom he would suggest, thinking he might name you. But do you know what in fact he did say? And solemnly? 'Why don't you marry my sister Mary, and bring her to the right religion?'" He smiled. "Poor little Edward. Ned's making him into a fanatic reformer too. But you see, my love, if I were truly as ambitious as my enemies say, I would repudiate this secret marriage and wed myself to the next in line."

Katryn looked at him soberly. War in August. She came slowly toward him. She sat beside him on the bed and put her arms around him. If aught should happen to him—

He pulled her down beside him, and began to kiss her. In between his caresses he whispered, "Write Edward, sweetheart. Tell him we're going to wed."

The sun shone, birds sang; the spring air was delicious. Katryn sat writing to Edward.

First she must explain how much she had loved Henry. She wrote carefully. How much she had respected and loved Edward's father; how deeply she had felt her duty toward him; how full of grief she was to realize that he was forever lost to her and Edward, except that they could always treasure his love for them, and never never forget it. So must we honor him, Katryn wrote. But she and Edward were both younger, and they must not yearn after the dead, but honor them in their hearts no matter what the rest of the world thought.

Edward wrote back quickly. My lord, my uncle, he said, had spoken with him, and he would deem it right and good, and it was actually his desire, that the Queen's Grace wed with his uncle.

Katryn wrote back, and this correspondence was kept from other eyes; as yet no one knew.

"I am thankful," Katryn wrote, "that you have given your permission for the Lord Admiral, your uncle, and me to wed. We shall be all part of the same family, now, and I shall be not only thy mother, but thy aunt who loves thee."

Katryn sealed this letter, and Anne looked up from her sewing. "When you are done, your Grace," Anne said, "there is a troublesome matter I must put to you."

Katryn looked surprised.

"Katryn"—for they were alone with Lucy— "a most amazing and horrifying tale has come to my ears. The meanest, most hateful type of gossip. I do not even know how to begin to tell you, you will be so outraged and undone! I myself was overthrown. But this lying rumor has it that there has been a man riding down to Chelsea; the villagers claim to have seen a man! And that he comes to see thee, and that there are some, within this house, who maliciously claim to have heard a man's voice in thy own chamber!" By this time Anne had risen and was facing Katryn, and Katryn saw plain she was furious with anger that any should demean the Queen's name, especially any member of her own household! Anne said, "I think you should discover who's at the bottom of this plot, and have them soundly beaten and tried for perjury!"

"By all the saints," Katryn muttered. Poor Anne, she thought, and poor Lucy! Lucy was wringing her hands. "By all the saints," she repeated helplessly. Her husband was right; it was well they had already written Edward. What to say? I've been wed these three months past, she thought, and I have forgotten that no one is used to it save me; I have forgotten what a shock it is going to be!

Anne cried, "Aye, I didn't see how I could even tell thee! You who have been our model for five years since you came from Yorkshire! You, as Kate Willoughby says, our angel, our true Queen! A man in your chambers! Oh, Katryn, I think 'tis treason!"

Katryn said steadily, "It is true!"

Anne didn't believe it. "Have you taken leave of your senses, madam?" she asked. "True? How can it be true? You, our Queen, with a clandestine lover? Katryn!"

Katryn shook her head. "Nay, nay," she cried, "not a lover! Not a lover, but a husband!"

Anne stared at Katryn. "You are secretly wed?" she whispered. "I cannot credit it." Then she stopped. There was only one man who could then be Katryn's husband. Only one. "You are wed, then, madam," she said, "to the Lord Admiral, are you not?" Lucy gave a loud cry of despair. "My God, My God!" Anne was saying. "A year would ha' been too soon!"

Katryn squared her shoulders. "I ha' wed with the Lord Admiral," she said, "and first I want to say I am proud of it. In fact, in very truth I'd follow him to the ends of the earth in my petticoat. And as far as waiting a year—I suggested two years, but it was a foolish suggestion, I know it well. We waited long—long enough."

"Oh!" cried Lucy.

She is jealous, Katryn thought, losing me to a man; in her way, she wanted to look after me. But he will win her over.

"We ha' much planning to do," Katryn said. "We will ignore the rumor, and as soon as I consult with my lord, we will make our marriage known to all. There is not much time, I warrant. But it is time now for us to have a cup of wine, and drink. I would wish you to drink a wedding toast to us. I'll pour the wine myself."

"Nay, nay, madam," Lucy cried, as if by the very act of waiting upon herself Katryn had already abandoned her queenly rights. "I'll pour it, madam," cried Lucy, "and I'll drink, but then I am going to the chapel!"

Katryn took the cup from her trembling fingers. She said, kindly, "Lucy we shall welcome your prayers, and thank thee for them."

"I shall pray sorrow and distress do not descend upon thee," Lucy cried.

Katryn lifted the cup. Sorrow and distress? "Let us drink," she said.

Black-gowned arms raised the silver cups, and the three women drank. Lucy took the empty cup from Katryn's fingers; she replaced it and hers on the sideboard. When she came toward Katryn again, Katryn saw she was crying; Katryn made a gesture toward her with both hands, as though to grasp her and give her physical reassurance. Lucy fell on her knees.

"You have my heartfelt wishes, madam, and my prayers!"

Over the kneeling figure Katryn's eyes met Anne's. Anne tried a tremulous smile. She is trying to tell me not to put stress on Lucy's fear. "Please rise, Lucy," Katryn said.

Lucy did. At the door she said, "Bless thee, madam."

Katryn walked over to the chair she had left. "I hope," she said to Anne, "that we shall not need these prayers that are no doubt begging heaven from Lucy's lips at this very moment."

Tom Seymour listened quietly that night to Katryn's vivid description of the events of the afternoon. He was unusually grave, so grave that Katryn was finally impelled to ask, "But Lucy's fears—they are quite untenable. They do not cause you disquiet, do they, my lord?"

"Nay, nay, I was but considering the method of announcing our marriage."

"Oh," said Katryn a bit relieved.

"The court is at Hampton Court. Next week there is to be a banquet for the Scottish lords. In the afternoon, I would wish you to come to London. That night, we can appear together."

Katryn imagined the great Gothic banquet hall, filled with the glitter of the court on a state occasion. Her face grew a little pale. Tom Seymour grinned. "I've found that to take the offensive is best, and a surprise action even better."

Katryn traveled up to London by her own barge. The afternoon was sunny and warm, and she commanded her musicians to play. She held Elizabeth's hand in hers, and on the other side of her the little Jane Grey watched the river banks go by with all the normal entrancement of a nine-year-old.

But once within the familiar brick walls, once more within the great palace where she had spent so many of her years, the past seemed close about her and the future was drawing nearer. Still in filmy black mourning, with a long train fluttering behind her and a silken black scarf, Katryn stepped from her barge, and took anew possession of the queen's chambers.

The chambers bustled. Unpacking, amidst the sudden flow of greetings that began to bombard the chamber doors, Katryn began to feel disquiet. How could she face the court tonight? How could she? On the arm of a new husband! She could hear the gasps, the titillated whispers, the horrible bawdy remarks the men would make.

If only he were here! He would dispel the image of Henry. My God, she thought, I keep expecting Henry to come in—lumber in, as my lord put it. Try as she would, she could not keep her eyes from the door or her ears from listening for Tom's step. He would give her courage.

She had not seen him for a week, the longest time he had not come to Chelsea by night, except, of course, when he had been at sea. He had written a short note, saying that he was endeavoring to win over the Scottish lords, feting them every night at Seymour Place or other points of diversion in the city. Feting meant some manner of loose women, too, Katryn was sure.

She had spent the week making a new gown, which had to be done secretly with but Lucy and Anne's help, although Mistress Barbara was expert with lace and she had helped too. Tom Seymour had been explicit about her gown. "I want you to have a new gown," he said, "and it to be as elegant as possible; no white collars, either."

"I've made them famous," she said. "There is naught prettier than a white collar on a woman."

"I don't want you to expose your breasts, though."

"Oh," said Katryn. "You are always telling me what to do!"

"Aye, and I expect someday you will revolt," he said lazily. "Then I'll thrash you. It is a mystery to me that women pick on purpose a dominating man, and then fret and fume under it, or him, rather. And other women pick a man they can dominate, and they fret too, and yearn for that good thrashing which I may have to administer. In the future, of course."

"We haven't quarreled yet," Katryn said.

"No, but we will, my sweet." He laughed. "I'll let you pick the color of the gown, but I want you to wear those dazzling emeralds."

"Thank you so much," said Katryn, "and I'd already picked the color!"

"Green for Kendal," he said, "I can predict everything you will do."

"You are very maddening," said Katryn. "You make me out simple-minded."

"Far from it," he said. "If you are simple-minded, I'd fear for the whole of the male sex."

The gown was pale green satin, and it reminded Katryn very much of the gown she had made long ago at Tansfield, although the material was far finer and the lace fragile as only the Brussels lace-makers could create. Lucy laid it on the bed with its matching satin slippers. It was six o'clock, and the big chimes rang out over Hampton Court. When they died, Katryn could hear the river noises and other familiar sounds of the big palace; the windows were open and the air of the June evening, indescribably sweet, stirred through the chamber.

Katryn was sitting on her stool and Meg was brushing her hair. Anne was by the window seat and Lucy was fussily straightening the folds of the satin dress, so it lay perfect on the bed. Of a sudden, the chatter of Katryn's other ladies in the next room ceased.

He comes, Katryn thought. She heard his voice and turned toward the wide, enscrolled doorway, with its pretty gilt against the ivory paint. It was opening. It must be he, for anyone else would perforce knock on the chamber door of the Queen. Tom Seymour closed the door behind him as casually as if he had done this every day of his life. He stood there a moment; he bowed.

"Good evening, madam," he said, now coming forward to her across the room, while Anne and Lucy stood transfixed.

I warrant they didn't think it was really true, Katryn thought, until this very minute. "Good evening, my lord," she said.

He had reached her and stood behind her, meeting her eyes in the glass. He leaned down and kissed her bare shoulder.

Katryn's eyes flew to Anne, who was watching with wide eyes. Oh, he shouldn't have done that! He was walking over to the bed, inspecting the dress.

"Very fair, and the color is good," he said. He sent Lucy a smile, flashing suddenly in his dark face. "Are you going to forgive me," he asked, "for wedding the Queen's Grace?"

Lucy stammered. He took her hand. "I don't expect quick forgiveness, my lady," he said.

Lucy now sent him a tremulous smile. Katryn sighed with relief. He is being so kind to her, she thought. I was afraid he might pay her no mind. He was walking toward Anne; he leaned down and kissed her cheek.

"I think you wedded too quick, my lord," Anne said determinedly, as though she were obliged to speak the truth. "But you know Will and I hope for nothing but your happiness."

"Thank you, Anne," he said.

There was a moment's silence. Then he sat down in the chair, stretching out his feet and crossing them at the ankles. From the bed, Lucy spoke.

"Her Grace is not yet dressed, and if you would—"

Oh, thought Katryn, she is going to order him out. She held her breath.

Tom Seymour interrupted. "One of the pleasures of being wed is watching one's wife be dressed, or undressed."

There was silence. Meg began to brush Katryn's hair.

I'll never forget this, Katryn thought.

Lucy found her voice and offered Tom wine. He sipped it and told them of the events of the day, such as the ground being broken for Ned's new house on the Strand. He said then he wished to remove her Grace to Seymour Place this very night, and her train could follow later.

Katryn said, "If you should wish to accompany me, Lucy, we should be happy."

Lucy said that she would, and that she would also apprise the other ladies. The last hook on Katryn's gown was fastened, the last tendril of red hair caught into place. The great emerald chain caught the light.

Lucy said tremulously, "Madam, you are so fair."

"Thank you, Lucy," said Katryn. Lucy went ahead, backing about as she always did, to open the door. Katryn took Tom Seymour's arm. "Forth to battle," he whispered; he was smiling. In the next room all her ladies curtsied low, peering out to make sure they were actually seeing their mistress on the arm of a new husband. She swept on and Anne came behind, and then six of the ladies, holding gowns up and stepping lightly, not looking at anything now but the back of Katryn's shimmering satin dress. Thus the procession started forth, first for the gallery, and then the banquet hall itself.

"Everyone is gathered in the gallery below, and I have apprised your crier," Tom Seymour said low. No one could hear, for Anne kept quite a distance behind them, and the ladies were behind Anne.

"I had no chance to speak before your women," he said. "Now heed me, and listen close. They will say, you know, that we are founding a rival house, like the Tudors themselves, when a Tudor wedded with Henry V's widow, thus founding their line, by marrying a son with a Beaufort."

"Aye," said Katryn, although she had not truly thought of it. Her eyes gleamed for a moment. It was possible!

"Your eyes gleam gold like a usurer's," he said. "Only these are higher stakes than you ever played before, and put it out of your mind. We are not founding a rival house."

"Aye, my lord," said Katryn meekly.

"They will say, in my immense ambition I've snatched you as wife, for power, prestige, and all the monies you are accused of piling in your coffers."

Katryn held her head high.

"They will be jealous of your beauty, for now at thirty-three, you are more fair than I have ever seen you."

"Thank you, sweetheart," she said, giving him a dazzling smile. They were going down the steps.

"Do you think you can combat all that?"

"Certainly," said Katryn.

"Spoke like a true Border wench," he said, and it made Katryn think of her uncle. I wish he were here, she thought, but I never saw him again, for he died that very winter, two years ago. Two years—how fast they fled. But I wish he were here, among these throngs of people who are staring at us now—aye, staring; they are hardly even talking. She stepped down the last step, her ladies grouped behind her. The trumpets blew. Katryn's crier, at the foot, called out, "The Queen's Grace!"

Katryn inclined her head, men and women bowed long, low. At the end of the room, with back to the empty fireplace, standing where his father used to stand, a small figure waited.

Katryn made her way through the aisle left open for her, passing quickly along the bent heads and curtsying women. Edward came forward.

Katryn curtsied. Edward reached out his arms. "My lady mother," he said joyously. "My lady mother!"

19

The wind was light and could not have suited his purpose better, Tom Seymour thought. He slipped one arm through the heavy rat-lines, adjusted the glass, and swayed thus for a moment high in the shrouds, relishing the clean, wet, salt air, and the gentle motion of the *Salamander*'s lift and fall as she swam lazily toward the shore line.

The ship lay almost at the mouth of the river Esk, and astern her moved, just as majestic, twelve more white-sailed ships, gun ports already open, and the guns run out.

This light wind should soon dispel the morning mist, Tom Seymour thought. The Scottish army was to his right, outnumbering Ned's forces two to one. And the Scots had already begun their pre-dawn attack. Moving in closer, the fleet maneuvered as the morning lightened. There were the marshes to the right of the Scots, and here he was, in considerable force to their left. Visibility was good now, and the range nigh perfect. He gave the order to commence firing.

Then he gave the order for his boat to be lowered. He was leading the landing parties himself. The Scots would find themselves not only between the sea and the guns of the English fleet and Ned's land forces but, as Tom Seymour said, "We shall be ready with boats, and escort aboard all those who can pay ransom, to partake of English hospitality. After their efforts on the battlefield, the Scots should be grateful for our forethought."

The battle of Pinkie did not last long. And by evening, the English fleet was at the mouth of the Firth of Forth, and by morning of the next day, September eleventh, it was riding peacefully at anchor, its guns commanding the seaport town of Leith. Ned, having marched into Leith from the south, came aboard the *Salamander* for breakfast. "You did well, Tom," he said, wiping his mouth, and reaching for wine. "But I want you to go back. You have the appointment of lieutenant general of the south parts, during my absence." Ned was thinking aloud. "It may be a month before I return."

Tom Seymour did not arrive in London until the twenty-first of the month. By that time Katryn had been in the city for three weeks.

London was bustling. The summoning writs to Parliament had been issued in September; a great many town mansions were being readied and a great number were already occupied. None bustled like Seymour Place.

The news of victory in Scotland had arrived nine days before, and Katryn knew that her husband would be home as soon as the ship *Salamander* breasted the last billow between Leith and Southampton, for it was the policy of the two brothers not to leave England long at the same time. She knew Tom Seymour had been appointed lieutenant general during Ned's absence.

He had been gone six weeks. Katryn had spent her time moving from one manor house or palace to the other, interspersed with flying trips to London to see how the painting and redecorating of Seymour Place was coming along. The introduction of her household into a wholly male establishment presented problems. But now even the escutcheons on the great stairway were gilded bright and scarlet; the whole front wing and down to the gallery had been commandeered for her ladies, with Elizabeth's big pretty room last, nearest to the gallery. And on the first of September, when Katryn arrived from Hanworth with her train, and baggage carts piled with feather beds and all manner of hangings, the finishing touches could be put to the rooms before their lord arrived home.

He would be pleased with his principal London dwelling place, she was sure. The chamber where the lords of the council met was newly painted; the carved chairs boasted a cushion in each seat; escutcheoned screens stood at each side of the fireplace, and the sideboard groaned with plate, so the lord of the council could find refreshment easily.

The galleries were beautiful, Lucy thought. The window seats were newly cushioned. The September sun flooded the long room. Lucy said, "This will be the court, madam, with your Grace here."

410

Katryn nodded, absently. Ned's wife, the Duchess of Somerset had just left; she had come to call. Katryn knew she had been fiercely jealous of Katryn's new chamber of state, with her golden chair with the red-tasseled fittings, and by the sight of the Princess Elizabeth, and little Jane Grey, the fourth in line, and all the ladies, including Anne and Kate Willoughby. Her eyes had snapped, and she had talked endlessly of the wonders that Somerset House was going to incorporate, and then—well, then it would be plain which was London's most important household.

Toying with her scarf, Katryn went over to the window, which looked out upon the court. The Duchess was climbing into her carriage. She was as unwieldy as the vehicle, and Katryn wondered, with a sharp twist in her heart, if the Duchess was again pregnant.

Four days passed. On Sunday, Katryn's chaplains each preached a sermon, and most of the titled Londoners attended. The chapel at Seymour Place, once the residence of the Bishops of Durham, was justly famous and beautiful. After the service Katryn entertained. The Duchess didn't come; Katryn knew she was sitting alone. It is going to be easy, Katryn thought, to wrest the court from under the Duchess; she is so very dull. Moreover, Ned had turned fanatically somber. Previously a ruthless and greedy gambler, he had forsworn it. He had recently forbidden dueling; he frowned upon the dance. When Katryn thought of her Tom Seymour with his drawling wit, she knew which man the court would seek out. It was going to be no surprise to her that the privy council would meet mostly at Seymour Place, or that it would be here that visiting envoys and nobility would come; even the divines had more respect for Dr. Parkhurst and Dr. Coverdale than they did for Ned's chaplains.

Katryn went to her own privy chamber. From the virginals in the corner by the window came a cascade of sound as Elizabeth sat playing. Katryn picked up her pen. When Elizabeth paused a moment, Katryn said, "I am going to write to your sister, the Lady Mary. She is at Grafton; she just writ. We must make it clear to her that in London we should always be happy to have her with us, with a chamber set aside."

Elizabeth nodded, and then realized she should say something. "Aye, madam," she said dreamily, looking out the window.

"Elizabeth," Katryn said, "I know what girls your age think about;

dreams and nonsense. But truly, you must always be kind to your sister Mary, for one never knows."

Elizabeth looked up from the keys. Kate Willoughby, who as a widow had gratefully accepted Katryn's invitation to join her, smiled a little.

"The young resent practical advice, madam," she said. "They think it loses them honesty of some sort."

"The young have much to learn," Katryn said. "You are a princess, Elizabeth, and almost fourteen. Heed me, and practice kindness and courtesy to all, especially your older sister. Someday you may remember what I say, and be glad you obeyed."

Two more days passed. It isn't possible, Katryn thought, that all of September will see me without my lord. Worry intruded. A September storm blew down, and after it a day of fog. It was the twenty-second of September; on a night still foggy, Tom Seymour came riding home.

They had supper together before a bright fire, he in his woolen dressing gown, having gratefully doffed his wet clothes. Flushed with excitement and happiness, Katryn listened while he recounted the adventures of the brief battle and the voyage. Between watching him as he ate, and laughing at his tales, she was conscious of nothing but joy at having him home; even though, as he said, "I shall not see thee as much as I should wish, till Ned comes home."

"The privy council can meet here, my lord!"

"Aye, sweetheart, but I must make a trip to Wales. And then I must see Edward every day; in fact I must spend a good deal of time with the court."

Edward was at Greenwich. "Why cannot I come?" Katryn asked.

"Because the Duchess is with him, and—"

"I shan't quarrel with her, my lord!"

"You cannot come, sweetheart," he said. "The two of you cannot be in the same palace without causing trouble—who precedes the other, et cetera." He waved his big hand.

Katryn clenched her hands. She was about to speak. Tom Seymour got to his feet and took hold of both clenched fists. "Best save your strength, Katryn, don't waste it in protest." Katryn looked up at his face. His eyes were deep glittering blue. "I mean," he said, "I've been away a long time."

Ned came back to London on the eighth of October, and so the following day Tom Seymour returned to Seymour Place from Greenwich. Parliament convened, the days grew shorter and colder, and the fall winds had a sudden sharp bite to them, as if to warn of winter's approach.

Ned had not found the little Queen of Scots. She had been spirited away to a lonely castle and Ned had been helpless to discover her whereabouts; the Scottish lords dickered, and accepted money, but their little Queen still rested in her unknown hideaway. It made Katryn's head seethe with plans, for she had it in her mind that Edward should marry with the little Jane Grey.

Tom Seymour laughed when she confessed her plan. "She's not healthy enough, sweet," he said. "True, I wanted her under our roof and under our care, for she's such a little thing and half afraid of her parents, and I know very well she'd be a pawn to any strong man." He was thinking of Dudley. "For instance, Dudley has a number of sons; he would like one of them to marry her. Then—the crown."

"The crown?" Katryn asked, incredulous.

"Both Mary and Elizabeth could be passed over, on the grounds of illegitimacy, by an unscrupulous man with an army at his back. Oh, my God, darling, do you ever read history?"

"Of course," said Katryn.

He laughed. "Well, the union of the two crowns, Scotland and England, is practical. But more than that, Katryn, I very much doubt if Jane Grey could ever bear a child."

Katryn lowered her eyes. Was there pity for Jane Grey in his tones, or half-spoken contempt for a woman who couldn't fulfill her natural duties? Katryn suddenly felt sick.

"Abandon the little Jane as queen," he said.

Katryn hardly heard him. She went over to the sideboard and poured herself a cup of brandy. Tom Seymour looked slightly surprised. Recklessly Katryn gulped a big gulp. She choked.

He burst out laughing. He doesn't understand I'm undone, she thought. Her stomach burned. He had stopped laughing and was regarding her, and suddenly she thought, Oh, he is so handsome; I love him so much, if I could only have his son! He had risen and was coming toward her, a puzzled look on his face. What had he said before? Dudley has a number of sons.

"You should have a number of sons!" she burst out.

He gathered her close. Over her head, he said, "God forbid, sweetheart. God forbid." He squeezed her tight. "I want you just as you are."

"No, you do not," sobbed Katryn.

"Indeed I do," he said. "If you get pregnant I shall be extremely annoyed. I shall send you to my gloomy castle in Wales, and disport myself here in London with the ladies."

"No, you wouldn't," cried Katryn. "I know you. You wouldn't."

"But I don't want children," he said positively.

She could not mistake the sincerity in his voice. She raised her head and dried her tears, wiping them away with the back of her hand, to see him clear. He meant it. Was it possible? All men wanted children, especially men in high places. But he didn't care!

"You keep battering yourself against the stone; you keep wanting much; you cannot accept nay." He spoke quietly, leaning his elbow on the mantel.

Katryn's head was swimming. His image clouded and grew sharp. I love him so much, she thought dimly; if only I could have his child!

November began cold and wet. It rained unceasingly and so hard it was impossible to go abroad in the streets without acute discomfort. Nonetheless Seymour Place glittered, from the rain-whipped flags flying from its turrets to the glorious assembly of personages who went in and out its great carved doors—the prettiest women in London, Katryn thought, and the handsomest and most exciting men. The wines that flowed were as sun-warmed and sparkling as Kate Willoughby's black eyes, as hearty as Will Herbert's laugh. The Londoners gathered outside its walls en masse, it seemed, for here was a spectacle right within the city. From the Lord Mayor to the Lord Protector, from the princesses to the Queen, and to the Lord Admiral himself on whose wide shoulders adventure sat as plain as a signal. It was a better show than the Bear Gardens.

On the occasion of Katryn's birthday, she and Tom Seymour entertained at a banquet. "We should celebrate," he said, "now that you begin your thirty-fifth year."

Katryn said, "Why, I am only thirty-four!"

He laughed. "That's what I said."

"I don't like that way of putting it," Katryn said. "If the ladies hear you say that, and then add a year, they'll ha' me thirty-six, at least!"

"I see," he said gravely. "It is true that ladies' arithmetic has always baffled me a bit. If I were a shopkeeper, I'd go mad."

His grin is so engaging, she thought; he looks just like a little boy sometimes, when he's amused. If I only—

He leaned down to kiss her good-by. "Stop thinking," he said. "I can hear the winches turning."

Katryn's brow puckered. Ship talk, she thought, but he was gone.

The banquet was a great success. The next day in chapel, Katryn hardly looked at her prayer book and hardly heard the sermon. I am so fortunate, she thought. In the nine months since Henry's death, much has been accomplished. Even our much too hasty marriage—it was plain that the great mass of Londoners, and even the court, thought it thrilling and romantic. Jealousy, of course, always abounds, but the city, my city, still loves me as much as I love it. I should show my thanks. For a week, I shall make it known through my chaplains and criers, no one hungry will be turned away from Seymour Place, and in the mornings I shall hear petitions from the deserving.

The next day, Bess Bourchier Parr with her two youngest children arrived as a petitioner, she said, casting herself down before Katryn, who sat in her chair of state.

"Your brother has cast me out, madam!"

Katryn motioned to Kate Willoughby to take Bess away. She could smell the heavy odor of too much wine. During the next hour Katryn had difficulty keeping her mind on the favors asked, and when the last poor widow was given material for a decent shroud for her husband, Katryn rose. Now for Bess.

"My lord the marquis," said Bess, struggling with her husband's new title, "has divorced me, cast out my children, branded them as bastards, and wed another!"

Katryn looked at the children. The little girl—she was three—was sucking at her fingers. A black-haired boy of four stood sturdily silent.

"I'll take the children, Bess," Katryn said, "and thee."

She knew that Will Parr had probably gone recklessly through Bess's fortune. She said, "You should not have come as a petitioner!"

"What else am I, madam?" Bess asked.

At least, thought Katryn, you ha' borne four healthy children.

It was the twenty-fourth of November, a cold sleety night. Tom Seymour came home as wet and cold as the weather. "I'd like supper before the fire, in my own room," he said. "Please join me."

"But I had planned—" Katryn began.

"Unplan," he said shortly.

What is amiss? she thought. He looks annoyed and angry. She thrust back a sharp swirl of anger herself. He had spoke so sharply! "Unplan," he had said. Katryn tapped her foot as she gave orders to the groom of the chamber.

When she came into the room, the table was laid and he was drinking wine. He stood with his back to the fire; when he saw her, he dismissed the two servants in the room with a wave of his hand.

As the door closed, he said, "I'm annoyed because I have to go to sea. Ned wants two lonely northern Scottish castles taken by fleet action; he hopes to find the little Queen. The reason I am annoyed is that our informants tell us she is resident in neither of them. It's a waste of my time and money and men."

Katryn blurted the first words that came into her head. "But why you, my lord?"

He frowned. "Why not I? A December voyage north takes a fairly experienced man, unless we expect to lose a couple of ships."

"When," asked Katryn in a small voice, "do you sail?"

"As soon as possible. But there is no need to fret. Only you had better speak softly tonight; I'm as cross as a bear. And mayhap you had better come kiss me; you can always fix anything with your sweet kisses." He sent her a smile.

Katryn stood stiff. "It's not my fault Ned is sending you on a voyage! Blame your own brother!"

Tom Seymour kept the smile on his mouth, but his eyes darkened. "Ah," he said. Then, "I'm hungry."

It was Katryn's habit to serve him when they ate alone. She tried to push aside her sudden reluctance to do so; she wasn't hungry, and she wanted some wine too. Carelessly she piled some meat on his plate, and set it down. Then she helped herself to wine. Tom Seymour sat down.

"If we're not careful," he observed, as he buttered his bread, "we're going to have that quarrel I warned you about."

Katryn tossed her head. "Oh," she said. Then her mind turned to Bess. She sat down opposite him, and began to tell him of the morning's events.

Tom Seymour said, "Is Will's new wife—and I use that word with some reservation—is she the Cobham girl?"

"Aye," said Katryn. "What reservations do you have?"

He raised an eyebrow, and didn't answer.

"Has she been in your bed, my lord?" Katryn inquired icily.

Tom Seymour laid down his knife. "Tonight I want no words on your part about my previous actions, whatever they might have been, and no words anent my brother or my brother's wife, who, by the way, is expecting another child."

Katryn turned pale. Was that a taunt?

"Eat," he said. "It may improve your temper."

"My temper?" echoed Katryn. "It's you who confessed to temper!" Angrily she picked up a piece of fowl. It was hot. She swore. Then she said, "So I asked poor Bess to stay here, and live with me."

His next words were completely unexpected, and they were delivered coldly. "I won't have her here, Katryn. I refuse to give shelter to a female winebibber; she deserves nothing at our hands."

Katryn stammered incredulously, "But I've already offered—nay, promised her—the protection of my roof!"

"Disabuse her then," he said, "or I will. I won't have her here."

"I won't be ordered about," she cried. "Aye, I won't be! And the reason you won't have her here is because—"

He interrupted. "I called her a female winebibber, but I was being polite. Your brother is right; none of those children are his. She's an incontinent whore, and I will not have her here, and that is final. I know her ilk."

"Since she's been your mistress, I'm sure you do," Katryn cried. "Mayhap the children are yours!"

He looked bored. "Mayhap," he said. "You may keep the children." Now he looked at her hard. "You cannot have everything from life, Katryn."

He means children, she thought. "I can!" She got to her feet and turned her back.

Behind her he pushed back his chair. "There is a certain amount of ruthlessness in you. Am I supposed to bow down before it?"

"I want to be able to have whom I wish under my own roof! Yesterday you told Dr. Coverdale to preach no more fiery Anabaptist sermons! And he is *my* chaplain!"

"He may not so preach in my house."

"I don't need to stay here! It *is* your house; you've said it. But I've many houses! And in them Master Coverdale can preach as he wishes —aye, and Bess can come! And you, you—" Katryn looked at the big bed. "You can sleep alone!"

"Is that your final word?"

"Aye. I leave!"

He smiled. But Katryn backed away. "I expect," he said, moving toward her, "that all this would have reduced poor Lord Latimer to complete subjection?"

"I didn't need—"

"I see. He was always fairly passive. You even took the helm with Henry, and then extricated yourself neatly. But you won your point; did you not? Even with the King?"

"Aye," said Katryn defiantly. "And I'm not afraid of you!"

"You needn't be," he said. "I judge women fairly well. You'll like this lesson. It's late in coming, I'm sure; for sixteen years you've been overgorged, badly spoiled, like my pet falcon."

Katryn, near the door, tried to reach it. But she felt his fingers close over her arm like steel, and with almost studied violence he spun her around to face him.

"Like my pet falcon," he repeated.

"Don't you dare mock me," she cried. "Let me go! I don't want to stay here with you! I want to go back to one of my own houses, where I can be happy!"

His arms closed around her. His hand covered her eyes. His voice was lazy. "Poor little bird," he said, against her mouth. "We'll put the hood on you now, shivery and naked under your robe."

Katryn tried to struggle, to cry out. I am going to faint, she thought wildly, I cannot breathe. The mocking, brutal beast! His hand no longer covered her eyes, but she kept them tight, tight shut.

She wakened early in the dawn. Very early, she thought dimly, because there was still no sound in these parts of the great house. But the bed curtains were not drawn, and the room showed faintly gray. Beside her, one arm still across her, Tom Seymour slept.

In the still, dark room, Katryn felt the blood in her cheeks. If he wakens, I'll never be able to meet his eyes.

Tom Seymour stirred. He was awake. Katryn shut her eyes. But he isn't fooled, she thought, for he is turning me to face him. Her eyes flew open. Unaccountably, she thought, I am giving him a smile, the unrepentant beast.

"Do you love me?" he was saying sleepily.

"Aye," said Katryn, "but, sweetheart, it's almost dawn."

"I've no meeting." He yawned, and kissed her throat, and settled himself comfortably. "It's Sunday," he said. "Go to sleep, kitten, go to sleep."

On the thirteenth of December, Tom Seymour had been gone ten days. Restless and worried, Katryn decided to ride down to Chelsea with a number of her train, to stay only overnight and to bring back carts full of Christmas greens for decorating the great house. Riding back to London the next day, in the cold but clear air, she thought all had benefited by the brief excursion, but she was glad to be back in London again, where the news could reach her fastest. The next day it began to snow.

The snow fell thick, and the winds increased in volume. The winds truly howled, she thought, pacing the floor before her fire. In her mind was the picture of a sailing ship far far to the north, struggling close-hauled against the might of a North Atlantic storm. Ice would cover the bulwarks; shining ice would form on the rigging, and surely the timbers, oaken though they were, would groan as the green tons of icy sea water landed with a roar on the slanting decks. And through this picture she could hear his voice: "Never worry, I am a good sailor, I have a fine crew and a fine ship."

The next day was the fifteenth, and by afternoon the sun was shining on the white world outside. Katryn felt much better. Lucy was lacing her. Katryn said, "That's too tight, Lucy, on my breasts."

She looked at herself. "I wonder if I'm gaining weight?" But her waist looked as tiny as always. "It wouldn't do for me to be fat by the time my lord reaches home. And I hope, Lucy—oh, I hope it's before Christmas!"

But it was not. And no word came from Tom Seymour. Christmas passed, and Katryn tried to make it fine for everyone else. She entertained only family and friends. But with all my ladies, and Will and Anne, and Will Parr and his new wife, and Cat Knyvet and her husband, there must be a hundred people here tonight, Katryn thought, and I all alone.

During Dr. Parkhurst's Christmas Eve sermon, she alternately prayed for Tom Seymour's safety and hoped fervently he had not just taken possession of a Scottish castle full of pretty women, of course! After a month at sea, she thought, and plenty of wine, or that awful smoky liquid my father used to drink—I won't think of it, I won't! I'll pray. Tom Seymour's dark face floated before her eyes. If he could hear me, she thought, he'd say, "Mayhap you're confusing your maker, Katryn." Oh, she thought, if only he were home!

The day after Christmas, couriers arrived from Scotland. The two Scottish castles of Arbroath and Dundee had been taken by fleet action, but the little Scottish Queen had been resident in neither. The Lord Admiral was on his way home.

The weather was cold and mean, but there were no more storms. On New Year's Day, Tom Seymour landed in England and, riding hard, reached Seymour Place at nine o'clock in the evening. Katryn tried not to cry. She rubbed her cheek against his leather coat. He had brought a New Year's present, a beautiful Scottish cairngorm swinging on an intricate silver chain.

"Thank you, my lord," Katryn whispered, "but all I wanted was thee." And later that night, just before she went to sleep, she realized that it was the first day of the new year. It will be the very best in my whole life.

By the fifteenth of January she was sure that it would be, that her sleepy prediction had been right. She counted carefully. She must have conceived one of the nights in November before he had left.

But because it mattered so much, she confessed to no one that she thought she was with child. She waited two more weeks, and on the first of February, Meg, lacing her, said, "Madam, you've gained weight."

"Not much," said Katryn equably. Oh, I'm so proud, she thought; I'm almost dizzy with it. "Not so much, Meg," she said, "considering I warrant it's been two months, now."

Meg threw up her hands. "Madam!" she cried. "Oh, madam!"

Katryn's eyes sparkled. "I feel so smug, Meg," she said. "But not a word, wench. Not a word. Till I tell my lord."

But how to do it? she wondered. What would he say? That night she kept eying him covertly as he ate. She started to speak a hundred times, then fell silent.

Finally she said, "Mayhap you'll have to send me to that gloomy castle in Wales." She looked at him expectantly.

"What?" he asked.

He's forgotten he said it, she thought. "Nothing," she said, feebly.

"What are you talking about?" he asked. "What's amiss, Katryn? You've been fidgeting and squirming. Eat your supper; it's good."

"I know it," said Katryn tearfully. "I ordered it special for you."

Puzzled, he looked at her. "Now what have I said?"

"I warrant you never remember what you do say to me!"

"I never said I'd take you to Wales. And how do you know I'm going next week?"

"Oh," cried Katryn. "you said it in jest! That you'd send me to your castle in Wales if I—" She stopped.

"If you what?" he prodded. But she could see he was searching his memory, and suddenly he pushed back his chair. "Oh, God!" he said.

There was silence. Katryn swallowed. "Aren't you glad?" she whispered. "I am."

Tom Seymour rose. He came to her side of the table, and Katryn averted her face. "You swore," she said.

He leaned down and lifted her to her feet. "I seem to be guilty on all counts," he said, and he put his arms around her and tipped her head up with his hand under her chin. Through her tears her eyes were almost pure gold.

"I'm so happy," said Katryn. "Please be happy too!"

20

On the fifteenth of March, at seven-thirty, Tom Seymour requested the Lady Trywhit to attend him in his study. When Lucy entered the room, it was almost dark; the candles were burning and Tom Seymour looked up from the papers before him and rose. He told Lucy to take the chair on the other side of the flat desk.

Lucy seemed nervous and he tried to calm her a bit. "I have an early meeting here," he said, "and what I have to say, Lucy, will not be long in the saying. First, I have asked Dr. Huicke, of whom her Highness is so fond and in whom she has much faith, to reside here with us. You are to tell her Highness that we need a resident physician here, in any case." Lucy's eyes were fixed upon him with a certain intensity.

"Her Highness is very happy," she said, almost as though she found it hard to believe. Lucy looked at the man who was responsible, not only for her happiness but for her condition.

Tom Seymour said slowly, "No man, Lucy, could be happier or prouder of her Grace's expecting than I."

Lucy nodded. Then she remembered she should answer. "I'm sure that is so, my lord."

"Indeed, it is," he said forcefully, and Lucy eyed him with some disquiet. He was so overpowering to be alone with, Lucy thought, twisting her fingers together.

"And that damned carriage," he was saying.

Lucy jumped. Her mistress had just had made an open carriage, much daintier and more impressive than the closed carriage the Duchess of Somerset was accustomed to go about in.

"I don't know whether to forbid her the use of it or not," he said. "I have replaced the driver with a man I can trust, and the horses are both gentle and easily controlled. But I can just see it overturned on the street!" He paced back to the fire and swung around to face Lucy, who hastily dropped her eyes.

"Forbid her Highness the carriage?" she faltered.

"Well, for a few weeks more, mayhap, she can use it. But never, Lucy, in bad weather. Never! And never in crowded streets, or the narrow ones. I think mayhap I'll obviate the whole question." Lucy's eyes grew wide. Was he going to destroy the carriage? "I shall send her Grace down to the country."

"Oh, prithee, my lord," Katryn cried. "don't! Don't send me away! Besides," she said, "I have so much to do, and we are giving two parties next week, and think on all that must be bought for sewing on the baby's wardrobe, to say naught of mine! And I don't want to leave you!"

"Jesus!" Tom Seymour muttered.

"I am young and strong," Katryn cried. "And I shan't use the carriage; I'll walk!"

"Walk?" he said, looking appalled. "Walk? In this weather?"

"Aye," cried Katryn. "What's wrong with walking?" She jumped to her feet and began to pace back and forth.

"I wish to God you'd sit down." He sank down onto the bench himself and heaved a long sigh. Katryn almost giggled. He's the one who needs to sit, she thought. I'll have to divert him. "I asked Anne and Will to sup with us this eve," she said, "and stay and play whist. You'll enjoy that after your long day, and I promise I shan't stir from the house this day. I have much to do, and it's beginning to rain, so I shan't go out and you can rest assured nothing could hap."

He stood and leaned down to kiss her. "I'll see thee at seven, sweet," he said. But at the door he paused. "But in June—and don't bother to remonstrate—you're going to Sudeley."

June, thought Katryn, but that gives me two months. And I truly should go to Sudeley, for I know he wants the baby born there, and anyway, he'd not let me stay in London during the summer because of the sickness and plague. I shouldn't travel much after June, either. The rain spattered against the windows. Katryn went over and looked out. The lords of the privy council were arriving. She looked longingly into the court. But she had promised. I'll not go today, she thought, but tomorrow I shall. I can smell April in the air! Humming happily, she picked up her shawl and started down the hall to waken Elizabeth, and bid her good morning.

Off Tom Seymour's study was a small closet, the Bishop's retreat, which Katryn had redecorated as a small private dining room. There, at seven that night, Katryn and Anne sat down to supper with their husbands.

"Eat, Will," Tom Seymour said, "and the whist should take your mind off our troubles."

Katryn frowned. "What troubles?"

Tom Seymour shook his head at her. But Will suddenly said, laying down his knife, "By God, Tom, today I told Ned I would plough up my parklands afore I paid any such tax! And further, I told him he was a traitor to his kind! And wait until Katryn hears of the proposed two-pence-a-head tax on sheep."

"Two pence a head?" she whispered incredulously. "Why, that would—that would—I won't pay it!"

Tom Seymour suddenly chuckled. "I think we're going to avoid that, Will, for truth is I told Ned myself I wouldn't pay it. But hark to my sweet wife. Come, now, I want to be free of all that for a while. Let's eat, let's drink." He raised his glass.

"As long as we don't drink to Ned," Will muttered, and the faintest frown went over Tom Seymour's face. Then he applied himself to his food.

But Katryn knew he was worried. There was unrest in the city, and a great deal of vandalism, especially against the churches; and there were many respectable people who thought Ned Seymour responsible since he endorsed the destruction of imagery.

And then, the night of Katryn's party, two of the lords of the council sent word they were not attending. She discovered the reason.

"They'll not come because Ned is coming," she said to her husband. "And do you know why? Ned has removed the celebrated carving, the "Dance of Death," from St. Paul's and is installing it in his own new house!" She couldn't believe it.

Tom Seymour nodded. "I know," he said. "Gardiner was arrested today."

"Gardiner?" she breathed. A name from the past. "What has he done?"

Tom Seymour lifted his shoulders. "He was not in a position to do any real harm," he said, "for all his guile. But Ned seems to be under great strain. His is a terrible task, Katryn."

"So much of a strain that he steals from St. Paul's?" Katryn cried.

Tom Seymour said, "Things are proceeding poorly with the French, with the Scots. You know how Ned feels about the enclosures. He's going to forbid them. What Will Herbert said last night, a great many people are saying—he is a traitor to his kind." He rubbed his chin. "I said to him today, Ned, you have an insurmountable task. You should permit me to be the governor of Edward's person, and we should try to act more in concert. He looked"—Tom Seymour paused—"he looked at me as though I'd laid a knife at his throat. I was for a moment angry! 'You do not suspect, my dear brother,' I said, 'that I have designs on Edward's life!'"

"He doesn't let me see Edward," Katryn said. "He doesn't let Elizabeth see him. He holds him like a prisoner!"

"Yesterday I gave the poor little King some money. He told me he had no money at all, not even to tip his servants. Ned was black with anger. It is a damned curious situation, Katryn. Ned said to me in council meeting, today, that I had disagreed with him openly seventeen times. Katryn, he had counted, and kept tally!"

"Ned reminds me," said Katryn furiously, "of Richard the Third!"

Tom Seymour shook his head at her. "Richard was next in line to the throne. It availed him a great deal to do away with his nephews. Ned has not the shadow of a claim on England's throne. That is why the fight is so bitter and that is why many want him to be no longer regent; there can be a scramble for the regency; all may hunt it. Truthfully, the most pressing danger is Edward's health."

"They will never get Elizabeth from me," said Katryn sturdily. "Nay, nor little Jane either!"

Tom Seymour frowned deeply. She had no complete knowledge of the workings of the political scene, and it was no time to tell her. He said mildly, "These are not times to think with the heart, my love. Deviousness is the order of the day."

"I can meet that too!"

"If one could foresee how they will strike—" He broke off. "We must proceed on our way, Katryn, the best way we know how, with honor."

Katryn looked over at him. He was more serious than she had ever seen him. She said, "I've only two more weeks here with thee, and I do not want to go." For a moment she felt fear. She did not want to go! To leave him! There were many who wanted his life. Many!

"I sense you're fretting," he said. "Let me make it quite clear. There is no danger to me; more than half the council stand solidly behind me. As for Dudley and his minions, I go well armed."

"If they could strike betwixt you and Ned," Katryn said, "then—"

He raised an eyebrow. "A house divided? Well, I don't think Ned is so afraid of me or my friends that he would sign my death warrant. But you are right. That is what is being attempted. Distrust betwixt us is being attempted in sundry ways."

No one knew exactly who started the rumor. No one knew from whose lips it first came. But it struck Katryn with the full force of its slander and calumny, for it took the truth and twisted it vilely. It was Anne who laid it before her. And it was at Elizabeth that it struck the cruelest blow.

"They say," Anne said very low, even though she and Katryn were alone, "that Bess is mad in love. They say she is already Tom's mistress! They say she will never be fit to sit on the throne; that she is like to her mother! They say Tom has seduced her under your very eyes! They say all manner of vile things! They say he enters her room every morning, even when she is still in bed!"

Katryn said woodenly, "There is a washroom Tom fixed up at the end of the hall, just where the gallery begins. He passes Elizabeth's door, for hers is at the end." She wet her lips. "It is true that once, mayhap twice, he was without me, for usually, Anne, we go together to bid the princess a good morning. She is fond of both of us. And we always bid her a good morrow. But I remember once, a few weeks ago, he went in shirtsleeves and hose, and gave both Jane and Bess a spank while they were still in bed. You could hear them giggling. Mistress Ashley was with them, and she told me. There were maids in the room also."

Anne said, "This foul lie hits Bess hard. They keep repeating, like to her mother, the whore! She's like to her mother! Blood will tell."

"You do not need to tell me, I have heard it," Tom Seymour said. The anger he had first felt was past.

"But what shall we do?" Katryn cried.

"We cannot even deny it," he said, "for that would dignify a foul slander and somehow make it into fact. We will proceed as we always have. It is almost June. You are going to Sudeley. Elizabeth will have to go to Hatfield. Separated thus from my roof, the rumors will die out. My lips are sealed, Katryn. I cannot go about denying I have had some sport with a fourteen-year-old girl, who is your ward. But there are many who will deny it for us, take heart from that. No one, for instance could repeat it to Will without paying dear. But you and I and Bess—we shall have to ignore it. Dudley will not say this aloud, you know. I cannot accuse him of having started it; he will deny it, and say it is foul. I warned you, Katryn. I warned you."

"It is partly my fault," she cried. "Aye, it is! For I have always had difficulty in treating the princesses like princesses. Everyone— even Henry—used to say, you treat them just as if they were your own and your own family. I've not been careful enough!

Tom Seymour shook his head. "Nothing you could have done would spare or save Elizabeth. She is second in line to the throne. Her enemies will use every weapon. If she were not living here with you and me, it would be someone else. They are exceedingly fortunate in having me as a target also. You will have to tell her; that will be the hardest part, Katryn. And I have other news. Ned has taken over your royal manor of Fausterne, and given it to a minion of his. I pressed him today also for the jewels left you in Henry's will. He will not give them up."

Katryn's eyes gleamed. "I shall see Edward!"

Tom Seymour shook his head. "You cannot, Katryn; they would not permit you to see him." He said lazily, "My brother is wondrous hot in helping anyone, save me."

Katryn sat down suddenly on the edge of the bench, and Tom Seymour knelt beside her and hugged her.

"Oh, my sweetheart," he said. "Do not mind. We have plenty. And if we stand firm, they will cease the attacks sooner or later. I am going to send you to Sudeley. It is beautiful. There is an old story about Sudeley. The Botelers, who owned it, were accused of treason to the crown. Their lord suffered death and the castle became crown property. They say the Lord Boteler said, 'Ah, Sudeley. 'Tis thou who's the traitor, for being so beautiful to be so coveted.' "

Katryn cried, "And to give up Elizabeth!"

"Be brave," he whispered. "You are always so gallant. Remember you like the fight when the odds are the longest. And you will not have to give up Elizabeth permanently. Just till the baby is born. It gives a fine excuse; the rumor will die a natural death if Bess is not with you for a few months."

"I have only three," Katryn said.

"I want you to go to Sudeley before another ten days have passed," he said. She knew there was no arguing.

Katryn made ready to go. She called Elizabeth to her, and spoke with her privately. Katryn began slowly, hardening her heart.

"Yesterday," Katryn said, "I came into the room, and you were standing with my lord, close to him, and you had laid your hand on his arm."

Elizabeth's whole body stiffened. She gazed white-faced; her mouth drew down, and her eyes were like fire. Katryn saw she could not speak.

Poor child, Katryn thought. She is hardly grown, hardly wench yet. "Elizabeth," Katryn said, "you are not yet mature. So I must tell you plain. You are a princess, and it has always been difficult for me to think on that to the exclusion of all else. But you are a princess! And you must never, never, touch a man, even on the arm. There have been," Katryn said baldly, "evil things said of thee and my lord."

Elizabeth shivered. Her quick intelligence remembered her mother.

"My lord and I have talked long about this evil rumor that attacks your chastity and your very life."

"And his," Elizabeth said through her teeth.

Katryn thought, Ah, she does love him. No wonder; my husband is a young girl's ideal. She feels the first stirrings, and she thinks on him and what it must mean to him. She said strongly, "Elizabeth you are a princess. Someday you may be queen—aye, oftimes I feel inside you shall be queen! So we shall fight this, you and I, with our own weapons! We shall fight it, and fight it with pride. Hold your head high, and I shall tell you what we must do, and how you must deport yourself, and while you are away from me this summer, while my child is born, I shall even tell thee what to read, and what to wear. I do not go for ten days. During those days, we shall be seen close constantly. We shall be seen as the Queen's Grace and the Lady Elizabeth's Grace, the finest princess England ever had! And we shall treat with regal scorn those who would defame us." Katryn rose. It was almost time for services in the chapel. Elizabeth rose too. Out of long habit Elizabeth handed the Queen her prayer book, and her silken scarf for her head. Suddenly Katryn's eyes gleamed. "Hurry," she commanded.

At the top of the gallery steps, they stood together. Their ladies were behind. At the foot of the steps, the lords of the privy council were leaving, by ones and twos.

"Smile," Katryn whispered, as they began the descent.

Heads were uncovered quickly. Katryn and Elizabeth passed through. And within the sanctuary of the chapel, Dr. Parkhurst was waiting at the altar. Katryn paused before her pew. Her voice was sweetly clear.

"Master Parkhurst," she said. "It is our wish that today you preach on two thoughts which have occurred to us. That we should forgive our enemies, and that the Lord says, quite plain, 'Vengeance is mine!' "

On the ninth of June Elizabeth took her leave for Hatfield House, and it was now the morning of the tenth. Although yesterday's leave-taking of Elizabeth had been painful, Katryn had managed it with fine words. "I shall let you know immediately if I hear aught bad," she said, "and do all as I have commanded. And if we part without tears, I shall be very proud of both of us!"

Nevertheless Elizabeth clung to her. "God keep thee, madam," she mumbled. "And thy child."

Katryn swallowed, thinking of those words. Bess had such strength; she had hated to be apart from Katryn because she was to undergo the ordeal of childbirth. But now, alone for a moment in her bare room, for the hangings had already been put away, she was conscious of real sadness, almost worse than parting from Bess.

I have never been so happy as I have been here, she thought. Never in my whole life. And this deep sadness is that I am leaving my love. I cannot endure it! She gave a cry. I cannot!

Tom Seymour heard the cry. He loomed in the open door, coming quickly to her side. He took her arm.

"I cannot leave you," she cried.

"You are not leaving me," he said patiently. "I am taking you down."

"I know, I know. But then you will leave!"

"Sweetheart," he said. "Sweetheart, London is not safe in the summer for thee. And—"

She put her arms around him and sobbed. "I'll go," she said, "I'll go, as I promised. Oh, I don't know what is the matter with me!"

"You're having a baby," he said. "Come, sweetheart."

She looked around the room with tear-dimmed eyes. "I might never see this room again!"

Tom Seymour's eyes contracted, even the pupils. Then he said, "Why, if the house burns down, I'll build you a new one. As big as Ned's."

Katryn blinked back the tears. "Bigger," she whispered.

"Bigger," he said. "Now come. I'll carry thee."

Katryn put her arms around his neck. He was carrying her so easily, down the long gallery, down the steps, so that when he set her in her litter, she smiled brilliantly. "I shall love Sudeley, my lord," she said. "I'm sure I shall."

The Cotswold hills were golden with the light of sunset. The castle, its stone warmly yellow, caught the light. Sheep grazed on the rolling pastureland, and from the tower atop the chapel the castle bells rang out, welcoming its lord and lady.

"It's unearthly beautiful," Katryn said.

"It is yours, sweetheart," he said, "and the little knave's. Only though if he's like me, he'd rather be in your round little belly."

Katryn giggled. "It is that wondrous golden stone."

"Aye, and there is a special walled garden at the foot of the tower room where you shall be, and from that tower room you can see out over the hills. I shall think of thee, in the garden, in that room, when I am far away."

"But you will come in August," she said quickly.

"Aye," he said. "I will come in August."

I must be brave, she thought. I must. It is just that I can hardly bear to see him ride away.

"It is only six weeks," he said. "And they will go fast. Then I shall be here."

"If only you could stay," she cried. "If only we never had to go to London again! If only we could stay here, like my father stayed at Kendal!"

"We have all thought that, at times. To leave this mad world and to retreat." He sighed. "But it's not for us, I fear, Katryn. For a while, yes, but when the winter begins, you would think on London."

"I wouldn't," she said earnestly.

"One cannot leave the world behind," he said, "and most especially, you cannot."

"I'm not going to think about anything," Katryn said, "except that we shall sup together, alone, and you will be by me till tomorrow."

And later that night, wakeful, lying beside him, she found the disquiet that pricked her had disappeared. Of course six weeks would go fast! And how wonderful it was to lie here, so close. She rubbed his bare leg with her foot, and he stirred in his sleep and put one arm around her. Katryn sighed with content.

In the morning, before all the company, she was able to stand in the court and see him mount and ride away. The June day was dawning with a rosy light. I will be happy here, she thought. I will be happy, and partly because he loves Sudeley and I am where he wants me to be. I truly feel very well! I have not been sick one single day. And there is so much to do!

Katryn had been attended in her travel to Sudeley by a train of one hundred and twenty-five, and as June gave way to the first week of July, each day of summer seemed more perfect than the last. Katryn found herself thinking of the past.

It's because I'm not so active as usual, she thought, reclining in her cushioned chair in the garden. The roses were blooming and the sweet scent of stock hung heavy. She thought of Gainsborough. The memory of Lord Borough was dimmed with time; it was years and years ago—nineteen, almost. I was so young. She tried to recapture her feeling for him, but it eluded her. Mayhap I thought of him as a father; I hope I made him happy, for we were wed but a short six months afore he died. She thought of Lord Latimer, and her years at Snape Hall.

But there is naught I would undo, naught that I could undo, for all that my lord thinks he should have seized me by force that night so many years ago in the garden at New Hall. The love I bear him now, I should not have been capable of it then and—it is very complicated—and we are fortunate that, all these years we knew each other, at least we knew that the other was there. And we have so much time still.

She thought of Kendal. It rose before her, grim and gray, throwing its shadow against the green hills as black as the helm clouds of Westmorland. I'll probably never go back, she thought. This is my life now. Sudeley—and how beautiful it is. And yet, someday, perhaps this son I bear will go there, for it is his heritage, too. For this little knave of mine is going to inherit all I've struggled to get and have and keep! These vast spreading acres of Sudeley, all my manors and villages and pasturelands, even mayhap Kendal. And my lord, in but a few more years, should have an earldom to hand down to his son. And her son himself, being so endowed, would probably become a duke. The Duke of Kendal! Katryn thought. And he should marry with one of the Tudors, mayhap. Edward's children, or Mary's children; nothing less than royalty would be half good enough.

"Now this will be the day nursery, and the next room the night nursery," Katryn said. "And the tapestry that depicts the months of the year will be hung in here, and the chair of state with cloth of gold placed in here for me, and the little gilded bedstead, with the tester and curtains of crimson taffeta. It will be so pretty," Katryn exclaimed.

"As beautiful as though he were royal, madam," Lucy said proudly.

Katryn had walked into the night nursery. The cradle took her eye. It seemed impossible that in a few weeks there would actually be a head on that pillow and a little baby to tuck the satin quilt about. Katryn's eyes shone. "The bed for the nurse can go under the windows, and all these windows are to be hung with the heavy carpet against drafts."

She sighed. The days were flying past. The gentry from all about had been entertained, and there was a great deal of coming and going, couriers arrived and departed with letters and gifts. Tom Seymour sent down a parrot from London, and Katryn hung the cage in her privy chamber, and all the ladies were amused and delighted with the brightly colored bird. And if sunrise was beautiful from Sudeley's towers, then was sunset, lying golden on the hills, even lovelier. And each sundown brought the warm, waiting month of July nearer to its close.

On the first of August Tom Seymour came riding down to Sudeley. In the court, waiting with her ladies about her in their bright gowns, for she had seen him coming from afar, Katryn anticipated the sight of him; for though the days had truly gone by fast, yet it seemed so long since she had seen him!

He was so tanned! He's been to sea, she thought rapidly, and made him a little curtsy—the best I can manage without falling in a heap. She sent him a dazzling smile, while he took her hand.

They look so fair together, Lucy thought, even though she didn't quite approve of his lordship's drawing his wife into his arms. But all else did; even the grooms looked on in open approval.

"There is so much to say," Katryn whispered.

"Aye, except you look so well! That is the best thing you could say to me, sweetheart!" He surveyed her. "Your eyes shine, and your cheeks are pink, and you are a picture I couldn't wait to see."

"After you have a wash, we'll have supper together," Katryn said happily. Supper together—what sweet words. How supremely wonderful to have him here! It seemed as though the whole tempo of the great castle had changed with its lord home. When they were alone in her room, she clung to him. "I love you," she whispered. "And I have never been so happy."

The days proceeded, like heaven, Katryn thought. Sudeley was a world in itself, and Tom Seymour was assiduous in his care of it.

"It is my proudest possession," he said. "For my more than twenty years of labor, when I look at Sudeley, it is all worth it!"

He rose every morning before dawn, leaving her half asleep and warm and but drowsily conscious he had kissed her before he rose. Then he would ride out; as she had breakfast, she would watch him go from her windows. Every inch of the vast estate was inspected, from its rolling pastureland to its hunting preserves, its parklands, its villages. At dinner, he would be back in time to join her, except the days he went hunting.

"Nay, you must go," she said, "you love it so much." On those mornings she would be wakened by the baying of the hounds, as they scampered joyful and loud from their kennels out ahead of the horses, through the great castle gates.

He fixed up a farm cart with a seat and pillows. In this contraption he took her riding behind a plough mare. They jogged along slowly, with the picnic baskets piled in the back, over one of the grassy tracks beckoning into the hills.

After they had eaten, with the August sun high in the sky, Katryn lay on the blanket spread on the warm earth. Lying thus, close together, they would talk until Katryn dozed.

It was hard to believe that London existed. It was hard to believe it mattered that the little Queen of Scots had been safely transported to France. "I was at sea the three weeks of July, hailing every sail we saw, but it was useless," Tom Seymour said.

In July, too, he had come to grips with Ned. In front of the council Ned had accused him of suggesting that Edward should speak of his troubles to Parliament, or to the council, if he wished. Tom Seymour rose to his feet and asked Ned if it were not true that any English king had a right to come before Parliament. The lords of the council nodded their heads. They voted Tom Seymour an extra eight hundred pounds per annum. But Ned met the defeat with ill grace. And just before Tom had come to Sudeley, Ned's duchess had been delivered of another son. The child was named Edward.

"That's the third," Katryn said, open-mouthed. She lay back on the blanket. "Each time I think on it, I think Ned must be having delusions. To name all his sons after him! I wonder if he'll name the fourth one Ned?"

Tom Seymour frowned slightly.

"Speaking of Ned makes me think of London, though," Katryn said. "Now I think our child should be raised here at Sudeley, and all is ready, but in September, after you leave, I shall stay only till the end of October." She sighed, and she thought, Oh it is going to be wonderful to wear pretty clothes again! Until this moment I hadn't thought of it. But 'tis true, and next winter in London, she could be a wife again, too.

Tom Seymour said, "Your thoughts seem to have made a complete circle, by the expression on your face." He was lying on his stomach, his hand under his chin, looking down at her. "First you looked almost asleep and peaceful, and now you look as though you are planning a coup of some sort which will overthrow me entirely."

Katryn said, "I was thinking on the winter, and how wonderful it will be, and also to be able to love you."

"Oh," he said. "Well, I've managed." His eyes twinkled.

Katryn, with her eyes closed and her head on his shoulder, sighed a sigh of deep contentment.

"And," he said, "you have the most amazing philosophy. As though you are quite sure that every day will be exactly like this one—as good as this one, proceeding endlessly."

"I think it will be better," she said sleepily. "Tomorrow will be better."

He laughed. "Go to sleep, sweetheart. I'm sure you must be right. Tomorrow will be better."

And surely it will be better, she thought, because some tomorrow soon I shall have my child.

"You must not be disappointed if you have a daughter," he said. "I'm afraid you are so set on a knave."

"So are you," she said.

"Nay, I've tried not to be." In London he was endlessly the brunt of his friends' jesting. "I've never seen a man so proud of approaching paternity," Will Herbert had said. "That's all you talk of."

"I was afraid I was getting too old," Tom Seymour said.

" 'Tis true," Paget said. "After all, he's thirty-nine and his first legitimate child."

"I'm sure I'll have a son," Katryn said stubbornly. "And I've consulted with soothsayers."

He raised an eyebrow. "Well, Katryn, if you have a wench, she will probably confound plenty of mere men, starting with these soothsayers. Did you think of that?"

"No," said Katryn. She looked thoughtful. "She might," she conceded.

Tom Seymour chuckled. "Pity me with two of you, as you once said to me. I shall be clay in your hands, a mere shadow of a man."

Katryn sighed. "You would make a wonderful father for a wench," she said. "She would just adore you. But—" She glanced at him.

"I will never love anyone as much as I love you."

On the twenty-eighth of August Katryn felt an unfamiliar and yet familiar warning pain. She waited a few moments, a few minutes. The August night was warm and lovely; the windows were open. On the table before her was a big bowl of apples, the heavy candlelabra, and the deck of playing cards. She played one card thoughtfully, and uttered an exclamation of annoyance when Tom Seymour scooped it up. Then she said, "I think I am going to have my baby."

Tom Seymour dropped the cards. He started to get to his feet. "Where's Lucy?" he said. "Where's Huicke?"

Katryn said, "Marry, my lord, let's finish the game. I'm not a bit uncomfortable. What would Lucy do?" I shouldn't ha' told him, she thought; why did I? It'll be some hours yet. And I might as well play cards, and if I don't play with him, no one else is good enough to make the game worth the candle. She frowned. "I warrant I was mistaken," she said sweetly. "My game, my lord." She spread her hand.

"Damn," said Tom Seymour. "I didn't know you had that queen."

Katryn's eyes glittered. The pain crept slyly about her back, but it was almost nothing. Why, if I'd had to stay in one chamber like Jane, she thought, I'd have taken leave of my senses. Poor Jane. Katryn picked up the deck of cards and began to shuffle. "I used to win from Henry all the time," she said.

The night hours deepened. The stillness of August, lying heavy on the land, heavy as the harvest, was illuminated in the black skies by a brilliant moon. It shone in the windows of the room where Tom Seymour waited. Within Katryn's lying-in chamber Lucy cried, "Your Grace, pray don't get up again!"

Katryn slid to the edge of the bed. "I'm going behind my screen," she said with dignity. This wasn't as bad as they said. And it was perfectly natural. "Now if I had this same pain in my chest," she said to Lucy, "I'd think I was dying." She appeared again, walking slowly. Dr. Huicke restrained Lucy. "Let her Grace be," he said. "Let her Grace be."

Fifteen minutes later Katryn's baby was born. She lay still and quiet, but her eyes were bright. Then they closed and she dozed a little. I seem to be floating, she thought. Then suddenly she opened her eyes wide again. She spoke. "I had a knave, didn't I?"

Goodie jumped. All the ladies turned to look at the bed. Then Katryn realized that Tom Seymour knelt at the bedside. She smiled at him. Anne thought happily, how radiant she is! Tom Seymour slipped one arm around her shoulders. "Sweetheart," he whispered. "You—we—have the fairest daughter in the whole world. I give you my word. The fairest!"

Katryn sighed. Oh, well, she thought, I shall have more children, and the next one a son.

He said, "Her hair is auburn; her eyes are blue. You may not hold her yet," Tom Seymour said. "You will sleep. Huicke gave you a bit of opiate."

Katryn said, "I love you, my lord." Her eyes closed. She slept.

The first day of September was bright and sunny. Katryn woke and stirred. Everyone is so happy, she thought dreamily, and principally I and my lord. But Lucy's face was so—truly flushed with happiness, Katryn thought. Her eyes sparkled, Lucy's did.

"Oh, the baby, your Grace," Lucy said. "She is so fair, and perfectly formed!"

Katryn sat up. It is true, I have had my child! I have never been so happy! I have never felt like this! My own baby, and in a moment Anne will bring her, and for the first time in my life I will hold my own child in my arms. My heart is so full I can say nothing.

"Anne," she said. She sighed with pleasure. Her body felt free and light. "Anne," she said. "I cannot wait! Bring me the baby!"

Katryn held the baby gently. Her tumbled bright hair fell about her shoulders, and she leaned her head down to kiss the edge of the cheek. Why, she is beautiful! she thought. Wordless, she held the child. This was a matter for the senses, the smell, the feel, the sight. "How I love thee," she whispered. "How I love thee, my little one." Of course she did not hear, this mite, this morsel. But certes she could feel these were her mother's arms. Katryn touched the tiny hand, so pink. "I love thee," she whispered again. The baby's eyes opened. They were clear, deep blue. "Pray she keeps them," Katryn said. She could feel Anne and Lucy were near, and Goodie and Meg, and Mistress Barbara, and Joan. Joan was sniffing. Katryn suddenly raised her eyes. Against her breast the baby stirred. She kicked. "Look," Katryn cried. Her eyes met Anne's and Anne smiled. Katryn smiled too. "You're thinking I'm a very novice at this, for all my thirty-four years. But now I know I'd sooner died than give her up."

The baby was so sweet. She couldn't resist another kiss. "Aye," she whispered, her lips in the downy hair, "and I'd sooner died than give up your father's love, too." She raised her head. "This is the happiest day of my life," she said. She kissed the edge of the baby's cheek again. She was so little! I had forgotten, she thought, how little is a babe. Dr. Huicke's face swam before her blurred eyes. I should ask him, she thought, why I am so weary, but I warrant it is right I should be.

I should ask him, though, about my weariness. He was saying, "Your Grace, I am going to take the babe. You are not recovered yet."

Katryn felt him lift the child from her.

"Nay, thou art still weak, my love," Tom Seymour said.

The faintest frown crossed Katryn's face. I cannot ask Huicke about my weariness now, she thought, for my lord will hear, and it is worrisome to him. She saw him lift the baby from Dr. Huicke's arms. He sat down next the bed in a chair placed there, with the baby in his arms. Oh, thought Katryn, how wonderful! Our own child! She bit her lip.

"Don't weep, sweetheart," he whispered. The others had drawn away to the other side of the room. "Don't cry. I'll read you what I wrote to Ned."

"Ned?" asked Katryn. "And how you hold her! Just as though you'd been a father many times over!"

"I've learned fast, whilst you slept." He sent her a flashing smile. "See how sweet she sleeps on her father's arm? I need only one arm." He took a deep breath and looked down at the baby, and Katryn thought, Oh, I am going to weep again. He is so loving. My own sweet love. What was he saying? The words were going by. "The Queen's Grace was delivered of the fairest daughter in the whole of England." He has writ that to Ned; he is so proud, she thought, as proud as if I'd given him a son. It truly made no difference to him. Her eyes shone. He is so happy. I shall think nothing about feeling so weary.

She said low, "You didn't want me to have a child, because you were fearful."

The blue eyes met hers, and there was a watchful look in them. "Aye, sweetheart," he said. "That is true."

"I was so blind," she said. "I have never loved you more than I do now."

"Katryn," he said. "Katryn."

The room swam. Am I going to faint, she wondered. She saw he had risen suddenly and was handing the baby to Anne.

"Prithee, my lord," she said, and she knew she said it for she could hear the words, "don't leave me. Don't leave me!" She felt his fingers close over her hand and his arm under her shoulders. She clung tight. But I am swooning, she thought dimly, and she closed her eyes.

She woke, and it was afternoon. Dr. Huicke was bending over her. He felt her head. "Do you have any pain?" he asked low.

"Nay," she said, "except a bit. In my stomach, and in my head. Should I have stayed in bed more?"

"Nay, you did fine, and wondrous brave. You need sustenance," he said.

"I will try," she whispered.

They brought her chicken broth. She swallowed the soup. "I'll be better tomorrow," she said. Sleep and rest will cure me, she thought, sleep and rest.

The next day when she woke, she remembered the baby. For a moment she lay content, but slowly she became conscious of pain, an odd sort of pain. She felt hot, and she threw back the coverlet.

"I wish you'd bathe my head, Lucy," she said. Tom Seymour's face swam before her. Suddenly she knew what she wanted. "Pray lie down here beside me, my lord," she whispered, "and hold me close."

Within his arms, she closed her eyes again. She was safe now. She sighed again. Surely this was Snape Hall, and he was picking whispered. "Stay by me."

Was she dreaming? She could feel his arms, she could feel his weight on the bed and the touch of his hands smoothing her forehead. Where are we? she wondered. At Snape Hall? She could see it so plain; was this the day she had waited on the battlements? How fleet like a deer she had run down those steps to greet him! Now her legs felt like dough, with little pricking aches along them. She sighed again. Surely this was Snape Hall, and he was picking up the lute. "I'm going to make love to you," he said.

Katryn lay still. What day was it? She heard low voices. Were they talking about Jane? But Jane was dead. She slept.

She dreamed. She was screaming, lying on her bed, with Henry in the next room. Would he come? Would Henry hear her and come to her? Other, she would die, and Anne too, and Lucy! "Anne," she cried. "Anne!"

"I am right here," Anne said.

"Thank God," said Katryn. "I was dreaming." She opened her eyes. "You are still beside me," she said low. "Stay with me, my lord. Stay by me."

It must be morning, she thought. I've slept away the night. It must be Saturday. She wrenched at her thoughts, worrying at them. It must be Saturday, and I have had a baby. Surely I have a baby; I've not dreamed it. But this morn I am sick. For the first time, since that horrible day years and years ago, I am sick. She tried to raise herself.

"I fear I am sick," she whispered.

Tom Seymour said softly, "I know it, sweetheart. Now lie still, and Lucy will bathe thee with some cool water. Are you hot?"

"Aye, very," she said. "But don't leave me!"

"I won't," he said. "I'll never leave you."

"Oh, please don't," she cried. "Please don't. When you are right here, I am safe! I don't think I'll die, though, for what should you do without me? I don't think," Katryn said, "that God will let me die."

"Of course He won't," Tom Seymour said.

She felt the cool water. She kept tight hold to his hand. The water, and the smooth cool linen towel felt good. She sighed a little. "My legs hurt," she whispered.

They bathed her legs. She kept hold of his hand. From the next room came the sound of crying. "Is that the baby?" she asked.

"Aye," said Anne, "but she is just hungry. She is very well, Katryn."

The crying stopped.

"She's being nursed," Anne said.

Tom Seymour was holding something to her lips. "What is it?" she asked.

"Just watered wine, with a bit of sugar." His voice was far away, but he was near; his hands were holding her.

She gulped. It tasted good. She was thirsty. "Tastes good," she whispered. "I feel better." She was less hot.

"Is this Saturday?" she asked.

"Aye," he said.

"Let me know," Katryn said, "when it is Sunday. I shall ask Master Coverdale to preach in here."

She saw Anne again—or was it her mother? She tried to see Anne more clearly. Then she remembered. She had just come home. She had just come in the door, and she called, "Mother! Mother! It's I, Katryn, come home again!" She stared at Anne. "But you are not mother," she said, dimly. "You are Anne."

Anne said, "Mother is dead, Katryn."

Katryn cried, a little gasp. "Pray hold me, my lord," she said. "Hold me tight."

The room was full of sunlight, and someone moved to close the curtains. "Nay, leave it be," Katryn said clearly. "Leave it be, for I must think. Is it Sunday?"

"Aye, Katryn," Tom Seymour whispered.

"Have you been here all night?" she asked. "I thought you were."

"I've not left thee," he whispered, "except to wash, and let your sheets be fixed."

"I am sick, my lord," she said. Her voice shook a bit. "I am sick, and I am afraid."

"Sweetheart," he muttered. "Do not fear!"

"I am sick, and I should make my will. I know I should. Where is Huicke?"

"Here, madam," Dr. Huicke said, his voice very low.

"Well, fetch me Dr. Parkhurst, and you two shall witness this will. Nay, command me not for I shall do 't!"

There was quiet in the room. She could hear her own voice echoing about. After a bit Katryn said, "Has someone fetched quills and paper? For I am ready." Her brow furrowed. I have a child, she thought, a female child. I must think. "I leave all my jewels, to be divided equally between my baby and the Lady Elizabeth's Grace, my dear daughters."

Her clock was striking. Idly she wondered what time it was. "Are you writing?" she inquired. Surely someone must be writing this down. "I don't have much strength," she said. "And I leave all else, all of which I am possessed—and I wish it were a thousand times more—to my lord and husband."

Katryn tried to raise her head. Tom Seymour lifted her a bit, propping her up on pillows. The clock struck again, silvery notes. Marry, she thought, this is taking a long time. "I wish no masses said for my soul," said Katryn, "and so give alms to the poor, in the amount of what the masses would cost. Now give me the pen." Certainly she had to sign it; she was sure she should. She took a deep breath. I must be strong enough to write, certes I can write! Marry, it was difficult. She felt the pen in her fingers. She saw the paper. She wrote slowly. "Katryn, the Queen, Lady Seymour." But there was something else she always wrote. She drew the initials then, slowly. "K. P." She sighed deeply. Her fingers dropped the pen. "Oh," she whispered. "Ink on the counterpane." The blot swam.

Black clouds descended on Katryn. The day passed. She dreamed. She spoke. "You are taunting me again," she cried. "Always mocking! Nay, I do not apprehend!"

Lucy stiffened at the words. Tom Seymour gathered her close. "My love, my love," he whispered.

"I dream," she answered. "I dream of thee and me. Always you, all my life, always you. You will come and get me. I am sick, here at Gainsborough. But I will get well, and you will come and take me away. Please take me away!"

"I will," he said. "I will."

"I must be delirious," she said. "I have much pain. Much pain. Like Jane. That is what you were saying, was it not? You feared this, did you not? Is that why, my lord, you didn't want a child?" It was very clear, now. She opened her eyes. Here was her room, and alongside of her Tom Seymour. "I see all of you," she said clearly, "and I shall not die! How can I die with you all about?"

Dear God, she prayed, I cannot die! I cannot leave him. I cannot leave him. "I am thirsty," she added.

"I cannot control my thoughts," she said. The room was dim and vast.

"She has forgotten the child," a voice said. What child? Katryn thought. I am burning hot. I am afire, I think. A cold cloth was laid on her head. She talked. She said, "What day is it?"

"Tuesday," he said.

"Don't leave me," Katryn said. "I feel hot, but I am going to get well. Who is that? Dr. Parkhurst?" Had he come to shrive her? The room was black and hot. "Hold me, my lord," she whispered. "As we have slept together before, hold me now."

The little clock chimed the half-hour. Tom Seymour looked across at it. The hands stood at two-thirty. Slowly he removed his arm from beneath Katryn's shoulders. He leaned down and kissed her on the lips. "Katryn," he said. "My dearest love."

He stood by the side of the bed. Dr. Huicke went over to him. Dr. Huicke wept unashamedly. "My lord," he muttered, "you must let me—give you—"

Tom Seymour evidently did not hear. He said, "I will go now and make the arrangements. I wish her Grace laid under the altar here at Sudeley."

The day was Wednesday, the eighth of September. The castle bells tolled. The chapel bells sounded, and the choir sang. Dr. Parkhurst could not preach, so Dr. Coverdale read the sermon. And afterwards, Lucy and Anne went with Tom Seymour into his study. Anne was trying desperately not to cry in front of him. She wanted to put her arms around him but she did not dare. She had never seen a man look like this. He doesn't even see me, she thought; nay, he doesn't even know we are here. And yet he is speaking to us.

"Anne," he was saying, "you are to dismiss the household."

"Dismiss the household?" Anne quavered. Has he too forgotten his child, as Katryn had done in her delirium?

"Aye, except for the baby's nurses. Dismiss all. I am leaving."

"You are leaving?" whispered Anne.

"Aye," he said.

"Where?" asked Anne.

Tom Seymour looked at her blankly. "Where?" he echoed. Then he said, "I go to Kendal."

Anne almost cried out. But Katryn is not there, Tom, she thought wildly. Search as you will you shall not find her now.

"I go now," he said.

"By yourself, my lord?" Anne asked very low.

"Aye," he said. "Good-by."

"Good-by," Anne said.

She went with him, trotting at his side, to the open doors. She went out into the court. A groom held his big horse. Anne saw the saddlebags.

A hush lay over Sudeley. The glow of ruddy light fell onto its yellow stones. On the Cotswold hills lay the September sundown. Tom Seymour mounted. The gates stood open. He did not look back. He rode out the gates, and into the west of the setting sun.

444